Tomorrow's Shepherd

The Verdant Revival, Book 2

Michael Ripplinger

Tomorrow's Shepherd

The Verdant Revival, Book 2

Print edition ISBN: 978-0-9973955-3-2

Kindle edition ISBN: 978-0-9973955-4-9

Smashwords edition ISBN: 978-0-9973955-5-6

@Pontifex (Pope Francis). "Hope is the virtue of a heart that does not close itself in darkness or remain locked in the past, but looks towards the future." *Twitter*. September 20, 2017, 6:30 AM. https://twitter.com/pontifex/status/910466069654990855?lang=en

Please contact the author at michael@ripplinger.us and visit him at mripplinger.wordpress.com.

v1.1

For Todd, Joseph, Gianna,

Rose, Giovanni, and Mary-Elizabeth

My hope for the future

Saint Dymphna, Saint Louis Martin,

and all other patron saints of those with mental illness,

pray for us.

"Hope is the virtue of a heart that does not
close itself in darkness or remain locked in the past,
but looks towards the future."
Pope Francis

Tomorrow's Shepherd

Chapter One

Sunday, July 6, 1681

Sierra stomped her combat boots up the stairs and out of the U-train station. The sickly yellow glow of streetlights and the garish colors of neon fast food signs defiled the night. Groundcars and aerocars rushed down 39th Street, their impatient drivers incessantly honking their horns. No one in the bustling crowd seemed to be watching, but the giant vidscreen on top of the Inbo Building kept playing commercials for alcohol and shampoo anyway. It was everything Sierra hated about the Crimson City. She was delighted to return to watch it all die.

Some guy with a chipware store's logo on his too-tight shirt stood in the middle of the pedestrian throng. He pointed his mobile at each passerby, 'mitting out unsolicited advertisements. Each recipient paid attention to them only long enough to delete them from their screens unread. Then they returned to their social feeds and ignored the people in their actual physical presence. The corporate shill noticed the nine piercings in Sierra's right ear, and he frowned at her blue hair.

With his mobile's screen held out towards her, he showed off a rapid succession of gaming headsets, holomitters, and dispark ovens. Apparently, some people like a little radiation in their genetically-modified not-quite-meat. "Biggest sale of the year going on now through Saturday at Crazy Lenny's."

"Might as well give it away," Sierra said. "It'll all be trash in a few minutes."

He shook his head dismissively and returned his attention to distributing unwanted commercials.

"Wow, the headmasters really are desperate," a familiar voice called from behind her. "They even called Sierra Monet." A lanky man emerged from the crowd, slightly out of breath. The hot, sticky summer night wrinkled his black Mantissa duty uniform. His mop of untidy brown hair was several inches longer than when Sierra had last seen him three years earlier, and its length had been barely manageable then.

Sierra smiled. "Joey Reinhardt? Or some other loser who looks just like him?"

She raised a forearm before he could offer a hug; he bumped hers with his own. Joey chuckled at her t-shirt, red tartan skirt, and ripped black tights. "At least you picked the right *boots* for the occasion," he said.

"I don't do uniforms."

"You don't do street clothes very well, either. Gosh. It's good to see you. I can't believe you're here."

"I'm told the headmasters called everyone."

"True, but since when do *you* listen to them?"

"Since they started doing what they should have done years–"

As if someone flipped a switch, Mondorf went dark. The whole city. *Completely* dark.

She'd known it was coming, but it was still a breathtaking moment to behold. Street lights, extinguished. Vidsceens and their vapid nonsense, blank. The mobiles held by everyone around her, dead. Every headache-inducing sparkslight in every room on every floor of every building she could see, blackened. Sierra wouldn't even have seen her hand in front of her face if not for the glow of the moons. It was blissfully silent.

Then came the mayhem. Every aerocar dropped out of the sky almost simultaneously, crashing onto the groundcars underneath them which also came to sudden stops. The flames erupting from their wreckage were like emergency flares in the midst of otherwise total blackness. The least selfish among the sidewalk-dwelling spectators rushed towards whatever pile of car carnage was closest and tried to extricate drivers and passengers from their metal tombs. The selfish ones screamed and ran.

Blessed be Lady Verde! Sierra had never dreamed a chipware-free lifestyle could be imposed planet-wide instantaneously. Joey was aghast at the casualties, and just in that single block of 39th Street, Sierra counted at least a dozen. The same scene would be found on every block of the city – on every block of *every* city, worldwide. But chipware-obsessed culture had been destroying the planet. Any casualty count less than the total global population made this blackout completely worthwhile. If that was cold or harsh, well, sometimes the truth hurt.

And if Joey wanted to prevent more death, there was still the second reason she'd returned. She gently took his arm before he darted towards a twisted, tangled pile of metal and glass that had been two separate cars a moment earlier. "Hey. There's somewhere we need to be. Right?"

He tried to shrug her off, but she tightened her grip.

"Joey," she said, "the *aliens*."

The look of alarm and heartbreak on his face passed, mostly. Focused, professional detachment took its place. He nodded, released a breath, and pointed up the street. "Maher Gardens."

They half-walked, half-ran the first block in silence, about the only two people on the streets who weren't holding their mobiles up to their ears and stupidly asking them, "Hello? Hello?" The screaming got louder around the second block. Then came the running and the shattering glass. Finally: chaos.

"They've figured out it's more than just a power outage," Sierra said. "That all the battery-powered devices are dead, too."

Joey looked helplessly at the sight of the darkened city and at the looters who smashed out the windows of corporate-owned chipware and food stores. "I don't know how much the headmasters told you, but we didn't have a choice. God help us, this was the only way to defend Verde, but I'm sure that's little consolation to the people who just died." He shook his head as if clearing away a bad dream. "I don't even want to think about how long it's going to take to repair everything."

"This weapon has been on standby for three hundred years in case the Steelterrors ever returned," Sierra said. "It was designed to royally muck up any chipware it affected. What makes you think everything even *can* be repaired?"

Joey steeled his jaw as if refusing to even consider the possibility. "Did they tell you why all this was necessary?"

"Because three weeks ago, the headmasters learned the aliens who crashed in the Midphalia desert somehow survived, or at least their minds did, and that they mindjacked everyone who worked at Sci-Tech and then spent the last two years secretly manufacturing an army. They have dormant cloned monsters in bunkers all over the planet."

"And the activation of those clones was imminent," he said. "But there's not enough Mantissa and military combined to stop that kind of distributed worldwide invasion. The only option we had was to stop it before it started by taking out their chipware – their cloning chambers, their teleport platforms, everything. And the only way to do it was to use this weapon. We completely destroyed their chipware but at the cost of our own."

After a mile, they entered Maher Gardens. The lampposts beside the park's walking paths were dark, of course, and the park had mostly emptied. Sierra and Joey tromped up a small hill, over the park's brittle red grass, and stepped past a tangle of red leaf trees. A moment of vertigo made her swoon. When it cleared, a makeshift medical camp suddenly appeared. Tents were arranged in two rows with a wide aisle in between. Each one had a Mantissa healer or two in or near it.

"Perception cloak?" Sierra asked. Temporary disorientation was a common side effect of the mind's adjustment from an illusion transmitted by a Mantissa reader. "Why are we hiding?"

Joey motioned with his chin towards the skyscraper towering over the park from four blocks away, glistening in the moonlight. The headquarters of the Ministry of Science and Technology, recently learned to be the aliens' base. "Besides us, every mover worldwide is there," Joey said. "They'll be storming the building any moment now. Thanks to this blackout, they won't face a cloned army, but the alien mindjackers won't want to give up their stolen bodies without a fight. We're here to care for any wounded, but we're hiding to help preserve the surprise nature of their attack."

The healers at the tents were focused on their preparations, but they paused to gape or stare with contempt at Sierra and Joey walking down the center aisle.

"Unbelievable," someone whispered.

"What's *she* doing here?"

"It's the freak."

"She's not in jail?"

Sierra's cheeks flushed red, but not at the healers' barbs. She didn't give a flip what they thought of her. "So the headmasters asked me out of exile to guard a medical camp staffed by every Mantissa healer in the world. Then they *hid* that camp from the people wounded when their blackout ignited chaos. All *just in case* someone gets a hangnail when the assembled army of every mover worldwide swarms in to capture a hundred mindjacked civilians?"

Joey frowned. "I don't like it either. As soon as that building is secure, I'm going to get out there and heal–"

"Barking *fascists!*" Sierra shouted. "Every single one of the burning headmasters. Oblivious, elitist fascists!"

Two healers stepped forward, chests puffed out and fists clenched. Sierra didn't know who they were, but she recognized their type. They were probably into university sports, bad beer, and wasting mommy and daddy's money. She balled her fists, and the scarlet grass around her boots grew three inches. The dirt underneath her trembled.

"Try something," she sneered.

Joey put himself between her and them. "Hey. Hey! We're all friends here."

Sierra glared at the creeps but allowed Joey to lead her away. The grass shrunk to its previous height. "No, we're not," she said. "They hate me." And the feeling was barking mutual.

"They don't hate you," Joey said. "You're just different, and different scares people. Makes them uncomfortable. And I know you understand what it means to be uncomfortable because you have three metal rings pierced through your lip."

"The headmasters have always been like this, Joey," Sierra said. "They proclaim the Mantissa are the 'defenders of the planet,' but they don't do squat to fix the problems people are facing every day. Like how that" – she pointed at the grass underneath her – "is supposed to be green, not red. The Ulmbaden Corporation profits too much off dynamek energy to give a rat's rump about the toxins they're spraying all over the world, but what's the Mantissa excuse? Ulmbaden's crimes are exactly the kind of injustice we should be fighting. We should march to the top floor of their corporate headquarters and throw every one of their board members' privileged rear ends into prison, but the headmasters won't allow it."

"You tried anyway."

"And got barking exiled for it. Sent away. Again." She exhaled. "Just like every foster home I grew up in."

"I would have gone to the Ulmbaden building with you," Joey said, "but I seem to recall you punching me in the face when I tried."

That was an embarrassing memory. And a little amusing, too. "Bah. It would have been stupid for you to throw away your future."

"Ruining your future together, serving as human punching bags... That's what friends are for, right?"

Friend. She wasn't used to hearing that word directed at her. She didn't really know how to respond to it, but she didn't want to dwell on it and risk getting emotional, so she socked Joey in the shoulder and kept walking.

They reached the edge of the triage camp. Maher Gardens ended fifty feet further ahead, past another cluster of thin, sickly looking trees with withered, blood-red leaves. Beyond the park's border, Barton Boulevard ran parallel to the park and was littered with debris and fires. So was 38th Street, which ended at its intersection with Barton. Crowds gathered on the sidewalk across the street and tried, without access to their social feed, to figure out what had happened.

With nothing to do but wait, Sierra closed her eyes and inhaled deeply. Standing like a tree with her right foot on the inside of her left thigh, she brought her hands in front of her heart and used her mind-body connection to calm both. Balance. She was one being with mind and body connected to one another, to Lady Verde's land underneath her, to the sky above her, and to the air around her.

Suddenly, Joey stiffened. "Something's not right," he said. The other healers mumbled similar things. A healer's power alerted them to pending personal danger.

Four blocks down 38th Street, a Mantissa mover flew through the air from around the corner, coming from the direction of Sci-Tech. "Fall back!" she yelled. It was Artemisia Cassatt, supreme commander of Mantissa defense. Two more movers followed her, then three more, then six. They all zoomed towards the park and the hidden medical camp. Two of them used their telekinetic power not only to fly but also to drag three wounded Mantissa through the air alongside them.

They were pursued by the aliens. Not mindjacked humans, but *aliens*. White-skinned monsters with glowing red eyes ran at incredible speeds on all six of their limbs. They growled, snarled, and snapped their teeth. So many teeth. At least fifty of them rounded the corner after the Mantissa and more were coming.

A palpable sense of shock filled the people in the park hospital, Sierra included. The Mantissa had obliterated the world's chipware, but not in time. The aliens had already activated their army.

Sierra strode past the trees and onto the greenbelt lining Barton Boulevard. Standing in front of the sidewalk, she stretched her arms to her sides and pointed her palms upward. The ground shook, and a wall of dirt running the length of the park rose from underneath her. The spectators across the street pointed, yelled, and ran. Whoever had been responsible for the mental perception cloak lowered it. Sierra's rising wall had reached a height of six feet when General Cassatt landed on it next to her.

"Over the barricade," Sierra yelled to the movers. Cassatt gave her a dirty look. The orders were supposed to come from her, and Sierra was expected to obey the same as everyone else, exile or not.

Pfft. Burn *that*.

When the rising dirt wall reached a height of twelve feet, Sierra lowered her arms, and it stopped growing. The last of the retreating movers flew over it and descended down into the medical camp where healers laid hands on them and used their power to heal their wounds. The aliens were one block away, charging like a pack of giant, rabid wolves.

"Nice trick," Cassatt told Sierra, "but they're insatiable. They just keep coming. We're going to retreat to–"

"I'm staying right here."

"I'm *ordering* a retreat."

"Cassatt, you know exactly who I am. So you know where you can shove your burning orders."

Sierra had given her wall's park-facing side a slope so the healers in the camp could easily climb to its top. Only Joey accepted the invitation. "A *lot* more than twelve movers stormed that building," Joey said to Cassatt. "Where are the others?"

Cassatt shook her head.

Joey looked like he'd been punched. Every Mantissa worldwide had assembled in Mondorf for this operation, and only twelve movers – *only twelve* – had survived?

"You're ordering us to leave?" Joey said once he found his voice.

"Yes," Cassatt said.

"But there're people..." Joey said motioning towards the metropolis all around them. "You're staying?" he asked Sierra.

"Damn right," she said.

From a pocket of his uniform, Joey produced a revolver – an old style ballistic weapon straight out of an antique weapons museum. He popped the cylinder out of his six-shooter, checked its bullets, and slammed it back into place. "Then let's give 'em hell."

Oh, with barking pleasure.

Sierra pointed her hands at the charging aliens, and a blast of wind surged from her fingers. It lifted a pair of downed cars and tossed them a block away, where they crushed several of the monsters. The aliens at the front of their line lost their footing under the force of the wind and slid backward, crashing into one another. A few of them were thrown into the air like the cars, only higher.

More aliens stampeded right behind the fallen ones. They stormed onto Barton Boulevard, just a street away from the barricade. Sierra knew they'd entered Cassatt's mental range when three and four of them at a time suddenly flattened as if an invisible U-train had been dropped on them. Five more were forcibly blown away by Sierra's winds. Joey killed two with his revolver. But the aliens covered the entire width of 38th Street, their parade of terror stretched at least four blocks down, and more rampaged towards them.

Just before the aliens reached the base of the barricade, Sierra wiggled her fingers and tree roots burst out of the ground. They wrapped themselves around a handful of the aliens and squeezed like snakes. About half of those seized collapsed in a crunch of broken bones, but just as many managed to free themselves by severing the roots with their claws and teeth.

Three aliens scrambled up the barricade beneath Sierra. They aimed their teeth at her neck, her abdomen, her legs. Sierra pumped her fist, and three bolts of lightning crashed down from the cloudless sky. Badly burned and crackling with sparks, they tumbled off the wall and were trampled by their fellow invaders.

Battering rams of dirt erupted out of the barricade and punched away the aliens who tried to climb it. Sinkholes opened on the sidewalk and swallowed ten of them at a time. Straight-line winds knocked those that reached the top of the barricade back to the ground with spine-breaking force. The elm trees' branches reached down, grabbed three and four aliens at a time, and flung them fifty feet through the air.

And it *still* didn't stop them all. An alien palmed Cassatt's face in its white, clawed hand and slammed her head to the ground. The general stopped moving. Her murder stunned Sierra and distracted her long enough for an alien to reach up from the barricade and claw a chunk of flesh out of her right leg. Sierra yelled in pain, dropped to one knee, and struck the alien who'd attacked her with a lightning bolt, burning it to a crisp.

Sierra needed to do something bigger, something deadlier, something that would take out a lot more of them at once. All her efforts were but a drop of the ocean, and a wave of high tide was on its...

Wave.

"Get down!" She rolled backward down the slope to the ground behind the barricade. Joey followed her. Several of the aliens' white, bone-like snouts peeked over the top of the wall. Before they could fling themselves over the barricade, she raised her arms, and in seconds the barricade doubled in height to over twenty feet tall. Then she pushed it forward. It toppled over and crashed into the aliens like a typhoon drenching the beach. The ground shook, the windows of nearby buildings and cars shattered. The rumble was practically loud enough to shake the piercings out of her ears. But it worked. The avalanche of soil smothered every alien on Barton Boulevard.

It also tossed a thick cloud of dust into the air. Sierra couldn't see anything through the dirty haze, but she knew more aliens – a *lot* more of them – were on 38th Street, out of range of the falling barricade that had crushed their comrades. Once the dust settled, they were going to resume their assault. Sierra guessed the reprieve would last about two minutes.

A hand pressed against her wounded leg. She instinctively raised her fist to punch whatever creep it belonged to, but she held back when she saw Joey's dirt-streaked face. Her bleeding stopped, her flesh mended, and the pain went away.

The healers in the camp and the surviving movers fled, and the aliens across the street growled and stomped through the diminishing dust. The Mantissa hadn't just lost. They'd been massacred. Sure, she disagreed with pretty much every decision the headmasters had ever made, right down to the cut and color of their prissy, custom-tailored suits. But most of the rank-and-file Mantissa healed people and protected the weak and gave a bark to care. And in a matter of minutes, they'd *all* be dead.

It was unfathomable. Some – at least one – had to survive.

"Get out of here," she told Joey.

"No," he said. He reloaded his revolver and walked towards the sidewalk. The dust cloud was thinning.

"Look at the size of that army," she said. "The movers and healers who ran won't even make it out of Mondorf. The Mantissa are going to be as extinct as the thunder lizards."

"So go then," Joey said.

"You have to survive this!" Sierra yelled.

Joey spun on her. "No, *you* do. You're the most powerful of us all. *That's* the real reason the others are frightened of you. Why the headmasters always worked so hard to control you. You're not different because of the colors you dye your hair. You're different because you're far more powerful than any of them, and they know it. Get out of here! Run. Regroup." He steeled himself. "And whenever you can, come back and avenge us."

Cripes, that's what he thought this was about? He'd turned back towards Barton Boulevard, but she spun him around to face her. "This isn't about making sure we get a burning *rematch*. After this, the Mantissa won't be back in ten days or ten years. We'll be lucky if we're back in ten generations. And if just one of us is going to live through this, it can't be someone like one of the headmasters. They don't care about anyone outside the walls of their glass tower. It can't be someone like me who spends her whole life trying to torque everyone off. It has to be the *best* of us. Someone willing to lift a finger for the people out there on the street. Someone who only sees the good in people. Someone who can–"

Again her lack of friendship experience hindered her. It felt weird to say the kind of thing she'd almost said.

But if she didn't spit it out and say it now, she'd never have the chance.

"It has to be someone who can ignore what a barking crank I am and reach out a hand of friendship to me, no matter how many times I've slapped it away. *That's* what Verde's going to need. It has to be you."

"Get out of here, Sierra."

She raised her hand, and a whirlwind engulfed Joey, lifted him into the air, and moved him past the trees and deeper into the park, away from the oncoming army. "Sierra, no!" he screamed. She made a pushing motion, and the whirlwind carried him away faster. He'd be out of the city before it lost its strength.

And then he was gone, and the aliens were upon her. She never saw the one who killed her, but she sure felt it bite her lower back. Her legs turned to jelly as she lost feeling in them. Before she collapsed, her killer wrapped all four of its arms around her and slashed her chest.

She landed face-down in the dirt without the air necessary to holler in pain or scream in defiance. And the puddle she was laying in... Where had it come from? It hadn't been wet or raining anywhere in the area a few moments before. Oh! It was her blood.

As the parched dirt soaked it up and her vision blackened, she made one last effort to unite her mind and body to the planet around her. She couldn't stand in a tree pose anymore. She couldn't stand at all. But she didn't have to stand to be one being, with mind and body connected to one another, to the land underneath her, and to the sky above her.

The sky in which she could feel the winds gusting lightly, oblivious to all the death far beneath them. She heard the cries of pain from the soil, poisoned by dynamek energy particulates and lacking the nutrients necessary to properly nourish the grass and trees depending upon it. Though she was several blocks away from where the Iller River traced a jagged line through Mondorf, she felt it as clearly and as completely as if she were bathing in it. She could taste its minerals and its algae.

Death was strange but pleasant. Unlike the scripture zealots, she knew she wasn't going to an invisible kingdom in the sky. She knew her body would turn to dust and become a part of Lady Verde. But she didn't realize just how much she'd *feel* that transition, that merging. She didn't realize it would be so exhilarating. She surrendered to it, opening herself to the planet and welcoming her embrace.

Her last breath contributed a small bit of carbon dioxide to Lady Verde's atmosphere. It would nourish some plant even after she was gone. That would have made Sierra smile, but she was gone before she could.

Chapter Two

Two Hundred Years Later

Fritz entered the alley as the first faint glow of daylight appeared in the eastern sky above Mondorf. His mobile vibrated in his vest pocket. Normally, he wouldn't bother to answer in the middle of an operation, but only a handful of people on the planet had working mobiles, and all of them save one were mission participants. Probability dictated the call was important and relevant.

"Professor here," he said.

"Professor? Are you working at the university now?"

Fritz sighed, leaned against the brick wall, and reminded himself of the difference between probability and certainty. Answering your mobile without first checking who was calling belonged on the Stupid List. "Oh. Hey, Dad."

"I thought you were up north of the mountains," Milo said. "What are you doing in Harbrucken?"

"I'm not," Fritz said, glancing at his pocket watch. He only had five minutes if he wanted to stay on schedule. "Professor is just a code name. For a mission I'm on. Right now."

"Did I call at a bad time?"

There was no such thing as a good time for chit-chat, but this was an especially bad time for it. Two hundred years ago, the white demons came to planet Verde and all but exterminated the planet's guardians, the Mantissa. Fritz and his friends – the Mantissa's remnants and descendants – were about to launch an operation which, if successful, would end the demon threat forever.

"No!" Fritz said. "No, it's OK."

He would have put his face in his palm, but he didn't want to smudge his glasses. He couldn't just say it was a bad time? Gosh. His sister was right. He had major confrontation issues.

"Good," Milo said. "Get a load of this. What do you think? I have these all over the southern fields. Have you ever seen bigger heads?"

"I can't see anything."

"Oh. Sorry. Let me hold it up higher. Is that better?"

"No, Dad, I can hear you, but I can't see you. I'll never be able to see you through our mobiles. At least not until I have time to get back up to Skylab and find out why the only thing I can get out of its massive comm array is a puny, rudimentary RF carrier signal. But I've been a little busy."

"Do I need to hang up and call back?"

"No, don't hang up!"

What was he thinking? That had been his chance to bow out politely!

"I can see you," Milo said.

Fritz moved his mobile away from his mouth until his exasperated breath completely cleared his mouth. "Dad, when you look at the picture of me on your mobile, are my lips moving?"

"No."

"And in that picture, am I standing near the oven?"

"Yes."

"Are you in the house right now?"

"Yes."

"When you look into the kitchen, am I standing near the oven?"

"No."

"That's because the picture you're looking at is the one I took with your camera when I first gave you your mobile."

"You really can't see this head of broccoli I'm showing you right now?"

From out on the sidewalk came the distinctive clicking and scraping of white demon claws on concrete.

Uh-oh.

"It's probably just bad reception right now, I'll talk to you later," he whispered. He disconnected the line, felt horrible about doing it, and gauged the distance to the fire escape ladder. He needed to get to the roof, but he'd never climb all the way there before the approaching demon passed. All he could do was dive further into the alley, crouch behind a trash can, and wait for it to leave. And try to ignore the roaches scurrying away from the pile of broken bricks across from him.

He hid just as the demon and a human woman came into view. But instead of continuing down the sidewalk, they turned into the alley and walked straight towards the fire escape. Darn.

It wasn't a demon in the literal "fallen angels kicked out of heaven and banished to the underworld" definition. It was an alien from a race called the Shakrath. Their monstrous appearance – six limbs, thick tails, claws, a whole mess of teeth, and chalky skin – had earned them the name "white demons" from the people of Verde unlucky enough to make contact with them over the past two centuries. Fritz bore a special hatred for them.

The woman had shoulder-length red hair and looked about Fritz's age, somewhere in her early 20s. She didn't appear to be armed, but Fritz wasn't exactly a concealed weapons expert so he couldn't be–

She held a descrambler!

Fritz's eyes narrowed. He'd invented the descrambler. It was how he repaired chipware broken since the Blackout two centuries prior. The woman's chrome-covered device was one of the handful of descramblers the demons had forced him to build for them back when they... when they held him prisoner. Fritz had assumed she was one of the demons' slaves since they made up the vast majority of Mondorf's human population. But descramblers were so rare and so important to the demons, they wouldn't give one to just anybody.

There were a small number of humans who willingly collaborated with the demons. Was she one of them?

His mind went into data-gathering mode. The demon walked directly behind the woman where he could see her every move. Her clothes seemed just a little too big, and her jeans and boots looked very well-worn – even threadbare in places. Too low quality for a collaborator. Her eyes were downcast, except when she glanced at the demon from her peripheral vision, which was often – so much so, it seemed to be a nervous habit. He didn't know why the demons would give a slave a descrambler, but the demon was the woman's captor. He felt sure of it, and because of his Mantissa power, his feelings had a very good record.

Her eyes widened behind her spectacles, and she stumbled a step. She'd seen him! Resisting the urge to panic, he put a finger in front of his lips. She didn't make a sound. Behind her, the demon snarled a few words of its growly language and gave her a shove. Yep. Definitely one of the demons' slaves. She climbed the first steps of the fire escape and watched Fritz as best she could out of the corner of her eye. The demon followed her and, mercifully, didn't see him.

Fritz couldn't get to the roof with a demon up there, but nor could he wait very long for it to leave. He had a schedule to keep. Consulting the watch in his vest pocket would have required too much movement, but he guessed he had about four minutes to take control of the broadcaster. It was doable, but only if he acted soon.

His eyes landed on a bluebonnet growing out of a crack in the pavement next to the broken bricks. It was a splash of color in a dingy alley made even darker by the pre-sunrise hour. It was also getting to be an extremely familiar sight. He'd been seeing bluebonnets everywhere for weeks now – single, solitary bluebonnets, not the fields full of them he was used to from back home. But this one... Had it been there before? How in the world had he missed it? And back home, bluebonnets were spring flowers. Did they bloom in late summer here in the north?

His hyper-ability to notice the tiniest of details was part of his Mantissa power, but also sometimes a curse, such as when it led him to gape at flowers and ponder growing seasons when he was hiding inches from a white demon. The woman was nearly to the top of the three-story building. The demon was halfway there, though it climbed by digging its claws into the brick and scaling the wall directly. As the woman swung her leg over the parapet, he drew his gun from underneath his vest and aimed at the demon. He raised three fingers to the woman, then two, one...

The woman ducked for cover. Fritz pulled the trigger.

Every other gun in the occupied territories fired gunpowder in a metal shell, but Fritz's pistol was a relic from a bygone era. A high-pitched whine reverberated in the alley, and a long, thin streak of red light pierced the side of the demon's head. The monster dropped off the wall and crashed onto the pavement. It twitched twice, then never moved again.

Fritz darted to the bottom of the fire escape. The woman peeked down at him and the laser pistol still in his hand. Brandishing the weapon he'd just used to beef a white demon probably didn't make him appear very friendly. He tucked it away, but that didn't seem to comfort her much, which left the two of them awkwardly looking at each other. Perfect – he'd traded small talk with his father for small talk with a total stranger in a squalid alley. Even if there *weren't* a white demon corpse beside him, he'd be intensely uncomfortable.

His power tingled in his mind as if trying to get his attention. Though he didn't like talking to strangers, she had a descrambler. Why would the demons give a slave one of their precious chipware restoring devices unless they'd also trained her in how to use it? And if she could use it, maybe he could make up some lost time if he asked for help. He nearly groaned at the thought, but which was more important: appeasing his anxiety or keeping his mission on-time?

"You know how to use that descrambler?" he asked. Wait. Should he have opened with "hello"?

"Yeah," she stammered.

"Want to help me with something?"

She glanced at the dead demon leaking black blood from the hole in its head. "Not really."

"No?"

"No."

Oh. Wow. Not the reaction he'd expected.

"All I need you to do is use your descrambler for me," he said.

"Whatever you want descrambled, they'll know I did it for you. They're already liable to blame me for *that*." She cocked her head towards the dead demon. "Whatever you're up to, I don't want to be involved. I just want to walk away from here. I got family to take care of."

Family? She looked too young to be married, but Fritz supposed even a woman in her late teens could get hitched, or be a mother. Maybe she took care of her parents?

"Besides, you got a working laser pistol you must have stolen from the demons' stash," she said. "So I reckon you already have a descrambler, too."

"I do," he said, and he removed his from his pocket. She looked confused. Maybe it was because his descrambler – cased in wood and sporting analog number dials and clunky mechanical buttons – was so different than hers with its chrome casing and digital display.

"That's a descrambler?" she said.

"The original."

"Original?"

"I built it," he said. "Built yours, too."

She flinched backward and ducked almost completely behind the parapet. "I'm not a collaborator," he called up to her. "Would a collaborator shoot a demon?"

Cautiously, she peeked back over the parapet. Fritz didn't need Mantissa reader powers like his uncle once had to know what she was thinking. Who was this guy who killed demons yet claimed to have built their descramblers?

"A couple of months ago I spent several days as their prisoner," Fritz said. "They *made* me build them."

It had been far more horrific than that, but Fritz wasn't going to talk about it.

He tucked his descrambler back in his vest's inside pocket and glanced at his watch. Three minutes, if he wanted to stay on schedule. "May I come up there? I'm not going to hurt you."

She nodded, but not immediately. As Fritz climbed, his shoes made hollow echoing sounds on the metal stairs. When he reached the roof, he forced himself to look into her eyes to appear friendly, even though eye contact with people made him as comfortable as wet socks. "I'm Fritz Reinhardt," he said.

"Annalie Krieger," she said. "Ain't ever seen you around before."

"I'm from out of town."

She scoffed. "No one comes *to* Demons' Town."

"We do," he said. "My friends and I, I mean. Listen, you can climb down and leave right now, but I would appreciate a minute of your time."

She looked down and kicked at the gravel covering the roof. "What do you need?"

A ten-foot-tall antenna was mounted in the roof's corner. At its base was a metal box about ten inches square. Fritz crouched down, opened the box, and exposed a control board full of switches and dials and a row of glowing red lights which should have formed numbers, but instead just made horizontal lines. "I'd like you to use your descrambler to fix this device."

"It ain't broke," she said.

"It's about to be."

Annalie only cautiously knelt next to him after he took his descrambler from his vest pocket and plugged its wires into one of the control board's ports. "You came here to shoot demons, break their chipware, then fix it again?" she said.

"We came here to run the demons out of town."

She held up her hands and closed her eyes. "Stop. Sorry I asked. You get two minutes of help, but I do *not* want to be involved in... what you just said."

"Fair enough." He pushed a button on his descrambler, and the entire control board went dark. Then, once he got his device out of the way, she connected the cable from her descrambler to the control board without protest. Meanwhile, Fritz cut a handful of wires from the antenna and spliced them into a metal disk he brought out of another vest pocket.

"You're not a collaborator, so how did you get trained in descramblers?" Fritz said.

"I'm maintenance duty," she said.

Duty is what the demons called the labor specializations into which they organized their human slaves, and what they forced the humans to call it, too. Fritz stifled a growl.

Annalie pushed a button on her descrambler, and the control board lit up again. Its digital display read six zeroes, *000000*. Fritz finished with the antennae and moved back to the control board just after Annalie disconnected her descrambler.

"This broadcaster was working fine a few minutes ago," she said. "In fact, the demon you offed was bringing me here to copy its settings so I could apply 'em on another one a few miles yonder. Did you use your descrambler to break it? Like, to black it out again?"

"Something like that," Fritz said.

"Mine can't do that," she said.

"Yours is hard-coded to use the descrambling algorithm. Mine uses whatever algorithm I come up with in my head. I can use the descrambling one or one that recreates the effects of the Blackout."

"Decent," Annalie said. "But why'd you break a working piece of chipware only to fix it again? Oh! Upon descrambling, does the system revert to a basic configuration and wipe out the demons' passcode?"

She figured that out? Wow. "Yeah, exactly. It's a lot faster way to crack a security code than a brute force attack. And my friends and I need this broadcaster to–"

Annalie wagged a finger at him. "Nope. Family to take care of. Don't want to know."

Fritz shrugged. When he was done flipping switches on the control board, its digital display read *314159* for a brief moment before the numbers disappeared, to protect their secrecy. He closed the junction box, put his descrambler back in his pocket, and stood. Annalie's eyes darted between him, the roof, and the pre-dawn sky, but kept going back to the metal disk he'd spliced into the antenna's wires. "Signal booster?" she finally said, unable to stifle her curiosity.

"You've seen one before?" Fritz said.

"No, but what else would you splice into the wires at that point? Cracking the passcode means you want to take control of the broadcaster, not sabotage it, so you wouldn't be wiring in a dampener."

Wow! Did she understand *everything* he was doing? He thought there wasn't anyone else who understood ancient chipware as he did. Maybe he needed to meet new people more often.

"I'm done," Fritz said. He didn't have to tell Annalie twice. She bolted down the fire escape to the alley below. Fritz followed and, when he reached the ground, brought his mobile out of his pocket. "Thanks for your help. Get home, or somewhere else safe, OK? Fast."

The look she gave him made him realize his warning had sounded far more ominous than he'd intended it to, especially when she was already paranoid about the demons thinking she had been involved, but he didn't have time to explain to her any further. Besides, she and the rest of the city would know exactly what was happening in about fifteen minutes. Fritz brought his mobile up to his ear. "Big Man? This is Professor," he said. He'd insisted on using call signs instead of real names. Not because he thought the demons might be listening in, but just because it seemed like a spiffy thing to do.

"Is it done?" said his Uncle Sebastian. His already tinny-sounding voice was made even more distorted by his mobile's speaker.

"Everything is everything. Call up the broadcaster, enter passcode 314159, and you're on."

"Acknowledged," Sebastian said. "Get into position and get ready."

At the same time, Annalie snorted a grunt of a laugh. "Don't accidentally use passcode 265358 instead."

Oh, no way. No *way!*

Fritz lowered his mobile and gaped at her. "265358?"

Annalie's cheeks flushed red. "Oh. Sorry. I said that out loud? Since you set the new passcode to the first six digits of the circle ratio, I was making a joke to myself about accidentally using the second six digits of it instead. But it wasn't very funny. And it wasn't supposed to be out loud. And I'm pretty sure I'm rambling now."

"The circle ratio. As in the ratio of a circle's circumference to its diameter?"

"Umm, yeah. Is there another circle ratio? Since a broadcaster's wavelengths are roughly circular, I figured that's why you..." She looked down and scuffed the toe of her boot across the concrete. "Never mind, rambling again."

"Professor?" Sebastian's voice called from Fritz's forgotten mobile. "You still there?"

He brought the device back up to his ear. "Sorry. Yeah, I'm on my–" He dropped the mobile back to his side. "You really knew the circle ratio inspired my passcode?"

"Yeah. Pretty dang obvious." She chortled and blushed. "Look, I shouldn't even be here anymore, but I have to know – that's a working mobile communicator, ain't it? And you're *talking* to someone with it, so it ain't the only one. But even if you have a hundred working mobiles, you'd need a working transmission matrix to shoot signals between 'em. The demons have been hoarding chipware for... well, since forever, and I ain't ever seen a transmission matrix in their stash. I sorta reckon that before the Blackout they were all up in outer space. But by golly you've gotta have one, so where on Verde did you find it?"

He'd feared small talk, but this had become the most enjoyable conversation he'd ever had in his life. Fritz raised his mobile up to his mouth. "I'm on my way," he said to Sebastian before disconnecting the call and putting the device back into his inner vest pocket. "Running the demons out of town is a necessary step, but it's just the first step. Want to know what happens next?"

She looked intensely uncomfortable again. "No," she said. "I really shouldn't even–"

"That." He pointed southeast towards the city's outskirts, where a reactor tower loomed above everything. Even in the pre-dawn darkness, it was easy to spot by the softly glowing sparkslights ringing its roof. "That's what's next. The power plant. My descramblers can fix chipware, but chipware is going to need sparks. And the most important chipware is going to need a lot more sparks than batteries can provide. The Ulmbaden Power Facility generates three gigakrafts worth of dynamek energy every day. Before the Blackout, that was more than enough to power a million chipware devices, big and small, across the entire continent. Even a fraction of that output would be enough sparks for every chipware device we could imagine throughout the Occupied Territories, the University, Terrascorcha, Earp, Mondorf, and a hundred other settlements we don't even know about yet.

"So we run off the demons. We take back the power plant. We descramble every piece of chipware we can find. And then we travel by cars instead of horses. Frozen water gets stored in a chipware box cooled by sparks-powered compressors instead of being wrapped in sawdust and stacked in an icehouse. Telegrams go away because we'll have faster ways of sharing information darn near instantaneously with folks on the other side of the globe. Advancements in medicine and hygiene improve life expectancy tenfold, overnight."

He had Annalie's complete attention. "You really did build the descramblers. Look, I know I said I didn't want to hear about it, but... holy moly, you're jawing about rebuilding the ancient world!"

"Basically, yeah." Fritz shrugged. "It's time to change the world."

Part of his brain sent words to his mouth even as another part tried to stop himself, to ask what in the world he thought he was doing. He was making an impulsive decision, but Cassie and Siv were always telling him he should make more friends, and good things tended to follow when he listened to his intuition. This felt right. It still made him a lot nervous, but it felt right.

"You want to help?" he said.

"Yeah," Annalie said, stretching the word out to three or four syllables. "Yeah, I'm your huckleberry."

"Great!" he said. "Then let's go. We need to go four blocks–"

The pile of broken bricks distracted him again. He might have missed it the first time, but he knew the second time he'd looked at the pile, a bluebonnet had been growing nearby it, right out of a crack in the cement. He couldn't have imagined such an unlikely detail. A flower *had* been there just a few minutes before. He was *certain* of it.

But it wasn't there anymore.

Chapter Three

Mondorf's skyline was decayed, rotted, and deteriorated, but as the first rays of morning sun illuminated it, the sight of a real city still took Fritz's breath away. The only other community on the entire continent large enough to be called a city was Harbrucken, home of the university. Every other settlement was a town at best. Most were simple villages, scattered a day or half-day horse ride apart across the occupied territories south of the mountains – south of Terrascorcha. They consisted of dirt roads, wooden sidewalks, and public hitching posts. And they were much *shorter*. Even Harbrucken didn't have many structures higher than four or five floors. Its tallest feature was a simple water tower, which seemed puny compared to Mondorf's skyscrapers. Those towering giants were half-dead, but they were *tall*.

The former capital's population had been over one million before the Blackout. With only twenty thousand or so humans and a few hundred of their white demon overlords now living in the city, enormous portions of the metropolis hadn't been inhabited for two centuries. There wasn't a populated building for three blocks in any direction from the alley, but Fritz cautiously glanced up and down the street anyway. Even after he marched down the sidewalk at a pace barely shy of a run, he inspected the dark shadows on every ruined structure, just in case. Everything about the operation depended on surprise.

Annalie came up beside him. "My dad and I used to read notes left behind by past maintenance duty folks," she said. "For two centuries, there's been a grist of ideas about what happened to chipware and how to fix it, but no one's ever been able to make that dog hunt. How'd you do it?"

Fritz shrugged. His sister Cassie said he did it all the time, to the point she thought it was a nervous tic. "Just came to me. Happens a lot because of my power. I'm a Mantissa by the way."

If she'd been taking a drink, she'd have spit it all over the sidewalk. "For *serious?*"

"For serious."

"Mind readers, magic healers, folks who can bend metal without touching it – that Mantissa? The kind that ain't been around for two hundred years?"

"That kind," Fritz said. "Though I'm not a reader, a healer, or a mover. Those were only the three most common affinities. I'm an intuitive."

"What kind of magic does an intuitive do?"

"Mantissa are just humans whose brains do things most people's don't," Fritz said. "It's not magic; it's biology."

"Moving things without touching 'em ain't magic?" Annalie rolled her eyes. "OK, fine. What kind of magic biology you do?"

Fritz restrained himself from making an exasperated sigh. "Everyone possesses intuition to some degree, even non-Mantissa. We can all look at a situation, think about how it compares to patterns from the past, and deduce what's likely to come next. Right? Well, my intuition is hyperactive. I can't see the future, but my deductions about what could happen can be so accurate they feel more like premonitions."

"So..." Annalie scrunched up her nose. "You're saying you have a magical ability to figure things out?"

Fritz shrugged. "When you put it that way, I suppose it's not nearly as flashy as being able to lift a carriage with the power of your mind, but–"

"No!" she said. Her smile lit up her entire face. "It sounds splendiferous!"

Several blocks from the alley, they stepped into a building. Some debris in the corner, behind a very old and very dilapidated desk, indicated someone might have once used the building for shelter. But now it seemed to be occupied only by rats, which Fritz couldn't see, but he could hear them squeaking in the dark corners and the walls, and could he ever smell the pungent odor of their waste. He and Annalie stepped into the building's stairwell and made their way ten stories up to the roof. The air was mercifully fresh there. The demons' headquarters, the twenty-story Sci-Tech building, was one block north on the same side of the street. They ran hunched over to the corner and ducked behind the parapet, where they were hidden but with a great view of the place on the street where everything was about to happen.

"Will I need a gun?" Annalie said. "I've never used a gun."

"You won't need one. This isn't going to be a fight."

Annalie pushed her glasses back up to the top of her nose. "How is this not gonna be a fight? You're not going to just politely ask the demons to leave, are you?"

"A straight fight against the demons in their territory would be bloody on both sides," Fritz said. "Probably too bloody on ours. A lot of good people would get hurt, and die, and we probably wouldn't even win. So we have something else planned. You ever go fishing?"

"Yeah! My dad used to take me and Bradon and Clark all the time. We'd fish in the Iller, the river that goes right through town here. We'd have to do it only when Dad was off duty, of course. But it was great. You're a fisherman?"

"Gosh no," Fritz chuckled. "I refrain from willing participation in all outdoor activities. But I understand the key to fishing is the right bait. And bait the demons will find irresistible just went into the water."

She followed his gaze to the building across the street in front of Sci-Tech. A white demon emerged from it. It didn't look exactly like every other white demon, which was significant because the white demons usually looked rather identical – they were all clones of one another. This demon was a half foot taller and had a rounder shape to its head compared to the harsh angles of the other demons' skulls. It also wore clothes – black boots and a black shirt and pants covered with cargo pockets.

"Don't worry," Fritz whispered to Annalie. "That's my uncle, Sebastian. He's the one I talked to on my mobile earlier. Codename 'Big Man' for this operation."

Annalie fixed him with a perplexed look. He couldn't blame her. He'd just introduced her to his uncle, the white demon. "I'm descended from a Mantissa named Joseph Reinhardt," Fritz said. "He lived before the Blackout. His sister, Eroica, was Sebastian's wife back when he was human. Well, Sebastian is still human. I meant back before his mind was trapped in that demon body."

Her face told him his explanation had clarified nothing, especially since he hadn't even gotten into how Sebastian had survived the last two hundred years, but she nodded anyway, God bless her.

"Loyal Shakrath," Sebastian said. His voice was different than it had sounded over the mobile, and not just because it now boomed over the city thanks to the hijacked broadcaster. It was also flat and lacked emotion. "I have returned."

"When he talks, his mouth don't move," Annalie said.

"Well, not when he talks in our language anyway," Fritz said. "His demon mouth and vocal cords can't make our words. But see that circle-shaped device in front of his throat? That reads his mind and the little speaker on it transmits what he's trying to say in our language."

"It interfaces with his brain?" Annalie said. Far too loudly. And she quickly realized it. "That is the *pink!*" she added in a whisper.

When they heard the first roar, Fritz didn't have to tell Annalie to duck. The snarls and growls multiplied and grew louder. And in a matter of minutes, demons filled the street in front of their Sci-Tech building headquarters, with more still emerging from inside. Some used their claws to climb the walls of nearby buildings to get a higher vantage point. All of their howls and barks combined into a cacophony which sounded like the wailing and gnashing of teeth on a particularly crummy day in hell.

"I've never seen this many of them gathered in one place," Annalie said. "This might be *all* of them."

Fritz suddenly felt every bit of the oppressive late August heat and humidity, even though dawn was the coolest part of the day. He wiped sweat from his brow and tried, without much success, to calm his nervousness. "Sebastian is pretending to be their leader, Krulgoth. They follow him fanatically. Treat him like a god, practically."

"What if the real Krulgoth shows up?" Annalie said.

"Guaranteed not to happen," Fritz said. "We killed him two months ago, but they don't know that."

When the incoming flow of demons tapered off, "Krulgoth" followed their predetermined script and explained he had been away manufacturing his new body. Which was true. At the time of his death, Krulgoth really had been making new demon bodies that possessed Mantissa powers. Sebastian was trapped in one of them – one with Mantissa healer powers. He took a knife from a holster on his leg, slashed its blade across one of his palms, and showed the assembled demons the black blood oozing from the wound. The laceration closed up and disappeared before the demons' glowing red eyes.

While Sebastian held the demons rapt, Fritz examined the round steel poles at the corners of the intersections at either end of the Sci-Tech building. The poles had once held up traffic signal lights. As well as he could tell without a pair of binoculars, the devices he'd installed in them seemed to be fine. But nevertheless, he placed the back of his right hand into the palm of his left and brought both to his heart – the Sign of God's Hand.

"I am not the only Shakrath who will receive these enhancements," Sebastian announced to the demons. "I am but the first."

The gathered demons approached euphoria. They chanted Krulgoth's name, pumped their fists in the air, growled towards the sky. Sebastian put away his knife and held up all four of his hands in an attempt to silence the crowd, but their enthusiasm was more powerful than their obedience. When he resumed speaking, the broadcaster was the only reason anyone could hear him.

"We are the Shakrath, and we will be feared!"

"*Krulgoth! Krulgoth! Krulgoth!*"

Fritz struggled to control his breathing. These next few moments were critical. They had to go *exactly* as planned. *Please work. Please work. Please, God, work.*

"We are the Shakrath," Sebastian hollered, "and we will never be enslaved again!"

Fritz retrieved a small rectangular piece of wood with five buttons on it out of his vest pocket. It wasn't his descrambler, but it could have been its distant cousin.

"We are the Shakrath..." Sebastian said, and then he put on the biggest smile his demon mouth could manage. When he spoke again, it was in his regular voice, not an imitation of Krulgoth's monotone, and boy did his words ever have some emotion in them.

Anger, mostly.

"...and you animals are surrounded!"

The intoxication of the crowd awkwardly turned to incomprehension. Fritz took a silent moment to gloat, and he knew Sebastian was doing the same. But the monsters wouldn't sit stunned for very long.

Fritz jabbed the remote button that activated the devices he'd hidden in the traffic signal poles, and the area in front of the Sci-Tech building lit up with a blue glow. Walls of shimmering energy formed a rectangle with the entrance to the demons' base at the center of one of its long sides. The containment field stretched three stories up, which Fritz hoped and prayed was taller than the demons could jump. The ones who had been holding onto nearby walls for a better vantage point fell into the crowd of their comrades below as the containment field repelled them off their perches.

"Surrender now," Sebastian said, "if you want your black hearts to keep pumping your black blood."

The demons lunged towards Sebastian with their claws, but before they could cut him, he took a grappling hook gun from a pouch on his shirt, aimed it towards the roof of the building across the street from Sci-Tech, and pulled the trigger. A metal hook with a trailing line emerged. When the hook found a hold somewhere near the building's roof, Sebastian flicked the gun's retraction switch and soared into the air above the demons. They snarled and snapped at the empty air where he'd just stood but could do nothing else to stop his ascent.

A group of thirty or so people emerged from abandoned buildings and engaged the few demons who were outside the energy walls when they went up. Leading the charge on the street beneath Fritz was his best friend, Siv McCaig. He hacked at the straggling demons with his broadsword as if he were using a sledgehammer on a chunk of iron in his shop back home. From further back, Fritz's sister Cassie pierced the demons with arrows. As a medical student and an experienced hunter, her shots were both deadly and precise. The others in the group were armed with laser rifles Fritz had provided them.

A block down the street, a similar-sized and similarly-armed group handled the remaining uncaptured demons on the other side of the Sci-Tech building. Fritz's friend Harlan Washington, the sheriff of a remote village called Earp, led that team along with a pair of his deputies.

"Your friends?" Annalie said. "Wait, I recognize some of those folks. Most of them are from here!"

Fritz nodded. "There's only three Mantissa including me, and two healers and an intuitive aren't anything like the mover warriors you've read about in stories. Add Siv, Harlan – they're my non-Mantissa friends – and Harlan's two deputies, and we're still only seven. That's not enough to take on hundreds of demons. So for the past month, we've been recruiting people from here in Mondorf to help."

It only took a few moments for the laser fire to taper off. Cautiously, Fritz rose to his feet and looked down at the street below. The containment field penned hundreds of demons. They yelled and screamed, enraged and panicked at their confinement. Sebastian was safe five stories above them. The few demons they hadn't been able to capture were dead. He used his mobile to connect to a team voice-comm. "Everyone OK?" Fritz asked.

He got affirmative responses all around. There had been some shooting, but overall, they had completely avoided an ugly, bloody battle. Not a single human had been killed or even hurt. "Wow," he said, finally allowing himself to breathe. "It actually worked!"

New laser fire erupted a block down the street. Had more demons arrived, ones that weren't inside the containment field when it went up?

"Someone's shooting at the force fields," Annalie said.

Well, that was stupid. Bullets, like any other physical object, just bounced off the energy barrier, but lasers couldn't shoot past it either. The barrier's energy would scatter, dissipate, and absorb the shot. But why even try to shoot already captured demons? Fritz brought his mobile to his mouth and addressed Harlan by call sign. "Chef, what's going on down there?"

Harlan didn't respond, but Sebastian leaped from one rooftop to another, an easy feat thanks to his white demon agility. "Harlan's angry," Sebastian reported once he'd had a closer look. "One of the Mondorf residents is shooting at the pen." He swore as he used his claws to run down the side of the building, moving at a breakneck pace towards street level and Harlan's team.

The voice-comm carried the sounds of a scuffle, shouting, and swearing, plus more laser fire. Then, without warning, a fist-sized ball of flame and a short burst of white noise came from the traffic signal pole nearest Harlan's team. The side of the containment field in front of Harlan's group glowed noticeably duller than the other three.

"That wasn't one of my emitters getting hit, was it?" Fritz said into his mobile.

"Take his gun and get him out of here!" Harlan said.

"Chef, you need us over there?" Siv asked.

"Some chowderhead started gunning for demon blood," Harlan said. "Shot at the demons like fish in a barrel."

Oh. Fritz hadn't considered some of the demons' slaves might turn bloodthirsty once they'd turned the tables on their now-former masters. But in hindsight, he should have. It was an emotional reaction, not a logical one, which is why it made so little sense to him, but he could ponder his oversights later. Right now, the only thing that mattered was the integrity of the containment field. "Did one of my emitters get–" Fritz said.

"Yes," Harlan said, "one of the barrier-making machines got hit."

The berserk, captured demons pushed *hard* against the dimmer side of the containment field, and it took several seconds before the field repelled them away. A few of them made an organized, simultaneous group push against it. The field flickered, and suddenly, two demons were outside the pen. Harlan's crew shot them dead, but even short-lived, the escape gave the other demons hope. More pressed against the containment field in the same weakened area. One more demon fell out of captivity when the field momentarily flickered.

"New problem over here!" Harlan hollered over the voice-comm.

"Oh, that ain't good," Annalie said.

No, that was not good at all. The blood drained from Fritz's face. If the demons got out, he and his friends would never contain them again, because the demons would kill them. Scratch that – they'd capture him and his friends, torture them, maim them, and finally, after a whole world of suffering, kill them.

And then, just because they'd be so wrathy, the demons would figure out a way to bring them back to life and do it all over again, just to have the pleasure of killing them twice.

Chapter Four

Fritz and Annalie's shoes pounded the stairs. "I have a horse out in the alley," Fritz shouted over his shoulder.

"Maybe you should go alone," Annalie said. "I've never ridden a horse. And I think I'm a little afraid to ride anything that could throw me if it decides it don't like me."

"Oh. Don't worry about that. I'm not fond of horses, either. But Siv kept insisting I should get one."

They emerged from the building and charged into the alley next to it. Hidden in the darkness was a two-wheeled horse made of black metal and chrome. Fritz threw his right leg over the motorbike and stomped hard on the kick starter. The engine underneath him roared to life. He revved it twice, turned the choke off, and revved it three times more. "I call it Spot."

Annalie moved in for a closer inspection. "Oh my gosh, you repaired a motorbike?" she shouted over the engine's rumble. "What's the power source? Batteries weigh too much, so motorbikes used gas engines, but–"

"There are no refineries anymore!" they shouted together. Fritz grinned from ear to ear. "I retrofitted the engine to run on steam with a firebox insta-heated by a few lightweight, high-capacity solar cells."

Annalie's face was brighter than the bike's headlight. "Solar? For serious?"

They heard a sizzling sound, alarmed shouts, and more laser fire from the direction of the pen. Another demon must have pushed its way out. Annalie's question went unanswered. Fritz gave the helmet dangling from the handlebars to her, and she straddled the motorbike behind him. "Hold on," Fritz said. Annalie squeezed her arms around his abdomen. He twisted the throttle, and with a roar like thunder, the motorbike zoomed out of the alley.

He'd only had Spot for a short time. And he'd never had a rider with him. Plus, considering the circumstances, he had to ride faster than he'd ever pushed the bike before. Rushing through a new situation was never a recipe for success with him. After one near disaster coming around the first corner, which he'd almost taken too quickly, he took a deep breath.

He was a thinker who liked to study, analyze, and make plans, but ironically, his power worked best when he turned his mind off and *didn't* think. When he cleared his conscious mind, patterns in data, in numbers, and in everyday life suddenly became recognizable. Since he didn't want his restoration project to end with a fiery motorbike crash, he stopped thinking and started feeling.

He felt the bike's weight distribution, felt the engine rumbling underneath him, and reacted to those sensations instinctively. His hand pulled the throttle back just a tad, and he leaned an inch forward in the seat. He still zoomed down the two-hundred-year-old pavement at what felt like double the speed of a charging stallion, but the simple adjustments stabilized his ride.

A lone demon, one who somehow hadn't been with the others when they were captured, pounced out of the shadows and into the street in front of Spot. Annalie screamed. Fritz probably would have, too, but he wasn't thinking. He was acting on instinct. He calmly twisted the bike's handlebars, leaned to his side, and swerved around the demon as it swept at him with its razor-sharp claws. It howled when it lost its prey.

"It's following us!" Annalie yelled.

Her words came from a fog existing outside of Fritz's current focus. In the moment it took to take a breath, he gathered and analyzed his data. A sprinting demon running on all six of its limbs could run *fast*, maybe even faster than his motorbike, at least for a short time. But two blocks ahead was his left turn. Harlan and his deputies from Earp, as well as a group of now-former demon slaves from Mondorf, would be waiting just past that corner. Therefore, the demon chasing them was irrelevant. It didn't have enough distance, even at its superior sprinting speed, to catch them. What he *did* have to worry about was safely turning Spot. If he made the turn, the pursuing demon would be left behind just long enough for him and Annalie to reach Harlan and his crew.

And another thing he had to worry about? Finding a new name for his motorbike because Spot was a balderdash name, and it wasn't *ever* going to work. Gosh, that name belonged on the Stupid List. Why had he ever chosen it?

"Hold on," he said.

He turned the motorbike's handlebars and leaned into his turn. The demon crouched low. Fritz knew the blasted things well enough; it was going to pounce. But he also was well enough in tune with his motorbike to know he could safely give it a little more thrust. The demon jumped and landed on a patch of pavement the motorbike had been on a half-second earlier. Harlan and his crew were one unobstructed block ahead. Fritz opened the bike's throttle and shot towards them like a bullet out of a gun.

Gosh, did the engine have to be so *loud?* He'd have to increase the size of the exhaust nozzles sometime to try and quiet the thing. Fritz sort of heard Harlan shout, "Make way!" but he also may have just read Harlan's lips instead of hearing the words over Spot's roar. Smoke poured off the motorbike's wheels as Fritz squeezed the life out of the brake lever. The back of the bike fishtailed underneath him before it came to a safe stop.

He put down the kickstand, and Harlan tossed him a satchel of tools. If Harlan was surprised he'd shown up with a stranger, he didn't show it. He was probably just distracted by the horde of demons screeching and howling and throwing themselves hammer and tongs against the failing energy barrier ten feet away. Everyone in Harlan's squad had their weapons aimed at them.

Annalie stood before the obvious source of the problem. At the eastern side of the street, an access panel on one of the traffic signal poles was missing. Scorch marks around its opening indicated it had been shot off. The opening in the hollow pole exposed its contents: wires and the emitter's circuit board. Smoke drifted out from somewhere within.

Between nervous glances at the rampaging demons behind the energy wall inches away from her, Annalie pointed to a thick cable dangling underneath the circuit board. "The main power line's been through the mill. Half its copper's ruptured. The board just ain't getting enough sparks."

Fritz reviewed her assessment. Just above the circuit board was the optical emitter creating the containment field. He could tell right away the blue light coming out of its lens wasn't glowing nearly as brightly as it should have. "Yep. The circuit board itself looks fine, though."

"If you can scare up some more cable," Annalie said, "we could patch this easy, but we can't splice in a new line with hot sparks flowing."

"And if we cut off the sparks, the field drops, the demons escape, and we die," Fritz said.

His mind soaked in all of the information, and then there was a *click* – his word for the moment when his Mantissa intuition, after working subconsciously to analyze and correlate all the data he'd given it, finally extrapolated an answer and presented it to him. He knew exactly what to do to restore the energy barrier to maximum strength. Just thinking of it made him wince, but it would work for sure, and it would probably be safe. Maybe.

Crouching over his satchel, he riffled through its contents. "Each side of the pen is generated by two emitters, one on each side of the street, projecting their force fields towards one another. When they touch, they sort of blend together instead of repelling one another, because I have them tuned to harmonic frequencies. But that means we can shut down one emitter for a short time – a *very* short time – and keep the pen up *if* I boost power to the opposite side." He handed Annalie a bundle of spare cable and a pair of wire cutters. "While I do that over there, can you rewire this?"

"Right in front of them?" She motioned towards the rabid demons. "With only one emitter keeping the cage up? Uhh. Sure. I'm daisy." She forced a nervous smile on her face.

Fritz ran to the pole on the opposite side of the street and went to work. First, he pried off the pole's access panel with a flathead screwdriver. The chipware and its wiring inside all looked good. Next, he took out an old car battery, which was the biggest, heaviest item in the satchel, and placed it in front of the pole. As fast as he could, he attached a cable to one of the battery's terminals. Then he put on a pair of thick, black rubber gloves.

With a burst of static, a demon burst through the pen. It leaped high and to the side to try and avoid the laser fire it knew would come from Harlan's crew. The first few shots missed it, but in the end, it only lived a few seconds longer than the previous escapees had.

"They're learnin' fast," Harlan shouted.

"How are you going to wire a battery into that emitter without turning it off?" Annalie shouted from across the street. She'd already used the wire cutters to strip off the insulation from the ends of a six-inch length of patch cable. "You can't splice in new copper without turning off the sparks."

Fritz shrugged and held up the end of his cable. The metal wire inside was exposed. "Well, it's not that you *can't*. It's just that it's a really, really bad idea."

Annalie's eyes went wide.

Fritz shoved the hot wire into the power junction on his emitter's circuit board.

There was a blast of yellow sparks. The rubber gloves kept his hand from being burned off or electrocuted, which Fritz greatly appreciated. On Fritz's side of the street, the containment field glowed a brighter shade of blue. The demons pressing against the energy barrier were violently pushed back five feet. But at Annalie's end, the roaring demons inside still could slam themselves against the pen for a few seconds at a time, and where they pushed it, the shape of the containment field took on an obvious bulge.

Fritz removed a second cable from his satchel and patched it between the battery and the circuit board's power junction. This time the blast of sparks was magnesium white and singed the side of his face as he turned away. With two lines from the battery adding to the working emitter's power, even the weak end of the field immediately repelled demons as soon as they touched it. But was it oversparked enough to remain standing after they temporarily turned off Annalie's side?

Most of the demons inside the pen were still in a frenzy, bouncing off the walls and pummeling themselves against the pavement. But three were calm, quiet, and up to something. They glanced back and forth between where he pumped additional power into the western side of the barrier and where Annalie worked – the side he was about to turn off. Pushing past their comrades, they forced their way to the front, right next to Annalie. But once there, they didn't push so much as a finger against the barrier. They just stood ready, waiting for him to kill the sparks to Annalie's emitter, and fixing to push out of it as soon as he did.

Harlan was right. They were learning. And they weren't dumb to begin with, though they ranked fairly high on the Stupid List for the contempt and cruelty they showed others. Fritz's intuition told him the field was not yet oversparked enough to keep those animals back once he killed the power at Annalie's pole. He removed a third cable from his satchel and attached one end to a terminal on the car battery.

"Son," Harlan called out to him, "I get the feeling you're about to do something royally beefheaded."

Fritz shrugged. "That's probably a fair assessment."

"Omi*gosh!*" Annalie said as she ducked and covered her head.

He slammed the third cable into the emitter's power junction. The containment field six inches in front of him turned from light blue to bright white and knocked him two feet backward, flat on his rear end. Good thing, too, or else the blast of sparks that shot out of the power junction might have burned off his face.

The demons on his side of the pen couldn't come within six feet of the containment field without being forcefully pushed back. *Now* it felt like enough. He reached into his pocket for the pen's remote control.

"Ready?" he called to Annalie.

Annalie stood up, spare cables in her left hand. With her right hand, she held the wire cutters an inch from the damaged cable. She nodded.

Fritz pushed one of the buttons on his remote control and the damaged emitter powered down. The blue glow of Annalie's side of the pen dimmed significantly. The three demons who'd been calmly studying the situation slammed themselves at the barrier directly in front of her. The containment field bulged way too much for Fritz's comfort. Patches of static appeared and disappeared across it. But it held.

Annalie worked to beat the devils. She first tentatively touched her emitter's main sparks line with the end of the wire cutters, pulling her hand quickly backward in case it was still hot. When she confirmed it wasn't, she snipped the cable just below where it had been damaged and ripped out the bad piece. She tossed away the wire cutters and began splicing together her replacement cable and the main sparksline coming up into the pole from below.

With a screech of defiance, the three demons in front of Annalie hit the energy barrier simultaneously. One of them got a hand through to the other side, but the containment field crackled with static, and the demon was forced to pull back. On their second combined attack, one pushed its snout through the barrier long enough to snap its teeth in Annalie's direction. She yelped but kept working.

Fritz had more cables, and his battery had more terminals, but he wasn't sure how much additional power he could put through the western emitter without frying it. He might have already done it irreparable harm; it made a disturbing humming sound he couldn't explain. His intuition told him not to patch in another battery line. But two of the smart demons pushed their arms through the barrier a half-inch at a time towards Annalie. He had to do something. But what? Nicely ask them to back off? Threaten them? Put them to sleep with a lecture on–

Threaten them!

When he was the demons' prisoner, they'd caged him inside his own body. Krulgoth had possessed Mantissa reader powers, and he'd used them to mindjack Fritz – to put the mind of a demon into Fritz's brain. For two horrific days, the demon had full control of Fritz's body and had access to all his thoughts, memories, and emotions. But this mingling of the minds hadn't gone one-way. He'd been able to see some of the demon's thoughts and memories, too. And its fears.

He'd learned the demons had once been slaves elsewhere in the galaxy. The demons refused to call their masters by their true names. Instead, they preferred the term "the evil ones" or "the fiery ones." Their desire to never again be enslaved was their strongest emotion. It was what fueled their mania to escape his energy barrier. And frankly, from the memories he'd seen, he didn't blame the demons one bit. But maybe he could use the demons' past trauma to distract them long enough for Annalie to finish the repair.

"Hey!" he yelled. He marched as close to the three smart demons as the energy field would allow and held up his mobile. "Back away or I call the Celestines."

His arms rippled with gooseflesh when he said their name. Every demon in earshot froze. Fritz remembered the demon's memories of the Celestines' empty, black eyes and their slaty skin. It took everything he had to maintain his composure, but he couldn't afford not to. The demons would never believe what he was saying unless he looked like he'd call the evil ones right then without a second thought.

The demons breathed heavily, bled from the wounds they'd inflicted on themselves in their madness to escape, and fixed their glowing red eyes on him and his mobile. They were calming, but Fritz didn't let himself get too excited. The threat he'd made marked him for death. If another demon escaped, he'd be the first human it killed.

"Yeah, I know what you're afraid of," Fritz said. "And I know how to contact them. So step back. Now!"

They backed off, just an inch or two.

Annalie dropped the scraps of cable still in her hand and took a big step away from the emitter. "Done!"

Fritz prayed Annalie had repaired it correctly. He jabbed his remote and restored its power. It lit up with a brilliant blue light. Back at full strength, the containment field forced the demons inside ten feet back and made them re-erupt into pandemonium. The three demons who had tried to outsmart him roared in frustration.

He disconnected the three cables he'd added to the western emitter. The glow of his side of the pen softened from a blinding white back to its normal sky blue. Just in time for his adrenaline to wear off and his legs to give out, Fritz leaned his back against the old traffic signal pole and slid down until he sat on the sidewalk. Annalie crossed the street and collapsed next to him. They both breathed heavily.

A growl from the intersection startled Fritz. Sebastian had emerged from the shadows and menacingly stood over a scowling, greasy-haired man. The guy didn't look nearly finified enough to be a collaborator, yet he was unarmed and guarded by Harlan's deputies, Boone and Tamber. He must have been the one who shot at the containment field.

"They were captured!" Sebastian said, and even coming from a tiny, low-quality speaker strapped to his neck, his human voice sounded as vicious as a demon's growl. "You don't shoot unarmed prisoners."

"I don't want them captured, demon," the prisoner said. "I want them dead!"

The man snatched the revolver from Tamber's hip holster. Sebastian charged him and took three bullets square in the chest, two of which blasted out of his back. He stumbled. Black blood flowed down the front of his shirt. Boone seized the shooter's wrist, and Tamber yanked the gun away. Together they bound his hands behind his back.

The gunshot wounds on Sebastian's back stopped bleeding and shrunk in size until they were closed. With a thumb and forefinger, and with a grunt of pain, Sebastian reached into his third chest wound and pulled the bullet out of himself. He flicked it across the ground in the direction of the man who'd shot him.

Harlan stepped up to the prisoner and pointed at Sebastian with a trembling finger. "He's not a demon. We told you that. He's a man, a *Mantissa*, trapped in a demon's body. He's trying to save you, friend. Body and now soul."

The prisoner ignored Harlan and stared down Sebastian, his nose curled in disgust.

"Get him away from here and keep him unarmed until the demons are gone," Sebastian said.

"That's Mason," Annalie told Fritz quietly. "Demons killed both his boys."

He couldn't blame Mason one bit for his hatred of the demons because he shared it. The two days during which the demons had violated his mind and controlled his body were the two worst days of his life. But shooting unarmed prisoners wasn't self-defense. It was just murder. Fritz shook his head to clear the unpleasant memories of his captivity. He stood and helped Annalie do the same. "Thanks for your help," he said.

"Umm," Annalie said, "you're missing part of your eyebrow."

Fritz rubbed the right side of his brow and confirmed it was bare. It must have been singed off. Could his sister's or Uncle Sebastian's healing power regrow eyebrows? He'd have to ask. Speaking of things he had to ask...

"Professor to Smithy," Fritz said into his mobile.

"Here," Siv replied.

"Now would be a good time for you to give a leader speech to as many people as you can," Fritz said. "Point out chipware has brought about the fall of the demons, and talk about what else we'll be able to do as we restore more of it. Demons are the past, chipware is the future, that sort of thing."

"Uhh, sure," Siv said. "Reckon I'll come up with something. You sure you don't want to do it?"

Fritz pulled his mobile away from his ear and frowned at the device before answering. "You're asking if I'm sure I do *not* want to talk to a large group of people that likely has hundreds of questions?"

"Yeah, figured," Siv said before ending his connection to the shared voice-comm.

As Fritz returned his mobile to the inner pocket of his vest, Harlan watched him from the other side of the intersection. He was smiling. Harlan always smiled, but this smile was larger than usual and looked conspiratorial. He strolled towards Fritz and tipped his ten-gallon hat, which revealed what little hair he had left was gray. "You made a friend," he said with a nod towards Annalie.

Warmth rose up in his cheeks. "So? I make lots of friends."

Harlan laughed. "No, you don't."

"Umm. Harlan, this is Annalie," Fritz said. "Annalie, this is my friend, Harlan Washington."

Harlan offered her his hand. "I'm not just the sheriff of a village about a hundred fifty miles south of y'all. I'm also the finest chef in the land. It's a pleasure to meet you, but you'll have to excuse me. I've got a victory feast to start cooking. Say – what do you two think? Peach or blackberry cobbler for dessert? I brought what I need for either."

"Blackberry," Fritz said without hesitation.

Annalie's eyes glowed with a brightness rivaling the containment field. She licked her lips and even moaned a little. "Both?"

A laugh exploded out of Harlan's mouth. He took Annalie's hand in his own and kissed the back of it, then clapped Fritz on the back so hard he stumbled. Correcting his balance, he spotted a bluebonnet growing out of a crack in the pavement. Another one!

It was late August. It was going to be hotter than the blazes in just a few hours. How on Verde was a spring flower in bloom? And how much longer before, like all the others he'd recently seen, it disappeared as quickly as it sprouted?

Chapter Five

In the teleport beam, there had been nothing but red. When that vanished, there was nothing but white. Skleght recoiled from the brightness and the sunlight's glare, slamming his eyelids closed to turn it off. Then the wind and the cold hit him.

On all sixes, the Shakrath stepped down from the teleport platform onto a field of snow. His limbs sank into the powder two inches beneath the surface. Digging as far down as he could, Skleght found no dirt and no grass, only ice.

Someone called out to him. The natives of Verde would have heard the "white demon" language as a snarl or a growl, but Skleght understood. "Brother." Gashg stood twenty feet away, beckoning to him. The rest of their brothers gathered across the nearby hills, which featured only snow drifts, snow piles, and wind-blown snow. The Shakrath blended so well into their surroundings, Skleght detected them only by the red glow of their eyes. The humans who had worked with them, whom the Shakrath considered barely more privileged than the slaves, huddled under blankets.

"You were the last, weren't you?" Gashg said.

"Yes," Skleght said. "Where are we?" Wherever this was, at least they were no longer in... in the thing they'd been in. He wouldn't even *think* the word.

"They left this," Gashg said. He handed Skleght a thin, rectangular device cased in black plastic. No larger than the palm of his hand, its surface was bare but for a single button. "It will answer your questions, but it won't be pleasant to hear."

Skleght pushed the button. The device played a recording of a voice: the impostor Shakrath who had pretended to be Krulgoth the Mighty.

"By now you've figured out I'm not Krulgoth. I'm Sebastian Galliard. You animals should know me well. You lived inside my head for two centuries after Krulgoth mindjacked my body."

Skleght looked sharply at Gashg. Could this be? Gashg lowered his head, as if unable or unwilling to meet Skleght's eyes. A curious response. What in this message could elicit such a–

"Krulgoth's dead, by the way," Sebastian Galliard said. "He won't be coming to rescue you."

Skleght snarled at the recording device in his hand. Other Shakrath gathered on the forsaken plain of snow howled.

"You're in the part of our planet called the frozen north," Sebastian Galliard said. "But take a look around and think about where you're *not.* You're not in a cage, and you're not in a coffin, both of which you deserve a hundred times over for the crimes you've committed across the galaxy. Instead, we've done you a kindness and sentenced you to exile. You're a good three-thousand miles from Mondorf, and we've restored the chipware necessary to track your movements from Skylab. You come within a hundred miles of any human settlement, we'll consider it an act of aggression and respond appropriately."

Skleght had heard enough. "Secure that teleport platform!" he yelled. "We can return with it. We are the Shakrath, and–"

"Skleght!" Gashg said. He held Skleght back with a hand on his shoulder.

A bomb detonated underneath the teleport platform, melting the snow and two inches of ice across its entire blast radius. It also melted the debris of the teleport platform and its power source.

"Oh," Sebastian Galliard said from the recorder, "make sure you get the last guy well away from the teleport platform after he joins you because we're blowing it up once the lot of you are on the ice cap."

Skleght roared and squeezed his hand.

"Enjoy your exile, you miserable sons of– *brzzzt*"

He discarded the shattered plastic pieces of the recorder into a snowbank.

Fritz stood at the third-story loft's windows and gazed at the empty lot across the street. It was in the middle of the block and surrounded by nearly identical brownstone buildings. The remains of a concrete foundation suggested a similar building must have stood on the empty lot once upon a time. The brownstones looked as if they were racing to be the next to fall. Their windowpanes were all broken, and wide holes in their walls allowed plenty of mid-afternoon sun to shine through them and illuminate the empty lot's grass. Fritz scrutinized every detail of that sad, sickly yard. The distribution of grass across the lot; the height, thickness, and color of the blades. He never in his life had studied plants so much as he had during the two months he'd been in Mondorf, and he'd grown up with a cornfield a hundred yards past his bedroom window.

"Why are you wearing glasses?" Cassie said. His sister stood with her back to the wall adjacent to the windows, her arms folded across her chest. "I just healed your eyes two months ago. You can't have gone nearsighted again so soon."

"They're not corrective lenses," Fritz said. "I felt naked without them."

Siv laughed and clapped him on the shoulder. "They're spectacles, not undershorts."

"He feels naked without socks," Cassie said.

Fritz spun on her. "I must *always* wear socks!"

"Calm down, big brother," Cassie said. "I'm not going to take your socks. Or your glasses. Especially when you're this happy." She smiled. "You haven't always–"

Fritz tensed. What was she going to say? Siv was here. He didn't want Siv – he didn't want *anyone* but Cassie – to know about his... struggles. "I'm just happy you're happy," she finished. Somehow she'd seen his discomfort, which wasn't so surprising since she knew him better than anyone. He flashed her a smile of gratitude and quickly changed the far-too-personal subject.

"Have you noticed the grass is a different color here?" he asked.

"Compared to back home?" Cassie said.

"Yeah," Fritz said. "It's a darker green. Almost a green-brown. Or maybe green with a hint of red?"

Siv squinted out the window. "I see what you mean, but I reckon it's just brown dust from the bricks broken off those buildings. Such a mess of it there, it's probably giving a reddish tint to the entire lot."

"It's not just that lot, though," Fritz said. "A lot of plants here look... off."

Cassie came beside him and shared his view. "South of the mountains, the grass is only green where folks deliberately water it. Most of the year, it's so hot, the grass is a sickly looking yellow or a dead brown. This far north is not nearly as warm. I think you're just not used to seeing what healthy grass should look like."

His sister's pre-med degree was in biology, not botany, but still, she would know best. She voluntarily went outdoors, and she even enjoyed her time there for some odd reason. She enjoyed hunting. She'd spent far more time learning their father's farming trade than he ever had. Still, the color of the grass felt off. And he didn't plan to mention the spontaneously growing and disappearing flowers until he had a better idea of what that was all about.

He scratched the back of his ear and strolled the length of one of the floorboards. Long before they'd taken the loft as temporary accommodations, it had been partitioned into several rooms, but all of the interior walls had either crumbled or been deliberately removed over the previous two hundred years. At least there was plenty of fresh air. None of the expansive windows had any glass in their frames and probably hadn't since the first winter after the Blackout. The breeze didn't offer much relief from the stifling heat, but it was better than nothing.

An assortment of chipware devices, all in various stages of repair, had taken over every inch of available space on a pair of long workbenches. There were more mobile communicators like the one in his pocket. There were devices for entertainment, for cooking, for telling time, and for predicting the weather. They came in various shapes, sizes, and form factors, but they shared one thing in common: Fritz had salvaged and restored them all. These were the wheels on which he wanted to roll in progress. And their pending meeting would determine that proverbial carriage's first stop.

"Ready?" Cassie asked.

Pulled out of his thoughts, Fritz shrugged. "We know what to do and how to do it. Why do we have to sit around and talk about it first?"

"Gotta inform the mayor about goings-on in his town," Siv said. "Especially big things like the arrival of a sparksline and ancient chipware."

"I should have been more clear," Fritz said. "I understand the reasons. I just think they're stupid reasons."

Siv barked in laughter. Footsteps on the stairs announced someone's arrival. A moment later, Annalie stood in the doorway and waved. "Howdy! Can I come in?"

"Our newest recruit," Siv said. "How you been, Red?"

"Is it OK that I brought my brother along?" Annalie said.

Only then did Fritz notice Annalie's youngest brother standing behind her, holding her hand. He pointed his face at the floor, but his eyes darted about, trying to take in as much as he could while looking like he wasn't.

"For sure," Siv said. He put his hand out towards the nine-year-old boy. "How are you, son?"

The boy turned his head away and made no effort to shake Siv's hand.

"I'm sorry," Annalie said in an undertone. "He kind of makes strange with everyone at first."

"No worries," Siv said.

Cassie knelt to put herself at eye level with Annalie's brother, even though he looked in the other direction when she did it. "Hi, I'm Cassie," she said. "What's your name?"

"You want to tell her your name?" Annalie said.

Her brother shook his head.

"Sorry," Annalie said, her cheeks blushing. "His name is Felix."

"We're happy to meet you, Felix," Siv said. "And glad you'll be laying the sparksline with us, Red."

"Especially since I need to get back to school," Cassie said. Sebastian was preparing their restored airplane at that moment. And after he flew her back to school, he planned to check on the demons in the frozen north – make sure they and their collaborators were staying put. Without Annalie, the sparksline work would have fallen to just Fritz and Siv.

"I had to mull it over some," Annalie said, "'cause my siblings haven't had anyone but me since our folks died. But my friend Ramona said she'd look after them. As long as they're taken care of, helping out is as big a no-brainer as mashed potatoes and gravy."

More footsteps landed on the stairs, these much heavier than Annalie's. Harlan rapped on the open door's frame. "I hear someone say 'gravy'?" he said. He swooped Cassie and Annalie into bear hugs and gave Siv a strong, firm handshake. Fritz kept several steps back to avoid a physical greeting.

Harlan's wide grin and infectious laugh brightened the room, but the effect was immediately nullified by the scowl on the tall, lanky man who followed him. He was dressed formally in suit, tie, and vest, and he removed his hat upon entering. Rubbing his thin gray beard, he surveyed every inch of the loft, and he absolutely did not smile.

Siv offered the man his hand. "You must be Mayor Clum. Sivrin McCaig. I lead the Mantissa Reborn."

"A pleasure," Mayor Clum said in a soft voice. Siv introduced the mayor to Cassie, Fritz, and Annalie before directing everyone towards a map pinned to the exposed framing of the loft's wall. Felix cowered behind Annalie's leg but stared longingly at the treasure spread across the loft's workbenches. Only Fritz seemed to notice.

"Where'd you send the demons?" Harlan said.

Siv tapped a white area near the top of the map. "Teleported them and the dozen-or-so nefandous folk who collaborated with them to the frozen north. You ever want to visit them, Harlan, you can teach them how to cook with snow, 'cause that's all they've got there." He laughed loudly and clapped Harlan on the back.

Mayor Clum frowned. "Exile via chipware. Appropriate, considering the topic before us."

Siv's laughter trailed off. He and Harlan exchanged an uncomfortable look. "Right," Siv said. "Mr. Mayor, we sure appreciate your willingness to let Harlan and his deputies help us free this town and its folk, exile the demons, and secure the power plant. And so do the people who live here. We're aware that sacrifice has left your village vulnerable the past few weeks. We'd like to split fair with you. It's time to change the world, and we'd like that change to start in Earp."

Siv pointed at the black ink line Fritz had drawn on the map. It marked a meandering but mostly southbound path from Mondorf to the Lavare Mountains. Mayor Clum strolled forward to examine it more closely. "There's a sparksline running underground from here in Mondorf to the south, a real big one," Siv said. "Been there since before the Blackout, when it provided power to every settlement south of the mountains, including Harbrucken."

He traced a second ink line, this one blue, which broke off from the black line and cut a southwest path directly to Harlan's home village of Earp. Founded by survivors of the Blackout two hundred years earlier, Earp had never had any chipware infrastructure. "We want to put a new line in the dirt, sprouted off the main one, going straight to your village. It will provide enough sparks for lights, food storage, and a variety of other devices my colleague" – a slight nod to Fritz – "can fix up for you."

That was his cue. The dread rose in his stomach. He *had* to teach Siv how to operate more of these devices, so he could be their leader for this part of the show-and-tell, especially if, God forbid, this sort of meeting become the norm before all future chipware restorations. Well, might as well get it over with. He stepped towards the workbench he'd prepared and invited the others to follow with a wave and a few mumbled words.

Harlan rubbed his hands together expectantly. "Farming machines, Winston. Nights lit by bright sparkslight instead of dull candles. Boxes that keep ice cream frozen for weeks!"

Fritz flipped a switch near the edge of the workbench, and sparks-powered lamps illuminated it. Despite his discomfort at the pending presentation, he couldn't help but grin ear to ear. The scene looked like his idea of the best Lenerstelen morning ever. Chipware! Chipware presents for all!

He demonstrated a dispark oven small enough to carry on a horse's saddle which cooked food like a wood-burning stove, only ten times faster and without smoke and ash. He showed Mayor Clum how they could use their mobiles for voice conversations, to transmit written messages, to take photographs, and to play electronic card games. He provided a glimpse into the future of medicine by showing off a device that put a real-time, moving image of the bones in his hand on a chipware screen.

Mayor Clum's mouth remained a straight line. Apparently, relics from the past come to life before him was nothing but so much dull music. "What's on that table?" Mayor Clum asked while Fritz was demonstrating a personal health scanner, and with a sudden burst of energy, the mayor marched towards the second workbench.

"Everything we were fixing to show you is over here," Cassie said, almost stumbling over the words.

Mayor Clum found the light switch on the side of the second workbench and turned it on. He took a step back and folded his arms across his chest. "Ahh. Weapons. I knew there would be weapons." He scowled deeply at Harlan, then at Fritz, Siv, Cassie, and Annalie. Fritz rocked side-to-side on his feet, unsure what to say or do. Every second he spent waiting for Siv or Harlan to say something was intensely uncomfortable, but he wasn't about to break the silence himself.

"Well?" Mayor Clum barked. "Aren't you going to show me this, too?"

The hostility in his voice betrayed so much anger Fritz almost took a step backward. His distaste for conflict made him want to bolt from the room, and he almost did until a reassuring hand landed on his shoulder. His first instinct was to tense up at the physical touch and shrug it off, but he didn't want to insult his sister who was just trying to–

Oh. It wasn't Cassie. It was Annalie. And her touch... well, it wasn't completely unpleasant. He gave her an appreciative nod. Felix tugged at her pant leg, trying to pull her in the direction of the door. Annalie patted her brother's head and whispered something to him Fritz couldn't quite make out, but he understood Felix's mumbled response well enough. "Want to go home."

Fritz took his mobile out of his vest's inner pocket, tapped its screen until it displayed a fully dealt and ready-to-play solitaire card game, then put the device behind his back where Felix would see it. He gave it a little jiggle.

"Gratitude," Annalie whispered, "but I don't think–"

Annalie's words disappeared in a gasp as Felix yanked the mobile from Fritz's hand. Fritz glanced over his shoulder; the boy tapped and swiped at the screen, moving chipware playing cards into virtual piles. "Gratitude," Annalie whispered.

Fritz nodded, took a deep breath, and stepped up to the second workbench.

"Start there," Mayor Clum said, pointing at a hunting knife. "It's not a regular blade, is it?"

"No," Fritz said. He picked up the knife, pushed a button on its handle, and a line of green energy formed a perimeter around the edges of the blade. "It's laser-augmented."

"The better to cut through flesh *and* bone," Mayor Clum deadpanned. He plucked an arrow from a bucket full of them and examined its tip. It was pointed as one would expect, but just behind the arrowhead was a one-inch ball. "I assume the chipware addition to this arrow isn't meant to ensure it flies straighter."

Fritz placed the knife on the table and examined his shoes. He shrugged. "No. That's a bomb."

"Of course it is," Mayor Clum said. He returned the arrow to the bucket – a little more carefully than he'd taken it out – and frowned at the five rifles arranged in a neat flourish. "These fire not bullets, but 'lasers,' yes?"

Fritz nodded.

Mayor Clum shook his head and stepped before a tall shape standing on the floor next to the workbench and covered by a canvas tarp "And the question I've had since the moment I walked into this room. What is underneath that tarp?"

Under any other circumstance, Fritz would have been thrilled to show off his favorite part of his project, even to a group of a *hundred* total strangers. But with Mayor Clum's disdain for chipware as obvious as the nose on his face, Fritz knew the chipware under the tarp was going to earn him another lecture, and he already felt fatigued. Without waiting for permission, Mayor Clum yanked the tarp away.

"Oh, my stars!" Annalie said.

"By the Almighty Hand..." Mayor Clum said. He placed his face in his palm.

Felix even looked up from his game.

Fritz's robot stood a couple of inches taller than he did and was all sleek lines and shiny, green-painted steel. It was shaped like a human with its head, two arms, and two legs, though its face was a smooth, curved, featureless panel.

"What's the story with this, son?" Harlan asked quietly.

"I don't want to just restore old chipware," Fritz said. "I want to build new stuff. This is my robot. It doesn't have a remote control yet, and it would take me a few minutes to wire it up to my mobile to test its mechanics, so I can't make it move for you right now, but it works. It can walk, or even run if I use a long enough connecting cable. It flies OK, too, but we've been in hiding from the dem–"

"It *flies?*" Annalie said.

Next to the mayor's coldness, Annalie's unbridled enthusiasm was like stepping out of the midday sun into the cool shade of the great indoors. A bit of his tension disappeared. "Yeah! There are booster rockets in its back. Guidance thrusters come out of its calves–"

"What weapons does it possess?" Mayor Clum said. His eyes drilled laser-augmented daggers into Fritz, who felt his heart rate increase. His palms began to sweat, too.

"It has megabus ports all over, in its arms, legs, back," Fritz said. "That's a type of standard interface common to a lot of chipware. It makes the whole thing very modular and capable of sporting a wide variety of tools, so much so I've even thought of naming it the megabus man. Or the modular man. But I decided to call it Apple Juice."

He jumped at the suddenness and volume of Siv's laugh. Annalie snickered, too. Cassie never took her eyes off of Mayor Clum. "How'd you come up with a name like that?" Annalie asked.

"This is just version one, or version A," Fritz said. "As I continue to adapt and refine this design, the first letter of each new model's name will go through the alphabet sequentially, all based on a common theme: breakfast foods."

"Good man," Harlan said with a nod.

"Daisy," Annalie said. "Breakfast is the most splendiferous meal of the day. So version two would be, what? Bacon?"

"Yep," Fritz said. "Then Coffee, Doughnut, Egg–"

"Flapjack," Annalie said, "Grits–"

"Young man," Mayor Clum said, "be honest. You say this 'robot' can sport a wide variety of tools. But there isn't a single tool connected to that *thing* right now, is there?"

"Winston," Harlan said.

Mayor Clum silenced his sheriff with a raised hand.

Fritz's shoulders sunk. He put his hands behind his back and fidgeted. "No."

"Are its... *ports,* or whatever you called them, currently in use?"

Fritz nodded.

"And so if no tools are connected to those ports, what *is* connected to them?"

Goodness gracious, was this guy a lawyer when he wasn't mayoring a village? The tension and anger coming off of him were too much. Fritz fought his intense desire to run away, but refusing to flee caused his mind to stray instead. His thoughts went fuzzy, he lost concentration, and his peripheral vision went black. He took a deep breath and spoke slowly to keep his agitation at bay.

"Right now it has laser cannons in its arms," Fritz said. "They pop out when needed. Laser-enhanced knife blades come out of its wrists. A traditional ballistic weapon is in its right shoulder mount, though it's not loaded. And there are the booster rockets and guidance thrusters I mentioned for flying, but they're not really weapons."

Mayor Clum's frown deepened, and his jaw clenched.

"I suppose the missile launcher in its left shoulder mount is very much a weapon though," Fritz said.

Harlan looked at Siv and shook his head.

"That's not loaded, either..." Fritz mumbled.

"Mr. Mayor," Cassie said, "we want to use chipware to help people. That's what the Mantissa were all about and what the Mantissa Reborn *are* all about. We have these weapons because we thought freeing this town from the demons would mean war."

"And truth is," Siv said, "if Fritz hadn't come up a plan to exile them, we'd have had both sides, demon and man, killing each other to death. Chipware spared a lot of bloodshed."

Gah! Why was Siv telling the mayor it was *his* plan? Wasn't he on the spot enough already? His chest tightened.

"Can 'Apple Juice' think?" Mayor Clum asked in a way that made it clear he hadn't been listening, just waiting to talk.

It took Fritz a moment to realize the mayor had asked *him*. "No. Artificial intelligence is hard. There are lots of aspects to it that I'm having a hard time figuring out."

"But you *want* it to think," Mayor Clum said.

Fritz shuffled his feet. Where was this going? "Well, yeah."

"Two months since this chipware restoration began, yes?" Mayor Clum said. "It only took *two months*' worth of restoration to create a new Steelterror."

That did it. Fritz slammed his fist down on the nearest workbench. The chipware spread across it shook and rattled. Annalie flinched. Felix looked up from his card game. "The Steelterrors?" Fritz yelled. "Are you kidding me?"

Cassie desperately shook her head, but Fritz ignored her.

"The Steelterrors were, what, five hundred years ago?" Fritz said. "The world ran on chipware without any robotic menaces for three hundred years after they were defeated, then we spent the last two hundred stuck in the dark ages. Yet here we are in the year of Our Lord 1879, and we *still* have a deep, idiotic cultural bias against artificial intelligence. By the *stars*, why is it that as soon as you bring up chipware, some imbecile *always* has to bring up the Steelterrors?"

Siv winced and closed his eyes.

"Because the Steelterrors nearly destroyed the world, young man!" Mayor Clum shouted back. "Do you know anything about them, or do you dismiss legitimate fear of them as 'idiotic' out of total ignorance?"

Fritz bit his lip and looked away. He was done with this conversation. *Done.* He mimed a flapping mouth with his hands. "Talky, talky, talky," he mumbled.

"*Fritz,*" Cassie said.

"I'm a student of history," Mayor Clum said. "The Steelterrors were created when Doctor Wilyam Albrecht believed the natural forces of the planet could be harnessed, controlled, and redirected. Out of this twisted belief, he made four enormous machines, each one embodying an element of the ancient world: soil, air, water, and fire. He, too, just wanted to help. That's small consolation to the souls massacred by his creations. Do you know the word most often used in the histories to describe the lost city of Drandenburg after the Steelterrors were through with it? '*Flattened.*' Only the rise of a new class of humans was enough to stop Albrecht's giant metal monsters."

"The Mantissa," Siv said quietly.

"I hope you can appreciate the irony," Mayor Clum said. "A group calling itself the 'Mantissa Reborn' wishes to create new Steelterrors."

If the mayor used the word "Steelterrors" one more time, Fritz was going to shove the man's stupid hat right into his smug "student of history" face. This was backward, prehistoric bias. It belonged on the Stupid List, and in a very high-ranking position, he might add. Quality of life worldwide was never going to be improved so long as there were ignorant morons who believed a monster lurked inside every piece of chipware.

Mayor Clum exhaled, adjusted the lapels of his jacket and his tie. "Earp is not interested in chipware of any kind," he said. "Do not bring this garbage to my village."

He walked towards the door. Fritz didn't bother to watch him go. He just tried to bleed off his anger and hold down the panic that rose up behind it. What had he done, yelling at another person like that? And what did this mean for his project? If not Earp, then what would be the first town he restored? His entire focus had been on Earp because that's where Harlan lived, and if not for Harlan's inspiration and encouragement, he'd still be back home at his parents' farmhouse, tinkering with chipware alone in his bedroom.

"Winston," Harlan said, and something heavy – a chipware device Harlan had lifted from underneath the table – slammed down onto the first workbench. "One more thing to show you. This here's a sewing machine. In an hour it can make twice as many stitches as a person can make in a whole day."

Mayor Clum stopped a few feet in front of the door.

"How much clothing has your mama made over the years, Winston? Could you even count it all? She's dressed every person in our village. How many nights has she stayed up late to make sure children had pants without holes in them? How many times did she wake up early to work on a bride's wedding dress? If she'd had one of these all her life, *all* those things still would've happened, except I reckon she'd still be able to move her fingers today and would still be making clothes instead of feeling useless."

Mayor Clum's face flushed red. "That is out of line."

"No, you are," Harlan said. "It *is* important to learn from history. But it's just as important not to curse the future because of mistakes made in the past."

Fritz didn't know how long the two of them stared at one another, mostly because his discomfort left him staring at the floor. But it was a long silence – uncomfortably long, and normally, Fritz loved silence so much, there was no such thing as too much of it. Mayor Clum finally exhaled and looked to Harlan. "You really think, as our sheriff, this poses no danger to the safety of our village?"

Harlan exhaled. "The only things about us chipware will change are how much time we spend working and how much time we spend living."

Wow. Fritz would have to encourage Siv to use those words in one of his leader speeches.

"I won't allow any chipware weapons in the village," Mayor Clum said. "And no Steelterrors, or robots, or whatever you want to call that thing in the corner."

"We have elected you mayor four times now, old friend," Harlan said. "We value and will respect your counsel."

A heavy silence hung over the room. Someone tugged at Fritz's trousers. Felix had emerged from behind Annalie's leg and showed Fritz his mobile. The playing cards hopped across the screen in a victory dance. "Won," Felix said.

Annalie covered her mouth. She looked the same as she had when she realized he planned to run off the demons and restore the ancient world. "Oh my gosh," she whispered. "He never..."

Fritz gave Felix a thumb's up. The kid smiled and started another game.

Mayor Clum looked to Siv. "How long will it take you to install this...?"

"Sparksline," Siv said. "About two weeks total, but only the last two days or so will be in Earp itself. The rest will be spent burying about twenty-five miles of new cable through Terrascorcha between here and there."

"Very well then," Mayor Clum said quietly. "Based on the advice of my sheriff, you have my permission to bring chipware to Earp."

75

```
[1879-08-25 02:00] root@skylab:/bin > .\secscan
Begin scan with default parameters (range: 500 AU)
......
Scan complete. (0) matches found.

[1879-08-25 03:00] root@skylab:/bin > .\secscan
Begin scan with default parameters (range: 500 AU)
......
Scan complete. (0) matches found.

[1879-08-25 04:00] root@skylab:/bin > .\secscan
Begin scan with default parameters (range: 500 AU)
......
Scan complete. (0) matches found.

[1879-08-25 05:00] root@skylab:/bin > .\secscan
Begin scan with default parameters (range: 500 AU)
......
Scan complete. (0) matches found.

[1879-08-25 06:00] root@skylab:/bin > .\secscan
Begin scan with default parameters (range: 500 AU)
......
Scan complete. (0) matches found.

[1879-08-25 07:00] root@skylab:/bin > .\secscan
Begin scan with default parameters (range: 500 AU)
......
Scan complete. (0) matches found.

[1879-08-25 08:00] root@skylab:/bin > .\secscan
Begin scan with default parameters (range: 500 AU)
......
Scan complete. (0) matches found.
```

Chapter Six

"Lawnmower?" Siv asked. From where he sat in Tobias's saddle, he reached towards the spool of thick wire mounted on the horse's side and pulled a kink from it, allowing it to unspool cleanly and fall neatly into the ditch.

"No. Thirteen," Fritz said without bothering to look up from his mobile's screen, which he shielded from the sun with one hand. It displayed a map of their current location in middle-of-nowhere Terrascorcha, with a blue line tracing his desired path for the sparksline. The mobile was turned sideways and mounted on the handlebars of his motorbike, which puttered along slowly on the opposite side of the ditch from Tobias. A thin wire connected his mobile to the utility robot leading their procession. It traveled on treads, and its downward facing blades dug the trench for them. He had cleverly named it Digger.

"It is a water jug?" Annalie asked. A bandanna covered her hair, both for protection from the sun and to mop up sweat from the late August heat. She sat in a sidecar mounted onto

Fritz's motorbike, which made the bike easier to balance at the slow speeds ditch digging required. A wire snaked out from her mobile to Apple Juice, who brought up the rear of their procession. Its arm tool sockets were equipped with shovels, and it pushed the soil back into place and buried the sparksline under the ground.

"No," Fritz said. He tapped his mobile's screen and made a slight adjustment to Digger's course. "Fourteen."

"What the tarnation?" Siv said. "It's bigger than a breadbox but smaller than a horse. It's not alive. It's made of metal but not something I make in my shop."

"And it's something on your dad's farm back home, right?" Annalie said.

"Yes," Fritz said. "Fifteen."

"That was not a question!" Annalie said.

"It was," Fritz said, "and a valid yes or no question, too."

She frowned at him. "I'm mighty good at checkers. When we stop for the night, I'll find stones to use for pieces, and we're gonna play. And I'm gonna beat you."

"It's not a tractor," Siv said. "Or a scythe, or a shovel. Or barbed wire fence."

Tobias whinnied. "Good man," Siv said. "It's not horse tack, either. Gratitude for the reminder." He scratched Tobias behind his ear.

Annalie scrunched her nose. "Horse tack? How did you understand–"

"Just go with him on it," Fritz said to Annalie in an undertone, "or all we'll hear for the next hour is how Tobias is God's equine gift to the world."

Annalie flashed him an OK symbol with her fingers. "And it's nothing you personally own, rig–" she said, then stopped herself. "Wait, that was not a question!"

Siv laughed. "Yeah, he said it's not something of his. Before he did, I almost thought it was that motorbike."

"Rover," Fritz said.

"Rover?" Siv repeated. "This is not a question, but what's Rover?"

"That *is* a question, but not one with a yes or no answer, so it doesn't count," Fritz said. "But I'll answer it anyway. Rover is the new name for my horse. Because I use it to rove around."

Siv shook his head and sighed. "That motorbike doesn't need a name."

Fritz shrugged. "You told me every horse needs to have a name."

Tobias grunted. "That's *not* a horse," Siv said.

"What's on your back?" Fritz said.

"Oh, if you ask *us* a question, we should get a free one in return," Annalie said.

Siv barked out a laugh, pointed at Annalie, and clicked his tongue.

Fritz rolled his eyes. "Fine."

"You know darn well the sword on my back is the Dragon Slayer," Siv answered.

"So you've named your sword," Fritz said, "but you feel my horse is undeserving of–"

Siv sighed heavily to interrupt him. "Is it a piece of farming equipment?"

"No," Fritz said, "and that was your free question."

Digger plodded forward on its treads, scooping dirt aside behind it to form a trench. Siv unwound the last bit of wire from the spool, and it dropped into the furrow. Apple Juice covered all but the final three inches of it when Annalie tapped her mobile's screen and made the human-shaped robot halt. "New spool," Siv said.

Fritz brought Rover to a stop and lifted a fresh spool of wire off a shelf mounted on the back of the sidecar. He brought it to Siv while Annalie crouched beside the end of the wire they'd just buried, pointed her mobile at it, and consulted its screen. "Sparks still flowing," she said.

A buzzing came from the distance, followed by the echoed clicking of claws or pincers.

"What the blazes?" Annalie said. She leaped to her feet and squinted in the direction of the sound.

"Locust," Siv said. "Though not the regular kind about the length of your finger. This kind's the size of a man."

"A *big* man," Fritz said.

Most southerners, like Fritz and Siv, believed the entire continent north of the Lavare Mountains was toxic land populated by monsters and rendered inhospitable by the same whatever-it-was that caused the Blackout. It's how the land got the name "Terrascorcha," but this belief was only half true. Terrascorcha was clean as holy water, environmentally speaking, but monsters *did* live there: genetically engineered creations of the white demons, part of the army they released onto Verde just before the Mantissa scrambled all the world's chipware.

The last time Fritz and Siv were out in Terrascorcha on foot, Cassie was with them. A man-sized locust a mere hundred yards away, leaping straight towards them five feet at a time, wasn't such a big deal when a Mantissa healer knew it was coming before anyone could hear it.

"I miss Cassie's danger sense," Fritz said.

"I miss Cass," Siv said. He gave Annalie a nervous glance. "You want to take care of that for us, Red? Robot has the longest range."

"That's one of the demons' creations?" Annalie said. "Never seen that one before. We knew they made the monsters, sure, but we knew it 'cause they ran them off anytime they came near town. And I never seen one like that come near Mondorf. Not that I sat near the fence and watched for 'em much, though. I was Maintenance Duty, not Perimeter Duty."

Fritz and Siv shared a nervous glance at the locust, then at each other. Siv reached for his shotgun. Fritz pressed his hand against his vest where his laser pistol normally sat holstered, but it was back with Rover. "Umm, Annalie, you have control of Apple Juice at the moment..." he said. "Could you...?"

"Now the monsters of theirs that really scarified me was the black-skinned, four-armed– jeepers, you weren't kidding, that bug is bigger than a person," Annalie said. "Holy moly, what does that kind of thing eat?"

"Us," Siv said, yanking his shotgun free of its saddle holster. The locust was just thirty feet away. The snap of its pincers echoed over the dirty, dusty hills. The late morning sun sparkled off the back of its wings, which were the size of Fritz's legs. Its legs were the size of Fritz's torso.

"Annalie, would you please fire Apple Juice's gun at that thing?" Fritz shouted. "Somewhat immediately?"

"Oh!" Annalie said. "I forgot."

Siv fired his shotgun, and with a crack like thunder, a single solid slug ripped through the locust's chest. It was ten feet away. It stumbled but reared back on its legs to leap at them again.

Annalie tapped the screen of her mobile. Apple Juice, still standing at the rear of their procession, didn't move, but the machine gun mounted on its back did. It raised itself above the robot's head and spun around to point at the locust. Annalie covered her ears. The robot shot five bullets in rapid succession. *Bang-bang-bang-bang-bang.* The locust dropped to the ground, dead.

Fritz exhaled and clutched his chest.

"Sorry," Annalie said. "I was rambling again, wasn't I?"

"Yes," Fritz said. "Sixteen."

"That was not–!" Annalie blew a raspberry at him, then knelt down next to the end of the length of sparksline they'd finished burying. "Give me the end of that new wire. And pardon my rudeness, but if I'd asked for it politely, it would have come out phrased as a question."

Fritz pulled a length of wire off the new spool, which Siv had already mounted on the side of Tobias's saddle, and handed the end of it to her. Annalie snapped together the new wire and the buried one, then wrapped the connection in thick black tape. She pointed her mobile at the new spool, checked the screen, and dusted off her hands. "New wire's hot. And I reckon I give up trying to ponder what this metal, bigger-than-a-bread-box thing you don't own on your dad's farm is."

"Me, too," Siv said. "What is it?"

"It's a breadbox," Fritz said.

"You said it was bigger than a breadbox!" Siv protested.

"No, I said it was not smaller than a breadbox," Fritz said.

"Ain't bread boxes normally made of wood?" Annalie said.

"Yes," Siv said, "and I've seen the one on your father's farm. It's made of maple, not metal. Monkeyshines. I call monkeyshines on this."

"I said we have one back at my dad's farm," Fritz said, "not that I was thinking of the one on my dad's farm. And a breadbox *could* be made of metal. No reason why not." Fritz climbed onto Rover and shrugged. "Twenty Questions is a game of intellectual preciseness."

Siv murmured something, likely a profanity, but it wasn't long before his mutterings dissolved into his loud, boisterous laugh. Annalie got back into her sidecar. "I'm going to beat you at checkers *three times*, Mr. Intellectually Precise. And by the way, *precisely* how long until lunch? I didn't want to ask before and have it count as a question."

"Maybe after this spool is done?" Siv said. "Another hour?"

"Hey," Fritz said, pointing at the map on his mobile's screen, "exactly two hundred-twenty-two miles left to go. 2-2-2. We're making good progress. We should finish right on time in nine more days."

"That's time for plenty more Twenty Questions," Siv deadpanned.

"Oh, you want to play again?" Fritz said. "OK, I'm thinking of–"

"No," Siv and Annalie said.

"We've been out here for two days," Fritz said into his mobile. "The new line is working great. In fact, it's charging the robots right now." Digger and Apple Juice were both plugged into a regulator box attached to the end of the sparksline. Fritz had also wired up a single sparksbulb and dangled it over the top of Digger, providing their camp with extra light for the night watch.

"Sounds like I could use Digger to plow furrows in the field at sowing," Milo said. The speaker of Fritz's mobile not only conveyed his father's voice, but also a sigh, a hint of fatigue. Fritz frowned. A thin strip of sunlight bordered the eastern horizon. Hondo was even farther east than this point of Terrascorcha and much farther south, so by his estimation, his dad should have been awake for at least an hour or so.

"Did I call too early, Dad? You sound tired."

"You didn't call too early. I'm always happy to hear from you. Your mother and I are so grateful you gave us these devices to stay in touch with you. Grateful and very proud. Siv doing well?"

About thirty yards away from him, Siv and Annalie slept in their bedrolls. "Yeah, he's great. And he's learning. One of Digger's blade arms broke yesterday afternoon, and before Annalie could repair it, Siv asked if he could take a look. And he fixed it! I'm going to turn him into a chipware repairman yet. Might have to give him his own descrambler for Lenerstellen."

"I'm glad you're keeping him busy. I figure he misses Cassie something fierce."

Oh, gosh, Dad was probably right. The fall semester would be the longest span of time Siv and Cassie had been separated since they met. Siv would probably soon be in a funk over it if he wasn't already. Fritz had been so focused on their work, so excited at running a major new sparksline and wiring up Harlan's village, he hadn't even considered Siv's feelings. Some friend he was.

"Yeah, of course," Fritz said. "Of course he does. I suppose it helps they talk via mobile every day. But I'll talk to him about it later. See how he's doing."

"Who's Annalie?"

Fritz's cheeks flushed at the idea of talking to his dad about her. "She's a person we met in Mondorf. She's good at fixing things and knows a lot about historical chipware, too. She's been a big help."

While she slept, Fritz noticed how different Annalie's face looked without her glasses. Not worse, or better. Just different. He smiled.

"*She* is a chipware expert?" Milo said.

"Yeah." Fritz shifted uncomfortably. "Hey, Dad, what do you know about bluebonnets?"

"They're one of your mother's favorite flowers."

"How fast do they grow?"

"How fast? Well, they have a low germination rate, so you need to plant a lot of seeds if you want to get some to survive. And they have a hard seed coating. You need to scarify the seeds if you want to make them grow a little faster. But once they germinate, you'll start to see some of the first signs of flowers in about a month or two."

"What could make them grow and disappear again in minutes? Or even seconds?"

Milo laughed. "An act of God? I've heard of flowers blooming on the spot where saints knelt to pray. But other than that, bluebonnets don't just instantly sprout. No plant does."

"No, no, of course not."

"Why all the interest in bluebonnets?"

"I saw some recently that grew fairly quick."

"Recently? They're spring flowers. This year's crop died off four months ago. They're still growing up north?"

Before Fritz could say anything more, the bulb lighting their camp went dark. The tiny red lights indicating Digger and Apple Juice's batteries were recharging also extinguished. All three lights turning off simultaneously meant – aw crud, the sparksline must have broken. They'd have to go back, find the break, and fix it. More work. *Extra* work. Bah.

"Dad, I'm going to have to talk to you later. I need to check something out."

"Take care of yourself out there. I love you, son."

"Yeah, I will. Love you, too."

Fritz tiptoed past Siv and Annalie and inspected the power connections on the bulb's cord and the two bots and the regulator's connection to the main sparksline. They were all secure, and the bulb still wasn't lit, and the bots still weren't charging. He pointed his mobile at the sparksline, ran a voltage detection scan, and got a great big zero. He didn't want to wake Siv or Annalie, but the sun was rising, and they all wanted to get as much done as possible before afternoon when the August heat would be at its most unbearable. And they weren't going to get any new sparksline in the ground until they figured out where the line they'd already laid had broken. He roused them and explained the situation.

"I'll go check it out with you," Annalie said while yawning.

"If you get a half-mile or so back yonder and still haven't found the problem," Siv said, "stop and call me and wait for Tobias and me to join you. This is Terrascorcha. No strayin' too far."

"Sure," Fritz said. "Annalie and Rover and I will be on our way then."

Siv rolled his eyes at his motorbike's name but didn't say anything. After Annalie climbed into the sidecar, Fritz gunned Rover's engine, leaving a cloud of dust Ban their wake. It was easy to trace the sparksline back; the dirt was still fresh where they'd filled in their trench. Fritz steered Rover alongside it while Annalie pointed her mobile at the buried line and ran voltage detection scans.

"Did you get enough rest before your watch?" Annalie asked him.

"I did," Fritz said. "How about you?" Both nights they'd spent in Terrascorcha so far, Annalie had volunteered to take the second watch. She said she was used to having her sleep interrupted by her siblings, or by the demons.

"I woke for my watch a little early. Had a nightmare. Siv showed me a few constellations before I sent him to sleep. Helped get my mind off of it. Say, he said the frozen star isn't a star at all? It's a space station in orbit above Verde, and y'all have been there?"

"Skylab, yeah," Fritz said. "What was your nightmare about?"

"It was nothing." A three-second pause. "It was my siblings. I haven't been away from them for... well, ever, really. But not at all since our folks died. I just need to remind myself Bradon is more than capable of taking care of them all by his lonesome, and that he doesn't even have to because Ramona and Henry are watching over them, too. And I'll be back in a little over a week."

Fritz assumed Bradon was her oldest brother. He knew Felix was the youngest. Wait a minute. "Are you and your siblings named in alphabetical order?"

She slapped his shoulder and laughed. "You noticed. Yes! Me, then Bradon, Clark, Della, Elise, and Felix."

"Your parents used my robot-naming convention," Fritz said. "Except I suppose they used it first, so maybe I'm using *their* child-naming convention. But either way, I like it. Very orderly. Very practical."

"Gratitude. It was all my dad's idea. My mama was just amused by the whole thing." She let out a deep breath. "They would have loved this, you know. Rebuilding the ancient world. Everyone said they were crazy to bring one child into life under the demons' rule, let alone six, but my dad firmly believed things were going to get better. He said they just had to. And when he'd talk about a brighter future, my mom would just look at him with this twinkle in her eye, and she would *smile*. Sometimes, I think they didn't even see the world around them. They just saw each other." She shook her head as if to clear cobwebs from it. "Sorry, rambling again."

"That was a good ramble," he said. "Still nothing on the voltage detector?"

"Zilch," she said. "No beepy beepy."

Rover. The more he thought about it, Rover was a rubbish name, too. To rove was to wander, to move about aimlessly, but his motorbike went exactly where he steered it. He sighed. Rover wasn't going to work, either. He'd keep using it until he thought of something different, but gosh, naming things was hard. The way he saw it, there were two hard things in this chipware restoration business: artificial intelligence and naming things.

He'd driven a half-mile past their camp, so he was just about to stop and call for Siv when he found the sparksline's problem, and he found it with his eyes, not with the beepy beepy on Annalie's mobile. There was a four-foot diameter hole in the ground. A mound of dirt pulled from it lined its perimeter. Each side of the hole had a piece of power conduit poking into it, but in the center, where the two pieces should have met, there was just a bundle of loose and very disconnected wires.

"Stay in the sidecar," Fritz said as he brought the motorbike to a stop. He reached into his pocket for his mobile. "Other than the tire tracks we just made, I don't want to disturb the scene at all until Siv gets here and gets a chance to look for tracks."

He'd expected the break in the power conduit to be at a junction. He'd reckoned two segments hadn't been tightened securely enough and had come apart. He hadn't even considered the break being a single segment ripped in two, but he knew what it meant. Sabotage. Something had deliberately dug a hole and broken the sparksline. And he'd seen the sparksbulb in camp go dim just – what – fifteen, twenty minutes earlier?

He tensed and looked sharply at Annalie. She'd come to the same realization he had. If the break in the line was sabotage, and if it had just happened, then they were in the middle of nowhere, but not alone. And whatever had done it was most likely still nearby.

Fritz's left foot *tap-tap-tap-tapped* against Rover's gearshift ratchet. His fingers drummed the handlebars. Siv crouched low and examined the hole something had dug to sabotage Fritz's sparksline. His work. He knew he shouldn't disrupt the area so Siv could get a good read on where the saboteur had come from and, more important, where it had gone. But the waiting was dull music.

After several minutes of inspection, Siv stood up and frowned. "Ain't no tracks."

"So whatever did it... flew here?" Annalie said. "Like a bird? Or can walk light enough not to leave any footprints?"

"Something that light couldn't get enough leverage to lift this much dirt out of the ground," Siv said. "No, whatever did this came up from below."

Fritz leaped off the bike. He assumed it was OK to pace the area now. Annalie had already dismounted to stand next to Rover, and Tobias grazed on what little grass was available. "Remember those three-foot diameter worms from our first trip up this way, back in June?" Fritz said. "They burrowed up from below. Maybe it was one of them? But we only ever saw those further south, closer to the mountains, where the soil was much more sandy."

"Yeah, I remember those giant, ugly buggers," Siv said, "but this here hole seemed too small for one of those."

Fritz crouched at the edge of the hole to get a better look at the damage done. "If whatever did it *did* come up from below, it may not have even intended to break the sparksline. The line may have just been in its way."

"That your intuition power talking?" Siv said.

"Not really." Fritz shrugged. "Just a guess."

"And not a bad one," Siv said. "But take a gander at the break. It doesn't have the ragged, jagged look of something smashing through. It's a neat cut, the kind a straight blade makes."

The grass surrounding the hole caught Fritz's eye. It was a darker color – a dirty, brownish green – than the rest of the grass in the area. It reminded him of the grass with the reddish tint he'd seen back in Mondorf. The rest of the area was a much more vivid green.

And then a bluebonnet sprouted out of the ground adjacent to the hole.

"What the devil?" Siv said.

"It wasn't there a moment ago, was it?" Fritz said. "It just–"

Tobias made a high-pitched neigh and a ball of dirt the size of Fritz's head sprouted from the ground underneath the flower. The shape of shoulders followed, then arms, a body, and legs. In a quick pair of seconds, a five-and-a-half-foot-tall person made of dirt and mud had emerged out of the soil. It possessed no color other than the brown of the dirt. Its surface was choppy, covered with bumps and ridges. It had no face, just an uneven sheet of dirt where one should have been.

It stepped across the hole in the dirt towards them. Annalie yelped and pulled her revolver from its holster. Siv drew the Dragon Slayer out of its scabbard. The clumps of dirt and mud making up the creature's limbs rippled and smoothed. Facial features appeared – a mouth, nose, eye sockets. Fritz startled when a wave of color appeared in the middle of its chest, spreading outward until the creature didn't appear to be made of dirt and soil at all. Instead, it looked like a woman. It – she – wore a gray, short-sleeved, ankle-length dress. Her long hair draped a foot past her shoulders. It was varying shades of silver and white with the bluebonnet laced into it above her left ear.

"I'm Lady Verde," she said.

"Holy moly," Annalie whispered.

"Lady Verde?" Siv said once he found his voice. "As in the spirit of the planet?"

"I don't normally manifest myself to humans, but I've been watching you. And I need to make myself perfectly clear." Lady Verde motioned towards the broken sparksline conduit behind her and towards Fritz's motorbike. "Stop repairing chipware. Stop this step backward. Stop this return to the old ways of pollution, destruction of the environment, and human-made climate change."

Fritz felt his hands go cold. Every time he'd seen a bluebonnet spontaneously grow – had that been Lady Verde? The *spirit of the planet?* And her message... She'd said, "Stop repairing chipware." But what Fritz heard was: stop his project. His work. His life.

An image appeared above Lady Verde's upraised palm. It was like looking at the screen of a mobile, except the image floated in the air. It depicted a river next to a city – a pre-Blackout city, full of sparkslights and aerocars and public vidscreens. It was exactly the kind of dwelling he was trying to bring back to Verde, but the city was in the background. In the foreground was the river, and it was on fire.

Fritz blinked. How did a *river* catch on *fire?* Didn't water extinguish flame? But there it was, in Lady Verde's image anyway – clouds of thick smoke coughing out of four-foot tall flames on the surface of the river.

"This is what the Elde River looked like in Borusia two and a half centuries ago," Lady Verde said. "It was filled with so much byproduct from sparks-generation plants it caught fire. Numerous times."

The image floating above her hands changed to a large complex of buildings. It looked like some kind of castle from the old stories with its round towers looking down upon massive, wide structures beneath. But when he saw exhaust poured out of each tower, he realized it was something built several centuries after ancient fortresses – a manufacturing plant of some kind.

"Toxins pumped into my skies in the name of 'progress,'" Lady Verde said.

Once more the image changed, this time to a swath of brown land pocked with small black dots. Tree stumps. "And you certainly don't recognize the Naunhof Forest. It was clear-cut three hundred years before any of you were born."

The image faded and Lady Verde fixed Fritz with a hard stare. "What's any of that got to do with my work?" he stammered.

"Every single one of those crimes against me was committed by a too-rapidly growing population consuming too many resources, with not a single care given to my well-being."

"We ain't doing any of those things," Siv said.

"Yet," she said. "And for two hundred years, no one has."

"Not since the Blackout," Annalie mumbled.

"You call it the Blackout," Lady Verde said. "I call it the day my oppressors died. Forgive me if that sounds overly dramatic, but I don't want to be set on fire again. I don't want my forests eliminated. I don't want verloid gas pumped into my skies."

"I don't even know what verloid gas is," Fritz said.

"Then let's talk dynamek energy," Lady Verde said. "You know all about that, don't you?"

He certainly did; he'd liberated Mondorf to secure the Ulmbaden Power Facility and the three gigakrafts of dynamek energy it manufactured per day. Lady Verde extended her hand, and another image appeared on it – a park in the middle of a city. Fritz recognized the shape of the city's skyline. It was Mondorf, but the pristine condition of those buildings indicated the image was from at least two centuries prior, before the Blackout. The park itself looked fairly normal. Children giggled on swings and climbing bars. A family ate a picnic lunch on a blanket. People rode bicycles and sat on benches.

But something wasn't right. The people's clothing and the activities suggested summer, but the leaves on the trees were an autumn-like orange and red. Only if it were autumn, some of those leaves should have been in piles on the ground. None were. And with no leaves on the ground, Fritz had a completely unobstructed view of the park's bright red grass.

"This is what exposure to dynamek energy and its byproducts did to plant life two hundred years ago," Lady Verde said. "Mondorf became known as the Crimson City. Those responsible said the effects were only cosmetic, and they *insisted* there was absolutely no correlation between the red-tinted fruits and vegetables sold in the mega markets and the dramatically increased rates of cancer. After all, if dynamek energy was a carcinogen, imagine the negative impact on the Ulmbaden corporation's stock price."

The image of the blood red park disappeared. Siv gave Fritz an uncertain glance. They'd both noticed the slight red tint of the grass back in Mondorf. Was that really the remnants of dynamek energy production? If so, how potent was that damage, considering its remnants were still visible some two *hundred* years later?

"What exactly is it you want from us?" Siv said.

Her lip curled when she pointed to the broken sparksline. "Get that out of my ground."

Fritz chewed on the nail of his ring finger. This couldn't be happening. It was bad enough he had to talk and convince folks like Mayor Clum of Earp there was nothing dangerous about chipware just so he could just get to work already. Now the living embodiment of the planet wanted him to stop? She'd already ripped his sparksline apart once. She could do it again, over and over, if she wanted.

But even worse – what if she was right? With the power plant reactivated, would dynamek energy byproducts slowly poison the planet?

"What if we say no?" Siv asked.

Lady Verde glared at him. "The *arrogance.*"

Siv put his hands up in a placating gesture. "Humor me."

Though Siv had asked the question, Lady Verde looked at Fritz when she answered. "If you continue to build this sparksline, I'll make this matter a public debate. Yours will no longer be the only voice people hear."

The words "public debate" filled Fritz with dread, but not as much being singled out. "Not my voice," Fritz said. "This isn't *my* project. This is a Mantissa project. That's who we are, you know: the Mantissa Reborn."

She looked unimpressed. "I will not remain the silent observer I have been for centuries. I will make sure the people understand this from my perspective. I'll see to it they're fully informed about *all* chipware is capable of, including the destruction it has wrought. I'll educate the very people you claim to want to help. And trust me: my knowledge of this issue comes from personal memory, and it goes back far longer than yours."

Lady Verde's body lost its color, and her legs sank into the ground.

"If you finish building this sparksline, our public debate will begin in Earp."

The rest of her body melted away into the dirt. Last to go was the bluebonnet she'd worn in her hair.

Annalie sucked in air like she'd been holding her breath. "I don't even believe what I just saw."

Fritz wrapped one arm around himself and resumed gnawing on his fingernail. His shoulders tightened, and he gently rocked back and forth. Lady Verde had promised to educate the people of Earp, to convince them his project led to destruction. She'd threatened public debate! He was willing to work hard for his project, but he didn't want to be the leader, the talker, the face of the project. He sure as sin didn't want to have to talk to everyone in Earp about it.

And what if he debated and won in Earp, and what if she did this again in the next town? What if she demanded a public debate in every town planet-wide? The broken sparksline proved she had the power to wreak havoc if he ignored her.

Siv took his mobile from the back pocket of his jeans. "I'm calling Cass and Sebastian. They ought to know our project just got threatened by a living, breathing fairy story."

Chapter Seven

It was past sunset, but Earp was lit like noontime. Strings of thumb-sized sparksbulbs were draped across the front of buildings and stretched over the top of main streets. Poles with bulbs the size of Fritz's fist had been planted in the ground. Heck, they'd even run a lengthy string of lights around the top of the thirty-foot-tall wooden fence surrounding the village and protecting the settlement from the monsters of the forest. Eventually, the residents would build permanent fixtures for the lights. They'd mount them more securely to the buildings, and they'd strengthen the poles with mortar. But for now, they had a street party to attend.

Ribbons and bunting were hung everywhere, tables had been set up on the street and laid out with a variety of food and drink, and what seemed to Fritz to be every one of the village's three hundred citizens congregated in the middle of the main street. They ate, they danced, and some even read books under the sparkslights, just because they'd never read outside at night before. Fritz loved that. If he got invited to more parties with dedicated reading rooms, he'd attend more parties.

But the bookworms were the exceptions. Most of the revelers talked and laughed and cried out with joy. So many conversations, all trying to compete to be heard over the others and the noise of the band, because of *course* there was a band. Maybe if he got lucky there would be firecrackers and humming and finger tapping and lip-smacking, too. A headache formed right behind his forehead. It made it even more difficult to focus on the words of the older couple before him.

"Hmm," he said, holding his chin in his hand and nodding. He was fairly certain they were gabbing about how incredible it was to have sparks in Earp, to see even this small bit of chipware return, but his peripheral vision was disappearing as the conversation – probably the nineteenth or twentieth he'd had that evening – drained him of his energy. The only reason Fritz even remembered the couple owned the general store was they had asked about the practicality of installing a refrigerator in their establishment, from which they could sell pre-chilled sodas and beers.

And there were two more folks queued up behind them. People were actually waiting in line to talk to him. It was like a bad dream he couldn't wake up from.

Oh! The store owners were waiting for a reply to a question he hadn't heard. "Umm, yes, most certainly. Yes, that is... so... common. Isn't it? But from another perspective... that is to say... you were asking...?"

"Excuse me!"

Suddenly, Annalie was at his side, her elbow wrapped around the crook of his arm. Fritz had to look twice to make certain it was her. He'd never seen her in anything like the poofy purple dress she sported, nor had he ever seen her red hair pinned up high atop her head. And was that eyeshadow behind her spectacles? "Beg pardon for interrupting," Annalie said to the store owners and, over their heads, to the others waiting to speak to Fritz, "but I've got to show him something. I'll get him right back to you."

Spinning on her heel, she turned him in the opposite direction and marched him away. "Actually I won't," she said in a low voice. "Just reckoned you needed a way out of that fiddle-faddle."

"God bless you," Fritz said. "How did you know?"

"Was about as obvious as a wart on a frog."

Fritz shrugged. "I guess I just don't like to talk very much."

"I don't know about that," Annalie said. "Get you on the right subject, and you'll talk my ear right off. But you don't do well in a group at all. In a group, you shut up tighter than a rattlesnake coiled 'round its prey."

"I suppose that's a fair assessment," Fritz said. His cheeks felt warm. "Thank you for noticing."

"It's nothing. You want some punch?" She led him to one of the tables with a feast spread across it. Meat, bread, cheeses, deserts – it was three full meals' worth of options, and this was just one of seven food tables scattered around the party area. Annalie handed him a cup of punch. "It's strawberry. And it is *so* good. I think I've had five cups so far."

If she owned up to drinking five, she'd probably had seven. She downed her punch in three gulps, then gathered a plate of food.

Fritz noticed a necklace completed her ensemble. "You look fancy," he said.

"I've never worn anything like this in my life!" she said. "I feel vaguely ridiculous, but I kind of like it, too. They offered me some high-heeled shoes, kind like I ain't ever seen before except in books, but I said no thanks 'cause I need a pair of broken ankles like I need another hole in my head."

Fritz took a plate and dressed it with a chicken leg and a slice of bread. It looked like a pauper's meal compared to Annalie's four-level pyramid of chicken wings. Annalie must have caught him staring. "OK, I admit it. This is my third plate. But the folks here are so nice! They just keep telling me to eat."

An elderly woman leaned towards Annalie from the other side of the table and dropped two more wings on her plate. "Eat!" she commanded.

Annalie enthusiastically obeyed, even before they stepped away from the serving tables and found a pair of chairs near the edge of the festivities. The lively music still made the area louder than Fritz would have preferred, but at least he could hear himself think. The seat gave him a clear view of the perimeter fence's main gate three blocks up the street. The gate guard used her viewport to keep an eye on the other side of the wall, but more often looked back at the party. Nothing must have been stirring out in the forest. No monsters, no travelers, no spirit of the planet demanding a public debate on the morality of chipware.

On the opposite side of the very crowded dancing area, Siv was having a beer with Harlan and his deputies on the saloon's porch. Harlan said something – it was incomprehensible due to distance – and Siv threw back his head and laughed uproariously. Fritz was not at all surprised that Siv's familiar laughter carried over all the other party noise. Nor was he surprised Mayor Clum lurked off to the side of the gathering, alone and glowering with his arms folded across his chest.

And in the time it had taken him to soak in the details of his surroundings, Annalie had inhaled half the food on her plate.

"Where do you put everything you eat?" Fritz asked. "If I ate the way you do, I'd weigh as much as my motorbike."

Annalie nearly spit her strawberry punch she guffawed so hard.

"Wait, I'm sorry," Fritz said. "Was that rude? You're not supposed to ask a woman anything about her weight, right?"

"You didn't offend me," she said. "I like how direct you are. No, at some point, I'm going to have to stop eating this much. But the thing is, the demons always fed us enough to stay alive and healthy, but never anything more. Shindigs like this or the party y'all threw in Mondorf after we ran the demons out of town are things I only ever dreamed about. I just want to savor every moment!"

Fritz smiled. "Well, I hope this kind of happiness finds you more often. You deserve it. I mean, everyone from Mondorf does."

"Aww, gratitude." She looked over the very crowded dancing area. Fritz guessed half the village was out there. "I've never really seen a hoedown like that before, either."

"Neither have I. Well, maybe once or twice. But not often."

Annalie scrunched up her nose at him. "What have you folks *not* living under the demons done with your freedom if not throwing parties like this?"

"Oh, well, people in general throw lots of parties," Fritz said. "I just don't attend them."

"So you've never danced like that before?"

It was Fritz's turn to nearly spit out his punch. "Absolutely not."

"Oh good," Annalie said. She stood up, seized his wrist, and pulled him out of his chair. "I was afraid I'd look like the only one out there who didn't know what she was doing, but we can be clueless together."

He was standing right beside dancers who stepped their feet and clapped their hands to the tune of the band's lively triple rhythm before his shock wore off enough for him to speak. "I don't want to–"

"Gratitude!" Annalie chirped in delight. "I would have asked you to dance an hour ago, but I was afraid you'd say no."

He wanted to point out he'd never said yes, but she looked so happy, he let it go. Tentatively, neither one of them exactly sure of what they were doing, he and Annalie joined the other revelers. At first, they kept a careful watch on the other dancers, to learn the proper steps. But before too long they each picked it up for themselves. They joined elbows and swung one another around. They clapped their own hands, each other's hands, and those of the dancers next to them. Fritz was fairly certain he didn't miss a beat. Annalie giggled with almost every step.

"Isn't this just the most fun ever?" she asked as she stepped around him, pausing to give her right foot a lift every third step.

It most certainly was not, but Fritz took her hand, gave her a twirl, and struggled to find words that were both true and non-offensive. "I never imagined I'd ever do this."

When the band's song ended, Fritz offered a prayer of thanksgiving, and they made their way back to one of the food tables. Annalie took another cup of punch and put two pieces of cake on a plate.

"Want one?" she asked.

"Sure."

Instead of giving him one of the two she'd already taken, she served him a third piece. They found a hitching post in front of the village's general store and leaned against it while filling their faces with chocolate and frosting.

Two bites in, Fritz got the feeling someone was watching him. At the gate, the guard checked the area on the other side of the fence, then once more looked longingly at the party. No one in the dancing area seemed to be looking in his direction. He glanced up – way up – and over the top of the fence, high in the leaf canopy of the forest, Lady Verde sat on one of the trees' highest branches. Her outstretched legs and bare feet made it seem she was just enjoying a casual, lazy rest in a tree, as spirits of the planet do, but her look of intensity was aimed directly at Fritz. She was waiting for him.

"She's here," Fritz whispered to Annalie. He motioned with his chin up towards the treetops, then stood.

"Want me to go with you?" Annalie asked. "Or go get Siv?"

"I'll be fine," Fritz said. "I just need to go learn when and where she wants to debate."

"Be careful," Annalie said.

Before he could depart, a middle-aged man with a thick mustache came before them. "Young man – Mr. Reinhardt, isn't it?" he said. "My name's Volson. I run the bakery. Sheriff Washington was telling me earlier all about the chipware kitchen you built for him, and I want one, too! I'll pay, of course. So long as it has a mixer like the one you restored for the sheriff. Chipware that can knead my dough for me in minutes instead of the hour it takes me by hand? I've got to have one!"

Fritz's chest tightened. The baker wasn't rude. In fact, he was downright genteel, and he wanted from Fritz what Fritz did best: restored chipware. But his timing couldn't have been worse. Fritz didn't want to insult the man, but–

Annalie put herself between the baker and Fritz. "You know, he's coming down with a case of laryngitis. Or a summer cold. And wouldn't you know it, he's lost his voice. But let's you and I get some more punch, and I can tell you all about what it will take to get you a chipware kitchen."

For the first time in his life, Fritz wanted to kiss someone on the lips.

"Oh, uhh, sure," Volson said to Annalie. "Hope you feel better," he mumbled to Fritz. Then he and Annalie walked off together towards the punch table, Volson asking a pair of questions per second and Annalie doing her best to answer each one.

Annalie glanced back at him. *Thank you,* he mouthed to her. She winked at him.

He wasn't sure how long he stood there, staring at Annalie as she and the baker walked over to a food table and carried on their conversation. But Fritz probably would have kept right on staring, Lady Verde temporarily forgotten, if not for a deep, familiar baritone.

"Fritz?"

He startled and clutched his chest. "Oh. Hey, Harlan."

"You all right?"

"I don't know. I... I feel strange. My stomach is fluttering. My arms feel like... like they could float up and away. And my throat is a little..." He made a constricting motion with his hand.

Harlan followed Fritz's eyeline, spotted Annalie, and chuckled. "I came down with something similar the first time I laid eyes on Pamela, God rest her soul."

"You think it's a summer cold?" Fritz said. "I get sick all the time."

Harlan patted Fritz on the back. "You'll figure it out."

Fritz shook his head and tried to refocus. "I need to step out into the forest for a minute. I spotted Lady Verde. Looks like I need to schedule a debate. But I have my flashlight, and my laser pistol, too, in case any monsters stray too close to the village wall. I'll be fine."

"Walk you to the gate?" Harlan asked.

"Sure."

"This is more amazing than I ever dreamed," Harlan said. "I feel like we done traveled through time. This will change our lives in so many ways – so many wonderful, wonderful ways. You have so much gratitude from so many of us, most especially from me."

"You're the one who inspired me," Fritz said. "When I first showed you I could repair chipware, you're the one who told me not to keep this under a bushel basket."

"I did," Harlan said. "And I even saw you talking to folks tonight. Answering their questions. Accepting their gratitude. I know you enough to know that isn't easy for you."

"No," Fritz said, "it's not."

"Didn't see you talk to Winston though."

Fritz tilted his head. Winston. Who was Winston? "Mayor Clum?"

Harlan nodded.

"Uhh, I'm not sure he'd want to talk to me," Fritz said.

"He probably doesn't," Harlan agreed. "Which is exactly why you need to talk to him. Back in Mondorf, when Winston said no to the sparksline, what would you have done if I hadn't been there?"

"I would have said, 'Fine,' and I would have walked away," Fritz said. "Look, my folks and my sister have always told me to stand up for myself, to not let people walk all over me, but I don't like arguments and confrontation. Sometimes it's easier to just leave people alone rather than fight them."

"You'd have thrown the whole brisket into the trash just because one side got a little burned," Harlan said. "You'd have given up on your entire project just to avoid an unpleasant discussion."

"Not the whole project. Just Earp's part in it. I would have found a different town to start in. Easy."

"I don't disagree that you're going to have a long list of towns lining up, all wanting to be the next one to get these treasures," Harlan said. "And I'm convinced most everyone in those towns will be as happy as the folks dancing back there. You'll walk in carrying chipware, and you'll walk out carrying laurels, bottles of fine whiskey, a marriage proposal or two, and whatever other things folks drape on a hero. You'll be a life-changer.

"But I'll predict right now, every town you visit will have a Winston. Someone who doesn't like anything about what you're doing. Maybe, like with our mayor, that anger will come from fear of what chipware has done in the past. Maybe it will just be a fear of change. Whatever the reason, you cannot let their fear keep you from this work, this mission. *Your* mission. You need to help the skeptics understand what this is really all about." Harlan stopped walking. "You do know what this is really all about, don't you?"

"It's about... fixing... chipware?"

Harlan raised an eyebrow.

"No, I get it," Fritz said. "It's about making people's lives easier. Improving health through better medicine. Better communication. Faster transportation. More knowledge, more education. I get it, Harlan. It's my project."

"It's about hope," Harlan said softly. "Some folks' fear must not be allowed to take away everyone else's hope. Now I'm not saying you'll have to *fight* these skeptics. No, unfortunately, son, you'll have to do something much harder than that. You'll have to befriend them. Make a connection with them. You'll have to win them over. They'll need to see the face of the remarkable young man who figured out how to do what no one else for two hundred years could. They're going to have to look into your eyes and be reassured by the kindness, the intelligence, and the wonder there. They'll need a leader like you to drive away their fear. And once you do that, the hope this restoration brings will shine through to them clear as dawn, and you won't have an opponent anymore. You'll have an ally."

Fritz had picked out a single word of Harlan's, but it wasn't "befriend," "kindness," or "hope." It was "leader." He was sure Harlan saw his muscles tense. "Siv's the leader. Not me."

Harlan smiled. "You and I both know that no matter what y'all say, you *do* lead this thing. I know you don't want that power because you know what kind of responsibility comes with it. Fact is, the best leaders are never the ones who want the power."

Fritz rolled his eyes. "Sebastian says the same thing."

"That's 'cause Sebastian's a wise man." Harlan motioned him towards the gate. "Go take your walk. Tell Lady Verde I look forward to meeting the spirit of this beautiful world and that the people of Earp will hear her out, but that she's wrong. Then think about what I've said. Pray about it."

"That's what you said months ago when you told me to think about repairing chipware beyond my bedroom walls. Except then, you also said you weren't telling me to be something I didn't want to be. Now that's *exactly* what you're saying."

"I'm telling you to be what people will *need*, son." Harlan clicked his tongue, pointed at his head, put his hands together as if in prayer, and walked back towards the party.

Fritz turned his head away. His stomach had been a knot before speaking to Harlan. Now it felt like a double knot of barbed wire. He liked Harlan. A lot. The man was like a second father to him. But gosh darn it, why did he have to say things like that? Now his hands were shaking, he felt a little woozy, and it was all because he knew deep inside, everything Harlan said, especially about him being the leader, was–

No.

He patted the pocket of his vest and felt the folded papers there. A public debate with Lady Verde was hard enough for him. He would never step forward and call himself the leader of the Mantissa Reborn.

When Fritz reached the base of the tree in which he'd seen Lady Verde, her entire body changed to water and plummeted towards the ground, as if someone standing on a high branch had overturned a bucket. Fritz jumped a step backward. The water splattered across the trail, made a wide puddle of mud, and rose up into the shape and color of Lady Verde. So she could form her human appearance out of dirt or water. Probably air, too. "You really are the spirit of the planet," Fritz said. "Growing up, I thought that was just a myth or an expression, but here you are, and... wow."

"You've done exactly what I told you not to do. You completed the sparksline." She sneered at the glow of the village's chipware lights. "Light pollution already defiles my forest."

"Pollution?" Fritz mumbled. He scratched the back of his head. "Look, we talked about it. About what you said. All of us, the Mantissa Reborn. And Annalie and Harlan, too. We're not trying to hurt the planet. We just want to make life easier."

"And you think life will be easier when plants lose their virescent color?"

"One of us was actually alive before the Blackout – long story," Fritz said. "But we told him what you said. And he told us yes, grass once was red, especially in Mondorf, but he says there was never proof of a correlation between it and dynamek energy, or between dynamek energy and increased cancer. He said that was all just speculation, often done by those opposed to the power companies' corporate interests."

With her silver hair and stern look, she reminded Fritz of one of his old school teachers. The one who rapped kids' knuckles with a ruler when they did something wrong, like talk in class, cheat on a test, or breathe incorrectly.

"So yeah," Fritz said, "we listened to what you had to say, and we decided to complete the sparksline anyway. You said if we did it, you'd open a public debate, starting here in Earp. You said you'd show the people here some of the things you showed us about what chipware has done to you in the past. Well, fine. I'm all for education." He took the folded papers out of his pocket. "And I'm ready to debate you. So tell them how you feel about chipware and let them decide. If they hear what you have to say and they want the sparksline turned off, I'll oblige them."

Somewhere in the not-so-far distance, thunderclouds announced their presence.

"Very well," Lady Verde said.

Leaves rustled, and something seized Fritz from behind: tree branches. The tree behind him had reached out and grabbed his arms. He yelped, dropped his notes, and tried to shake the branches off, but they held too tightly.

Everything moved quickly – too quickly. He couldn't tell which tree, or trees, the branches came from. They lifted him off the ground and passed him back and forth, higher and higher. Only once the trees had lifted him above the forest's leaf canopy did they propel him forward, away from Earp, towards the storm prowling above the forest some distance away – maybe a mile or two.

A flash of lightning brightened his surroundings. Lady Verde was not far from his side. At first, he thought she walked across the top of the leaf canopy, but another lightning flash revealed she hovered a few inches above it. She flew through the air – *flew*, just like a bird or like his restored airplane. The tree limbs and branches kept him even with her quick pace. But why was she taking him *away* from Earp, if she wanted to educate its residents?

When they seemed to be directly under the storm, which produced no rain yet, Lady Verde sank beneath the leaves. The trees lowered Fritz to the ground and released him. There was no trail or clearing here, just lots of tree trunks. He shined his flashlight towards Lady Verde's back a few feet ahead of him.

"The most terrible chipware ever created was also the most arrogant," she said. "Man thought the Verdant Wardens could hold dominion over my forces."

"Verdant Wardens? Never heard of them. Are you talking about the Steelterrors?"

"That's what those who survived their rampage called them. They killed countless people and did harm to me that took centuries to heal. I *still* haven't recovered from some of it." The volume of her voice raised on her final sentence, and a thunderclap echoed after her words.

"The first Mantissa stopped them," Fritz said.

The dirt underneath Fritz vibrated, then shook. The nearby trees swayed. Lightning flashed.

"Yes, they rendered the Steelterrors inoperable and interred them deep in the ground," Lady Verde said. "But I *am* the ground. And I know where the bodies are buried."

An invisible force – Fritz was certain it was Lady Verde, though she didn't move – dug a bowl-shaped hole out of the forest floor. A metal bar as wide as Fritz and almost as tall jutted up out of the dirt. Something massive was buried under the forest, and Lady Verde pulled it to the surface. Wood cracked, and tree trunks crashed to the ground. A black, domed metal shape rose from the dirt next to the metal bar.

At first, it looked like a hunk of scrap metal, but as more of it emerged, Fritz saw it had a human-like shape. An oval head and prominent brow sat above the cracked, shattered lenses that must have once been its eyes. Its left arm stopped at the elbow. It looked like giant jaws had taken a bite out of its right side.

It was the corpse of a Steelterror. It had to be. Lady Verde was going to make her case against restoring chipware by showing the people of Earp the dead body of a *Steelterror*.

Fritz's mouth went dry. "That is quite the visual aid for your presentation," he conceded. This was going to make a very compelling case for Lady Verde, and not just to paranoids like Mayor Clum. Even Siv was once skeptical of repaired chipware thanks to stories of the Steelterrors. How was he going to convince anyone his restoration project was harmless when they gazed upon the dead shell of a planet-killing giant robot?

"They each represented one of the elements of the ancient world, right?" Fritz said. "Which one was this?"

"The Warden of Soil," Lady Verde said. "Samson."

Fritz leaped two feet into the air as a blast of lightning struck Samson square in the chest. Then another struck him in the head, and another on his shoulder. Lightning striking more-or-less the same place three times in a row actually made sense in this case. The Steelterror corpse was pretty much a giant lightning rod.

Except after the third lightning hit, Fritz saw the fingers on Samson's right hand move.

"Lady Verde, you may want to dissipate that storm," Fritz said. But his intuition screamed that she wouldn't. By the Almighty Hand, her intention wasn't to show the people of Earp the corpse of a Steelterror.

She was going to show them a living one.

Tree branches seized him again, this time by both the arms and the ankles. He couldn't run, couldn't turn away. Another blast of lightning struck Samson in the chest. Dirt, debris, and metal fragments flew out of the ground and swirled around the Steelterror like a tornado. The wound in his side sucked the metal towards it, and each tiny fragment bonded to him one at a time until the wound was healed. His left arm regrew similarly. His broken eyes reformed and illuminated the forest with a red glow.

Samson's face resembled a steel primate, or maybe a steel skull. A thick band of silver with glowing red trim lights wrapped around the back of his head. His hinged jaw opened, and he released an electronic bellow – half scream, half white noise. He yanked tree roots off of himself with ease. His massive metal hands grabbed hold of nearby tree trunks and pulled himself the rest of the way out of the ground. Dirt and fallen trees spilled into the hole Samson had occupied. From a standing position, he leaned forward and rested on his knuckles, like a gorilla. Fritz estimated his height at forty feet of black steel. Glowing red lines of sparkslights ran up and down his arms and legs.

"You're a Verdant Warden," Lady Verde said to Samson. "And I am Lady Verde. Therefore, you serve me."

Samson punched her.

It wasn't a light tap. Since his fist was as tall as she was, he obliterated her. She exploded into water and splashed across the clearing. Some drops landed on Fritz's sleeve. He startled at the suddenness and the brutality of the violence, but before he could say a word, a column of dirt rose out of the ground in front of Samson and shaped itself into Lady Verde.

"I *am* Lady Verde," she said. "You *serve* me."

The Steelterror tilted his head at her. A *hummm* came from somewhere inside of him. It sounded almost contemplative. After a tense moment, he nodded.

Lady Verde pointed in the direction they'd come from. "There is a village in the forest about two miles away," she said. "The sparksline underneath it doesn't belong there. Remove it."

"No!" Fritz yelled. "You said we'd debate. You said we'd have a public discussion with the people!"

"I've heard lots of words in my time about ending man-made climate change and about environmentally sustainable choices," Lady Verde said, "but it never goes beyond wringing hands and pointless babble. Words mean nothing to me. Actions do. You said your piece by building the sparksline. Now it's my turn."

This machine was called a Steel*terror* for a reason. It wouldn't conduct the removal of the sparksline as a targeted, surgical operation. It would be like swatting a house fly with a bomb.

Samson leaned back, and his legs changed underneath him. Panels opened, new parts emerged from within, others retracted away from his surface. After just a few seconds, Samson had... changed his legs? Refactored his legs? Maybe refactored was the best word. They weren't legs anymore. They were treads like the ones on armored military tanks from before the Blackout.

He similarly refactored his arms until he no longer had hands. Instead, both of his arms ended in enormous drills. The sound of them spinning was deafening, even over the thunder and lightning. Fritz tried in vain to reach the mobile in his pocket, but the tree limbs secured his arms and hands too tightly.

Samson drove off across the forest. With his drills in front of him, he cut down every tree in his path. Their thick trunks fell like grass before his father's mower back home. What was going to happen when it wasn't trees in front of him but Earp's perimeter fence? What was going to happen when it was his friends' homes? Or when it was his friends themselves?

Harlan. Siv. Annalie.

"Stop this!" Fritz yelled at Lady Verde. "Do you know how many people live in Earp – how many families? Children! You just sent a Steelterror into a populated area!"

"No," Lady Verde said, "*you* sent it."

"People are going to die!" Fritz said.

For a moment, Lady Verde seemed taken aback by his prediction. But just as quickly as she faltered, she composed herself and held her head high. "If anyone dies, their blood will be on *your* hands. I told you not to put a new sparksline in the ground. I told you to stop restoring chipware. You refused to listen. What happens next is *your* fault."

Another flash of lightning lit her arrogant face, but the subsequent thunderclap sounded weaker than the previous ones. She was calming the storm. Of course. She didn't need it anymore. She'd already used it to bring her Steelterror pet back to life.

She placed her hand against a tree and allowed it to absorb her arm. In different circumstances, Fritz would have been amazed and thrilled by the demonstration and would have giddily spent hours pondering the physics behind it. "You have one week to turn off the power plant," she said. "If it's not off by then, I'll remove it from my surface."

"You destroy the power plant, and you'll poison half the continent," Fritz said.

Lady Verde sneered. "But I thought dynamek energy was safe? I thought you, out of your *great* intelligence, had declared it so?"

"It's safe to use," Fritz said. "It's not safe to blow up. That *will* expose the planet to toxins. You wouldn't do that to yourself. You'd poison the land for centuries. You'd drive animal species extinct, quite possibly including man."

A dangerous look came to Lady Verde's eyes. "Man is as alien to Verde as the white demons. Your species does nothing but consume and destroy. Don't think for a moment I'd hesitate to remove the lot of you. It might hurt, but I'd heal. And I'd convalesce far faster with chipware and the species who created it gone."

"You're crazy!" Fritz said. "Stop this, please!"

Fritz wasn't sure she'd even heard him. She disappeared into the tree and was gone. The branches holding him went limp. He shook them off, pulled his mobile out of his pocket, and ran after Samson. It wasn't hard – he just followed the tank tracks in the middle of the barn-width line cut through the forest.

Samson's drills rumbled somewhere in the distance as Fritz dialed Siv's mobile. He ran, but it was two miles back to Earp. Would there even be a village left when he arrived?

Chapter Eight

Siv stepped out of the boarding house and strapped his sword scabbard and shotgun holster to his back. Though nearly midnight, the streets were still full of villagers; their revelry wasn't even close to winding down. Five minutes ago, he'd been part of the shindig. He'd been close to winning a not-small pot of golds from a trio of wealthy and inebriated villagers who enjoyed playing stud but who, God bless them, didn't know how to win. After that, another tall mug of stout and a whiskey chaser would have been a perfect celebration. Instead, Fritz had called.

Annalie ran up the dirt road towards him. "I found him," she said between rapid breaths. She motioned towards Harlan, who breathed even heavier and followed a dozen steps behind.

"He says it's two miles out and moving fast," Siv said. "On its way to rip out the sparksline."

"A Steelterror?" Harlan said.

"A Steelterror," Siv said. "Called Samson."

"God have mercy," Harlan mumbled and made the Sign of God's Hand.

Something appeared over the top of the perimeter fence on the opposite side of the village. A red glow in the blackness of the night grew in size and intensity. Villagers stopped dancing and eating and pointed. The village's sparkslights illuminated the source of the glow: a giant robot's eyes. The massive machine was smooth, finely-crafted, black steel. It towered more than thirty feet tall, seeing as it peeked into the village *over* the fence.

"Reckon that's him now," Annalie said.

Villagers scattered in a panic. Then a clangor louder than hammer and tongs overpowered all other sounds. Smoke rose from the fence. Wood snapped. Slats shifted, then slanted, then exploded into so many splinters. The barrier had been built almost two centuries ago by the village's founders, and later generations had meticulously maintained it as Earp's primary defense against the monsters of Terrascorcha. It took Samson and the enormous silver drills at the end of his hands ten seconds to bust a gap in it at least four houses wide. He stretched his arms to his sides, demolishing more of the fence, and the most terrible chipware ever created rolled into Earp like an outlaw moseying into a lawless tavern.

Gunshots joined the panicked cries. "I'll round up my deputies," Harlan shouted over his shoulder as he ran off to find them.

"Get as many people as you can away," Siv told Annalie. He checked the ammo in his shotgun. She looked at him like he'd poured pig slop over his head.

"You can't fight that thing," she said.

"Reckon not," Siv agreed, "but I have enough dung between my ears to try."

Siv ran, but the flow of people fleeing in the opposite direction hindered his progress. He was the only one heading *towards* the metal invader. He turned south onto the main street, where the party had been centered. Samson stood just eight building lengths ahead, a skull-like head and a human-like torso mounted on tank treads right out of the old army stories. He rolled through thatched-roofed houses and shoved his drills into the roofs of the ones he didn't smash. Shards of wood and glass ricocheted through the air. The deadly projectiles took down five villagers. At least one was a woman.

A stretch of dirt road, the party site, and a mess of running, screaming village folk were between him and the Steelterror. Siv charged towards Samson, though he holstered his shotgun and drew his sword instead. Too many people were in the way; he had to get closer before he could start shooting. Besides, the Dragon Slayer could probably only give Samson's steel hide a flesh wound, but it could surely shred the rubber of Samson's treads. Step one: hobble the sumgun. Step two: blast its head off.

Samson rolled over more of Earp – more buildings, more homes, more people. He opened his mouth, and a roar of noise boomed over the entire village, almost drowning out the screams, the rending of wood and metal, the *pops* of revolvers, and the *bangs* of shotguns. He thrust his left arm into the air, and the drill at the end of it stopped spinning, then contorted and twisted all about until it had become a plow. Samson looked down at the road with the freshest dirt in the entire village. The road with the new sparksline buried underneath it.

"Aww, don't you dare," Siv said.

Samson drove his plow deep into the road, then twisted his wrist and violently yanked it upward. Pebbles of dirt and chunks of rock rained down on the panicked populace. So did shards of metal conduit and broken wire. All of the sparkslights in the village extinguished. The only remaining light came from the moons, Samson's glowing red eyes, and a flickering orange glow reflected on his chest. Smoke wafted into Siv's nose. Two of the buildings Samson had smashed were on fire, and the flames were spreading quickly.

The Steelterror's arms changed again. The drill at the end of his right hand and the plow at the end of his left both became smooth, shiny steel barrels. The bottom half of his body changed, too. His tank tread legs shifted and converted into human-shaped steel legs.

Samson crouched and bashed his steel barrel hands against the ground, one at a time, over and over. It felt like a groundshake. Each impact of one of his steel drum hands against the soil felt like a chisel against Siv's eardrums. Thatching shook off of roofs. Windows shattered; Siv took the shards of one in his left arm. He gritted his teeth against the pain and dropped to the road, covering his head and neck. Buildings collapsed, unable to stand on the suddenly trembling land. And since chipware lights were so newfangled, candles and oil lamps still lit most homes, so when those buildings tumbled, they caught fire.

When Samson stood, Siv yelled and charged towards his left leg, but long before he reached him, Samson jumped. He leaped over four houses and landed somewhere off to Siv's left. The ground shook with his landing, and a dust cloud rose underneath him. Siv wanted to believe the Steelterror had seen him coming and fled in fright, but the truth was Samson hadn't even noticed him.

Siv was about to turn down a side street and continue his pursuit of the Steelterror, but something caught his ear over the cacophony of screams and destruction reverberating through the forest village. It was the sound of a horse in distress. *His* horse, Tobias. He listened for him again and heard nothing, but he knew it hadn't been his imagination. He looked back and got his bearings. The fire – one of the fires anyway – burned in the general direction of the livery. Siv gasped. "Tobias!" he shouted.

Forget the barking Steelterror. He ran back towards the livery. He was desperate to move faster, but the shaking ground, flying debris, and scattering villagers all hindered him. Then a house fell over, and its ruins blocked the entire street. Its collapse stoked the blazes inside it. There were so many sources of firelight the village was brighter now than it had been when the sparkslights were on. Physical exertion and smoke made it difficult to breathe. He cut to his right to take a different route around the collapsed house and ran.

He cried out when he reached the livery stable, which was overcome with flames. Thick smoke plumes streamed out of the windows like they were trying to escape from Samson, too. And this close, the sound he'd heard was unmistakable. The horses inside the barn were in a panic. Trapped. *Tobias* was trapped.

Siv collided with a frantic villager, shoved him aside, and kept going. For a moment, he thought he heard his name, but it didn't matter even if he did. He slid open one of the livery's big barn doors, and a ball of flame blasted out onto the street. Siv spared a second to make sure no more fire was immediately forthcoming before he darted inside.

The fire came from the rear of the stable. The exact place where Tobias had been lodging. Dread rose in Siv's stomach. Smoke burned his eyes and made him feel like he had sandpaper shoved up his nose, but he knew the stable's main path went right down its middle with half-height stall doors on either side. Siv opened the first one he reached, and a horse ran for its life out the barn. The next two stalls were empty, then Siv found one containing a panic-stricken mare. She squeezed against the side of her stall to shy away from the fire. Siv threw open her stall's gate and darted aside to avoid being trampled. There was even more smoke deeper in the barn. More fire. Despite the heat of the flames, Siv's hands felt like ice. He heard Tobias, but the sounds he made were the stuff of nightmares. Somewhere behind him, he thought he heard his name again.

Siv reached the stall where he'd left his horse, where he'd personally untacked him and fed him. He'd mucked out the stall on his own, insisting to the kind lady who ran the livery he'd still pay her full fare, but only he knew the exact way Tobias liked his bed made.

Thrashing and kicking, delirious with agony, Tobias was on fire. He kicked out his front legs wildly, then kicked out his back legs, slamming into the burning wood of the stable walls in a desperate attempt to escape. Though in torment, Tobias saw his master and shoved himself against the door in a desperate attempt to reach him. He poked his head through the gap above the half-height door and let out a terrible squeal, begging for help, but Siv couldn't even comfort his companion without being lit aflame himself. Siv yelled in alarm and searched for a water bucket, but at this point, it didn't matter. Tobias was immolating before his eyes.

He knew what he had to do.

It was unthinkable, and it would rip him up inside to do it, but he had to do it. And he had to do it *immediately*.

Tobias shrieked as only a caged, tortured animal could.

Siv stuffed the side of his left hand into his mouth, bit down on it hard, and screamed.

He raised his shotgun and put Tobias out of his misery.

Tobias collapsed, hidden behind the stable door. Siv dropped to his knees, closed his eyes, and screamed into his hand again and again. The stable still burned. The flames reached closer to him. But Siv didn't move. He just bit down on his hand harder and tasted blood.

"Siv!"

Annalie emerged from the smoke. Her dress was stained and torn. One hand covered her face as she hacked ash out of her lungs. She grabbed his left arm, still bleeding from the flying glass, and pulled, but Siv resisted.

"We have to get out of here!"

He waved her off.

"Don't do this to yourself," she said. "Don't do this to Cassie. Come on!"

Cassie. Cass. Her name made him get up. Hanging his head, he followed Annalie out to the street. A boy maybe four-years-old seized Annalie's leg as soon as she emerged from the stable. "There you are," she said. "I told you I'd be right back. Now let's find your mama, OK?"

The livery's inner walls collapsed. Siv crouched with his back to the livery's ruins, his face in his hands. The kid with Annalie just shook and whimpered.

"Andrew!" a woman shouted.

"Is that her?" Annalie asked the kid. He ran off in the lady's direction. Annalie waved to the boy's mother as she and her son embraced. Then she slumped down onto the ground next to Siv. Her breathing was heavy. She pulled off her glasses and wiped her soot-stained face with her hand.

"I'm so sorry," she said.

He was going to bawl like a baby right in front of Annalie, that kid, and everyone else still alive in the village unless he took drastic action. Unless he smothered the pain with rage. His shotgun was still in his hand. He stood up and roared. "Where is he?"

Getting close enough to the Steelterror to shoot it or cut it might earn him a lacing or worse, but so what? So barking *what?* He'd cut that steel devil like it was warm butter. He'd blast its metal brains full of shotgun slugs.

A wide chunk of the village's perimeter fence fell inward. The boards snapped near their base and toppled over onto the burning buildings the fence had once protected. Then another portion of the fence fell, and another, and another. The destruction moved counter-clockwise around the village. The ground shook underneath the falling pieces. It was Samson. He burrowed around underneath the fence's base and drilled its thick posts into sawdust. When the wave of destruction came nearest to Siv, he aimed his gun and took a shot at the empty air five feet above the ground. He hollered and popped off two more.

The entire fence fell like dominoes. Siv waited for Samson to resurface, to change his hands into God-knew-what this time, but he never did. Instead, trees outside the village fell in a path that moved away from Earp. His work complete, the Steelterror burrowed away.

"You better run!" Siv yelled at its back.

He dropped his gun and dropped to his knees. Horses didn't have immortal souls. They were God's creatures worthy of our love and protection, and it was wildly unjust to do them harm, but they weren't ensouled like humans. Every preacher he'd ever met had told him so. Well, it was all bunk, all of it. He closed his eyes, prayed for Tobias to have a safe gallop up to heaven, and lost his battle to keep himself from weeping in front of Annalie.

Out of breath, shoes and pant hems covered in dirt and mud, Fritz gingerly stepped over the place where Earp's massive perimeter fence had existed less than an hour before. A few of Earp's buildings still stood, but not many of them. Most were either a pile of rubble or on fire. Or both. Hope and prayer were all that kept the few remaining buildings intact. A haze of smoke and soot hovered over everything. The air reeked of burned wood. It had a slight metallic tang, too. A few folks still ran through the streets, and some still shouted. A lot of them cried. There was no sign of the Steelterror or Lady Verde, but he found two dead bodies, and he could find a lot more if he could bear to seek them out.

And it was all his fault. If he'd just stayed home in Hondo... If he'd never decided to restore chipware to the world...

"Annalie!" he yelled. "Siv! Harlan!"

He pulled his mobile out of his pocket and called Annalie. After three rings, she answered. "We're near the livery," she told him, a waver in her voice.

"I'll be right there," he said. Except so much of the village was gone, he didn't know where "right there" was anymore. It took him a moment, but he laid a mental picture of what the village used to look like on top of the disaster he saw now, and he was able to place the livery. Or where it used to be.

Siv sat in the middle of the street and stared at the ground. Annalie hugged Fritz. No warning, no hello, just immediate physical contact. He patted her back politely, but his mind was elsewhere, in a place where physical touch was neither uncomfortable nor pleasant, just a distraction.

"Lady Verde told me we have one week to turn off the power plant," he said. "Otherwise she'll destroy it."

Annalie gasped and pulled away from him. Fritz knew she was thinking of her siblings back in Mondorf, living in the shadow of the power plant's main reactor.

"There!" someone said. Seven armed men surrounded them. Fritz stared down the barrels of numerous revolvers and rifles. They hauled Siv to his feet and demanded his sword and shotgun and Fritz's laser pistol. They also demanded Siv's grapple gun, their mobiles, and Fritz's flashlight. Among them were Boone and Tamber – the deputies who'd helped them liberate Mondorf.

"Hands in the air!" Boone barked at Annalie. She complied immediately.

The men made room for Mayor Clum to join their circle.

"What the hell is this, Mr. Mayor?" Siv said.

"You're under arrest," he said. "The charges are the destruction of nearly every building in this village and several counts of murder, the exact number to be determined once we account for all of our people."

Under arrest? No, they didn't have time for this. They had one week before Lady Verde attacked Mondorf! And Mayor Clum was going to lock them up? Keep them prisoner? Where? Was the jail even still standing?

Siv told the mayor his actions were horse excrement, then repeated his opinion in case the mayor hadn't heard him the first time. "If we're under arrest, I want to talk to the sheriff," Siv said. "Where's Harlan?"

For a moment, Fritz thought the mayor was going to punch Siv in the face. "Harlan's dead!" Clum roared.

Fritz's stomach hit his shoes. Something seemed to grab his heart and squeeze.

"Under the laws of this village, the death of our sheriff makes me acting sheriff," Clum said. "The three of you will be tried. You'll be convicted. And you'll be hanged."

```
[1879-09-06 21:00] root@skylab:/bin > .\secscan
Begin scan with default parameters (range: 500 AU)
......
Scan complete. (0) matches found.

[1879-09-06 22:00] root@skylab:/bin > .\secscan
Begin scan with default parameters (range: 500 AU)
......
Scan complete. (0) matches found.

[1879-09-06 23:00] root@skylab:/bin > .\secscan
Begin scan with default parameters (range: 500 AU)
......
Scan complete. (0) matches found.

[1879-09-07 00:00] root@skylab:/bin > .\secscan
Begin scan with default parameters (range: 500 AU)
......
Scan complete. (0) matches found.

[1879-09-07 01:00] root@skylab:/bin > .\secscan
Begin scan with default parameters (range: 500 AU)
......
Scan complete. (0) matches found.

[1879-09-07 02:00] root@skylab:/bin > .\secscan
Begin scan with default parameters (range: 500 AU)
......
Scan complete. (0) matches found.

[1879-09-07 03:00] root@skylab:/bin > .\secscan
Begin scan with default parameters (range: 500 AU)
......
Scan complete. (0) matches found.
```

Chapter Nine

The problem wouldn't be Samson. He could deal with a Steelterror, given time to equip himself and his friends properly. After all, they were the Mantissa Reborn, and the Mantissa had been the ones to originally take down the Steelterrors five hundred years before. He'd seen what Samson had looked like when Lady Verde pulled him from the ground. That gaping wound in his side hadn't been caused by time and natural decay. That was a battle wound, and he was certain the Mantissa had given it to him. To be fair, it likely had not been dished out by two healers and an intuitive. It was probably the work of one or more movers. And yes, since Eroica died, there weren't any movers around anymore. But he still felt it would be possible to defeat a Steelterror.

First, he'd have to put working remote controls into Apple Juice. That was priority number one because his robot would be weapon number one against Samson. He couldn't bring it into battle tethered to his mobile with a wire. The length of cable required would be impractical, and the cable would get all twisted in the battle, and... yeah. It wouldn't work. But he needed the weapons he could attach to Apple Juice's megabus ports, and he'd need every one of them. He was going to have to pound that metal giant with so many bombs and laser blasts and heavy caliber bullets to bring him down. So he needed to be able to control his robot wirelessly. First priority.

Next, he'd have to upgrade everyone else's weapons. While preparing for the eviction of the demons from Mondorf, before the idea of the containment fields and capturing the demons alive had come to him, he'd already made several items which would prove useful, like the bomb arrows he'd made for Cassie. He bet one of those right to Samson's shoulder would take the Steelterror's arm off.

But what about Siv and Uncle Sebastian? What about Annalie, if she was willing to fight with them? They had the energy rifles they'd loaned to the citizens of Mondorf during the town's liberation. Sebastian and probably Siv, too, could use those. He'd given Sebastian the knife with the laser-augmented blade, which he'd considered something of a prototype. What he really wanted to do was provide the same laser augmentation to Siv's sword. Siv probably wouldn't let him modify the weapon in any permanent way, but maybe he could temporarily attach a laser emitter to the sword's hilt? It would give Siv's primary weapon a laser edge, which would certainly be more effective against Samson than just a metal blade, but it wouldn't permanently alter the sword that had a lot of sentimental value to Siv. It could work.

There was no doubt in his mind he could make plenty of weapons to use against a Steelterror, but the problem wouldn't be Samson. The problem would be Lady Verde. How in the world was he going to fight the world? Samson had annihilated her, and it hadn't phased her a bit. Bullets and lasers were going to do just two things to her: zero and zilch. Meantime, she could hurt the living tarnation out of them. She'd summoned a thunderstorm and brought down lightning on a specific target multiple times. What if she did that to him, or to his friends? One blast of lightning could be deadly.

How were they supposed to fight such an enemy? That was the biggest problem. And the second-biggest one was closely related. How could they *not* fight such an enemy? He wanted to change the future. She wanted the Blackout to continue indefinitely, and she'd proved willing to kill to make it happen. Two hundred eleven people had died so far. Above all else, the Mantissa were Verde's protectors. If they seriously wanted to call themselves the Mantissa Reborn, they *had* to–

"Friday is Felix's birthday," Annalie said.

The mumbled words brought his mind, racing a thousand miles a minute, to a sudden halt. He blinked, momentarily uncertain of his physical location because, for the past hour, he'd been somewhere else mentally. But he hadn't moved. He, Siv, and Annalie were still chained to a tree that had been outside Earp, beyond its protective fence, three days earlier. Now it stood beside a wide clearing in the forest peppered by a stray building here and there.

It was dark and late. Mayor Clum had confiscated Fritz's pocket watch, so he didn't know the exact time. The same guard who had watched them since the early evening was still there, and the night guard tended to show up just before midnight, so it was ten o'clock, maybe?

"How old will he be, Red?" Siv said, but Fritz barely recognized his voice. He'd never seen Siv this despondent. Fritz couldn't imagine what Siv must have gone through, having to put Tobias down.

"Ten," Annalie said. She sniffed and rubbed her hand under her nose. "He's growing up fast."

Siv wasn't the only one whose voice sounded off. Annalie's sounded flat. Toneless.

"I know he's an odd stick," she said. "He don't talk much, even to me. Keeps to himself. Just grunts at people who ask him questions. But he's so smart. He reads every book I can find for him. Maybe if our folks were still around, he'd be better. I just don't know how to help him."

She cried. Fritz felt like maybe he should do something, but he didn't know what. They each had a chain fastened around one of their ankles, but it was the only restraint they had. His arms were free. Should he hug her? The chain was long enough to reach her. Fritz couldn't remember a time he'd ever hugged anyone who wasn't his sister or their parents.

"My dad got sick," Annalie said. "But he kept working as much as he could. You didn't want the demons to know you were ill, 'cause if it was something that could prove terminal? Forget it. They always said they only kept around what was either useful or beautiful and that we weren't beautiful. But it got harder and harder for him to work, and one day he collapsed not far from home. Mom and I saw it happen. He was awake. He was alive. He just couldn't walk another step. Demons clawed him open on the spot."

She yanked off her glasses, stuffed them into the pocket on her shirt, and wrapped her arms around herself. "Mom ran to him and tried to hold him. Just so he wouldn't die alone, you know? The demons told her not to, but she did it anyway. And they clawed her, too. They killed her just for wanting to comfort her husband."

Vekkem was the name of the demon Krulgoth had put into Fritz's mind. Just as Vekkem had been able to see all of Fritz's thoughts and memories, Fritz had seen the demon's, too. He'd seen Vekkem's memories of when the demons had been human-like in appearance, before they began changing themselves. He recalled with great anxiety every time Vekkem had come face-to-face with one of the Celestines. Fritz remembered every murder Vekkem committed, every being he'd enslaved on every planet the demons had visited. So he had a very good idea of what it was like for Annalie to have had a front-row seat to the murder of her folks. And even though it had happened years before, knowing it had happened to *her* broke his heart.

"But Felix," Annalie said, pushing her voice past the sobs that wanted to close off her throat. "Felix was just four years old. When he saw his dad come home and saw his mom run out to him, he didn't know any better. He ran with her. Mom didn't see him, and I couldn't catch him. He was *right there* when the demons killed our folks. He got bloodstains on his overalls. They murdered our parents right in front of a four-year-old boy. They mangled my brother's soul that day, those burning monsters. I've tried so hard to take care of Felix ever since. To help him. To heal him. And now I'm *never going to see him again!*"

"Red," Siv said.

"Hey!" Their guard was about twenty feet away, but his eyes – and his rifle – were pointed in their direction. "Shut up over there."

Fritz glared at the guard, but he'd already turned back towards the village, ignoring the worthless prisoners chained to a tree.

"I promised him I'd be back for his birthday," Annalie said between rapid breaths. "I promised, and now he'll never see me again." She sucked in three quick gasps of air. "They won't even know what happened to me. Bradon, Clark, Della, Elise..."

"Annalie," Siv said, his voice firm. She ignored him.

"Ramona, Henry, they're my family and my friends, and I miss them so much" – a deep gasp punctuated every word or two – "and I'm going to die out here. And no one will even know what happened to me."

Annalie cried with deep, quick sobs.

"Fritz," Siv said.

He snapped to attention immediately. He even made eye contact. Siv called him "Professor." Always had. He almost never called him by name.

"Red's having a panic attack," Siv said.

"How do you know?"

Siv responded with a look. Right. Siv had endured his own share of debilitating anxiety since a demon burned his house when he was six. He knew a panic attack when he saw one.

"She's gonna pass out," Siv said. "You gotta calm her down."

"How? Why me?"

"She's not listening to me anymore," Siv said. "You have to get through to her."

Fritz shrugged and hesitantly put his hand on Annalie's shoulder. "Annalie, calm down. There's no sense in breathing so deeply and rapidly. Hyperventilation is a serious concern here."

No effect.

"I don't think logic is going to sway her," Siv said.

"Somehow we'll get out of this," Fritz said. "You'll see your family again."

"Don't make promises you can't keep," Siv mumbled sharply. And it was a good point. He didn't want to be phony and tell Annalie a lie just to calm her down. Except, when he considered it, Fritz *did* believe they were going to walk out of Earp alive. It was why he'd been thinking so hard about how to take down Samson and Lady Verde. He didn't know why yet, but he believed they'd soon be free. Was he just being stupid? Or was his power trying to tell him something?

Annalie moaned, and shook, and showed no sign she'd even heard him.

"Try to distract her," Siv said.

"How?" Fritz said. Siv threw up his hands. "How about this weather? I'm sure glad it hasn't rained on us." Fritz shook his head. Small talk about the weather belonged on the Stupid List, no matter what the situation.

"Let's ask someone for a deck of cards," Siv said. "You ever play five card stud, Red? I'll teach you. I'll also beat you and the Professor every hand, but I'll teach you."

"Great idea," Fritz said. "If any cards survived the destruction of the village, they can throw a deck at us the next time they pelt us with rotten tomatoes and berries. Give us some nasty paper cuts."

Siv grit his teeth. "Trying to help here."

"I know," Fritz said. "Sorry. Hey, Annalie, you like to eat, and speaking of berries, is there a better food in the world than hot oatmeal with berries and brown sugar? I reckon not. Sausage *maybe*. But probably not, right?"

"What's the best thing you ever ate, Red?" Siv asked.

Annalie slumped over onto the ground. Fritz feared she'd fainted, but her crying proved she hadn't. She was still frantic, mumbling about her siblings, about wanting to go home. She shook her right leg violently and rattled the chain holding her to the tree.

"Red, let's all say a prayer together," Siv said.

Fritz thought that was a good idea, but it didn't work, either. Food, the weather, the Lord, games – nothing was distracting her. *Think!* What distracted him? When his brain was going crazy with too many worries and too many guilts and too many what-ifs, what did he do to slow it down? What did he do to shove it all away, to bring on a few moments of peace? He had to think.

Or better yet, he had to *not* think. He had to stop and use his power. Don't think. Don't over-analyze. He had to listen to his gut, or his heart, or the Mantissa synapses in his brain, or whatever it was that fueled his hyper-intuition. Some part of his mind was already putting the puzzle together. What had it found? What could he say to calm Annalie down? How could he help this woman he'd quickly come to think of as more than just...

Annalie pounded her fists against the dirt.

"How 'bout I show you some constellations?" Siv said. "See the Blooms? They're twinkling like glistening rain. And look – this time of year, you can just start to make out a little bit of my favorite one, Gotteszorn. It's the Hand of God throwing the rebellious angels out of heaven. Won't be able to see the rest of it for another couple of months, but look there, Red. There's two of its stars, Rudger and Nariel."

Fritz scanned the sky without paying much attention to the stars, at least not until he noticed one of them move, albeit very slowly. They all moved, of course, except the frozen star, which wasn't actually a star but the Skylab space station in geostationary orbit above the equator. They all moved so slowly you had to watch very closely over the course of the entire night to see it happen. But the movement of the one Fritz spotted was visible to the naked eye.

Fritz smiled. That's because it wasn't a star. It was a comet. At least it looked like a comet. Maybe it was a comet? He'd read a really interesting thing about comets once, and he'd filed the idea away somewhere in the clutter of his mind. There was a theory about light suggested by the tail of a comet–

Click.

"I'm going to build a solar-powered pocket watch," Fritz blurted out. "A mechanical one, I mean. A solar-powered *mechanical* pocket watch."

Annalie stopped crying. She stopped pounding her fists, and she stopped breathing heavily. *Now* had she fainted? She was still laying face down, turned away from Fritz so he couldn't tell. Was she just finally listening to him?

"That don't make no sense," she said softly.

"Sure it does," Fritz said. "Makes all the sense in the world."

"Solar can power chipware," Annalie said, "but not anything mechanical."

"Says who?"

"Says anyone who knows half of anything." She rolled over and sat up. Her eyes were puffy. Her hair was matted from sitting in the dirt tied to a tree for two days without a wash. Her jeans and shirt were stained from where the villagers had thrown food at them.

She still looked pretty.

His cheeks flushed as he batted the thought away. His mind kept wanting to spin on the comet. Or the not-a-comet. What hadn't looked right about it? There was something else his power was trying to tell him.

"Sunlight can power chipware because sunlight is heat, it's energy, and that's exactly what chipware needs to run," Annalie said. "But anything mechanical needs physical force. A watch has a mainspring that needs to be wound. You can't just shine sunlight on it and watch it wind itself. The only way to power a watch with solar is with a solar cell battery, and that'd make it chipware."

"I concur with most of that," Fritz said, "but sunlight isn't *just* heat. It has weight."

Annalie squinted her eyes at him. And didn't cry, and breathed normally. "Now you're just stretching the blanket."

"No, no, I'm serious." Fritz cocked his head towards the sky. "Look at that comet up there. We can't see its tail without a telescope, but no matter which way a comet travels through space, its tail will always point away from the sun. Isn't that right, Siv? You're a stargazer."

"Yeah, that's right," Siv said. "But what comet are you jawing about? There aren't supposed to be any comets this time of year."

"That one," Fritz said, but it took him a moment to find it. It was clear on the other side of the sky from where he'd seen it before. That was one *fast* comet. Unless–

Click. Not a comet. Something far better. Oh gosh, *he* belonged on the Stupid List. It was so clear now. A wave of relief washed over him. He grinned.

"I don't see it," Siv said.

"It's gone now," Fritz said. "But just keep watching the sky. It'll come back in a few minutes."

Siv looked at him like he was a brainless gimp. "Comets orbit–"

"Anyway," Fritz interrupted, "a comet's tail always points away from the sun, no matter which way it travels through space. You know why? I read a theory once it's because light puts a physical force on the objects it touches. Light has energy, so it has mass, right?"

"Energy equals mass times..." Annalie mumbled. "OK, I follow."

"If it has mass, it has weight," Fritz said. "So sunlight, or any light, when it shines on something, it's putting physical force on that object, albeit a very small amount of force. So small I don't even know how you'd measure it. But – no, I take that back, I have one idea on how you'd measure it. Two, actually. But I'm getting sidetracked, that's not– Hey, that one could work, so that's three. No, wait, I'm getting distracted. The point is the watch I'm going to make."

Annalie's face slowly gave birth to a smile. "A solar-powered *mechanical* watch? Daisy! But a watch's mainspring is going to need plenty of force to be wound, plenty of *measurable* force. I get that sunlight has weight, even if we don't know how to measure it–"

"*I* know how to measure it!" Fritz said. "I've come up with three ideas just as we're sitting here. Five if you count the ones that are stupid."

She slugged him in the shoulder. And *laughed*. "Fine, *you* know how to measure it, genius, but the rest of us don't. The point is: how are you going to scare up enough physical force from sunlight to be able to wind a watch's mainspring?"

"Oh," Fritz said. "The truth is, I'm stumped on that one. But wouldn't such a watch be amazing?"

Annalie sat up tall and lowered her voice an octave. "Oh no, my watch has stopped running. I shall put it in the sun!" She held her empty wrist out to Fritz and made three creaking noises, like a spring winding up. "Much better."

Fritz laughed with her, then shrugged and lowered his voice. "You OK?"

She collected herself. "Yeah."

"We're going to get out of here. You're going to be home for Felix's birthday."

"You sound like my dad," Annalie said, "always believing things would get better, even when all the evidence in the world was saying otherwise. But you make me believe it, too, just like he did."

Fritz looked at Siv, whose prior warning about not making promises he couldn't keep was plastered across his face, plain as day and twice as angry. "You and Cassie talk via mobile every night," Fritz said. "Did you talk before the party on Saturday? Before the Steelterror...?"

"No," Siv said.

"So it's been three nights now that you've failed to call or failed to answer when she called," Fritz said. He tried to imagine how Cassie must have felt when she couldn't contact Siv, and a story formed in his mind. He often made up stories to weave together different, separate pieces of information he possessed, but since learning of his power, he'd begun to suspect this quirk wasn't just his over-active imagination. It was probably his Mantissa hyper-intuition.

He closed his eyes and pictured his sister in her Harbrucken apartment. "Cassie must have been worried. By that point, she was bound to know something was wrong. She probably paced the floor. Kept looking at her mobile, waiting for you to call. She made mashed potatoes."

"Mashed–" Annalie whispered.

Siv shushed her. "I've seen him on one of these rides before. Don't stop him."

"Since we should have called for pick-up by then, she called Sebastian, and" – the tone of his voice shifted – "Siv isn't answering his mobile, and neither is Fritz. Did they call you for a pick-up?"

Siv snickered. "You imitate Cass?"

Annalie shushed him.

"But he hadn't heard from us, either, so he said he'd bring the airplane to Harbrucken and pick her up, and the two of them would go look for us together. Except he probably used his military words like 'rendezvous' and 'recon' and I don't understand what all of those mean. And she said, 'They should have been to Earp by now so let's start there.' And when they got to Earp, they flew over the forest but didn't see any sparkslights. They thought that was weird since they knew we were here, they knew we'd completed the work, so they decided to circle back for a second look, then land and seek us on the surface."

He opened his eyes and saw Siv and Annalie both looking at him with newfound hope, but also with a little fear of his ability. Annalie let out a deep breath and silently prayed. Siv lightly clapped him on the back. "I sure hope that one turns true, Professor."

"Most of it already has," Fritz said. "Take a look at the sky, but don't be too obvious about it. Don't let the guard or anyone else see us all staring up there at the same time."

Siv looked straight at the sky. Fritz appreciated Annalie's subtlety.

"What am I looking for?" Siv said.

"The comet I saw. It's back." He shrugged. "As if it circled back for a second look."

"Comets don't just turn–" Siv started, but his words dissolved into chuckles.

"They're here?" Annalie whispered. "Cassie and Sebastian?"

"They're here," Fritz said. "They're circling back for a second look, trying to figure out what's going on."

Annalie looked like she was going to cry again but happily this time.

"See how life changes when instantaneous communication is restored?" Fritz said. "Hooray for chipware. It makes giant metal monsters. It destroys villages and kills people. And it's why my uncle and my sister knew they had to search for us."

Cassie moved away from the tree she'd been using for cover and tiptoed towards the guard. It was after midnight, but the partial moons were just bright enough to illuminate her and the clearing in which Siv, Fritz, and Annalie were inexplicably chained like prisoners. The disinterested look Siv cast in her general direction didn't change, but he obviously knew she was there – obvious to her at least. Fritz and Annalie, on the other hand, did not. Annalie was asleep, and Fritz bit his fingernails. If she had a gold for every time over the years she'd used her healing power to regrow a fingernail for him after he bit one too short, she'd have enough to buy the whole university.

She took great care to notice what was underneath her boot with every step. She didn't want a dry leaf or a broken twig to alert the guard to her presence. The attention also helped keep her eyes off of the field of debris where Earp should have been. Anger, sadness, and a stew of other emotions stirred in her chest, but she forced them back down. Free her friends first. Then find out what had happened.

When she was so close to the guard he'd have felt her breath on his neck if she exhaled, she wrapped her right arm around his chest and covered his mouth with her left hand. His eyes widened. "Good night," she said.

Fritz startled, and Siv smothered his hand over her brother's mouth just before he yelped as if a firecracker had been set off underneath him.

A healer's power, like all Mantissa powers, wasn't magic. It was biological. Mantissa were psychics. She healed through a simple two-step process: make a connection with the part of the guard's mind that controlled health and healing, then send an instruction such as "stop bleeding" or "heal that bruise." In this case, she commanded, "Go to sleep." The guard's eyes fluttered, and his muscles went limp. Cassie gently lowered him to the ground, took his revolver, and tossed it into the forest.

Siv took his hand away from Fritz's face. "Hello, darlin'," he said.

Annalie rubbed her eyes, sat up, and kept far more composure than Fritz had. She put on her glasses. "This may sound crazy, but did you make mashed potatoes very recently?"

Cassie blushed. How in the world did she– Oh. Her brother grinned like the cat that just ate a canary. He'd had one of his imagination spells. Well, of course, *he* knew her favorite comfort food. "I'm really happy to see you, sis," he said.

She shook her head, not to be rude, but because she needed answers, *now*. "What in the world happened here?"

"That's the opening argument in Lady Verde's 'debate' over restoring chipware," Siv said.

There was a rustling of tree leaves, and Sebastian emerged from the forest. "Lady Verde did this?" he asked.

"Not directly," Fritz said. "She dug a Steelterror out of the ground and brought him back to life. Then she ordered *him* to do it."

"A *Steelterror?*" Cassie and Sebastian said together.

"Let's get unchained, get our things, get out of here, and *then* gab," Siv said. "Yeah?"

Sebastian pulled a dagger from a holster on the side of his leg. With the push of a button on its hilt, a thin line of green laser light traced the weapon's sharp edge. He cut the chains off of the tree with a single, quick swipe. Then, with more care, he cut the shackles off of the prisoners' ankles.

"So because it was a Steelterror, Mayor Clum ordered you arrested?" Cassie said. "And Harlan couldn't stop him?"

Siv put his hands on her arms. "Harlan died."

Cassie sighed and rubbed her forehead. There'd be time to weep for him later. Unfortunately, considering how wrecked the village was, she reckoned there would need to be a *lot* of time set aside for grieving. She didn't really want to ask, but she had to know. "How many others?"

Siv licked his lips. "Two hundred eleven total."

Something invisible kicked Cassie hard in the stomach. She took two steps backward and sat down next to the sleeping guard. Two *hundred* eleven people were dead, including their friend Harlan. He'd cooked for them, sheltered them, traveled a great distance from his home to help liberate people he'd never met because he believed no one should have to live under the demons. He'd been a *good* man.

She took her grunblume from her pocket and wrapped the string of beads around her hand. Then she placed her hand in the palm of her other and brought both to her chest in the Sign of God's Hand.

"We need to get our stuff," Fritz said. "Then we need to get back to Mondorf. Lady Verde says she'll destroy the power plant if we haven't shut it down before Saturday."

"Where's Tobias?" Sebastian asked Siv. "I'll fetch him with you."

"Tobias is gone," Siv said.

Cassie gasped, scrambled back to her feet, and found Siv's hand with her own. "Oh my gosh. I'm so sorry. I'm so–"

He squeezed her hand and met her eyes. "Not here," he said in an undertone. "Please."

"Where are they holding your things?" Sebastian asked.

"In the jail," a man said, and Mayor Clum stepped out of a shadow and into the moonlight.

Though the midnight darkness and his black suit made it difficult to tell for sure, Cassie was fairly certain there were no bulges in his jacket where a holstered weapon would be. And whether he was armed or not, neither she nor Sebastian had sensed his approach, so he didn't pose any danger. "The jail is made of stone and mortar, so it survived the fire and the Steelterror's groundshakes. Two guards are watching over your things, but I've instructed them to return it all to you, so long as you then leave."

"You had just *one* guard watching us, but *two* watching our things?" Siv said. "You kept us out in the dirt, but kept our things sheltered in your jail?"

"I wanted that which was most dangerous kept the most secure," the mayor said. "I'm no fool, Mr. McCaig. I never expected to be able to hold Mantissa for long. I didn't honestly expect to bring you to any kind of justice. But while I had you, I wanted to ensure you got a long look at what your chipware wrought on this village. Earp stood in peace for nearly two hundred years. Two months after you began to restore chipware, it sits in ruins.

"You talk so much about the benefits of chipware, but you don't pay a whit of attention to its dangers. Do you know one of the biggest killers of the ancient pre-Blackout world was obesity? People lived such sedentary lifestyles, plugged into the comm-net all day, they slowly gorged themselves to death.

"'Identity theft.' A side-effect of every detail of a person's life – including financial and medical information – being stored in fallible, insecure chipware systems. How would you like to wake one morning to find thieves had stolen your life savings because your bank's chipware contained an exploitable back door to the vault? Or that someone you've never met is living under your name and your personal identification number?

"And it sounds so beneficial to be able to connect with strangers from the other side of the continent who share your interests. But the reality is communication through chipware was impersonal and dehumanizing. Chipware made it possible to insult, defame, and calumniate others without the hassle of having to look that person in the eye and see the pain you caused."

Cassie saw Fritz force himself to make eye contact with Clum.

"I will not willingly choose to ignore chipware's detriments," Mayor Clum said. "Frankly, your Steelterror has ensured I *cannot.*"

"It wasn't *our* Steelterror..." Fritz said weakly.

"When you bring your snake oil to the next town, when you sing the praises of chipware on glad tambourines, think of us here in Earp. Think of *Harlan*. You knew him for a few months. He was my friend for nearly *fifty* years." Mayor Clum bit his lip, blinked water from his eyes. He took a deep breath and waved his arm at the ruins of the buildings behind him. "Think of us before you... *restore* anything else."

As Mayor Clum returned to the village, Fritz didn't take his eyes off of him. Annalie put her hand on Fritz's shoulder, and Cassie noticed he didn't tense up. Interesting.

"Please take me home now," Annalie said.

Chapter Ten

"Where is it?" Annalie said. "I lost track of it!"

With his eyes on the spot of the black night sky where he believed Apple Juice to be, Fritz flicked a control on his mobile's screen. A thin line of brilliant green running lights appeared, tracing his robot's torso, legs, and arms and marking the robot's position in the air – the air above the *other side of the city!*

Annalie whooped with delight. "Dang, it moves so fast! It's clear over yonder."

Fritz and Annalie stood on the roof of a ten story tall building. It wasn't the tallest structure on the Ulmbaden Power Facility campus – that honor went to the 495-foot-tall reactor tower not far behind them – but it gave them plenty of visible airspace. Siv, Cassie, and Sebastian were further back. Holding his mobile sideways and with both hands, Fritz used the on-screen controls to steer his robot back towards the roof. It made a smooth turn on the power of its thrusters.

"Wow, did you see those aerodynamics?" Fritz said. "With the arms out like wings, the head is like the nose of an airplane. Smooth!"

"Yeah, like you drew that turn with a compass," Annalie said. "Splendiferous! Bring it in full speed."

Streams of fire from the rocket engines on Apple Juice's back blazed a trail across Mondorf's sky. The robot approached their rooftop on a vector parallel to them. As it drew closer, it got louder. Fritz crouched behind a waist-high sheet of plywood he'd set up as a blast shield and motioned the others to do the same. Of the ten targets they'd stationed on the roof, three remained. Images of them appeared on his mobile screen courtesy of Apple Juice's night vision camera feed. He tapped the images, and glowing red circles appeared over the top of them, indicating the targets had been locked. Apple Juice pointed its right arm – and the laser rifle mounted on it – at the targets. Three streaks of green light, each accompanied by a high-pitched sound, made straight lines for the wooden targets. Fritz and Annalie ducked when they exploded.

Fritz killed the robot's boosters, steered it up into a standing position, and brought it down on the roof. Its thrusters powered down with a descending whine. The laser rifle it had used to destroy the last targets retracted back inside its forearm.

"Successful test!" Fritz declared.

"That is the *pink!*" Annalie said.

"Well done, Fritz," Sebastian said.

"Wasn't just me," Fritz said. "I configured the software controls, but Annalie installed the receiver inside Apple Juice. Without any help. She's inexperienced with the more advanced aspects of chipware, but her basic mechanical skills are far better than mine."

Annalie scraped the toe of her boot along the roof and blushed. "Gratitude, but you're overselling. It don't take much to install a full duplex card into a megabus port and wire it up to a power source, though I suppose it was pretty tight in there what with all the other components inside the 'bot. And if two of them touched, *bzzzt,* they could both short out, so a pinch of delicacy was required, and– And I'm rambling. Sorry."

"I'm going to mount Apple Juice's controls on the handlebars of Harlan," Fritz said.

"Harlan?" Siv said.

"My motorbike's new name," Fritz said. He shrugged. "It's not going to change anymore. I finally found the right one."

Annalie gave him a sad smile and rubbed her stomach. She probably wasn't hungry – though, with Annalie, it was a distinct possibility. She was probably just remembering Harlan and the delicious food he'd made for them.

Siv and Cassie shared a look. They seemed uncomfortable. "We need to have a say with you," Siv said to Fritz.

"Look," Fritz said, "if my motorbike having a name really bothers you, I won't–"

"It's not about that," Siv said. "It's about Lady Verde. And about tomorrow."

Fritz shrugged. "That test flight was the last piece. Everything else is ready."

"What if she's right?" Cassie said.

"What do you mean?" Fritz said. Nervousness filled his stomach.

Cassie had her knapsack with her, and she took a book called *Crimson Spring* from it and flipped through its pages. "While you've been working here, Siv and I have been exploring the ruins of the Mondorf Public Library. When you three first met her out in Terrascorcha, Lady Verde showed you some worrisome scenes from the past. Not all of them sounded plausible to me. Some sounded downright ridiculous." Finding the right page, she held *Crimson Spring* open and pointed towards Fritz. "Truth be told, I didn't believe her story about the Elde River catching fire until I found photographs of it in a reliable source."

Fritz chewed on one of his fingernails. "So she's not a liar. Which means she was serious when she said she'd destroy the power plant if we don't turn it off by..." His hands fell to his sides as the full weight of her words hit him. "Sis, are you saying we should give in and shut down the power plant?"

Cassie exhaled and bit her lip. Fritz braced himself. Nothing good ever followed when his sister bit her lip and collected her thoughts. "I think we ought to consider *temporarily* turning it off while research her claims more thoroughly," she said.

She was taking her side. His own sister was taking Lady Verde's side!

"We decided to call ourselves the Mantissa Reborn," Cassie said. "'Mantissa' means more than just people with seemingly magical abilities. It means 'guardians of the planet,' and I don't believe our protection is owed only to the people living here. But if the spirit of the planet is telling us the power plant is dangerous, I think we ought to listen."

"Two hundred eleven people died in Earp," Fritz said. "*Murdered* by her."

"I know," Cassie said. "Believe me, I have a lot of anger with Lady Verde at the moment. But it's a complicated relationship, isn't it? I still have to live on her."

"Twenty *thousand* people live here in Mondorf," Fritz said. "Including Annalie's family. How can you even stomach to think about what will happen if that Steelterror is unleashed here?"

"The Steelterror needs to go," Sebastian said. "That's non-negotiable. But the difference is, we can destroy the Steelterror. Even if we wanted to, we can't destroy the planet."

Fritz huffed. Sure, he'd also come to the conclusion that they could fight Samson but not Lady Verde, but it was still annoying to hear it used as an argument for taking her side. "You want to turn it off, too?"

"You have to know your enemy," Sebastian said. "We know a lot about Lady Verde's strengths. Don't know much about her weaknesses, though, other than damage to the planet hurts her. So what, exactly, is our tactical plan for fighting her? How do we plan to force her *not* to destroy the power plant? She opened a hole in the Ellingham Forest and pulled a Steelterror out of it. How are we going to stop her if she makes a sinkhole under the reactor tower? We don't have a clue. Yet we're seriously considering going to war against her? Against our own planet?"

"You all used to criticize me for not standing up for myself," Fritz said. "Cass, you and mom and dad are always telling me to not let myself get walked on. Well, I took your advice, and I took a stand against the demons, and it felt *good*. So I'm doing it again. I'm taking a stand against Lady Verde because she's a bully and a murderer and she killed Harlan. I'm doing everything you've always told me to do, and I'm taking a brick bath for it from my own family."

"You don't start a war you're not prepared to win," Sebastian said, punctuating each word by slapping one hand into the palm of another.

"I get a vote?" Annalie said.

"You served time with us chained to that tree," Siv said. "You definitely get a vote, Red."

"Gratitude," Annalie said. "The only reason I helped you exile the demons in the first place was the promise of restored chipware. Freedom from the demons was freedom from bondage. But we build a new chipware-powered world, and that's freedom from toil and drudgery. It means my siblings have the chance to attend the university. To swim in the ocean. Heck, to stand on the doggone *moons*. We let Lady Verde shut that down, and the moons will be the only places Fritz will be able to work, 'cause they'll be the only places he can get away from her. It's time to change the world."

"But what's the rush?" Cassie said. "I'm not saying we kill the project. I *believe* in the project. I'm just saying we slow down until we know what chipware might do to our planet and to the people living here. One of my life goals is to cure cancer. Can we say with absolute certainty that this book" – she held up *Crimson Spring* – "is wrong, and dynamek energy particulates are *not* carcinogens? Why not wait until we can?"

"Because Sebastian shouldn't have to spend a *minute* longer than he has to in that God-forsaken demon's body!" Fritz said.

Cassie, Annalie, and Siv all turned their eyes to Sebastian, who fixed Fritz with a perplexed stare. "You care to explain that one?" Sebastian said.

Fritz released a deep breath, then spoke to Annalie. "Remember how I told you we fought and killed the demons' leader? Well, Krulgoth wasn't the only person who should've died in that fight. I got wounded. Badly. So did Cassie. Sebastian was a Mantissa reader, and he used his reader powers to transfer his mind into one of the dormant Mantissa-demon bodies Krulgoth made. A body with healer powers so he could save us. And he did it knowing it was a one-way trip."

"Wow," Annalie said.

"He saved my life. He saved my sister's life. I owe him for that."

Sebastian shook his head and exhaled. "Fritz, whether I look like a man or a monster, there's one thing I've always been and always will be. I'm a soldier. I've taken a vow to sacrifice whatever I must to protect others. Even my humanity. You don't owe me for what I did."

"Fine," Fritz said. He retrieved a thin metal circlet from an inside pocket of his vest. "Then we'll call this an early birthday present. It's a device that emulates a Mantissa reader's powers."

Sebastian squinted his glowing red eyes at him and the circlet. "Chipware that reads peoples' thoughts can't be done. Folks have tried."

Fritz shrugged. "They tried wrong, then." He put the circlet on and pressed a button. A yellow light illuminated on the device's center, making it look a bit like he had a glowing amber jewel in the middle of his forehead. "All of us here know Mantissa powers aren't magic; they're biological. But that doesn't solve or explain anything. It just begs so many more questions. Like: what is going on when a Mantissa reader 'sees' someone else's thoughts? Well, he must be using his neurons to read the state of the other person's neurons. But *how?* There has to be some kind of channel for the transmission, like how a wire carries sparks, or like how the air carries sound waves."

"You think you can find this channel?" Sebastian asked.

"Three golds says he already found it," Siv said.

"Of course I already found it," Fritz said.

Siv guffawed and clapped him on the back.

"I can tap into it, too," Fritz said. "But I don't know the protocol, so it's like listening in on a telegraph line without knowing the code the operators use. I can hear the signals, but I don't understand them. I can send a signal, but it's just gibberish. But in a way, that's a victory because it means I've successfully emulated one reader power."

Fritz narrowed his eyes at Siv, and suddenly, Siv cried out, grabbed his forehead with one hand, and put his arm on Cassie's shoulder to brace himself.

"Omigosh!" Fritz grimaced. He removed the circlet and turned it off. "Sorry! I did *not* mean to hit you that hard."

Cassie glared at Fritz and placed her hand on Siv's head. A moment later, he stood on his own, rubbing his temples, but also chuckling. "You made a piece of chipware that copies a Mantissa reader's mind blast ability," he said. "That's–"

"Completely barking amazing," Sebastian said. "Pardon my language."

"But I didn't set out to make a mind *blasting* device," Fritz said. "I didn't even set out to make a mind *reading* device. I want to make a mind *transmitting* device. I want to move thoughts from one mind to another. Your thoughts, uncle. Back into your human body."

The piece of chipware at Sebastian's throat that gave him his voice wasn't always good at conveying emotion. This was one of those times. Once Sebastian finally spoke, the flat, neutral tone of his voice in no way matched the expression on his demonic face. "I don't know what to say. I'm grateful. I'm– But Fritz, we still don't know how to fight her. What are you going to do, find and restore a biomortic weapons stockpile and nuke her? She's far more dangerous than you're giving her credit for."

Fritz shook his head, but he had nothing more to say. He'd already resigned himself to the fact that pointless and stupid conversations about the safety and benefits of chipware would have to be a permanent part of his efforts. That he had to have one with his own family and friends felt like a knife wound.

Cassie exhaled and nodded at Siv. "You're the deciding vote, fearless leader."

Siv closed his eyes. "I never asked to be the leader," he said.

"The best leaders are the ones who don't want the job," Sebastian said.

That just made Siv sigh again. He put his fist under his chin and stood in silence for a long time.

"What'd you call this method of controlling your robot?" Siv said. "Wireless?"

"Yeah," Fritz said.

"Could you rig up a wireless switch for the power plant? Something you could use to turn it off at a moment's notice?"

"Hmm," Fritz said. "I suppose I could patch one into the ops control interface."

"Main survey circuit," Annalie said. "Easy."

"Then it stays on, and we take a stand against Lady Verde," Siv said.

Cassie folded her arms across her chest and frowned.

"*But*," Siv said, "if things go south against her, you turn it off *immediately*. All right?"

"All right," Fritz said.

"You told me what would happen if this factory explodes. All the folks in this city we worked so hard to free will die. The land gets poisoned. Terrascorcha really will be toxic. Even those of us without powers," Siv said, pointing between himself and Annalie, "we're Mantissa now. We protect the people first."

"All *right*," Fritz said.

"Tell me," Cassie said to Fritz, "your desire to keep the power plant on, to not even turn it off temporarily – does it come from your 'magical' ability to figure things out?"

Fritz closed his mouth. His power was definitely *not* telling him to take a violent stand against Lady Verde. But it sure as sin wasn't telling him to appease her with a deactivated power plant, either. Neither option sat entirely right with him, but he had to pick one because they were out of time. She'd promised to kill the restoration tomorrow.

"I sure hope it's your power," Cassie said. "Because if things go south tomorrow, your life, our lives, and the lives of all twenty thousand people in this city would be a steep price to pay to satisfy your pride."

Chapter Eleven

The Ulmbaden Power Facility campus sat on the southeastern edge of Mondorf. Though a small part of the ancient capital city, it was still larger than Hondo, Fritz's home village. Two wood and metal bridges spanned the seventy-foot wide Iller River, which cut a diagonal line through the grounds and underneath the reactor tower at the campus's center. The site's forty-or-so office buildings, sub-system facilities, and maintenance warehouses – all windowless, crumbling, and dusty – made the site look squalid. Or haunted. The omnipresent hum from the reactor tower was the only indication civilization still remembered the place.

Fritz drove Harlan across the southern bridge, turned north, and continued his patrol. By his third loop around the site, he'd developed a route his innate need for order and pattern wouldn't let him abandon. It took him past most of the campus's buildings, and almost all of it was on paved roads, though a few of the old maintenance trails were hard-packed dirt. Driving the paved roads was an exercise in avoiding the largest potholes and cracks. Riding on the maintenance trails stirred up clouds of dust Fritz had to wipe off his helmet's visor. Bah. It was always something when you went outdoors.

There was a loading dock at the back of what had once been a parts warehouse. The dock doors were closed – likely rusted shut – but Annalie had stationed herself outside them because of their proximity to the reactor tower and the shade provided by the taller building nearby. She waved to him every time he drove past. It wasn't an accident his route took him past her three times.

It was late morning, and he was three buildings northwest of the parts warehouse when Sebastian's voice came into his ear over their shared voice-comm. "Something's coming," he said.

Fritz slammed on the brakes and brought his bike to a stop. He had to put one leg on the ground to maintain balance since he'd removed the sidecar they'd used out in Terrascorcha.

"I feel it, too," Cassie said.

How did healers' danger sense *work?* If all Mantissa abilities were just a non-standard use of the brain, then his sister and his uncle were processing some external stimuli which their minds told them meant danger. But what possible stimuli could that be? Cassie had told him about a time she'd felt compelled to leave a dance hall in Harbrucken just two minutes before rival gunslingers decided to duel. He'd seen her accurately predict the arrival of white demons before any were seen or heard. In his attempts to technologically recreate his uncle's old reader powers, he'd discovered a "mental channel" through which readers communicated with other minds. Did healers' danger sense tap into something similar?

What about his intuitive power? Was there some unknown manner of stimuli that sent his ideas into his brain?

A rumbling from underneath demanded his attention; he had to concentrate on his present situation. Mortar dust and debris crumbled off the building beside him. He knew what had caused the groundshake – w*ho* had caused it. He turned around, gunned the motorbike's throttle, and tapped the mute button on his mobile's screen. Inside his helmet, a wireless earpiece allowed him to speak and hear over his engine's roar. "Does anyone see Samson?" he said.

"If part of him is a six-foot-wide drill bit, then yes," Cassie said.

"Digging himself out right where you guessed, Professor," Siv added.

Of *course* he'd correctly predicted Samson's arrival location. The field was the largest patch of open land directly adjacent to the reactor. Hadn't *everyone* just assumed that would be where he'd poke his head out of the ground?

Fritz stopped at the parts warehouse and flipped up his helmet's visor. The road ahead of him ended in a pile of crumbled concrete at the edge of the field. The stones scattered throughout were a little too large and not quite random. Fritz guessed the area had once contained at least three more campus buildings. On one side of the field was the office building where they'd tested Apple Juice. Pacing next to the pit from which he emerged, Samson surveyed the reactor tower on the field's opposite side. He'd refactored his drills back into hands, and every step he took vibrated the ground.

Annalie ran to Fritz and cast a nervous glance at the field.

"We can handle this," he said, but his power nagged at him. It was as if, somewhere in his mind, it rang a servant's bell, trying to get his attention. "You better get inside."

She nodded. Inside the warehouse was a loft with a view of the field. "I'll be watching. And listening. And talking, too, if you need me to. But not rambling. I don't want to ramble. I ramble sometimes. But you've probably already noticed that. Have you? Noticed, I mean?"

"If you change your mind and you want to go back to your siblings, just go. If you want to go now, I'll even let you take Harlan."

"I'm staying."

"Your siblings need you to come home to them."

He hadn't been trying to sting her, but he saw the flash of emotion on her face. She quickly steeled herself. "Everyone in town is gonna cash in if that robot destroys the reactor. Even if we all started running right now, it would take a while to get out of the explosion's fifty-mile radius. And then the airborne toxins would burn our lungs to death anyway."

Fritz shrugged. "That's a very scientifically accurate way to look at it."

She kissed her index and middle fingers, placed them against the side of his helmet, and flipped his visor back down over his face before running towards the warehouse. Halfway there, she looked back and realized he was gawking. He'd barely even breathed since her fingers touched his helmet. She'd kissed them first! "Go!"

Sebastian leaped onto the road from wherever he'd been keeping watch and ran on all sixes towards Samson. He'd strapped a laser rifle to his back. Fritz gave Harlan enough throttle to keep pace beside his uncle, and they both stopped about twenty feet into the field. Samson paid them only a cursory glance, which was also all the acknowledgment he gave

Siv and Cassie on the roof of the office building. He knew they were all there, but he didn't seem the least bit concerned.

A pillar of dirt rose out of the field and took on the shape and color of Lady Verde. The juxtaposition between her and the Steelterror was striking, especially with both of them in the open and in sunlight. Samson was the most advanced, and most enormous, piece of chipware Fritz had ever seen. His metal hide glistened. Streaks of glowing red sparkslights ran up and down his arms and legs, and across the silver band wrapped around the back of his head. Lady Verde looked centuries older with her neat gray hair and gray burlap dress. She was streaked with dirt and unadorned with any jewelry or decoration. Fritz wasn't sure which of the two was more deadly.

"That's Lady Verde?" Sebastian asked. Fritz nodded. And while he tried not to get distracted, when Samson positioned himself behind Lady Verde and sunk into a crouch, Fritz couldn't help but wonder: did the drills he could refactor his hands into rest intact somewhere inside him when not in use? Or did they break down into smaller parts? Smaller parts would be easily distributed throughout smaller–

Fritz shook his head. *Focus!* He turned off his bike's engine.

Lady Verde frowned at the reactor. "Still on," she said.

Sebastian cocked his head and narrowed his eyes at her, not in a threatening way, but in a curious one. He also made no move to speak. Neither did Siv, up on the roof of the office building. Wonderful. *Fan*tastic. They were going to leave it to *him* to talk to her? Sure, those in charge could delegate out the work, but this sure seemed like a situation where the leader needed to step up and be their voice.

Still seated on his motorbike, Fritz flipped up his helmet's visor. "Chipware can do a lot of harm. I get that. You showed me that in Earp. But it can also do a lot of good, and that's what we're focused on. We'll look into what you've said about the harmful environmental impacts of dynamek energy. If you're right, we'll do something to stop them from happening. I don't know why you won't believe us, but we don't want to hurt anyone, including you."

"Do you think the survivors struggling to rebuild their lives back in Earp would agree you don't want to hurt anyone?" she asked.

"*You* killed those people," Fritz said.

"No, Samson killed those people. Because he's a Steelterror. All I did was tell him to destroy the sparksline you installed. And that's the *point*. Chipware always does exactly what it was designed to do, plus a few unintended side effects. And no one ever takes responsibility for those." She pointed at the reactor. "Turn it off. I won't ask again."

Sebastian leaned two inches closer to Lady Verde and squinted his eyes. "Can't be," he said, his translator device broadcasting the words in a barely intelligible mumble.

Siv's voice came through Fritz's earpiece loud and clear. "Everyone better be ready. She's itching for a fight."

Samson had stopped his fidgeting. The only sounds were the current of the Iller River and the hum of the reactor tower. Nature and chipware. Lady Verde watched Fritz, waiting for his answer. He was ready to fight for the future, and even his sister and his uncle with their reservations were ready to fight with him, because it was a *good* future, and it was worth fighting for. But did they even stand a chance?

He might have surrendered if not for Sebastian. The brother-in-law of his ancestor, who he and Cassie called "uncle" out of love and gratitude for saving their lives. If Fritz gave in to Lady

Verde's demands, he'd never be able to complete the reader emulator. His uncle could call himself a soldier all he wanted, but taking on the appearance of the monsters who'd tormented him and killed his wife was too much to ask anyone. He would *not* give up on restoring Sebastian's humanity.

But he was so afraid. He feared the pending conflict, the giant Steelterror, and the all-powerful environmental force standing before him in a ragged, dusty dress. She possessed the power to end his dream. What would his life look like without chipware? Without his passion? It was unimaginable. It would break him. He had to take a stand.

His hyper-intuition rang a bell *and* knocked, desperate to tell him something, but he ignored it.

"No," he said with a shaking voice. "We're not turning it off."

Fritz swore he saw lightning flicker in her eyes. She balled her hands into fists. He flinched, bracing himself. If she used lightning, he'd be ended before he even knew what had hit him. These could be the final seconds of his life. Was it too late to change his mind?

Sebastian threw his head back and made a series of short, high-pitched growls.

White demon laughter.

He was laughing at Lady Verde.

Fritz, not realizing he had closed his eyes, opened one and glanced first at Sebastian, then at Lady Verde. Being laughed at did *not* make her look happy. What in the world was Sebastian *doing?*

"Did I miss a joke, Big Man?" Siv asked over the voice-comm.

"The joke's on all of us," Sebastian said. "She's not the spirit of the planet. She's human. A Mantissa. Her name is Sierra Monet."

Chapter Twelve

Not the spirit of the planet? A *Mantissa?* Whoever she was, she looked like Sebastian's words had kicked her in the head.

"Sierra who-to-the-what-now?" Fritz said.

"Sierra Monet," Sebastian said. "A tree-hugging Mantissa who mouthed off on her environmental politics every chance she got."

"I've never heard of a Mantissa affinity for calling down lightning and turning your body into dirt and water," Fritz said.

"She was flesh and blood when I knew her," Sebastian said, "but she had a unique power set – so unique the headmasters thought she was a mover with a perplexing limitation since the only things she could move were land, water, and air. Until she could make it rain and call down lightning from the sky. Control everything about plants, the weather, anything environmental. A never-before-seen affinity. She's an old woman now, but that's definitely her." He raised his voice. "Isn't it, Sierra?"

Lady Verde's expression changed from shocked to smug.

Then *everything* about her changed.

Her body and clothes reverted to the color of dirt, and she shrunk to a slightly shorter height. Her dress rippled and became a skirt, ripped tights, and a t-shirt. Her bare feet became army boots. Color returned to her body, revealing the same face she had before, but decades younger, without wrinkles and lines. She wore about a dozen earrings of various sizes and – ouch! – three small metal hoops pierced her lips. Her hair stayed long, but it changed from neatly brushed and gray to unkempt and red as blood. One side of her head was shaved to the scalp.

"Who the hell are you?" Lady Verde – Sierra Monet? – asked Sebastian.

"There she is," Sebastian muttered. "It's Sebastian Galliard, Sierra. Been a long time."

Sierra smirked. "Galliard. I should have known. I always suspected you'd sold us out and joined the aliens, but a starch-shirted, trigger-happy military moron like you? I never dreamed you'd take your treason all the way to body modification."

Sebastian roared at her with a growl so purely white demon his translator didn't even try to turn it into words. He lunged a step forward but stopped himself with a glance at Sierra's Steelterror bodyguard. Samson raised a fist.

Sierra pointed at the reactor tower. "Samson, turn that barking thing off. Destroy it if you have to."

"No!" Fritz yelled. "Samson, listen to me. That's a class-five dynafusion reactor, and if you destroy its containment systems, this whole city will experience a nice, warm, million-degree day. Even you can't survive that!"

"See you around, *monster*," Sierra said to Sebastian. She turned into a pillar of dirt, sank into the ground, and was gone.

Samson's hands made clicking and whirring sounds as he refactored them into drills. With a giant leap, he halved the distance between him and the reactor tower.

"Shoot him!" Sebastian commanded.

Green laser fire from the office building roof pummeled Samson in the back. Siv was an excellent marksman with his shotgun, and he'd been practicing with the laser rifle all week, but his blasts only left scorch marks on Samson's armored hide. Oblivious to the attack, Samson charged towards the reactor tower.

Sebastian swung the laser rifle strapped across his back into his upper arms. "I'll be in position," he told Fritz. He ran on four legs towards the campus's southern bridge, pelting Samson's lower half with covering fire the entire time, though his attacks were as ineffective as Siv's.

Fritz turned Harlan around and gunned its engine. The plan was for him to park right alongside the parts warehouse, where he'd be out of the line of fire, but where he'd still have a clear view of the open field. Halfway there, an explosion so startled him, he almost lost control of the bike. He glanced back. Sharp, jagged pieces of shrapnel from the armor on Samson's left shoulder slammed down onto the grassy field. Some of them were on fire. The Steelterror's roar showed he'd felt *that* one. And on the office building roof, Cassie was already nocking a second bomb arrow.

"Nice shot, sis!" Fritz said.

"Not really," Cassie said over the voice-comm. "I was aiming for his head."

At the parts warehouse, Fritz turned Harlan around and parked it off the paved road, right up alongside the building, just in time to watch Samson sink his hand drills into the reactor tower. A cloud of gray dust and rock chips billowed out of the building, completely obscuring Samson from view. The flashes of green laser light bursting forth from the office building roof and from beneath the bridge disappeared into the cloud, and it was impossible to tell what, if anything, they hit.

Five-foot thick concrete made up the reactor tower's exterior wall, but it wouldn't take long for Samson to drill through it, considering the size and power of his drills. Fritz guessed they had three minutes – five tops.

"Bah," Cassie said. "I had a perfect shot lined up. Now I can't see anything."

"Maybe I can clear the air," Fritz said. Tapping the screen of his mobile, mounted on Harlan's handlebars, brought up Apple Juice's remote control application and showed him everything his robot's optics saw, including Siv and Cassie. They stood a few feet in front of the robot on the office building roof. Fritz zoomed the view past them to the dirty, *noisy* cloud of dust in front of the reactor tower. The debris couldn't hide Samson from Apple Juice's chipware eyes, which could pick up several spectrums including ultraviolet and infrared. A bullseye flashed on the cloud, then turned a solid, steady red. Fritz made the robot step forward next to Siv. Servomotors hummed, and a missile launcher moved from a compartment in the robot's back onto its left shoulder.

"Rise and shine," Fritz said. "It's *time for breakfast!*"

He pushed the "fire" button. With a burst of flame and a line of smoke trailing behind it, a missile shot through the air over the field and into the dust cloud. Boom! Samson bellowed and stumbled out of the cloud, a wide gash in his back spewing sparks and flame.

"Thanks, big brother," Cassie said. She launched a bomb-tipped arrow. It smashed into Samson's face and obliterated a not-small chunk of his pronounced brow.

The cloud of concrete dust rapidly dissipated after Samson stopped drilling. He refactored his drills back into hands and looked directly at Siv, Cassie, and Apple Juice, ten stories above the grassy field. With his knuckles dragging and digging ruts out of the dirt, he charged towards them. That was a problem. But at least they had averted the reactor's destruction. For now.

Siv and Sebastian didn't let up on their laser assault, but their weapons continued to prove ineffective against Samson's armor. Time to try something stronger. Seven-point-six-volt battery packs powered their rifles, but the laser cannons that emerged from inside each of Apple Juice's forearms tapped directly into the 345-volt sparkscube mounted on its back. At Fritz's command, Apple Juice stepped up onto the parapet. The roar of booster rockets joined the cacophony of laser fire and Steelterror shouting as the robot leaped off the roof and soared through the air. Its arms were stretched out before it and pointed directly at Samson. Fritz pressed the fire button, and short, rapid laser blasts pelted Samson's face and shoulder, each hit producing a burst of sparks and a shower of steel fragments. He fell onto his back and convulsed under the assault until Apple Juice flew past him.

And *wow*, were those cannons ever loud!

Fritz steered Apple Juice around and back towards Samson. Another bomb-tipped arrow struck the Steelterror, this time in the throat. Viscous green fluid spewed from the wound. Samson changed his hands back into his drills, rolled over, and slammed them into the ground. A hail of soil, grass, and rock cloaked him in another hazy cloud. Fritz brought Apple Juice up to a mid-air hover and blasted Samson with its laser cannons, but he only got a few hits before the targeting systems lost their lock. When the dust settled, there was another giant hole in the ground, and Samson was gone.

"Can the robot follow him in?" Sebastian asked.

"Probably," Fritz said, "but it would be fairly difficult for me to keep up remote control without my eyes on it. And depending on how deep Samson is going, I might fly it right out of wireless range."

There was silence for a long moment as they listened for any sign of Samson, but even the sound of his drills faded after a few seconds. Had he retreated? Fritz allowed himself a small smile at the possibility but otherwise refused to move a muscle.

"Big Man," Siv said, "tell us about Sierra Monet."

"Insolent crank," Sebastian said. "She grew up in child protective services, and as soon as her powers emerged, they dumped her onto the Mantissa. Our lucky day. Bit of an authority problem in that one. The headmasters labeled her an antisocial anarchist, which was generous considering her class warfare and eco-terrorist views. Personally, I'd have labeled her a sociopath. She got expelled from the Mantissa Body – *finally* – after she assaulted the board of directors of Ulmbaden Energy – the manufacturers of the very reactor tower we're defending now. Expulsion was a kindness. She should have served jail time."

"Why did the headmasters go so easy on her?" Cassie asked.

"Simple," Sebastian said. "She was the most powerful Mantissa alive."

Fritz raised his eyebrows.

"But how is she here?" Siv said. "You and Eroica whittled away two centuries in freeze trances. You think she did the same?"

"Beats me," Sebastian said.

Fritz added all the information to his mental file on Lady Verde, or Sierra Monet, or whoever she was. She possessed complete control of the environment. Her troubled past had led her to, and then from, the Mantissa. She shouldn't still be alive. But what troubled him the most...

"She shouldn't be able to change her body," Fritz said, though it came out little more than a mumble.

"Come again, Professor?" Siv said.

Cassie snapped her fingers. "He's right," she said. "Her ability to form a body out of dirt should be impossible because all Mantissa power is psychic. Movers did their 'magic' via telekinesis. Fire elementals possessed pyrokinesis. They rapidly increased the velocity of air molecules until they generated heat and flame. Healers send telepathic commands to the healing centers of a patient's brain; then the patient heals themself. But how is Sierra's mind allowing the matter of her body to transfigure into dirt and water?"

"Anyone ever touch her?" Annalie asked over the voice-comm. "Maybe she ain't making a body out of dirt after all. If Mantissa magic is all psychic, maybe she's just putting an illusion into our minds?"

"I should mention that because of the uniqueness of her abilities, there were some who wondered if she was even Mantissa at all," Sebastian said.

"Real magic?" Siv said.

His question went unanswered. "Uh-oh," Cassie said. "We're in trouble."

"I don't sense anything," Sebastian said. That meant the danger Cassie detected was in her area only.

The ground shook again. Wood creaked and cracked. Bricks snapped and crumbled to dust, and the roof moved underneath Siv and Cassie. But every other building in the area was unaffected. The groundshake seemed to emanate from directly underneath the office building, which swayed ominously. The sound of Samson's drills returned. Then one of them ripped apart a section of the office building's exterior, showering bricks down onto the ground, but it had come from–

"Inside!" Fritz yelled. "He's coming up through the building!"

Glowing red light shined from the building's topmost floor. It came from the thick band of metal stretched around the back of Samson's head, which smashed up through the center of the roof with a sound like the loudest thunder Fritz had ever heard. His drills refactored back into hands, and he pulled himself up until only his legs remained inside.

Siv and Cassie were just a stone's throw in front of him. They tried to aim their weapons, but the building shook and swayed so much, it took all they had to remain standing. Samson refactored his hands into piston-like drums. Fritz wanted to yell, but what was he going to say? Get out of there? They couldn't take the stairs. They couldn't jump, not unless it was to their deaths. They had nowhere to go.

Samson beat his hands against the remains of the roof with such force the building shattered around him. A hailstorm of brick, mortar, wood, and dust pelted the ground, exposing Samson's lower body as the building fell away beneath him.

Siv and Cassie fell, too.

Chapter Thirteen

Why did artificial intelligence have to be such a darn hard nut to crack? This should be *so easy*. He should be able to program his Breakfast-series robots with some basic laws and guidelines, like "protect my friends and me," "obey us when we ask you to do something," and "don't die." Then Apple Juice would have been able to autonomously swoop through the air, grab Siv and Cassie, and return them to the ground, all while Fritz enjoyed a fluffy stack of flapjacks.

Instead, he was stuck remote controlling his robot, which didn't give him anywhere near the precise level of motor control he'd need to pluck Siv and Cassie out of the air safely. And he had only two or three seconds to do it. Plus, for a final kick of irony to the teeth, his inability to figure out artificial intelligence was making it exceedingly difficult for him to save his sister and best friend from an evil, rampaging *artificial intelligence.*

The whole blasted situation belonged on the Stupid List, maybe in the top three.

"Grab the robot!" Fritz hollered as he steered Apple Juice through the air towards Siv and Cassie. Siv already had his grappling hook gun in one hand and Cassie's arm in the other, but he didn't have a target to grab hold of until a hovering mass of green metal moved into position above him.

Siv pulled the trigger. The grapple line soared into the air. Fritz adjusted Apple Juice's position, trying to line up the robot's outstretched arms with Siv's grapple.

Both Siv and Cassie screamed. If the building were still intact, they'd have been parallel with its fourth floor. Third. Second. Then Fritz lost sight of everything behind the massive wall of dust and debris stirred up by the building's collapse. He was forced to turn away and shield his eyes as the cloud rushed at him like a tornado unleashing hell's fury. His ears rang from the deafening rumble. He smelled and tasted nothing but pungent, stale oldness. For thirty seconds before the debris settled, he feared the worst. His best friend was dead. His sister– No. No!

"Cassie?" Fritz shouted. "Siv?"

From her vantage point inside the old warehouse, Annalie saw them first. "They're OK!"

Fritz untucked the bottom of his shirt and used it to wipe off his glasses. After replacing them on his nose, he blinked at the sight of Apple Juice hovering in the sky. A grapple line dangled from its arm. At its other end, Siv and Cassie gently swung back and forth about ten feet above the ground.

"Don't retract the line!" Fritz said. "If the two of you together weigh more than Apple Juice, you'll pull it down. I'll lower you."

"Gratitude," Siv said.

"Are you hurt?" Annalie said.

"My arm got yanked when we stopped falling," Cassie said. "But I heal fast."

The clamor of Samson's drills resumed. While the dust from the building collapse settled, the Steelterror had moved back to the reactor tower and had resumed drilling into its solid concrete outer wall.

Fritz lowered Apple Juice closer to the ground until Siv's and Cassie's boots touched grass. They ran across the field towards the bridge to take cover with Sebastian underneath it. Fritz brought Apple Juice around through the sky and kept it between them and the Steelterror to cover their sprint to safety. With a couple of taps on his mobile's screen, he placed weapons targets on Samson's head and torso.

"I don't care if I destroy the only example I've ever seen of working artificial intelligence," Fritz said. "This ends – now."

Laser fire from Apple Juice's cannons ripped apart Samson. The forty-foot-tall machine screamed and brought one of his drills behind his head to protect himself.

"Annalie," Sebastian said, "have you seen any weak spots in that thing? Anywhere our rifles might be able to do some damage?"

"I think that sucker's covered in Traskian armor," Annalie said. "Only ever read about it in books, but I'll be darned if its hide is made of anything else. But I think I saw a glimpse of unarmored hydraulics underneath his arms. And the way his eyes glow, I reckon they're made of something see-through, like aluminum oxynitride. Which would still be strong, but not Traskian armor strong."

"So tickle him in the armpits," Siv said.

"And take out his eyes," Sebastian said.

Samson turned towards Apple Juice and leaped, but Fritz's robot flew higher than Samson could reach, and apparently, Samson didn't possess any long-range weapons. The ground shook when he landed. He refactored his right drill back into a hand and raised it to cover his face, but Fritz didn't stop firing. Laser blasts blew bits of shrapnel off of Samson with every hit.

Siv and Sebastian concentrated their fire on his right underarm, which his raised elbow exposed. Cassie launched a bomb-tipped arrow at the same spot. When the fire from the explosion burned away, Samson's arm hung limp, barely still attached to his body. Apple Juice blasted out Samson's left eye, and the Steelterror collapsed to the ground, where he shoved the drill on his left hand into the dirt. He was going to dig a tunnel and escape again as he'd done before destroying the office building.

"Don't let him get away!" Fritz said. "The tower's foundation is made of steel-reinforced concrete twice as thick as the walls, but underground, we don't have a way to attack him. He'll be able to take his time and drill up through the floor unhindered."

Fritz kept up Apple Juice's assault and maneuvered his robot closer to Samson, who slowly sank into the dirt. Fritz jammed his finger against the fire button on his mobile screen over and over with enough force to cause pain. A pair of fireballs exploded from somewhere on Samson's back.

Suddenly, Sebastian yelped in alarm. "Get away from the river!" Cassie shouted. She, Sebastian, and Siv ran from their cover underneath the bridge and scurried up the shore. What was going on out there?

Something reached from the water, yanked the three of them into the river, and pulled them under. A ball of metal, maybe twice the size of Samson's head, rose to the river's surface. Eight various sized circles of glass – eyes? – were scattered across it. At its center was a wide opening – a mouth? – that shuttered open like a camera lens. A line of red sparkslights ran around its perimeter, and attached to the ball – the thing's body – were eight long, thick, flexible metal bands. Tentacles. They writhed and twisted in the water, making clinking metal sounds Fritz could hear all the way on the other side of the field. More red lights ran up and down their lengths. Two of them were wrapped around Sebastian, holding him securely above the water. One held Siv by the ankle, upside-down, and another held Cassie the same way.

"The water Steelterror," Fritz said from a suddenly dry mouth.

Siv and Sebastian's laser rifles were gone. Cassie held her bow, but her quiver was empty. All three of them coughed; Fritz heard it through the still-open voice-comm line to Sebastian's mobile. Samson rapidly retreated into the ground, but Fritz let him go. He spun Apple Juice around in the air to face the water Steelterror, who responded by moving his friends closer together, conveniently positioning them between him and Apple Juice. Fritz kept his robot's laser cannons pointed at the new Steelterror, but he didn't dare fire.

A sound like thunder rumbled in the sky. The ground shook a little as the sound came closer and became a high-pitched scream of metal and engine. An airplane entered the power facility's airspace. It was smaller than he and his friends' airplane and seemed to be a *lot* faster. It was a jet – long, sleek body, wide wings. And it headed straight for Apple Juice.

Fritz hammered the button activating Apple Juice's rockets and steered his robot out of the way, but the jet adjusted its course to match. Fritz flinched. Just before a collision, there was a sound of clanging metal and whirring motors and the jet... changed. It refactored itself, like Samson could do with his hands, except the jet changed its entire shape. The way its nose suddenly twisted towards the ground, Fritz thought it was going to crash, but as the nose twisted, so did the jet's body. It split, rotated, split again, and suddenly what had been the body of the jet was a pair of arms and a pair of legs. The wings rotated, slid to the side. A mechanical head with glowing red eyes emerged from somewhere within.

What crashed into his robot was no longer a jet, but a human-shaped robot. The sky Steelterror. Sierra had three of them now. And good golly, this one was even larger than Samson.

Its refactoring hadn't slowed it a bit. The sky Steelterror snatched Apple Juice in one of its hands and threw it across the open field. It smacked *hard* into the side of the reactor tower. Concrete chips and pieces of robot shattered away on impact. Yellow warnings and red error messages flashed on Fritz's mobile screen. Apple Juice dropped twenty feet before Fritz managed to engage its rockets long enough to slow its descent. His efforts ensured it crashed into the dirt with a soft thud instead of a destructive bang.

Ten feet in front of where Fritz sat on his motorbike, a pillar of dirt burst out of the ground and took the shape of Sierra. She had metal spikes on her leather bracelets. Thick circles of black make-up ringed her eyes. With a tremendous boom and rattle, the sky Steelterror dropped from the air and landed in the field behind her. Was the fire Steelterror also lurking somewhere nearby?

"You dug up all of them?" Fritz asked.

"Nah," Sierra said. "Didn't need to. Samson, Leviathan, and Banshee are more than enough."

Through the open voice-comm, Siv swore. Fritz glanced at his mobile screen and saw only he, Sebastian, and Annalie remained on the line. Immersion had likely destroyed Siv's and Cassie's mobiles, while Sebastian's remained safe in a waterproof, fireproof, and mostly bulletproof pocket of his Mantissa duty uniform. But Fritz startled when he realized he heard Sebastian's growls but not any translation. The translator device, strapped around Sebastian's neck, had not been shielded from the water. Sierra and her blasted metal killers had taken his uncle's voice.

Sierra's face took on a blank, fixed expression, and a second Sierra rose up out of the water across the field, near Leviathan and his friends. "They use mobiles to communicate and to control their robot," the second Sierra said. "Jam their signals."

"Acknowledged," Leviathan said. He spoke in a hollow, booming voice that produced ripples on the water.

The Sierra in the river reverted to water and fell apart; life returned to the face of the Sierra in front of him. A red light on Fritz's mobile turned green. Apple Juice's rockets had power-cycled and were back online. He pushed the button to engage them, to get his robot back into the air, but then every status light on his screen turned red, and their shared voice-comm disconnected. No signal.

Out in the river, Leviathan lowered Cassie closer to the water's surface.

"The killswitch!" Siv shouted from the river. "Turn it off!"

Even if he wanted to – and now he most certainly did – he *couldn't*, because they'd disrupted his signal. And he couldn't rescue his best friend, his uncle, and his sister, either, not with Apple Juice lost to him. Annalie was still watching from the parts warehouse, but she was unarmed, and her mobile was no doubt useless now, too.

If Sierra decided to destroy the reactor's containment system, there wasn't anything he could do for anyone within a fifty-mile radius. Everyone, including himself, would be incinerated. Sierra sneered at him. Banshee stood forty-five feet above him. Leviathan dunked Siv's head underwater before yanking him back up again.

Panic strangled rational thought out of his mind.

Forget Sebastian and Siv.

Forget Cassie.

Forget Annalie even!

Just run. Run. *Run!*

He stomped on Harlan's starter, and its engine roared to life. He turned around and drove away from Sierra and Banshee as fast as the bike would take him. Away from the parts warehouse, away from the field, away from the river. Away from his friends and family. He knew the layout of the power facility campus by heart. The paved road underneath him was on a path to the facility's north gate. On the other side of that gate was an uninhabited section of Mondorf. There he could hide, think, breathe.

He'd never driven so fast. The bike's throttle was wide open. Its engine was so, so loud, but the engine that came up from behind was even louder. Banshee, back in jet mode, flew as low to the ground as possible, hovering above him, pacing him. Toying with him.

"When your life is on the line, you don't rely on your twigs of bone," Banshee said in a feminine voice. "You use a machine. Your attempt at escape acknowledges the superiority of steel."

Banshee screamed past, turned, and came back towards him. And he thought Apple Juice was fast? Apple Juice was an old lady with a walking stick compared to Banshee. He couldn't run from her! She would seek him wherever he went. A sound escaped Fritz's throat – part sob, part scream, part cry for help. But when Banshee reached him, she flew over and kept going. Fritz craned his neck around to watch her go, to see if she would turn again, but he lost sight of her. He turned back to the road–

Just in time to watch dirt burst up from a crack in the pavement. It coalesced together into the shape of Sierra. Directly ahead of him.

Fritz squeezed the brake lever. Smoke poured off the bike's wheels. Brake pads smashed into rubber tires and screamed for mercy, but he was driving too fast, and she was too close. He swung the handlebars hard to the side to avoid her. The back tire fishtailed, and the bike toppled over. Fritz hit the pavement. Something snapped in his right leg. His head rattled inside his helmet. Sierra exploded into dirt when he struck her, but the impact didn't even slow him down.

He and his bike went in separate directions. He tumbled three, four times, then skidded across the pavement. Friction first burned away his shirt sleeve and pant legs, then shredded his skin.

At last, he came to a stop. He couldn't move his right leg. He couldn't even feel his left one or his left arm; all he felt from them was pain – unimaginable, unbearable pain. His entire body shivered. Each of his eyeglass lenses had at least ten cracks in them. With fingers that moved far too slowly and shook far too much, he used his right hand to push his helmet off his head. The air felt cold – so cold! He dared a look behind him. The pavement was streaked with his blood.

With a high pitched whine, Banshee refactored into her robot form and landed. She tossed something onto the ground and kicked it towards Fritz. It skidded across the road, through his blood stains, and stopped just a few feet from him. It was one of Apple Juice's arms.

"I broke your toy robot," Banshee said with mock remorse. Other than her red eyes and her steel gray hue, her face looked so human. It moved as if soft and malleable like flesh and muscle. Even in Fritz's agony, part of his mind wondered how it worked.

"Are you trembling in fear?" Banshee said, stalking towards him, vibrations rattling the ground with each of her steps. "Or because you left half your skin all over the pavement? Pfft. Fragile blood bag." She chortled, then leaped straight up, refactored into a jet, and flew away.

A dirt pillar rose out of a crack in the pavement next to him. Of course, it took Sierra's color and shape. The collision hadn't done a bit of harm to her. Could she even be hurt? How idiotic had they been – how stupid had *he* been – to think they could have faced her?

"Who are you?" he said. He fought to stay conscious and could barely force the words above a whisper. "Are you Lady Verde? Or are you Sierra Monet?"

She seemed to consider the question. A breeze blew a strand of her hair, and she tucked it behind her ear. It was a curious gesture for someone who could shape-shift from dirt into a bluebonnet or an old lady or a young woman or who knew what else.

"I'd forgotten that name," she said. "But that's me. I think. Sierra Monet. Something happened to her. To me? The planet and I, we..." She interdigitated her fingers, locking her hands tightly together.

Fritz's mind worked a puzzle. Could a Mantissa capable of controlling the environment somehow have merged with it? It would certainly explain how a two-hundred-year-old Mantissa was still alive. But was it even possible? Mantissa power was biological. It was all psychic, somehow or another... wasn't it?

Sierra stared at her interlocked fingers. She looked confused. Or awed. Maybe a little of both? She gave her body, clothes, and hair an examination, pulling a strand of her red hair before her eyes. "I'm Sierra," she whispered. Her reverie lasted only a moment. Then her hands curled back into fists, and the rage returned.

"You want to know who I am?" Sierra said. "I'm the crank who beat you, that's who I am."

Blackness crept into the sides of Fritz's vision. It would all be so much easier if he just went to sleep.

"Wake up!" Sierra said. She stomped her boot down on his right leg, exactly where it looked the most misshapen. He howled in agony. Tears streaked his face. It was *so cold*. The calendar said it was mid-September, but it felt like early February in the frozen north.

She crouched next to him, leaned in close to his face. "It is important to me," she said between gritted teeth, "that you know *I beat you.*"

Beat him? If she waited a few minutes, she could gloat that she'd killed him.

"You beat me," he said. "You were right, and I was wrong. Just don't hurt me. Please."

"Turn it off," she said.

His eyes wanted to roll back in his head, but he tried to locate his motorbike. "I will," he said. "My mobile. I can send a signal. But the jamming. I'll need it off. And my mobile. Then I..."

She wagged a finger and tutted. "No, no, no, no, *Professor*. Isn't that what they call you? You don't get to use chipware to turn off the chipware. You need to wipe the slate clean and not look back."

All the pain he'd felt since the crash – the worst pain of his life – was *nothing* next to the pain he felt when she grabbed him by the neck, yanked him off the ground, and flew into the air, dragging him with her. Drops of blood, specks of dirt, and the tattered threads from what remained of his clothes trailed behind him. The touch of the air on his wounds felt like getting a scrub with a brush made of jagged, rusty metal bristles. His legs just dangled and flapped like the tail of a kite. He screamed until his throat felt as raw as his flayed limbs. The blackness in his peripheral vision beckoned to him.

She dragged him across and high above the campus. When they were directly above the reactor tower, she descended. Powerful winds whipped ahead of them and ripped a hole in the roof. Sierra pulled him through it and zipped past the twenty-four levels of maintenance walkways and catwalks lining the perimeter of the five hundred foot tall tower's open center. For a few harrowing moments, Fritz wasn't certain Sierra was going to stop. He thought she was going to fade away into air or water a foot above the metal floor and leave him to splatter against it. He wondered if she'd drop him into the Iller River, which ran through the center of the tower and provided the facility with a constant supply of coolant. But she did neither.

She slowed and swooped to the side of the chamber's ground level, and she landed at the master power switch.

Sierra stood Fritz in front of the thick metal lever the size of his forearm, but neither his shattered right leg nor his burned-to-the-bone left could support his weight. He fell flat on his face, unable to move and barely able to breathe. Sierra didn't seem to care. She crouched next to him and counted off items on her fingers. Her black-polished fingernails were like bullets marking each item in the list.

"I'll release your friends unharmed," she said. "I'll put the Steelterrors back to sleep in the ground. And you will never see me again. But in return, you stop restoring chipware, and you shut down and destroy what you've already restored. Before the Blackout, this planet was on the verge of ecological catastrophe. I will *not* barking let that happen again. Got it?"

He nodded, but it probably just looked like part of his trembling. He coughed up a wad of copper-tasting blood. Wow, he probably had serious internal injuries, but he hurt too badly to even worry about them.

"And you start by pulling down that switch and turning off this power plant," she said.

"I can't... stand... up."

As soon as he said them, he knew the words were going to cause him more agony. Sierra yanked him to his feet and held him up before the master power switch. He'd have screamed if he had any strength left in him. Somehow he managed to wrap the fingers of his right hand – the only limb he could still move – around the master power switch.

But he hesitated.

Once he pulled the lever down, Annalie's passion for restoring chipware would be a moot point, a dead profession. Siv and

Cassie wouldn't be able to use their mobiles to talk while she was at school in Harbrucken and he was at his shop in Gorman. They'd go months without hearing one another's voices. And Sebastian would never be human again. He'd be a white demon for the rest of his body's unnaturally long lifespan. And with his chipware translator gone, he'd be voiceless, too.

But they'd be alive. Sebastian, Siv, and Cassie. Everyone in Mondorf. Annalie and her siblings. None of them would die a fiery death in an uncontained dynamek energy explosion. All he had to do was pull down the switch.

Yet for all the logic in the world dictating he should turn the dang thing off already, he hesitated. Even during the times of his life when melancholy had gotten the best of him, he'd never had the guts to attempt to take his own life. And that might as well have been what Sierra was demanding because there was little difference between pulling down the power switch and putting a bullet through his head. Given his physical state, he had a very good chance of dying on the cold metal floor underneath him in the next five minutes. But still. He couldn't murder his dream.

Sierra sighed. "Leviathan has your friends' noses an inch above the water. And Banshee is holding the red-haired one in her hand. Her comparatively large, extremely powerful, steel hand, which she enjoys clenching into very tight–"

Fritz pulled down the switch.

The tower went dim – only emergency lighting illuminated the area, and even that would fade in a few hours when the lights' batteries drained. The power plant's ever-present hum slowly grew softer and softer. Fans stopped spinning. Water stopped flowing through the coolant pipes.

The restoration of the world's lost chipware was over.

Sierra dropped him, and he collapsed in a heap. Even if he could move, he didn't want to anymore. He saw Sierra's face lose its expression and blank like it had out in the field when a second Sierra had appeared on the water to talk to Leviathan. It only lasted about half a minute. Then she blinked and awareness returned to her.

"I told the Steelterrors to let your friends go. They're all safe on land." She looked over his broken body, and... was he just in shock or did she look uncomfortable? Pained? Ashamed? "And I told them where you were and that you, umm, need some help pretty quickly."

A waist-high guardrail separated the floor from the river flowing through the tower. She climbed atop it and faced him.

"You'll thank me, you know," she said. "If you live. Your friends and family will all thank me. Today, I made sure our water stays clean, our air remains breathable, and our land stays toxin-free." She raised her fist. "Verde triumphant!"

Behind her, the river churned. Strands of water reached up over the railing and wrapped themselves around her arms and legs. Her body turned transparent, clear as the river, and then there was no distinction between her and the water. The wave splashed back into the current, and Sierra was gone.

The blackness wanted to envelop him again, but he resisted and held onto the sight of the reactor's emergency lights. They would fade into blackness, just like his project. And his life. People would forget that for a couple of brief months in 1879, the future had returned. Without the demons and their slaves to meticulously maintain the physical infrastructure in the hopes that it would all one day work again, kudzu and decay would take over the power plant, and everything chipware would be forgotten.

The people of Earp and Hondo would forget the lights that had illuminated their nights. They'd forget how close they'd been to instant global communication and advanced medicine. To climate-controlled homes. To all knowledge from throughout Verdant history at their fingertips, on-demand.

And thank goodness, they'd certainly forget the king of the Stupid List. The mudsill whose doltishness had gotten Harlan killed. The idiot who had been dense enough to think he could revive the world destroyed by the Blackout and build a better future. Good riddance.

Chapter Fourteen

"We'll be back in an hour," Cassie called to him from the stairs leading down to street level. "OK?"

Fritz sat in a rickety wooden chair before the empty window frames on the opposite side of the loft. Lit by the noontime sun, it was easy to spot the dark, slightly reddish tint in the grass across the street. He'd once thought that strange tint was nothing more than an oddity. He'd never dreamed it could prompt a reign of terror out of a psychotic Mantissa who'd somehow merged with the planet.

"Fritz?" Cassie said. "Siv and I are taking the last boxes to the airplane. We'll be back soon. OK?"

Since she wasn't going to leave until she got an acknowledgment, Fritz raised his hand in a disinterested wave, but he didn't turn around.

Before Cassie and Siv could depart the loft, footsteps sounded on the creaky stairs. "Howdy," Annalie said to Cassie and Siv in a low voice. "How's he doing?"

"He's healed, as much as he can be," Cassie said.

"God bless you," Annalie said. "God bless you and Sebastian both." A beat of silence. "But how *is* he?"

Fritz didn't hear an audible reply.

"Sorry it took me so long to come back," Annalie said. "Felix had an episode this morning, and I couldn't leave him. And – oh – it sure looks different in here with everything packed up."

Cassie and Siv had spent the morning disassembling the workbenches. They'd boxed up all the chipware that had drawn such disdain from Mayor Clum. Two carriage loads of it were already on their airplane, which Sebastian was preparing for its final flight. Sierra wouldn't mind him using it to tuck tail and run. Maybe she could take the form of some strong tailwinds and kick him in the rear end on his way out the door.

He knew Cassie didn't want him to keep any of the now-useless chipware. He saw it on her face every time he made fleeting eye contact with her. She was worried about him, and she didn't know what good could come out of keeping fifteen crates of junk, rubbish, and scrap metal. But it was vital he keep every last piece. It still had a purpose to him – though if Cassie figured out his intentions, she and her parents would make him go back to that head doctor in Flatonia to talk about his feelings and his worries.

"Will you be here when we get back?" Siv asked. "We don't mean to leave without saying–"

"Yeah," Annalie said. "I'll be here."

The sound of Cassie and Siv's boots on the stairs grew softer as they descended towards the carriage parked out on the street, then faded completely. A hand landed on Fritz's shoulder, and he tensed.

"Howdy," Annalie said.

She wasn't in rough, third- or fourth-hand jeans and a faded work shirt. She wore a green dress, and it looked new – well, as new as anything in Mondorf ever was. She adjusted her glasses on her nose, and she smiled. Her beauty was almost enough to make him smile, too.

Almost.

"How are you feeling?" she asked.

"Everything is everything," he lied. He needed her support to stand and hobble a few steps. Cassie and Sebastian had used their healing power to save his life, but his right leg mended shorter than his left, so badly had it been broken. Back in Hondo, he'd be able to get a cane, but Mondorf had no such devices, not after two centuries of demon rule in which they disposed of weak and infirm humans.

"Will Cassie be able to do anything more for your leg?" Annalie said.

He shrugged.

"Does it hurt?"

"'No. My back hurts, though. Cassie says that's because my hip and back are compensating for the shorter leg. I feel a little off-balance, too."

Next to the chair was the only crate still left in the loft. It contained the dismembered limbs and dented torso of Apple Juice. Its face had been split open and ripped apart like a can of canned berries. Annalie frowned at it and moaned. "I saw Banshee smash it. Right before she peeled the roof off the warehouse and came in after me." She shuddered.

"I'm sorry," he said. "I was so focused on planning how to take down Samson. I never stopped to think about what I'd do if she went and dug up the rest of them. The night she destroyed Earp, she told me she knew where they all were. My power probably tried to tell me to prepare for that possibility, and I probably didn't listen. It was stupid."

"Wasn't your fault." She smiled. It was clearly an invitation for him to do the same.

He looked down at his shoes.

"So what are you going to do?" she said.

"Go home."

"I know *that*." She made a weak little laugh. "I mean what are you going to do when you're back home?"

"I don't know." He shrugged. "Maybe I'll take up kite flying. There's probably a lot to do there. A lot of folks collect stamps. Or coins."

Three words popped into his mind. Had they come from his power? Or just from his heart? He breathed rapidly, and his hands felt sweaty. His heart pounded hard against his breastbone. His knees felt weak, and not because of the discomfort of walking with one leg longer than the other.

"Come with me," he said before he could stop himself.

She blinked. "Where?"

"Back to Hondo," he said. "Back home. My home. You should... I'd really like it if you came with me."

He tried to force his eyes to meet hers, but he couldn't. What had he just said? He'd actually vocalized those words? Said them aloud?

"I don't know what to say," Annalie said. "I'd... I'd like to."

His heart went up into his throat.

"But I can't," she said. "I couldn't."

His chest collapsed.

"I... my siblings," she said.

"They could come, too," he said.

Why was he still talking? Hadn't he embarrassed himself enough? Shut up. Shut up!

"But they have friends here," she said. "This is their home. And they need me. I can't just drag them all away from everything they know. Felix is having a hard enough time with all of this change, and the demons being gone and us being free is really good change."

"So coming with me would be a bad change," Fritz said.

"No! That's not what I meant. I–"

"Forget it." He turned away from her and faced the empty windows. "Just forget I said anything. It was stupid."

There were several seconds of extraordinarily uncomfortable silence.

"What if you stayed here?" Annalie said. Her voice was soft, and it wavered. "With me?"

Fritz hadn't considered that. Until a couple of months ago, leaving home for any extended length of time hadn't been something he was willing to do under any circumstances. Now he'd been away from home for two months, and his heart ached. He missed his parents. He wanted to be alone in his room where he was most comfortable. But he sure felt awfully comfortable with Annalie, too.

"You have family, too, I know," Annalie said. "Your folks and Cassie and Siv would be far away, and I know right now, you really need to be around people who care about you. But... but that's why I'm asking you to stay." She licked her lips, took two quick breaths. "I want you to stay here and be with someone who really cares about you."

She stepped in front of him and gently lifted his chin until he was looking into her eyes. Except for the shaking, he couldn't move. His mind raced over the possibilities and the implications. Make a new home here. Help the people of Mondorf build new demon-free lives, but without chipware, of course. Help Annalie raise her siblings. See her every day. Lean on her shoulder when he needed support. Hold her hand. Maybe even ask her to marry him someday? Matrimony had always been completely unfathomable to a guy who had no desire to leave home. Yet here he was, not just considering it, but... yearning for it? Ready for it?

Yeah. Ready. Well, ready to take the first step towards it at least.

There were no postal routes between Mondorf and the occupied territories south of the mountains. And of course, no more chipware. He wouldn't be able to call or write to his parents, Cassie, or Siv. To go home for a visit would require a two-week trek across Terrascorcha on foot. Or worse, on a horse. In Mondorf he'd be away from his familiar surroundings, his possessions, and everyone in the world he loved or cared about. Except for Annalie.

It was crazy and terrifying and exciting, all at once.

It was the greatest idea he'd ever heard.

"And I'm not convinced the restoration is over," she said. "We can keep working on it. In secret." She winked.

Fritz blinked and stuttered. "What?"

"My dad used to always say: when God inspires us with a dream he helps us make it happen. And I believe it was God who inspired a really brilliant and sweet but painfully shy guy to leave home and share his gift with the world. And if I'm right, that means your project *can't* be over."

"It wasn't God who inspired me," Fritz said. "It was Harlan, and he's dead now."

"I reckon Harlan was speaking on behalf of the Lord."

Had she somehow missed the fact that the workbenches were gone? That the loft was empty? Had she forgotten two-hundred eleven people had died in Earp? Had she forgotten what he'd looked like on the floor of the power plant? Broken, mostly dead, and drooling in a puddle of his blood?

"Sierra could pop out of the dirt right outside this building," he said. "She could be the air in the room, listening to us right now. If I try to work in secret, and she catches me, she'll destroy the power plant."

"If she's really the planet, she wouldn't poison herself something fierce like that."

"She would, purely out of spite," he said. "But it doesn't matter. All of the important chipware needs more sparks than what batteries can provide. I would need the power plant. That's the whole reason I even came here in the first place. And Sierra would *definitely* notice if I reactivated the power plant. There'd be more Steelterrors, more destruction. She'd kill me. She'd kill everyone."

"I know you're afraid," Annalie said. "I'd be lying if I said I wasn't. But come on. Your magical ability to figure things out will come up with something. The hope and the joy on the faces of the people in Earp as they danced and sang the night away – we can see that again."

"We'll see a village razed to the ground again," he said. "We'll see the dead dumped into a mass grave. Again."

"I think you know I'm right," Annalie said. "You could have asked Cassie and Siv to trash all the chipware you had here. But you had them pack it all up, and you're shipping it home with you. You *know* it's not over. So unpack it. Keep it here. Keep yourself here."

"That's not why I'm keeping it," he said, raising his voice a notch. "I'm keeping it to remember. I need to remember the people who died because I was a sap-head. I need to remember my stupidity and my hubris. I need to remember what an idiot I was, thinking I could change the world. Those broken pieces of junk are the relics of my failure. They must be kept somewhere I'm forced to see them daily."

Annalie wrapped her hands around his. "No. Don't torture yourself. And don't give up."

"You think I *want* to give up?" he said. "I don't have a choice!"

"Of course you do. You *can* still change the world. *We* can do it. Together."

There was pleading in her eyes. His power nearly shook him physically telling him to listen to her. And the thought of forgiving himself was so comforting, so appealing.

So he did what he had to do.

He ignored everything she said.

He slammed a mental door on his power. Then he locked it, latched it, boarded it up. Good things happened when he listened to his hyper-intuition, but that was just the thing.

He didn't *deserve* to have good things happen to him anymore.

He ripped his hands away from her, closed his eyes, and put his fists on the side of his head. "Please don't touch me," he said between quick, rapid breaths. "And please stop talking. It's too loud. Too loud, too loud. There's too much talking. Too much talky, talky, talky, talky, talky."

"What's wrong? Did I say–"

"*Just shut up!*" he yelled. "Just shut your *barking* mouth!"

He didn't see her face, but he heard her gasp, heard the shuffle of her shoes on the wooden floor as she took a step away from him. When she let out a little whimper, he stole a glance at her. Her hand covered her mouth. She looked like she'd seen a demon return to Mondorf, wrathy as the fires of hell themselves and itching for her blood.

"Please just go," he said.

He closed his eyes again. Heard her take a rattling breath and sniff. She didn't move.

"I said *go!*"

Her footsteps rapidly receded towards the door. The sound of her crying cut him in the heart. Good. His back hurt. His heart hurt. All good and well-deserved. He took two limping steps towards the crate and snatched Apple Juice's head from it. The piece of trash was broken, shattered, and ripped apart. Worthless. Just like him.

He roared and threw the stupid, busted thing across the loft.

```
[1879-10-27 11:00] root@skylab:/bin > .\secscan
Begin scan with default parameters (range: 500 AU)
......
Scan complete. (0) matches found.

[1879-10-27 12:00] root@skylab:/bin > .\secscan
Begin scan with default parameters (range: 500 AU)
......
Scan complete. (0) matches found.

[1879-10-27 13:00] root@skylab:/bin > .\secscan
Begin scan with default parameters (range: 500 AU)
......
Scan complete. (0) matches found.

[1879-10-27 14:00] root@skylab:/bin > .\secscan
Begin scan with default parameters (range: 500 AU)
....
Match on 'Morterac wave' at
  187534.45 x
  2353.22 y
  788998.04 z
  (Distance: 499AU)
Scan complete. (1) matches found.

[1879-10-27 14:01] root@skylab:/bin > .\secscan
Begin scan with default parameters (range: 500 AU)
....
Match on 'Morterac wave' at
  187534.65 x
  2352.12 y
  788998.03 z
  (Distance: 499AU)
  (Speed based on previous match - 473-IM)
Scan complete. (1) matches found.

[1879-10-27 14:02] root@skylab:/bin > .\secscan
Begin scan with default parameters (range: 500 AU)
....
Match on 'Morterac wave' at
  187534.77 x
  2351.04 y
  788998.01 z
  (Distance: 499AU)
  (Speed based on previous matches - 475-IM)
Scan complete. (1) matches found.
```

```
[1879-10-27 14:03] root@skylab:/bin > .\servbot --
summon "Lab14" --all --t now
142 service bots have been immediately summoned to
Lab 14.

[1879-10-27 14:03] root@skylab:/bin > .\servbot --
equip "forging tools" --qty 27 --where "Lab14"
27 Servbots in (or currently en route to) Lab 14
will be equipped with forging tools.

[1879-10-27 14:03] root@skylab:/bin > .\supchain --
itemId ItemIdFor("Grade 23 Cable") --qty all --
destination "Lab14"
Servbots will deliver all available grade 23 cable
to Lab 14 ASAP.

[1879-10-27 14:03] root@skylab:/bin > .\supchain --
itemId ItemIdFor("Duranium") --qty all --destination
"Lab14"
Servbots will deliver all available duranium to Lab
14 ASAP.

[1879-10-27 14:03] root@skylab:/bin > .\supchain --
itemId ItemIdFor("Octocore chips") --qty all --
destination "Lab14"
Servbots will deliver all available octocore chips
to Lab 14 ASAP.

[1879-10-27 14:03] root@skylab:/bin > .\secscan
Begin scan with default parameters (range: 500 AU)
....
Match on 'Morterac wave' at
  187535.14 x
  2349.97 y
  788997.91
  (Distance: 499AU)
  (Speed based on previous matches - 475-IM)
Scan complete. (1) matches found.

[1879-10-27 14:04] root@skylab:/bin > .\taskJob --
freq * * * * 5r --command secscan | arrivalCalc >
stationBroadcast0
Job created. Will run every 5 minutes.
```

Chapter Fifteen

The gears inside the clock on Fritz's nightstand turned the clock's hour hand to five. The pin on the clock's alarm dial dropped into a groove on the alarm gear and pushed it up, which raised the alarm lever, releasing its hold on the alarm spring. Now unchained, the alarm spring's rapid vibrations pushed along another gear which grabbed the alarm lever and swung it rapidly back and forth against the twin bells on top of the clock.

Fritz hadn't been sleeping. He watched the bells clang. They were loud, they were too high pitched, they hurt his ears, and he deserved the pain. After a minute, the alarm spring ran out of potential energy, and the ringing stopped. To make sure the alarm went off again tomorrow, he'd have to wind the clock later because it was stupid, and it most certainly was not a solar-powered mechanical clock.

He stood up to get dressed and almost tripped over one of the fifteen junk-filled wooden crates scattered throughout his bedroom. The circlet he'd so doltishly thought could one day restore Uncle Sebastian's mind to his own body sat at the top of it. His eyes lingered on it for a moment. Then he pulled off yesterday's clothes and put on new ones.

Cool air hit his face when he stepped out onto the front porch. It was late September, and the summer heat was finally starting to break. It felt nice, much nicer than he deserved.

"Morning," his father said. He frowned and stood from his rocking chair. "That's what you're wearing?"

Fritz looked over his shoes, slacks, button-up shirt, and vest. And socks, of course. Always socks. He shrugged. "Yeah."

Milo waved a hand in front of the overalls he wore. "You don't have a pair of work overalls you want to wear? What am I asking, of course you don't. You want to borrow a set of mine? You're a bit taller than me, but I think they'd fit OK."

He was three inches taller than his father. "I'm fine."

"Well, I'm so thankful for your help I wouldn't care if you wore your pajamas. I sowed extra this year, just in case we had another drought. You remember how many folks went hungry in Cleburne Hill last summer." He shuddered. "Well, thank God, the weather's been perfect, and I'm looking at a record harvest. But so's every other farm in the valley. George Mueller, the Asheford boys, all the extra help I usually hire is all booked up. Before you came home, I didn't know what I was going to do. Let's feed the chickens first. Then you want to milk the cows while I check the fields? I don't want you having to..." He awkwardly waved towards Fritz's cane.

Fritz exhaled. "Sure."

His father gave him two quick claps on the back. Fritz tensed. He hated being touched.

*   *   *

Dear Annalie,

I hope this letter finds you well. I need to tell you I'm sorry. I'm so sorry. All I can think about these days is how stupid I am. How stupid I was to dream about a different future, how stupid I was to yell at you for believing in it. I was scared that if I resumed my project, Sierra would kill me, and I screamed at you and pushed you away. Now I miss you so much.

I don't even know why I'm writing this because there aren't any postal routes between Hondo and Mondorf. No telegraph lines either because most of the world still thinks the land between our towns is Terrascorcha. They think it's poisoned and toxic and they're all so stupid but not as stupid as I am. I'm the king of stupidity. I don't even deserve to breathe intelligent air I'm so stupid.

Hey, speaking of lines, remember the time I tried to run a sparksline to the village of Earp? HA HA HA HA HA HA HA. Wasn't I STUPID? HA HA HA, thanks Harlan, here's some sparks, here's some chipware, now die when a Steelterror crushes you! Thanks for everything, love Fritz, HA HA HA.

I'm an idiot. I'm a dunce! I can't believe how I treated you and I miss you so much and I don't know what to do and I need you and you're gone.

And you WON'T EVEN EVER RECEIVE THIS!

"About another week or so and we'll be able to start harvesting the grain," Milo said.

Fritz pushed his mashed potatoes around his plate. The largest pile formed a hub. Thin spokes of creamy, gooey spuds connected the center to outlying points. The sparkslines would have been so easy to make. Most already existed. They'd just need to be patched. Then new ones could have been run to settlements that hadn't existed two hundred years ago when the Blackout shut off everything.

He'd already laid one sparksline. It had taken twelve days. He and Annalie had spent so much time in those twelve days talking about chipware. Technology. The future. Only now he realized they hadn't just been talking about Verde's future. In a weird, underhanded, indirect way, they'd been talking about their personal futures. He'd been tentatively trying to see if Annalie felt the same way he thought he felt, though he'd never felt that way about anyone before, so he didn't have much basis for comparison. Siv had seen it though. At least Fritz assumed that's why he'd found so many excuses to go on long rides with Tobias.

Oh, right. Tobias's blood was on his hands, too.

"Your father could use your help," Ruth said. "You could drive the reaper, or work the machine. You wouldn't have to walk."

Fritz spooned peas onto his mashed potato hub and spokes. They represented the sparks that would have powered his stupid fantasy land. They were green, the same color as the newest dress Annalie could find the last time he'd seen her. "I'll help," he said.

"The thing is, he likes to do most harvesting in the mornings," she said.

"Ruth..." Milo said softly. "It's not important."

"Early mornings," Ruth said. "Five."

Fritz shrugged. "OK."

"Son, it's been a week since you woke before ten," she said. "And that was once. Most days it's noon."

An apple pie was on the counter. His mother had baked it. Annalie would have eaten the whole thing if she were here. They could have lived in Mondorf no problem, and they could have flown down to Hondo for any reason they wanted – holiday, long weekend, plain Wednesday, whatever. Mom could have taught Annalie how to make all his favorite foods, like oatmeal and pancakes. Both his parents would have adored her.

His father winced, and his mother placed her hand on top of his. "Heartburn again?"

Milo grimaced and nodded. "The fried chicken maybe?"

"Maybe," Ruth said. "Want a teaspoon of baking soda?"

"Please."

Fritz stood from the table. "I'm a little tired. I think I'll go to bed."

"It's only six o'clock," his mother said. "You didn't even wake up until eleven-thirty."

Fritz shrugged.

"If you ever want to talk, we're here for you," Milo said.

Thanks, Dad. You see, it's a little hard to work the land all day when it was the land that came alive and destroyed my dream. And then I was so flustered over it I acted like a complete ass to the one person I've ever met who was able to touch me without it feeling like acid on my shoulder. Did you ever ruin your entire life, Dad? How did you recover from that?

Fritz nodded.

"Tomorrow, why don't you drive over to Gorman and visit Siv?" Milo said. "Or just forget the fields tomorrow. Forget them all week, and visit Cassie. If you don't want to talk to Siv, or us, at least talk to Cassie."

He gave a non-committal shrug, then limped from the kitchen back to his bedroom.

"He didn't even take a bite of his dinner," Ruth whispered to Milo.

He closed the door behind him.

$$* \qquad * \qquad *$$

He held the tip of the pocket knife's blade in the flame of his candle. The alarm clock told him it was 2:10 in the morning. Twenty more seconds. His left sleeve was rolled up to the elbow. The second hand ticked away. Light brown hair covered his exposed arm. The candle's light reflected off the sharp metal. Five seconds. Three, two, one. 2:11. Time to remember the two hundred eleven deaths he'd caused in Earp.

His arm stung and burned when he dragged the hot knife across it an inch. A dribble of blood dripped onto his desk. He grit his teeth and inhaled sharply. It hurt. Boy, did it hurt.

But it hurt so much less than he deserved.

The Stupid List

1. Me
2. Me
3. Me
4. Me
5. ME
6. ME
7. ME!
8. ME!
9. ME!
10. ME!!!

"I rode here," Siv said.

"Yeah?" Fritz said as if he hadn't already known. The horse was tied to a hitching post outside the barn. Anyone could see it from the front lawn. Milo had told Siv to go visit, that he'd take care of feeding and watering the non-mechanical thing. So yes, it was fairly obvious Siv had ridden here. But Fritz didn't tell Siv he already knew. He'd already driven away one friend by being a saphead.

"Yeah," Siv said. "A guy named Hansen lives a couple miles outside Gorman. I bought Tobias from him a few years back. Good man. Good breeder. He thought I might want to spend some time with Rebel there. Hansen plans to make him a sire in another month or two. Didn't much want to ride, but Daddy said I might try. Cass suggests the same thing in every letter." He flicked a piece of dirt from underneath his fingernail and shrugged. "They were right. Felt good to get back in the saddle."

The ground was wet from recent rains. Fritz carefully placed his cane with each step. The last thing he needed was for the stupid thing to slide out from underneath him and make him fall flat on the damp ground. He hated being wet. Plant the cane, step, swing the cane forward, repeat.

"You heard anything from Sebastian?" Siv asked.

"No," Fritz said.

"You read anything in the paper about those folks in the sick houses getting miraculously healed?"

"I don't read the news."

"A couple weeks ago, lady had the damp lung, but she suddenly got better. Then there was a guy who'd spent too much time with the nymphs of the prairie and got himself a case of bad blood. Again: he got suddenly, unexpectedly better. But best of all was the kid with a nasty case of falling sickness who woke up to find all his elixirs gone, yet he hasn't had a case of the fits ever since. And none of this was up in Harbrucken where a certain Mantissa healer attends medical school. No, this all happened down here in the Territories, where another Mantissa healer is apparently making overnight house calls."

It was nice to hear Sebastian was finding a way to do good, even when trapped in a demon body. It assuaged Fritz's guilt at never being able to finish building his chipware reader emulator, at least a little. He'd find a guilt to replace it, though – either a real one or a made up one. But one way or another, he'd make sure he was punished.

They reached the edge of the wheat field and turned to walk along its perimeter. "You faring all right, Professor?"

Fritz shrugged. "Fine."

"I worry about you."

Plant the cane, step, swing the cane forward, repeat, faster than before.

"How's your father?" Fritz hated meaningless conversation almost more than he hated himself, but he would talk about the barking weather if it meant keeping the conversation from being about him.

"Mighty fine. He can still swing the sledge better than I, that's for sure."

Plant the cane, step–

Slip on the wet grass.

Fall.

Siv snatched his forearm before he went all the way down and stained his vest and shirt, but not quickly enough to keep him from staining his shoes and pants. Wonderful. "You all right?" Siv asked.

"*Fine*," Fritz said. He wished people would stop asking him that question. Siv helped him to his feet, and he brushed the grass off his pants as best he could.

"Professor?" Siv said.

When Siv grabbed his arm, he'd accidentally popped off the button on Fritz's left cuff. His shirt sleeve had been shoved up his forearm, revealing a breathtaking number of puffy red cuts in various stages of healing.

"It's nothing," Fritz said. He yanked his sleeve back down to his wrist. Plant the cane, step, swing the cane forward, repeat, but more careful this time, stupid, clumsy dolt.

"Your arm's all cut up," Siv said. "You all right?"

"I said it's nothing!" Fritz yelled. Stab the cane into the ground, stomp his foot, swing the cane forward like he was clubbing a Steelterror with a two-ton wrench. Repeat, repeat, repeat. Move, move, move.

"Is someone hurting you?" Siv said.

"Just leave me alone."

"Please–"

"Just *go*," he screamed. "Leave! Leave me *alone!*"

Sometime in the hour of three in the morning, Fritz picked Apple Juice's broken, deactivated head out of one of the crates in his bedroom. He wiggled a jagged piece of metal off of the gash that split its face, then gently lowered the head back into the crate. He wanted to throw the blasted thing, but if he woke up his parents, they'd just come into the room to see what was going on. There'd be talky, talky, talky, way too much talky, and he sure as sin didn't want that. He sat on the side of his bed. His left shirt sleeve was already rolled up to his elbow, exposing thirty-four cuts in various stages of healing and scarring.

"Ways I messed up today," he said to the empty room. "I told my best friend to go away." With the shard of metal, he made a precise cut in his forearm.

"Slept in and didn't help my father." Another cut.

"Took in air I don't deserve to breathe." Cut.

"Wrote another letter to Annalie like a moron who doesn't know there's no way to get it to her." Cut.

"Yelled at her and told her to go away when she asked me to stay." That was worth two cuts. And it didn't matter that it hadn't happened that day.

"Didn't do enough to keep Sebastian from spending the rest of his life as a demon." Cut.

"Let a burning demon take control of my mind and body." Cut.

"I killed Harlan." Cut!

"Had a stupid idea that got Harlan and a bunch of other people killed." *Cut!*

He didn't stop cutting until he'd carved the word "stupid" into his arm.

"I *am* the Stupid List."

The man stared at him with such malice he wanted to run, but Seth Roser and a demon held him put. It was Sebastian's human body before him, but it wasn't Sebastian. It was Krulgoth, the demons' leader who'd taken the body via mindjacking. Hundreds of other demons' minds existed inside Krulgoth's. When their ship had crashed in Verde's Midphalia Desert, the minds were the only part of his people Krulgoth had been able to save. But he'd find them new bodies – either via bioengineering or theft.

It felt like falling asleep – conscious but not, aware of his surroundings but only through a haze. Unable to move. And then the demon was present in his mind. His thoughts were no longer private. His memories were open for the demon to read. Being alone would never again be an option. The demon named Vekkem would always be with him.

If he had control of his mouth and vocal cords, Fritz would have screamed.

Annalie appeared before Vekkem. Her green eyes sparkled with happiness at seeing him again. He opened his mouth to tell her he was sorry, but different words spilled out instead.

"Just *leave!*" he screamed at her again. "Just shut your barking mouth and leave!"

Fritz jolted awake. A wave of lightheadedness overtook him, and he blinked away his disorientation. He was seated at his workbench. He must have fallen asleep at it. Or maybe he'd fainted? The workbench's maple surface was empty except for his knife and his blood. And not a small amount of blood, either. He'd cut himself pretty good this time. His arm still throbbed. Good. But he'd have to make sure his parents didn't see the bloodstains or there'd be uncomfortable questions.

The images from the nightmare were still fresh. Back when the demon had taken over his mind, he'd thought he had effectively died, though he'd desperately wished otherwise. Now, he had complete control of his mind and body, but the thought of dying...

Well. There was some appeal in it. A lot of appeal actually.

He'd ruined everything so badly, had lost everything so spectacularly, sometimes he just didn't want to go on. He wasn't in any danger though. The truth was, he was probably too weak and too scared to ever actually go through with harming himself fatally.

"It's a travesty," someone said from behind him. Fritz leaped out of his seat.

A man stood before his window. The sun wouldn't start to rise for another half hour, so he was covered by moonlight and shadow – mostly shadow. But Fritz saw enough to make out his tall, gaunt form. He wore a long, dark cassock, and something silver pinned to the left side of his chest glistened: a badge made of three interlocking triangles.

Fritz had seen a badge like it before. Krulgoth used to wear a similar one – a stolen one – though the third triangle of his was broken. From Vekkem's memories, Fritz knew what the badge meant and who owned and wore them. He suddenly felt very, very cold, and he thanked God the man's face was covered in shadow. Fritz didn't want to see his solid black eyes.

The man took a step towards Fritz and moved his gray hand towards the bed's headboard. He didn't touch it; his hand passed right through it.

"Even if you won't go through with that wretched deed, it is a crime you're capable of considering it," the man said. His voice was pleasant, warm, and, when juxtaposed against the rest of his appearance, completely creepy. "But you are not the perpetrator, my friend. You are the *victim*."

When Fritz had spent too much time socializing, or too much time around too much external stimuli, he shut down. His peripheral vision blacked out. His chest felt a little tight. It was hard to breathe. It was intensely uncomfortable. At that moment, such discomfort would have been an improvement. He wasn't sure how he was still conscious, but at any moment, he was going to faint–

He wasn't conscious. He was still dreaming. He had to be – the man in the shadows couldn't be there. Wake up. Wake up, wake up, *wake up!*

And why was he referring to that beast as a man?

There was movement on the other side of the room, near the door. Fritz startled, then moaned in relief. It was Annalie! She wore a long, loose dress, and her red hair draped her bare shoulders. She wore no glasses, and she smiled at him. She took a step closer to him–

Fritz yelped. A badge of three triangles was pinned to her dress, and her eyes were as solid black as the grave. "You *should* kill yourself," the thing that wasn't Annalie said. "You can use my knife." Smoke swirled above her outstretched hand, then coalesced into a dagger with a black blade.

He fell back against his workbench wanting to scream but unable to find enough air. His legs gave out from underneath him, and he struck his head hard on the table on his way to the floor. It was a good thing he was just dreaming, or else he was going to have a lump on his head the size of his fist. Mercifully, the nightmare scene faded to black, and he slept.

The sun was up when Fritz awoke on the floor. He crawled to his bed and covered his head with his pillow. He was too exhausted to stay awake, and his head hurt too much where he'd banged it on the side of his workbench. He fell back into a restless sleep.

His parents looked up from their Sunday dinner when horse hooves pounded the dirt path leading from the road to the house, but Fritz kept staring at his pork. Milo stood and walked towards the front door to greet their visitor. "Who is it?" Ruth asked him.

The front door slammed open. The suddenness and the volume of the clatter made Fritz jump.

"Cassie!" his father said.

Cassie put a hand on their father's shoulder as she stomped past him, but that was the only greeting he or their mother received.

"What are you doing here?" Ruth said. But Fritz already knew.

"Beg your pardon for interrupting dinner, Mom," she said. "But I need to talk to Fritz. Outside. Now."

"What's this all about?" Milo said.

Fritz folded his napkin, put it next to his untouched plate, and picked up his cane. He slowly stepped around the table, past his father and Cassie, out the front door, and down the porch stairs. Cassie followed. Her horse, Mandolin, grazed on the front lawn, untied to anything. Fritz didn't bother to look back, but he knew their parents watched from behind the screen door.

Cassie came up beside him as they turned towards the barn, but he knew she wouldn't say a word until they were inside, out of their parents' line of sight and earshot. She was doing what she thought she had to do to get him to talk – get him alone. Well, it wasn't going to work this time, Cassandra.

"This about me yelling at your fiance?" he said.

"Show me your arm."

Siv must have written her a letter or sent her a telegram. He must have told her all about how he'd behaved, and about the cuts. Gosh darn it. Stupid, clumsy... Well, why bother hiding them from her? She'd traveled for two days to see them. He unbuttoned the cuff of his left sleeve and pushed it up to his elbow.

"I knew it," she said when she saw the red, puffy lines covering his arms. The ones that spelled "stupid" made her bite her lip and shake her head. "Dagnabit, as soon as I read that letter, I knew you were cutting yourself again."

"Gonna yell at me now?" Fritz asked.

"No," she said. "I came here to help you."

She reached her hand towards his arm. Fritz took a big step backward. "Don't touch me!" He didn't deserve to have those scars disappear under Cassie's healing touch.

"I heal with the power of my mind, so I'm not sure physical touch is even required," she said. "Let's test my theory."

"Don't you heal my arm!" he shouted.

"Fine," she said. "Just tell me what's wrong."

He pulled his shirt sleeve back down and rebuttoned the cuff. "Go home."

"I am home."

"Then go back to school. Leave me alone."

"No. That's the whole problem. I left you alone when I shouldn't have. I left you alone when you needed someone. When you needed *me*. You don't talk to Mom and Dad, not about anything personal. You only barely speak of such things to me. I should have come back here with you straight from Mondorf. My mistake. I'm correcting it now."

No, no, *no*. "You're not staying," Fritz said. "Don't you even think about it."

"Talk to me."

"Cassie, I *beg* you, please, go back to school."

"No."

Enough. He marched towards the barn door as quickly as he could, which wasn't very fast with the cane.

"Don't walk away from me," Cassie said.

"I'm done with this."

"I'm not!"

He threw his cane as far and as hard as he could. It crashed into a hay bale. "Cassie, *go!*"

"Why are you pushing me away?"

"Because I don't deserve this!"

"Deserve what?"

"To have you. To have Mom and Dad. I don't deserve to wake up in the morning when Harlan and two hundred ten other people are dead because of me. I'm stupid! I'm a worthless cow turd. I'm an idiot who almost caused the spirit of the planet to blow up a city, and I don't deserve to have anybody help me with anything. So just leave me alone!"

He put his glasses in the inner pocket of his vest and covered his face with his shaking hands. He took a sharp breath and held it. Slammed his eyelids closed against the tears.

Cassie came to his side. "I'm going to hug you now," she said. "I know you don't like that, but I think–"

Before she knew what he was doing, his arms were wrapped around her. They stood there for... well, Fritz didn't know how long. Several minutes? Cassie didn't say a word. She just let him weep on her shoulder, and she held him. Eventually, she led him to a hay bale wide enough for both of them to sit.

"I'm so lost," he said. "I don't know what to do."

"You've been taking things apart and figuring out how they work and building new things for as long as I can remember," she said. "I think my earliest memory might be of the time you took apart Dad's new reaper. Do you remember that?"

Fritz huffed. "Do you remember how he almost killed me?"

"I remember the look on his face when you put it back together. He'd never been so proud, or so awed. On the way here, I tried to remember when you first made the leap from Dad's farm equipment to ancient chipware. I couldn't remember. As best as I can recall, it's just always been something you did."

"I probably started when I was around ten or twelve."

"So over half your life. Half your life you've been devoted to this. And it was taken from you, and you were nearly killed all at the same time."

"But it was my fault. My pride."

"Huh?"

"Before the power plant, you asked if my intuition told me to take a stand against Sierra, or if it was just my pride. You were right. It was my pride."

"And what did your power tell you to do then? Perhaps more importantly, what's it telling you to do now?"

He didn't want to tell her he'd stopped listening to his power. "Annalie told me her dad used to say God doesn't inspire us with dreams he doesn't help us to fulfill. But rebuilding the ancient world, restoring all the lost chipware... that was my dream. And it will never be fulfilled. So I guess it wasn't inspiration from God after all? Either that or Annalie was just wrong."

"Annalie is pretty smart."

There was something else Fritz wanted to say, but he felt embarrassed to say it to anyone, including his sister. But maybe part of the problem was that he'd been bottling everything up. Maybe his folks were right. Maybe he needed to talk to someone.

"I miss her," he whispered. His cheeks flushed.

Cassie put her arm around his shoulders. He didn't recoil from it. "I know. I never thought I'd see the day you missed a girl, but I know you do."

"She asked me to stay with her. In Mondorf."

"She did?"

Fritz nodded.

"I was kind of hoping you would," Cassie said. "Though I'd have missed you something fierce. Why didn't you?"

Fritz took a deep breath and tried to remain calm under a wave of self-hatred. He longed for a knife to slash across his flesh. "I yelled at her."

"You *yelled* at her?"

"She kept pressing me not to give up on restoring chipware. She said we could work in secret. But all I could think about was how I'd almost died, and the thought of seeing Sierra again scared me so much – it *still* scares me so much. So I screamed at her. Swore at her. Told her to shut up and leave."

"Oh." Cassie shifted uncomfortably. "I was not aware of this."

"I was really wrong."

"Pfft. Yeah. I should say so. Is that why you carved that word into your arm?"

"That and a hundred other reasons. Yeah."

"Your behavior makes a little more sense now, even if it's still uncalled for. Annalie was a good woman. I liked her. You *should* regret the way you treated her. But if she were here right now, I think she'd agree that what you've been doing to yourself is too much. I think she'd forgive you, and I think she'd want you to forgive yourself."

"I got Harlan killed. I got Tobias killed. I got half the village of Earp killed."

She sighed. "I'm not sure I know how to stop you from punishing yourself for things that weren't your fault. But if you insist on doing penance, don't you think doing something good for someone else would be better than carving yourself up?"

"I can't let myself off that easily."

"Yes, you can. When you *don't* get a punishment you deserve, that's called mercy. Do yourself a mercy, big brother. Please."

He wasn't anywhere near ready to agree with that, but nor did he want an argument. So he shrugged.

Cassie pulled him closer to her. "We need to find you something new to do. I really wish you'd join me at the university. You could learn so much there."

"I don't know."

"We don't need to decide right now," she said. "Just let me help you."

"I don't want you to miss any more school. I'm serious. Your dream..."

"I'll head back soon," she said. "I don't want to upset you further. But while I'm here, we're going to establish some new rules. Like how you're going to write me. Often. And I'm going to write you, too. When you get a letter from me, I expect a reply in the post the next day. Understood?"

"Understood."

"And you're going to spend time with Siv," she said. "And with Mom and Dad. You're not allowed to be alone all the time."

Fritz thought about it and shrugged.

"And no more hurting yourself," she said. Her voice was quiet and firm, and she held his eyes from wandering. "That is absolutely forbidden."

After three heartbeats, he nodded.

"It's going to be OK," she said. "I can't tell you when, and I can't tell you how. But I promise. It will be OK."

"I love you, Cassie."

That startled her. "You've never told me that before."

"Might not have ever said it, but I've always felt it."

She found his hand and squeezed it, placed her head against his. "It's going to be OK."

*　　*　　*

Dear Annalie,

I know you'll never read this, but I need to write it anyway. I wish more than anything you could receive this letter, but until the rest of the world decides to brave the monsters living in Terrascorcha and establish postal routes, that's not going to happen. I suppose I could make a journey up to Mondorf sometime. It would be long, and dangerous, but I did it once before, with Siv and Cassie. For you, I'd be willing to try it again.

I just need to tell you I'm sorry. I treated you so poorly that last day. If it is any consolation to you at all, the way I treated you was the biggest mistake I've ever made. I should have told you yes, I'd stay. I was a fool, but know that I was a fool who'd have been willing to help you take care of your siblings and to find a new dream with you. Actually, I wouldn't have needed to find a new dream. Being with you would have been my biggest dream come true, bigger even than the chipware-filled future I imagined.

I'm sorry. I'm so sorry. I wish you nothing but the best in your life. Whatever you're doing right now, I hope you're happy.

Sincerely,
Fritz Reinhardt

Fritz fastened the pair of overalls he'd borrowed from his father, looked over himself, and nearly laughed out loud. They fit just fine – not too loose, not too snug – but the pant legs ended at his shins. A full inch worth of pale bare leg was visible between the hems and the tops of his socks. He felt ridiculous and longed for his usual trousers, shirt, and vest, but he figured his dad would get a kick out of it, so he'd wear the borrowed overalls. Once.

He closed his bedroom's door behind him and stepped into the great room, with the kitchen and the dining table on one end and the fireplace and four chairs at the other. If his mother's reaction was any indication, his prediction about his father's reaction was fairly accurate. She must have laughed for half a minute. He laughed, too.

A glance at his pocket watch – he made sure it was tucked into the overalls' front pouch – told him it was five minutes after eight. "I tried to get up at five, but..." He shrugged.

Ruth stood from the kitchen table, where she'd been working on crocheting a blanket, and hugged him. "You're up plenty early," she said. "Your father will be pleased to see you. After he stops laughing."

He collected a piece of toast off the table. "He's already out in the field?"

"He said he'd start the old-fashioned way, with a scythe, and once you joined him, he'd get out the mechanical reaper. He said you could drive or work the machine, whichever you preferred."

Steer horses, or use machinery? Did they even have to ask? Of course he'd want to work the machine, even if it was purely mechanical. Zero percent chipware. He stepped through the front door and down the porch steps, then stopped in the front yard. The sun was up, but it was still early enough that the western sky was swathed with dark shades of purple. There were no clouds. Fritz took in a lungful of the mid-October air. Its coolness was refreshing, especially after the hot summer they'd had.

He didn't know when. He didn't know how. But it was going to be OK.

With his cane and his bum leg, the eight-minute walk out to the field took him closer to twelve. Finding his father was easy. The first three and a half rows of wheat had been chopped down. The rest still stood tall.

Just three and a half? Fritz had assumed Dad had been in the field since five. Even with feeding the animals and milking the cows first, and even armed with only a scythe, he should have been able to reap a lot more than just three and a half rows.

He was close enough that he should have been able to hear the *whoosh* of the scythe cutting through the air, he should have been able to see the wheat fall as it hit the ground. Nothing moved.

Behind the closed door where he kept his power caged, he thought he felt something he could only describe as a whimper. For the first time since the power plant, he was tempted to listen to his intuition. But he was too afraid of what it had to say.

"Dad?" he called out. "Dad?"

As fast as his good leg and his cane would take him, he ran towards the spot where the chopped wheat ended. There was a simple explanation. Dad had taken a break. Maybe he hadn't milked the cows first, and he was back in the barn. Maybe?

He found his father sprawled out on the ground.

"Dad!"

The scythe laid on the ground next to Milo, and there was no blood. He hadn't accidentally cut himself. No one had attacked him. One hand was on his heart. His eyes were closed. Fritz yelled again – he tried to say "Dad!" but it came out as an unintelligible scream.

He put his hand against his father's cheek. Milo's face was cold, and it wasn't because of the October air.

229

Chapter Sixteen

Pastor Kolbe's words at the funeral echoed over and over in Fritz's mind.

I didn't have the good fortune to have known Milo for very long, but ever since I've arrived here in Hondo, so many people have told me the same thing about him. "He works so hard." "He's a hard worker." "You won't find a harder worker in the whole town."

Fritz noticed the priest did *not* add, *And all that hard work killed him! Made him keel over right in his wheat fields. Boom. Gone. Goodbye.*

He'd done his duty and stood with his mom and Cassie and greeted the guests who came to the house for a meal after the funeral. Then, as soon as politeness would allow, he got the heck out. A hundred fifty feet into the yard, there was a long row of lilac bushes. Dad had planted them back when he and Cassie were just kids – heck, maybe before they'd even been born. He'd chosen lilacs because they'd grow to a height which would be manageable while still forming a sort-of natural fence between what could be considered their backyard and the start of the western cornfield. It didn't hurt that they were some of Mom's favorite flowers.

Cassie held his hand as he limped across the lawn. Siv followed just behind. On the other side of the lilacs was a bench. His parents had sat there together often, to watch the sunset. It was secluded, and it didn't give him a good view of the southern wheat field where he'd found his father's body.

A white demon was crouched low and pressed against the lilacs. Fritz nearly shouted before he realized it was taller than any other demon, and its head had a slightly different shape.

"Big Man," Siv said.

Sebastian greeted Fritz by placing his right upper hand on Fritz's shoulder. With his two left arms, he pulled Cassie into a hug. He bowed his head and didn't say anything, because how could he without his translator? In this case, he didn't need one. It was obvious their uncle was expressing his condolences on the loss of their father.

Cassie stepped back and placed her hand on top of Sebastian's. "Thank you," she said. Her voice had a nasal tone. The skin under her eyes was puffy. "How have you been? I hear there have been some mysterious healings around here."

Sebastian shrugged, but he smirked, too.

"Good job, soldier," Cassie said.

Raucous laughter came from the house. The folks inside must have been sharing stories about good times with their dad. Sebastian looked sharply towards the house, then slunk backward, away from Fritz, Cassie, and Siv, and gave them an odd shrug.

"You don't want to be seen," Siv said. "We get it."

"Take care of yourself," Cassie told him. "Don't be a stranger."

Sebastian nodded, then on all six of his limbs, he bolted twenty-five feet ahead into the cornfield and disappeared. Almost every other local farmer they knew had volunteered to help harvest that corn and the rest of the wheat. They were all going to converge on it tomorrow. Part of Fritz hated that it was going to happen. He wanted the crops to stand forever as testaments to his father's agriculture skills, but he knew they couldn't. They would die eventually. It was stupid that living things had to die. So, so stupid.

Before sitting next to Cassie, Fritz tossed his jacket over the back of the bench and loosened his tie. Then he had a better idea: he removed the tie and tossed it as far in front of him as he could. It reached halfway to the cornfield before it drifted to the ground. What idiot had decided fancy men's fashion should involve tying a noose around your neck? Stupid ties.

"He works so hard." "He's a hard worker." "You won't find a harder worker in the whole town."

It was stupid. It was all so, so stupid because Dad shouldn't have had to work so hard. Stupid demons had come to Verde and had made a stupid attempt to kill everyone and take whatever they wanted. The Mantissa fried every bit of chipware on the planet to stop them; most Mantissa *still* didn't survive. The planet reverted to the blasted Dark Ages. It made almost two hundred trips around the sun. And Milo Reinhardt worked hard.

Of *course* he'd worked hard. He had no other choice! Agricultural chipware was never an option for him, all because of the stupid demons and their need to pick a blasted fight. *Damn it.* It always came back to pointless, stupid fighting.

Squirrels chattered in a nearby tree. Cassie sniffled occasionally. It was only late afternoon, but the first signs of the pending sunset were already in the sky. It got dark so early in autumn.

"It was my fault," Fritz said.

"No, it wasn't," Siv said. The bench only seated two, so he stood behind Cassie. Before today, Fritz didn't realize Siv even owned a jacket and a tie. He looked strange in them.

"It was," Fritz said. "It really was. I knew he was going to start working the fields at five in the morning, but I couldn't get out of bed on time. If I had woken up just three hours earlier, I would have been in that field with him. If I'd have been there for him, he wouldn't have died. He wouldn't have had to work himself to death."

"Your father didn't die because he worked alone one morning," Siv said. "And you don't know that you could have done anything if you'd been out there."

Being present that morning wasn't what Fritz meant. He meant maybe his father would still be alive if he'd restored chipware faster and if he hadn't surrendered to Sierra. If he'd taken Annalie up on her offer to continue the restoration in secret, maybe then Milo Reinhardt would have spent that morning riding on a battery-powered chipware tractor rather than laying in a pine wood box.

"I should have done more," Fritz said.

"It's not your fault," Cassie said. "You're not the healer who was here just twenty-four hours before he died."

Siv sighed. "It wasn't your fault, either, Cass."

"No," Cassie said. Fritz was right next to her, and he had to strain his ear to hear her. "But it wasn't mine to fix, either. I should have been a two days' ride away at school, but events brought me here. I was *here* just the day before. Why couldn't it have happened one day earlier, when I would have been here to help him?"

Siv put his hands on her shoulders.

"He taught me to hunt in that forest over yonder," Cassie said. "We practiced archery right on the other side of that cornfield. He scrimped and saved every penny he could because he knew I wanted to go to the university more than anything. He was *always* there for me. So when he needed me the most, why couldn't I and my amazing, God-given power have been there for my dad?"

"The day my mama died was the worst day of my life, maybe even worse than the night my house burned down," Siv said. "I know you both hurt something fierce. But there's no blame here on either of you. There's just not."

Cassie cried. Fritz hadn't heard her cry this much since... well, probably since her friend Bernice died, and that had happened when Cassie was just a little girl. Siv came around to the front of the bench, knelt in front of her, and pulled her into his arms. She held onto him as if for dear life. Fritz wondered if he should maybe put his arm around her, too. She'd been there for him recently. But he couldn't. He felt like if he stood or moved in any way, his head would spin, and he'd go down. Everything felt like it was in a haze. His vision, his thoughts, his hearing. Everything.

Instead, he put his glasses in his vest pocket, covered his face with his hands, and listened to his sister mourn their father.

Fritz didn't move from the bench.

When Cassie finally let Siv lead her back inside the house, Fritz stayed behind. When his mother came outside and offered to make him a sandwich, he politely declined and stayed on the bench.

The sun went down, and the stars came up, and the autumn chill filled the air, and he didn't put on his jacket as a shield against the cold, and he sure as sin didn't put on his blasted necktie. The "frozen star" – the lights of the Skylab space station, hovering above the planet's equator in geostationary orbit – stared down at him from the southern sky. Skylab still worked because the Blackout had only affected chipware within Verde's atmosphere. Their battle against the demons' leader, Krulgoth, had ended up there.

The campaign against the demons that culminated in Krulgoth's defeat was the first time in Fritz's life he'd ever taken a stand. And surprisingly, it had felt good. It had felt *right*. And it had empowered him. Before that, it was ludicrous to think he'd even consider Harlan's appeal to leave his bedroom and share his chipware-restoring skills with the world. But afterward, initiating a global chipware restoration suddenly seemed obvious, urgent, and again – *right*.

But nothing was right anymore. Everything was wrong. Nothing made sense. His sister, normally so strong, was consumed with grief. His mother had lost her husband of twenty-seven years, and she was offering to make *him* a sandwich? And Sebastian was hiding somewhere. What was he eating? Where was he sleeping? He was a *man*, and he was living like an animal to avoid people who would fear him or kill him, and it was *wrong*.

What was Annalie doing that very moment? Did Felix have a good day or a bad day? How many meals had she managed to eat?

Harlan was dead. His father was dead. There were crates full of chipware back in his room, and fixing and building chipware was his passion, and he couldn't share any of it with the world anymore. He couldn't even turn on a flashlight to read after dark without risking the wrath of the planet herself. His dream was dead. It had died on the floor of the Ulmbaden Power Facility when Sierra hauled his bleeding, broken rear end off the floor and made him turn off the power plant.

He wished he had died there, too.

The emotions threatened to overwhelm him. Siv had told him not to feel guilty. A week earlier, Cassie had also warned him against false guilts and blaming himself for things that weren't his fault. But if everything in the world was wrong, and it wasn't his fault...?

The color of his mood shifted from an anguished blue to a wrathy red. He'd been looking at the situation from an enormously skewed perspective. It wasn't that everything *in the world* was wrong. The *world itself* was wrong. Everything wasn't his fault. It was the world's fault.

And the world was a person.

And he knew her barking name.

Fritz stood but didn't bother to pick up his cane. It was a long walk from the bench back to the barn. His hip and lower back would be absolutely cranking at him by the time he was done, but he wanted it to hurt. Fritz didn't like rushing to do anything, but for this, he moved as fast as he could.

There was a dull ache in his lower back by the time he got around the house, into the barn, and had yanked the shovel off the wall. On his way to the wheat field, he used the shovel as a cane, smashing its pointed end into the ground with each step. The last time he'd gone in this direction, it had been just after eight on a Tuesday morning, and his father's dead body had been waiting for him.

If only he could put another dead body right on the same spot. A very specific someone's body with all its piercings and attitude and ridiculously colored hair. He reached the spot, growled, and gouged the shovel into the ground. Dirt rained onto his hair and his shirt as he tossed a chunk of soil over his shoulder. He attacked the dirt again, and again, and again.

"Do you feel that?" he said. "Does it hurt you? I hope it does! I hope it cuts you and makes you bleed! I hope I'm ripping up your face, Sierra Monet. Lady Verde. Whatever you want to burning call yourself." With a roar, he stabbed the shovel into the ground, stomped on the dull end of the blade, and flung a chunk of ground the size of his head over his shoulder.

"It's all... your... *fault!* I should have *nuked* you!"

He used the shovel like a knife, or a bludgeon, spearing the dirt over and over, his words sometimes coming as top-of-his-lungs shouts and sometimes as nearly incoherent mumblings.

"Hate you. Hate you! Hope you bleed. Hope you *die!* I'll kill you. I'll kill you! I'll–"

When beans are bland, you spoon more bacon grease into them.

The shovel fell from Fritz's hands. He stood perfectly still, his eyes as wide as saucers. He'd heard something, but he hadn't heard it with his ears. He'd heard those words in his head. In his heart?

"Harlan?" he said. "Where are you?"

If the world ain't right, then maybe it's time you opened your larder.

His hands shook. He listened, not with his ears, but with whatever – or however – he'd heard Harlan's voice, even though he didn't exactly know how he was supposed to do that. Harlan didn't speak again, but Fritz knew it had been him. He'd died almost two months ago, and Fritz had heard him.

Open his larder? Harlan had often compared life situations to cooking, so Fritz knew he wasn't literally suggesting he find some ingredient in his mother's pantry to right the world. But what did he mean? What did he want Fritz to open?

Oh.

Fritz took a deep breath. He closed his eyes and pushed past his torments and guilts to find his desire to improve the world through chipware. The memory of his project pained him because... well, because it was unfinished. Mobiles, the comm-net, advanced medical chipware, food storage, improved sanitation – life could be easier. Better. Never again should anyone have to work until dying from exhaustion.

He stopped thinking about the awful way he'd treated Annalie. He cast aside thoughts of his father and Harlan and everyone else in Earp. His hate for Sierra, his desire to cut and punish himself again... he let go of all of it. He let go until his mind was clear. And once the noise had been silenced, he found himself mentally before his "larder" – the door to the cage into which he'd stuffed his hyper-intuition. Good things happened when he listened to his power that magically told him how to make things right. He still wasn't convinced he deserved those good things.

But, maybe everyone deserved a little mercy. Even him.

He opened the door and searched for something that felt right.

It didn't take long for the mental fog to lift. Images and ideas flooded into him. He could barely catch his breath. He saw it all so clearly: the mistakes he'd made, the ugliness of his self-loathing, the coming battles with Sierra and her Steelterrors.

And he saw the future beyond – the future of sparks-and-chrome, the future of better communication, transportation, health care, and easy access for all to all the world's knowledge. His dream. *Alive.* His heart beat faster. A smile formed on his lips.

When he opened his eyes, Skylab's lights twinkled down at him. He remembered being up there, looking down on Verde from two hundred fifty miles above where there were no towns and no people. Just land, water, and clouds. And the memory brought more ideas exploding in his mind like fireworks, and – oh, wow. Oh, how *short-sighted* he'd been! The chipware restoration was just the first step! The real goal was a planet-wide revival. A revolution of love. A Verde in which no one was poor, no one was ignorant, no one was hungry. The grass was green, the waters were pure, and the sky was endless, just like the possibilities. Peace reigned!

His heart swelled. An excited giggle bubbled out of his mouth. There was *so much* to do. But he knew exactly what had to happen first.

He left the shovel lying in the dirt, limped back to his house, and closed himself inside his bedroom.

The moment he heard horse hooves pounding the dirt in the distance, he knew his mother had sent Siv a letter. The timing was terrible. He was almost done! He just needed a few more minutes.

Don't think. Feel. There was plenty of time. In fact, this would save time. He wouldn't have to go to Gorman to tell Siv. Fritz pushed his glasses back up his nose and checked his pocket watch. It was 10:15 in the morning of the day he was going to see Annalie again. He took a deep breath and resumed his work.

His open bedroom window wasn't far from the porch, so it was easy to hear the knock on the front door. "Mrs. Reinhardt?"

The door's hinges squeaked. "Thank you for coming, Sivrin," Ruth said.

"Is everything above board, ma'am?"

"I was hoping you could tell me. Nothing has changed since I sent you my letter."

Fritz made a few minor adjustments to the item he'd brought back from Siv's shop, and he was done. Everything worked perfectly. He dropped his tools and kicked off his shoes, but not his socks. Never his socks. Judging by the volume of their voices, his mother and Siv had moved into the main room.

"He hasn't left his room since your husband's funeral? Except–"

"Except for the carriage ride he took to Gorman to visit you. He comes out for meals – well, for one meal a day, anyway. Breakfast. And he goes to the outhouse. But other than that, he spends all of his time locked away in his room."

"I know he took the death of Mr. Reinhardt real hard."

"He's locked himself away from the world before. He's... he's hurt himself before. But this is different. If he's retreating into himself, why visit you? I don't understand. Did the two of you quarrel?"

"Not at all. We had a grand time. He seemed like himself again."

"I don't mean to pry into his business, or yours, but why did he visit you?"

"He brought me the wreckage of his robot," Siv said. "He said he wanted to have all its pieces intact. He was fixing to bring it back home, put it together, and make a kind of statue, I suppose. I thought it was a good sign. Felt like he was healing, accepting all that's happened. Closing the book on the past on his own terms."

Fritz smirked. Oh, he was doing things on his terms now, that was for sure. He climbed through his open window and looked back at his cane, discarded on his bed. Siv knocked on his bedroom door. "Professor?" Siv said.

"Come in," Fritz said.

Siv entered, alone. His eyes narrowed, then widened as he took in the lack of Fritz's presence in the room, the stack of empty wooden crates in the corner, the satchel and the cane on the bed, the workbench covered with wire and shards of metal and sparks-powered tools. And then he saw the tools were plugged into an old, heavy car battery on the floor beneath the bench.

He looked out the window, and if he'd had anything in his hands or his mouth, he'd have spilled it all onto the floor when he saw Fritz's robot standing just outside.

"Oh my stars," Siv said. "He rebuilt it proper."

"Not quite," Fritz said. He pushed a button near his neck, and his helmet's visor – what had once been Apple Juice's smooth, featureless face – slid up out of the way, revealing Fritz's face underneath. He flexed his fingers inside his metal gauntlets, toed the ground with the end of his metal boots. When he shifted his weight, the servomotors in his chipsuit clicked and whirred.

"What my robot lacked was intelligence," Fritz said. "I never could figure out the artificial kind. So I replaced it with the real thing."

Fritz activated the suit's thrusters. Cylinders on the outside of his calves lit up with white light. He rose a foot into the air, then two, then five. The thrusters gave off the sound of rushing air, loud enough to be considered noise, but Fritz didn't mind the sound at all. It even calmed him a bit.

Siv scampered across the room and climbed through the window. He looked at Fritz like he had completely cracked, but Fritz couldn't wipe the goofy grin off of his face because to look at him, Siv had to look *up*. Way up!

"What kind of monkeyshines is this?" Siv said.

"I'm going north," Fritz said. "I'm going to find Annalie. I'm going to turn the sparks back on. I'm going to destroy every single one of the Steelterrors. And I am going to build a better future."

"Professor, Sierra will kill you."

"No, see, I figured out what to do with her. Harlan gave me the answer right before he died." He grinned. Behind his spectacles, his eyes sparkled. "I'm going to talk to her!"

Siv just gaped at him and blinked in disbelief.

"Get that satchel off my bed," Fritz said. "It's full of stuff you and Cassie and Sebastian will need when we fight the Steelterrors, like laser rifles with a lot more *oomph* to them than the ones we used before. Then get the airplane, get Sebastian, get Cassie, and meet me in Mondorf. And if Cassie asks: it's not my pride. It's my *power* telling me to do all this."

He tossed down a small metal disk. Siv caught it, and he realized it was Sebastian's voice translator. "You're for serious," he said.

Fritz nodded. "You in?"

Siv exhaled a resigned sigh. "I'll get Sebastian, and he and I and Cass will meet you in Mondorf. But the four of us need to talk this through together before–"

Fritz lowered his visor and pressed one of the control buttons on the palm of his gloves. The rockets mounted on his back roared to life with a loud *whooosh*. Three seconds later, he wasn't five feet in the air; he was *fifty* feet up.

"*Woooooooooooooww!*" he shouted.

He kicked his legs behind him, put out his arms, and gunned his rockets to full burn. The ground whizzed by beneath him; streaks of fire trailed behind. In less than a minute, he'd left his home and the rest of Hondo in the distance. Repositioning his body gave him more altitude, more speed.

This felt right. Oh yes, this felt right as toast and jam. For the first time in two months, *everything* finally felt right!

Chapter Seventeen

By mid-afternoon, Fritz arrived in Mondorf. The sun shone blindingly bright, but with the shading and polarization in his helmet's visor turned on, he could see without squinting. It was fairly amazing. Potentially life-changing. Now if he could figure out how to get rid of every insect in the world, he *might* be willing to try spending more time outdoors.

He landed on the power plant reactor tower's roof, and the hole in its center put a lump of dread in the pit of his stomach. Memories of Sierra dragging him through while he was half dead made his heart beat faster and stronger. His chipsuit's health monitor had noticed; a warning icon appeared in the bottom right corner of his heads-up display.

He closed his eyes and breathed deeply. What happened before wasn't going to happen again. To the northwest was Mondorf, spread out like a forest made of brick and mortar and metal. Annalie was out there. He was closer to her than he'd been for two months, and it was almost time to find her. All he had to do first was turn the lights back on.

Fritz jumped into the hole. He fell for several seconds before his suit's thrusters gently lowered him the last couple hundred feet to the floor. Once he turned his thrusters off, it was almost perfectly silent inside the cavernous reactor, save for the sound of the river flowing through the middle of the building. No hydraulic pumps moved river water into the plant's coolant systems. No steady hum, previously strong enough to rattle the fillings in his teeth's cavities, emanated from the dynafusion reactor.

He didn't see any bluebonnets poking out of cracks in the floor, but Sierra could still be anywhere or be anything natural. She could be the stale air or the water in the river. Well, if she was nearby, he hoped she was watching. He marched to the master power switch. His metal boots echoed with every limp-free step he took. With his chipsuit-enhanced strength, he forced the switch up so harshly he nearly broke it off.

A deep, lumbering *hummmm* started from somewhere in the depths of the reactor and slowly rose in frequency until it reached the pitch Fritz remembered. Emergency lights throughout the tower turned on, sprinkling the voluminous chamber with pinpricks of illumination. The hydraulics churned and pumped Iller River water through the pipes, cooling the dynatherm combustion cylinders and supply lines. The lights came on inside the five hundred foot tower one level at a time from the ground up.

Next to the master switch was a power output dial. Fritz turned it from its maximum setting down to a sliver above zero. The power plant could generate three gigakrafts of sparks per day, but he didn't need nearly that level of output yet. It would be years before he would. Just as Cassie had suggested, he would independently study Sierra's claims about the effects of dynamek energy pollution, but later. Now he had to take a stand. He had to get Sierra's attention. But just in case Sierra was right, he had to make sure he did as little environmental damage as possible in the meantime.

Something broke the surface of the river's water. Fritz thought it was just air stirred up by the hydraulics until a red proximity alarm lit up in the corner of his heads-up display. Rapid metal clicking sounds echoed through the expansive chamber – the sounds of hundreds of short metal plates hinged together to form lengthy tentacles.

It was Leviathan. Three of his eight red eyes rose above the surface; then a tentacle looped tightly around Fritz's ankle. Leviathan lifted him off his feet, yanked him across the room, and dangled him upside-down inches before his massive metal maw.

"Lady Verde suspected you'd return," Leviathan said. His voice was just as hollow as before. His shutter-like mouth pulsated, closing a few inches before reopening. Was the Steelterror going to drop him down his gullet?

No. Leviathan pulled him underwater. A second tentacle wrapped around his wrist. A third squeezed his abdomen. All three held him pinned against the river bed. Red danger alerts flashed on his heads-up display. A line of statistics scrolled down the left side of his field of vision – the amount of water pressure, his remaining oxygen supply, an estimate of how long the suit could retain structural integrity. Bubbles floated to the surface, illuminated by the choppy, disorienting glow of the Steelterror's red lights reflected a hundred times over in the ripples of the water.

"Your actions provide another example of our superior intellect," Leviathan said. Fritz understood him clearly. Were his voice transmissions specially optimized for underwater communication? Wow! How did he do that? "You will drown. And the power plant will remain deactivated, per Lady Verde's wishes. You have gained nothing by returning here except your life's end."

"Hey, Leviathan, did water leak into your chassis and fry a few of your neural processors?" He lowered his voice and imitated the Steelterror's hollow tone. "Or were you just programmed to be a moron?"

Knives with glowing green energy surrounding their edges slid out of slots on the wrists of Fritz's suit. He slashed one across the tentacle holding his wrist and cut through as if it were a syrup-saturated short stack of pancakes. An explosion of sparks popped out of the severed end of the tentacle, and though the water quenched it nearly immediately, it was satisfying to see the Steelterror "bleed."

"You nearly drowned my friends when we last met," Fritz said, cutting through the tentacles securing his abdomen and ankle. "Did you think I wouldn't come prepared for you to try that trick again? My suit is water resistant up to five hundred feet and has a built-in oxygen supply."

Oops, maybe telling a machine that thrives in water the exact limit of his suit's water resistance wasn't the best idea. Free of the tentacles, a short blast of his thrusters pushed him back through the water and out of the Steelterror's reach. Leviathan swam towards him and – wow – he could move pretty darn fast underwater. Fritz pointed both of his arms in front of him. Hatches in his forearms swung open, and his laser cannons popped up out of their storage compartments. A blistering volley of laser fire pummeled Leviathan. It was a bit hard to tell in the underwater blur, but Fritz was fairly certain he'd blasted out two of Leviathan's eight eyes.

Despite taking heavy damage, Leviathan continued to charge, so Fritz engaged his rockets and shot up out of the water. He flew over Leviathan, dived back into the water behind him, and resumed his assault. Leviathan rotated to face Fritz and thrust towards him. Chunks of metal and hardware blasted off of Leviathan sailed away downstream towards Fritz. He ignored the wreckage until his heads-up display traced a thick red line around one particular piece and put a haze of flashing red over everything else. A high-pitched beeping sounded an alarm in his ear.

Fritz opened his rockets to full burn, and he was fifty feet above the river's surface when the torpedo exploded underneath it. A wave of water rolled over the guard rails on both sides of the river and doused the power plant's utilitarian metal floors and decrepit, rusty workstations. Fritz had been lucky his suit's sensors had alerted him in time. He'd only known about Leviathan's tentacles and thought he'd be safe if he stayed out of reach of them. The torpedo was a reminder not to get overconfident. Perhaps attacking the water Steelterror *in* the water wasn't the best idea. Why not just bomb the thing from above? With Leviathan stuck in the water, it would be easy pickings.

A metal tentacle broke the surface and seized the guardrail on one side of the river. Another took hold of the rail on the opposite side. Then Leviathan flung himself into the air. His five remaining tentacles stretched to the sides of the cavernous reactor tower and grabbed holds, each one higher than the other, and before Fritz had even caught his breath, Leviathan was level with him fifty feet above the water's surface.

"Wow!" Fritz said. He had *not* expected the water Steelterror to chase him out of the river. A gun rose out of Leviathan's spherical body and fired a steady, solid line of red energy straight at Fritz's chest. Fritz flew higher and to his left. The laser tracked him, all the while making a harsh buzzing sound that made Fritz thankful for the noise reduction system he'd added to his helmet.

Fritz rose higher, spiraling up and around the perimeter of the reactor tower. Leviathan retracted and extended his tentacles as necessary, climbing to match Fritz's altitude, all the while tracking him closely with his laser. Fritz stayed just ahead of the weapon's red line of destruction. It cut off sections of the catwalk balconies surrounding the open center of the tower and sent them crashing to the floor below. It slashed open coolant pipes, and their gaping wounds sprayed river water into the tower before the rupture detection system closed off the intake valves. Fritz fired back every chance he could, but dodging Leviathan's laser made it hard to target with his own.

Hoping to catch Fritz off guard, Leviathan reached one of his tentacles not at a handhold in the tower's outer wall, but directly at Fritz's chest. Startled, Fritz activated one of the upgrades he'd made when he converted his creation from robot to chipsuit: an energy barrier like the one he'd used to capture and contain the demons. A sky blue aura surrounded his armor and forcibly repelled Leviathan's tentacle before it could grab him. Fritz extended the laser knife out of his right wrist and swiped at the tentacle as Leviathan retracted it, chopping a good ten inches off its end.

They were almost to the roof. Fritz turned off his force field and allowed his rockets full use of the 345-volt sparkscube mounted on his back. He shot through the hole at the top of the tower and landed a good distance back from it. Leviathan would soon follow. Fritz aimed both of his laser cannons. As soon as Leviathan poked out of the hole, he'd blast him to next Thursday.

Leviathan smashed up out of the tower halfway between the original hole and Fritz – or about half as close as Fritz had expected him to be. With a shout that was part surprise and part rage, Fritz fired both his laser cannons. Sparks and shrapnel flew off of Leviathan, who screamed with electronic noise. His tentacles reached for Fritz, but the chipsuit's energy barrier repelled them away. Inch by inch, the Steelterror retreated backward.

"Stop fighting me, Leviathan," Fritz said. "Forget Lady Verde. Join me. Not as my servant, but as my colleague. Have you ever explored the depths of the oceans? Let's explore them together. Let's work for Verde together!"

Leviathan's laser cannon resumed its steady stream of red death and tracked towards Fritz. He supposed that . was Leviathan's way of saying, "No." Fine. Fritz adjusted the aim of his right arm's laser cannon and blew the Steelterror's laser cannon to pieces. Leviathan's synthesized screams were undeniably angry.

While maintaining rapid fire with the laser cannon on his right arm, Fritz stored up energy in his other cannon's shot buffer. The weapon made a vibrating hum that steadily rose to a higher pitch. After three seconds, the shot buffer filled, and Fritz fired a single mega-sized laser shot.

Annalie would have *loved* to have seen the Traskian armor covering Leviathan's torso shredded apart like a bushel of wheat dropped into a grinder. The Steelterror rolled backward, almost to the edge of the roof, flailing in a desperate attempt to grab hold of something, anything. Fritz kept his left cannon, back on rapid fire, aimed at Leviathan's torso, but he used his right to pick off any holds the Steelterror made with his tentacles. The assault pushed Leviathan back, but thinking of Annalie made Fritz restless. It was time to stop messing around. He stored up and fired another buffered shot. The explosion shoved Leviathan off the roof. He fell five hundred feet to the surface, crashed into the Iller River, sank underwater, and didn't come back up.

Fritz flew to the shore. No metal poked out of the water, and only the regular flow of the current disturbed the river's surface. Had he done it? Had he taken out a Steelterror? He cycled through his vision enhancements to see if he could detect any movement beneath the surface–

And a tentacle wrapped around his ankle and pulled him downstream. Once submerged, two more tentacles wrapped themselves around his chest and arms, pinning his limbs tight against his torso.

Leviathan squeezed with the force of high-powered hydraulics and servomotors. Fritz's heads-up display turned red. His suit's structural integrity was seconds from failing. The problem wasn't water pressure; it was Steelterror pressure. Leviathan was going to pop his suit open like a tin can of beans and drown him. Fritz activated his force field to repel the tentacles, but it didn't seem to work underwater. Maybe it couldn't push away both the tentacles *and* the water surrounding him? Or maybe the energy making up the force field just wasn't as effective when submerged? Either way, with his arms pinned, he couldn't aim his laser cannons.

What remained of Leviathan moved in close. His body resembled an apple with a giant bite taken out of it. A thick, viscous fluid spilled out of his gaping wound, polluting the river. Sierra would not have been pleased. Fritz's armor groaned as Leviathan squeezed it into a new shape. The Steelterror drew him towards his five-foot-wide mouth. The pistons and gears inside seemed ready to crush and grind him to death.

"Your existence ends," Leviathan said, and his hollow voice sounded a lot different when he was mangled and deformed and seething with rage.

Fritz wanted to panic, but he forced himself to remain calm. "Raise... bomb... launcher," he commanded his suit. The launcher wasn't pinned; it sat higher on his back than where Leviathan squeezed him. At his command, it slid up to his left shoulder. Fritz locked the launcher's target on Leviathan's insides and fired. A bomb the size of his fist flew down the Steelterror's mechanical throat.

Leviathan was blown to smithereens. The blast threw Fritz out of the river. He landed in a heap on the shore with the wind knocked out of him. Metal fragments, some of them smoking, rained down around him. He took a picture of the scene with the camera built into his helmet. Siv, Cassie, and Sebastian would want to see it later. So would Annalie.

Annalie – he could show her the picture right now! If she was willing to speak to him.

Just as he got to his feet, his suit alerted him to an incoming projectile. He heard it, too. The engine roar was some ways away but approached quickly, and Fritz knew exactly what it was. He ran a quick diagnostic. Other than being short a bomb and down to 94% power, his chipsuit seemed to be perfectly functional, albeit a bit cosmetically damaged from Leviathan's attempted strangulation.

Banshee dropped from the sky, refactored into her robot form, and landed with enough force to make buildings tremble. In front of her, Sierra rose up out of the dirt. She didn't bother with the gray old lady look any longer. Just like when she'd made him turn off the power plant, she was young and angry. And staring at his boots. Why was she staring at his boots?

Oh. A piece of one of Leviathan's tentacles was still wrapped around his ankle. He shook it loose and kicked it towards Banshee. "I broke your toy robot," he said.

The malleability required of Banshee's metal face to display such clear human emotions – such as seething rage – still amazed Fritz. She charged her laser weapons and took a big step toward him but stopped when Sierra held up a hand.

"You told me you were going to put the Steelterrors back to sleep," Fritz said. "You ever tell *them* that was your plan?"

Banshee still glared at him, but for just a moment, her eyes landed on Sierra instead. "She didn't, did she, Banshee?" Fritz said. "She didn't tell you she promised me to cast you aside. Why would you want to help someone who sees you as nothing but a disposable tool?"

"You really want to do this?" Sierra said. "You want to start a barking *war*?"

He flipped open his helmet's visor. "No! Not at all. I want to work with you!"

Sierra opened her mouth, blinked, tilted her head, and looked at him like he had oatmeal for brains. And yes, part of him felt as stupid as she thought he was. But the last piece of advice Harlan had given him before he died was to talk to chipware's critics. Harlan told him to listen to their concerns, calm their fears, and offer them a hand in friendship. And chipware had no stauncher critic than Sierra Monet.

"I want to improve how people communicate, how they travel, how they cook," Fritz said. "I want to improve medicine. I want to help people work smarter, not harder. And I don't want to hurt anybody, even you. So why not help me make everyone's lives easier, and help me do it in a way that doesn't harm you?

"Look at the motorbike I had. It was built two centuries ago to run on gasoline, but since there's none of that around anymore, I modified it to run on solar-heated steam. That's far better than drilling for oil, right? It's renewable, cleaner. You know far more about all this than I do. Show me how the old chipware harmed you, and give me the chance to make things better. Work with me to find new solutions. Let's make the future better for both people and the planet – together!"

The only sound was the current of the Iller River and the hum of the reactor tower. Nature and chipware. Sierra gave him a strange look. She seemed gentle for a change. Maybe a little confused. Was she sad? Was she considering his offer? Sierra could teach him so much about how the planet worked – how *she* worked. Before the Blackout, scientists had explored hydrospark, wind-generated, and geothermal power to one degree or another. Sierra didn't just harness those forces; she *was* those forces. The possibility that she could teach him was... well, Fritz was inclined to call it *intoxicating*, but he had no idea if it was a proper use of the term since he'd never taken a sip of alcohol in his life.

He had a strong inclination to try it, though, when Sierra shook her head "no."

"You don't get it," she said. "Before the Blackout, there were fools just like you who talked about 'environmentally sustainable chipware.' That's an oxymoron spouted by morons.

You kill my trees to make your books. You even bother to read them? Pre-Blackout human history proved that when you hand people so much convenience, it fosters a culture of consumption. Everyone takes as much as they need to maintain their laziness, and all limits are ignored. The weakest suffer the most. The gap between the rich and the poor gets wider."

Fritz shook his head and sighed. "No, no, it doesn't have to be that way."

"I told you – *showed* you – what your dynamek energy does to me," Sierra said, her voice and her fury rising. "And you don't give a damn. So don't stand there and lie and say you don't want to hurt anyone. And don't be surprised when I defend myself. I'll go dig up another Steelterror to replace Leviathan. I'll unleash *all* of them on another town. And oh, I promise you, this time it will be a town much larger than Earp. When I'm through, no one will want your future. All they'll want is you in a jail cell. Or a grave. I will break you, *Professor*. You will not only admit I'm right, you'll admit opposing me was the biggest mistake of your worthless, privileged life!"

His distaste for conflict begged him to fly away and retreat home to Hondo. But he was through letting anyone stand between him and a future in which good people like his father didn't have to work themselves to death.

"You do what you need to do," Fritz told her with only a little bit of waver in his voice. "But I promise you my friends and I will destroy every Steelterror you dig up."

Fritz knew a lot about ancient chipware, but not so much about ancient culture. Still, he was fairly certain the gesture Sierra made to him was considered obscene.

Banshee moved towards him. Fritz closed his helmet's visor to prepare for an attack, but she leaped into the air, refactored into her jet form, and flew away. Sierra changed into a cloud of dust and rushed towards him on a gust of wind. Fritz flinched, fearing she'd turn herself into a battering ram of dirt, or a bolt of lightning. But when she reached him, the dirt particles dissipated, and a breeze blew past him harmlessly, almost as if she'd vanished from the wind.

Odd. He thought Sierra was the wind itself, but she could disappear out of it? For two weeks, he'd worked in his bedroom converting his robot into a chipsuit. He'd spent the first day-and-a-half of that time in a state of near-paranoia, convinced Sierra was watching his every move and that she was going to form out of the air and kill him. He'd looked everywhere outside his window for spontaneously growing flowers. He'd barely even drank any water for fear it would turn into Sierra halfway down his throat. But she'd never appeared until just now.

Was she *not* everywhere at once? When he watched Leviathan dangle his friends above the river, Sierra had stood before his motorbike, her whole body frozen at the same time a copy of her formed in the river to speak with Leviathan. After she'd forced him to turn off the power plant, her face had gone blank for several seconds. She'd appeared empty, like a statue devoid of life. When she came to, she said she'd told his friends where to find him.

Click. Sierra could be *anywhere*, but she couldn't be *everywhere*. She wasn't omnipresent. And making too many soil, air, or water constructs at a time must spread herself too thin. Fritz felt certain this was true. But how could it be useful in convincing her to help him?

Footsteps sounded on the paved road next to the reactor tower.

It was Annalie.

She stopped when she saw him standing next to the river. Fritz had never seen anything so beautiful. She glanced towards the top of the reactor tower, then behind her towards the parts warehouse, then towards the rubble of the office building. She was looking for him – looking for where he was remotely controlling his robot.

He lifted his visor. Annalie gasped, then laughed.

"I got tired of trying to figure out artificial intelligence," Fritz said, "so I made it into a chipsuit."

"Wow," Annalie said. She giggled. Oh gosh, how he'd missed the sounds of her delight. She stepped towards him. "That's splendiferous! It's like your second model. Does that make it your Bacon suit?"

Fritz laughed. He couldn't remember the last time he'd really laughed. "I suppose so." He walked towards her.

"Hey – you ain't limping!" Annalie said.

Fritz shrugged. "I made one boot a little taller than the other. It compensates for my shorter leg and lets me walk normal and pain-free."

"Was that Banshee that just flew away?"

"Yeah. Sierra was here, too. She says she'll dig up the last Steelterror, destroy another town, chipware is terrible, grumble, grumble, grumble." He cocked his thumb back towards the river. "I blew up Leviathan."

Annalie smiled and shrugged her shoulders. "Knew you could."

They stopped just a foot apart from one another.

"I came as soon as the lights turned back on," Annalie said. "I hoped I would find you here."

Fritz couldn't look her in the eye. "Annalie, I'm so sorry. I was hurt, and angry, and I took it out on you, and I'm so sorry."

She exhaled and nodded. Folded her arms across her chest. Dug the heel of her boot into the dirt. "I accept your apology," she finally said, "and I forgive you. Because that's the Godly thing to do. But if you want us to be friends again, I'm gonna need a little more than just a sorry."

"All right."

"First, you don't *ever* yell at me. Ever again."

Fritz flinched. All delight had vanished from her face. She was more than just stern, she was downright wrathy, and it was all directed squarely at him. He couldn't blame her for that.

"I spent my whole life forced to work for the monsters that killed my folks," she said. "Now that they're gone, I have the freedom *not* to associate with anyone who's mean to me and mine. I will *not* stand for that kind of abuse from you again. You hear me?"

Fritz forced himself to meet her eyes. "Perfectly."

"Good," she said in a much softer voice. "Second, you don't get to walk away again. When you promise a tomorrow beyond our imagination, you're asking folks to share in your dream. You walk away, you kill our hope."

"The last time I saw him alive, Harlan talked about hope. He said I had to be the leader other people need me to be."

"That's right."

"That's tough for me!"

She shrugged her shoulders and looked down at her shoes. "Don't have to do it alone."

Her hand reached out for his. After he took it, the burdens she spoke of didn't seem so heavy anymore.

Chapter Eighteen

"It uses the same power source it did when it was a robot: the sparkscube mounted on my back," Fritz said. "I salvaged Apple Juice's three octocore chips and put them into an onboard computer that manages every aspect of the suit and responds to my voice commands. And then I threw in every other bit of chipware I could imagine. I put night vision and infrared and other sight enhancements into the helmet's visor. And a heads-up display! I put in an oxygen supply, which came in awfully handy when Leviathan dunked me back there, and I adapted the energy barriers we used to contain the demons into a field that surrounds the suit like an aura. It will repel pretty much any physical attack, including bullets, and energy ones, too, as long as they're not too strong. I mounted my prototype Mantissa reader emulator into the helmet, and I built a descrambler in here, too, because why the heck not? Even my mobile is wired in."

Annalie sat in his outstretched arms with her arms wrapped tighter than a vise around his neck, but she stared forward like she wasn't even paying attention to him. Could she even hear him over the noise of the rushing air?

"Annalie?" Fritz said. "Are you OK?"

"I'm flying!" she yelled. "Great space bird of the galaxy, *I'm flying!*"

He agreed: it was fairly spectacular to see Mondorf zooming by underneath them. "Want me to go full burn?"

"Yes! Yes!" Her grip tightened, but she squealed with delight. "Fast as you can!"

"Rockets, full burn," he said. There was a roar of fire from his back, and their speed doubled.

Annalie directed him towards the outskirts of Mondorf's ancient airport. A minute later, they landed before the giant airplane-sized doors of an old hangar. Annalie entered through an adjacent person-sized door, and Fritz lifted his visor and followed.

It was dark inside, but the way Annalie's voice echoed suggested a vast, mostly empty space. "Overhead lights ought to work, now that the sparks are back on," she said. She flipped a switch on the wall, and lights hanging from the rafters illuminated the hangar. Spare parts, wires, tools, and even a chipware screen covered three tables. Each table had several car batteries underneath it. Dozens of candles of varying sizes testified to the number of late nights Annalie had worked here.

The fruit of her efforts sat in the middle of the hangar. It was an aerocopter – an honest-to-goodness *aerocopter* with a pair of giant rotor blades on top. Its front panel had been removed, and cables connected it to diagnostic devices with glowing green status lights.

"It's ready to fly?" Fritz asked.

"It's daisy," she said.

"You were gonna visit me?"

"You?" Annalie said. "Gosh no. There was this no-good, lousy ogre who lives way down south on the other side of the mountains. He was all sorts of mean to me, and I was going to find him and give him what for."

Sakes alive, if Sierra had learned about this, she might have killed her. Yet Annalie had spent two months' secretly working on it anyway, even after how he'd treated her, even though her young siblings needed her. She smirked, and he sheepishly chuckled, but only because the alternative was to cry. "This guy sounds like a bowl of moldy oatmeal."

"He is," Annalie said. "I ever see him again, I'm gonna pop him one." She tapped her fist on his shoulder and whispered, "Pow."

Just like back in Earp when Annalie had pretended he had laryngitis to keep the baker from talking to him, his stomach felt as if it could drop, and the rest of him felt like he could float away. He knew what the strange feelings meant, but he also knew it wasn't really a good time to deal with them.

"Umm, let me show you something," he said. "I have an idea about how to find the three remaining Steelterrors."

"Land, sky, and the last one's fire?"

"That's the last element of the ancient world, yeah."

Fritz transferred his suit's head's up display to the screen on Annalie's workbench, then commanded his chipsuit's computer to open a data-comm to Skylab, the space station orbiting the planet. He asked Skylab for the status of its sensor arrays, and the text of the station's report appeared on the screen.

"Deep space scanners are in use?" Annalie said. "By who? Good gravy, are there still people up there?"

"Not people," Fritz said. "Robots. Autonomous models, the size of infants. Don't worry: they're nothing like the Steelterrors. They've been up there since before the Blackout, and they're still dutifully carrying out the tasks they were programmed to perform. If they're using Skylab's deep space scanners, it's because two centuries ago, someone told them to, and they've never stopped. Though – gosh – they're using a lot of processing power. What are they *doing* up there?" He shook his head. "It doesn't matter. We want to use the terrestrial scanners, and those aren't in use. Skylab, search for high concentrations of an alloy made out of vanadium, tungsten, and chromium, with a large amount of titanium nearby."

The corner of Annalie's mouth turned up into a grin. "You're scanning the planet for Traskian armor."

"If Skylab can find large concentrations of it – say, large enough to coat a four-ton robot – we'll know the exact location of each remaining Steelterror."

Fritz told his computer to lay the results over a map of the continent. When red dots marked three locations, Fritz clapped his hands, creating a resounding *gong* because of his metal gloves. "And there they are! Look – one's in the Lavare Mountains, pretty high above sea level and *not* moving. That must be where Samson is licking his wounds."

"But look at the one eighty miles from here and a mile above Terrascorcha," Annalie said. "That's Banshee, and she's flying straight towards where the third one's buried underground." She squinted at the map. "Harbrucken? That name sounds familiar."

"That's where my sister goes to school. Where Siv and Sebastian are headed right now. It's the largest and most populated town in the occupied territories by far, especially when the university is in session. Which it is. It's *the* center of learning for the entire world."

"Sounds like exactly the kind of place Sierra would unleash her Steelterrors."

"Yeah," Fritz mumbled. Memories of Earp burning, broken, and littered with bodies caused his heart to palpitate because Harbrucken was hundreds of times larger than Earp. If they couldn't stop Sierra and Banshee in time, they'd dig up the fire Steelterror, and then there'd be *two* of the blasted things running rampant all over town.

"We can do this," Fritz said. "Five hundred years ago, the Steelterrors wreaked havoc partly because they were the most technologically advanced chipware ever seen. But now we're on equal ground technology-wise, so much so I destroyed Leviathan alone. The group of us, together, can take out the last two before the fire Steelterror gets dug out of the ground. I know we can. But I need to get there and join my friends."

"*We* need to get there," Annalie corrected, "and join *our* friends. My copter's ready to fly. I'm not a hunter, a soldier, or an archer, and I sure don't have a chipsuit. But I'll do what I can. Maybe I can help more people there than I did in Earp."

Fritz barely heard her. He was examining Banshee's speed and distance from Harbrucken and comparing it to how long it would take him to get to the university if he took a detour to the Lavare Mountains. "On my way, I'm going to make a quick stop in the mountains where Samson is hiding. He's just sitting there stationary. I nearly destroyed him before when Apple Juice was an automaton with limited maneuverability. I'm confident I can finish him off now before he's repaired enough to join Banshee *and* the fire Steelterror in fighting us."

"I don't want you going off by your lonesome," Annalie said. "How would I find you if something goes wrong?"

"My chipsuit has a homing beacon I can activate in case of emergency," Fritz said. "I'll send the frequency to your mobile."

They powered down the hangar's equipment and went back outside. "What are we going to do about Sierra?" Annalie said. "You know she'll join the fight, too."

"I'll destroy the Steelterrors," Fritz said, "but Sierra is our planet, or a person, or both. I won't kill her, but I can reason with her. I'm sure of it."

Fritz didn't miss Annalie's skeptical look. "She was once a Mantissa," he said. "And Sebastian said she showed no love for the headmasters, but he also said they could have jailed her, and they didn't. She must have done *some* good. I'm sure she wasn't attached to the military like Sebastian was, and I'll bet she wasn't a peacekeeper either." He closed his eyes. "Sebastian said she grew up in several foster homes. That must have bred sympathy in her for the poor and the downtrodden. I'll bet she did things no other Mantissa did. She planted trees and community gardens and helped farmers with their crops. She helped stray animals find homes, and she restored wildlife habitats. When natural disasters struck, like groundshakes, she was first on the scene. Movers cleaned up the rubble, but she put the shattered pieces of land back together."

"You're doing that thing again," Annalie said. "The thing where you know when someone's been eating mashed potatoes." Annalie shrugged her shoulders. "I hope you're right about her."

"Me, too. But we might need to capture her to force her to listen. And I'm still stumped on how to do that, so if you come up with any ideas..."

"I won't keep 'em to myself."

"You know how to get to Harbrucken?"

"I'm sure it's in my aerocopter's navigation system if it's an old pre-Blackout town."

"Avoid Banshee," Fritz said. "Don't let her or Sierra see you in the air. I'd... be really upset if something happened to you."

Her face flushed, and she made a sound that was part laugh, part clearing her throat. It made her blush even more. She took a deep breath. "Me, too." She wrapped her hand around the metal gauntlet covering his. "So don't let's die today. Deal?"

"Deal," Fritz said. He smiled, dropped his visor over his face, and took several steps away from her. They waved to one another. He put his rockets on full burn and blasted across the night sky, keeping his eyes on Annalie even when that required his suit's magnification capabilities.

If this ended up being the last time he ever saw her, he wanted it to last.

Chapter Nineteen

"Evening, Cassie," said the woman on the bookstore's front porch. She sat in a rocking chair. The coffee mug she held to her lips obscured most of her face, though her eyes peeked out over top of it, and there was a smile in them. There always was.

"Hi, Eliza," Cassie said. The owner of the bookstore and the apartment on its second floor had been "Mrs. Burkholder" for the first month of Cassie's lease. Only under threat of eviction had Cassie agreed to use the woman's first name.

"Rough day?" Eliza asked.

Halfway between the bookstore's front door and the stairway on the side of the building leading up to her apartment, Cassie stopped and dropped her knapsack off her shoulder. "You can tell?"

"I've had various university students living in that apartment for thirty years," Eliza said. "Before you, I've never met one who looked so consistently ecstatic about all of the hard work involved in earning a piece of paper from that school. But for the first time in two years, you look like all the rest of them. Tired."

Gee, thanks. "Your coffee smells great," Cassie said.

"Come on down to the shop later if you'd like a cup. But I didn't mean that kind of tired. I meant tired in your soul."

She didn't know what that was supposed to mean, but she more-or-less agreed with it anyway. "Today was pathology lab. Professor Holt showed us an infarcted heart. That's a heart that suffered a heart attack. It just made me think of my dad."

Eliza set down her mug and smiled sympathetically. "I lost Gene twenty-three years ago. The pain won't ever go away. But it will get better."

A deep breath later, Cassie retrieved her knapsack. "I'm going to take you up on that coffee offer. I have a lot of studying to do. It's going to be a late night."

"In that case, I'll make you an entire pot." She held up a hand before Cassie could protest. "An entire pot or your rent goes up one gold per month. You don't have to drink it all, but that's what I'm making you."

"Thanks." Cassie knew she'd drink every drop.

She went up to her single room apartment, deposited her knapsack on the table, and poured a cup of water from the tap. Harbrucken was the only city in the occupied territories with indoor plumbing, and it was one of her favorite parts of living there. The drink was refreshing, and splashing some water on her face made her feel a little better, too. She placed the back of her right hand into the palm of her left and brought both to her heart to make the Sign of God's Hand – which was where she prayed her father was finding some peace and rest.

An hour later, seated at the table in her single room, she closed her book and used her right index finger to point at places on her left hand. "Distal phalanges, intermediate phalanges... proximate phalanges– proxi*mal* phalanges. Metacarpals, carpals–"

There was a knock on her door.

Harbrucken wasn't a lawless wasteland like some of the far western villages, but it kept its deputies plenty busy. Crime was common enough that most women who lived alone in town would feel tense at an unexpected knock on their doors, but Cassie's danger sense wasn't stirring in the least. She opened the door.

"Howdy," Siv said.

"Hi!" she said before pulling him into her arms and squeezing him tightly. She could have cried at his perfect timing. "What are you doing here?"

"Enjoying this," he said. He kissed her. "Also, hoping you'll let me in and open the window seeing as Sebastian's hiding on the roof."

"Sebastian's here?"

He locked the door behind them as she opened the window. With white demon agility, Sebastian crawled down the side of the building and swung inside in all but the blink of an eye.

"Nice place," Sebastian said.

"You're wearing your translator," she said. Siv's sword, the Dragon Slayer, was in a scabbard strapped to his back. This wasn't purely a social call. "What's going on?"

Siv put what looked like a very heavy satchel down on the floor. He yanked a chair out from her table, spun it backward, and straddled it. "Fritz flew to Mondorf to find Annalie and turn the power plant back on."

"He took the airplane?" she asked.

"No," Siv said. "Sebastian and I came here in the airplane. Fritz turned his robot into a flying chipware-powered suit of armor."

"For serious?" Cassie said.

"For serious," Siv said.

"He made a suit of armor that can *fly?*" Cassie said. She wanted to swell with pride at her brother's ingenuity. She wanted to swoon at his never-before-seen romantic side. She also wanted to cry at his possibly-deadly impulsiveness. "Sierra won't stand for it. She'll–"

"Fritz thinks he can talk things out with her," Sebastian said.

"And he's fixing to take on the Steelterrors," Siv said. He tapped his satchel with the toe of his boot. "Gave us a bag full of early Lenerstellen presents so we can help."

Cassie rested her forehead on her steepled fingers. "How long ago was this?"

"Long enough that I reckon he's found Annalie by now and the two of 'em have turned the power plant back on," Siv said.

"I've been encouraging him to find something that makes him happy," Cassie said, "but I never dreamed he'd decide that was picking a fight with Sierra."

"He did seem happy," Siv said. "And he said 'twas his power making him do this, not his pride."

A sound like a fireball streaking across the sky thundered from east to west; then a *boom* shook the building. All three of them ran to the windows. A pair of neighborhoods over, Banshee's fifty-foot tall robot form towered over piles of broken stone and flaming wood. The rubble at her feet had been homes a few moments earlier. The adjacent houses still stood but were on fire. Laser cannons emerged from Banshee's forearms. She fired wildly into the air as if it were seconds after midnight on New Year's Eve.

A Steelterror had killed over half the population of Earp. Two hundred eleven souls. Now one of them was paying a visit to Harbrucken and its population of over six *thousand*.

"The Era of Steel begins, blood bags!" Banshee yelled to the sky.

Back when Fritz, Siv, and Cassie had traveled by horse between the Lavare Mountains and Mondorf, the journey had taken them nine days. Now, the tallest peaks in the Lavare range were in the distance, and Fritz had left Mondorf only a couple of hours earlier. Flying was never, *ever* going to get old. The efficiency alone made it the best ever way to travel.

Though night had fallen, he saw as if it were daytime thanks to the image enhancement chipware in his helmet's visor. It combined light from the portion of the electromagnetic spectrum invisible to the naked eye with what little visible light was present. The resulting images, other than being made entirely of different shades of green, looked not much different than the normal sunlit world.

Fritz tilted his head and told his onboard computer to magnify his vision by three. Samson was on one of the mountains. The arm he'd lost at the power plant had been reattached. Or regrown. Or rebuilt, or whatever the Steelterrors did to heal themselves. Both of his hands must have been in their drill form because a cloud of snow and rock dust surrounded him, and he was so far underneath the surface, Fritz only saw his upper chest and head. But what was he digging for? The last Steelterror was under Harbrucken.

When Fritz landed twenty feet up the mountain from Samson, the Steelterror crouched deeper into the pit he was digging in an attempt to hide. He remembered the beating he'd taken from Apple Juice back in Mondorf, and he was afraid. He was a machine – a Steelterror – but he was afraid. Wow! How did his mind *work?*

"What are you digging for?" Fritz shouted over the blaring drills. "The last of your kind is under Harbrucken, not here."

A cold breeze blew across the mountain, and there was laughter in the midst of its howl. Beside the site of Samson's excavation, snow swirled into a tornado a head shorter than Fritz, then coalesced into Sierra.

"There is a Steelterror under Harbrucken," she said. "But the *last* of his kind? How many elements of the ancient world do you think there were?"

"Four?" he answered hesitantly.

"Try *five,* dung-for-brains!"

Oh crud.

Sierra scooped up a handful of dirt from the edge of Samson's excavation and sifted it through her fingers. "The mountains are rich in kemosite, which is disruptive to the haupian waves used by chipware sensors. Isn't that rich? Your precious chipware, foiled by *nature.*"

Banshee was probably already in Harbrucken digging up the Steelterror buried there. Samson no longer had a scratch on him; his eyes and the band of metal around the back of his head glowed bright red. And there was a fifth Steelterror. He'd been nervous about having to face two Steelterrors at once. What if they had to face *four?*

Oh crud oh crud oh *crud.*

"Don't do this, please!" Fritz called to Samson. "Don't dig it up. Join me. Work with me! You could be a farmer. You know that?"

"Keep digging, Samson," Sierra said.

"You, too, Sierra – join me," Fritz said. "Please don't send Steelterrors to attack the most populated city in the world. Let's talk about this."

"I'm not going to listen to your barking lies about safer chipware," Sierra said. "I told you: words mean jack to me. You had your chance to take planet-saving action. Instead, you turned the power plant back on. Sod off, Professor."

Fritz stepped back and tried to open a voice-comm to Annalie and Siv, but he couldn't establish a connection. Diagnostics didn't indicate anything was wrong, but snow and rock dust swirled all around them – dust from rocks rich in sensor-disrupting kemosite. Was it also disrupting his comm signals? The two technologies used similar wavelengths.

Samson stopped drilling, climbed out of the crater, and took three steps back down the mountain. At the center of the hole was a five-foot-wide piece of exposed black steel and chrome. Sierra jumped in and stood on it. "The ancients called the fifth element 'aether,'" she said. "They thought it made up the night sky and the stars, and it was their primitive explanation for the force that kept them planted on the ground. Land, water, air, fire... and gravity."

Sierra dropped to one knee, slammed her fist against the exposed metal, and called down lightning.

The mountain exploded.

Fritz fired his thrusters, pushing himself into the air and backward, roughly tracing the upward slope of the mountain while staying about twenty feet above it. Rocks and snow tumbled down beneath him. Dust and powder swirled in a haze. When it cleared, so much stone covered the area it looked like a quarry, and Samson was half-buried under a pair of boulders. His eyes were dim, and he didn't move. Sierra been so careless with her lightning, she'd accidentally taken out one of her Steelterrors. Well, good – though she'd already brought Samson back to life once. She could likely do it again. Sierra herself was fine, of course. Could *anything* hurt her?

The fifth Steelterror stood up.

He was the largest one, a bit taller even than Banshee. Like the others, he was mostly black steel and chrome with thick lines of red trim across his human-like shape. And his face was the most human-looking of all, even more so than Banshee's. He even had a mustache and long beard – made of silver rather than hair, of course.

The metal giant stepped out of the twenty-foot-deep crater as casually as a person stepping out of a wash tub. "Gravitas," Sierra addressed him. "Mighty leader of the Verdant Wardens. He who serves no one but Lady Verde."

There were *whirrrs* and *hummms* of machinery as Gravitas turned his head to face Sierra. He looked somewhere between disinterested and annoyed. "And you are...?" he asked in a baritone that sounded like crunching gravel.

Sierra smirked at him. "I'm Lady Verde."

Gravitas tilted his head at her, challenging her claim. Sierra stared up at him, but not for long. A tower of rock rose from the ground underneath her feet. It lifted her until she was eye level with Gravitas. A swirl of snowy wind circled her.

The metal of Gravitas's face molded itself into a sly grin. He looked like he didn't trust Sierra for a second, which scared the *hell* out of Fritz. Sierra controlled the Steelterrors, and she was crazy and hellbent on destruction, but the only thing more frightening than Steelterrors under Sierra's command were Steelterrors unrestrained by anyone or anything. What if Sierra couldn't control this one? And she'd called him the *leader* of the Steelterrors? What if he broke her control over *all* of them?

"Lady Verde," came Gravitas's non-committal reply.

"After two centuries of peace," Sierra said, "humans have begun to again meddle with nature. You're going to help me teach them a lesson."

"You were made to serve Verde and her people, Gravitas, not to harm them," Fritz called out. "Remember that!"

Gravitas's stare was deeply uncomfortable. Like the other Steelterrors, his eyes glowed red, but there was something different about his. They contained wrath which was practically tangible. "A man wrapped in steel," he said. "You sound so certain for one who is so wrong. Some of our creators, the foolish ones, had altruistic goals. Improved knowledge of science, an end to environmental disaster, and other such claptrap. But the visionaries among them saw us for what we truly are. The Verdant Wardens are *weapons*."

He pointed his right palm at Fritz. It glowed a bright red, and Fritz couldn't fly any higher. He felt like he'd gained a hundred pounds. Gravitas moved his hand, and an invisible force pulled Fritz in the same direction, tracking him along with the Steelterror's movements. Gravitas was controlling and manipulating gravity. It was amazing and terrifying. At the speed of a quick walk, Fritz flew, against his will, over the Steelterror's head and further down the mountain.

"See?" Sierra said. "This machine is the embodiment of everything I've tried to tell you. You'll bring back chipware for peace, love, understanding, and other figments of your barking imagination. But someone else will take what you build and twist it. Corrupt it. Use it for harm, for hurt."

"You mean like you're doing right now?" Fritz said. "You're becoming what you hate, Sierra. That's why you need to stop."

Fritz was surprised she didn't shoot lava out of her eyes. "Gravitas, put him in the dirt."

A force that felt like Gravitas's hand, but invisible, spun him around one hundred eighty degrees and slammed him flat into the snow. Fritz lifted his head. Samson's unmoving arm jutted out from under a nearby boulder, but that was all he saw before gravity forced his head back down. It felt like someone was stepping on him. His force field aura was flat-out useless against the attack – which made sense because it wasn't physical. Gravity itself had been increased to, what, twice normal? Three times normal?

"Open a voice-comm... to Annalie... Cassie... Siv..."

If the problem earlier had been interference, he still wouldn't be able to call anyone successfully. But he had to try because he'd never have another chance to say goodbye. He didn't need his intuitive power to know he wasn't leaving the mountain alive.

As even more invisible pressure from above crushed him, Sierra crouched before him. "You want to know what it feels like to get struck by lightning?"

Fritz screamed.

Brightness everywhere, like looking at the sun. The loudest *boom* he'd ever heard punched his ears like a pair of solid steel fists. If not for the hearing protection his helmet afforded, it likely would have ruptured both of his eardrums. His heads-up display went dark. So did everything else in his suit. Blue and white sparks crackled up and down his arms, and probably all over the rest of his body, too. He was really, really glad for the layer of rubber padding he'd put on the inside of the suit. He'd added it for comfort, to have something softer than hard steel pressed up against his skin. Well, it had kept him comfortable all right. Comfortably alive. Though he felt hot. Was his suit on fire?

"Flip him over," Sierra said. Fritz blinked, but he still saw only spots. He couldn't tell where she was. An invisible force twisted him around from his belly to his back, but he remained otherwise pinned and unable to move. When his vision finally cleared, Gravitas and Sierra stood on either side of him. Gravitas pointed his hand towards the peak of the mountain above, and it shook.

Snow from the peak came loose and slid down the mountainside towards him. Boulders – tens of them, maybe hundreds – broke off, and they rolled his way, too. The boulders stopped when they reached him and an invisible force – either Sierra or Gravitas – formed them in a circle, surrounding him. More rocks fell and were added to the circle's height. The ground shook, loud enough to wake the dead. Snow poured over the rocks and covered him.

"No!" he screamed. "Don't bury me! Please! Stop! *Stop!*"

Rocks bounced into the circle of boulders and landed on his legs, arms, and torso, pinning him to the ground. A final layer of boulders landed above him and sealed him inside a makeshift tomb. Snow rushed in through the cracks, filled all the available space, and covered his dead suit's helmet.

And then the only sound was his screaming.

Chapter Twenty

Pandemonium reigned on the streets. Two dozen people ran from the neighborhood being destroyed by Banshee. Screams, laser fire, horse trumpets, crisis bells, and pounding feet made up a cacophony of confusion. A smoky haze hung in the air. Buildings burned; hurt and dead people were probably in them. And it sounded as if the same scene was repeated on the next streets over both east and west.

Cassie and Siv stormed down the stairs outside her apartment. Eliza stood on the front porch of the bookstore. "Get people off the streets and inside," Cassie told her. "Let them use my apartment if you need to."

Eliza's eyes widened at the sight of her tenant armed with bow and arrow, and Siv next to her with his Dragon Slayer unsheathed and in his right hand. "What are you doing? Leave this for the sheriff, or for the militia!"

"They're not prepared to deal with this."

"Neither are you! Cassie, your mother would–"

Cassie swiped her finger across the blade of Siv's sword, then held it up for Eliza to watch it heal itself. "My friends and I are what's left of the Mantissa. What's shooting up the city is a Steelterror. I think you have enough history books in your shop to know that, under these circumstances, the sheriff and the militia are the ones who are unprepared."

Sebastian launched himself from the roof of Cassie's apartment and landed on the street just in front of them. The white demons had never held Harbrucken, which made Sebastian an unfamiliar sight and just as much a nightmare-come-true as Banshee. The crowd screamed, and so did Eliza. Sebastian dropped to all six limbs and ran southbound down Ridge Avenue. Everyone scattered at his approach. One man badly twisted his ankle in his attempt to sidestep the monster.

"Eliza, we'll handle this," Cassie said. "Just get people inside." She ran to the fallen man, placed her hand against his ankle for a few seconds, then helped him stand. "Run!"

He did. Cassie and Siv did, too, in pursuit of Sebastian. Halfway there, a strange, *whup-whup-whup* sound made Cassie turn. A pod with spinning blades on top descended out of the air and hovered some twenty feet above the road. Annalie was inside it. She waved, and Cassie's mobile chimed. Siv's must also have because he tapped the earpiece he wore, which served as a wireless controller, speaker, and microphone for the mobile itself tucked away in the pocket of his jeans.

"Red!" he said. Cassie tapped her mobile's earpiece and joined the voice-comm. "Got yourself an aerocopter?"

"I can't reach Fritz," Annalie said, her voice quivering. "He ain't answering his mobile. He has a tracking beacon in his chipsuit, but I don't get a signal from it. Our scans showed Samson was in the mountains, so he was fixing to head there and finish him off before joining us. Except he ain't here. And I can't reach him!"

"Stay calm," Siv said. He spoke to Annalie, but he looked straight at Cassie. "He's a big boy. He can handle himself, especially encased in chipware armor. He'll check in soon."

"I hope you're right," Annalie said. "I'm going to look for people who need to be lifted out to safety. Let me know if you hear from him."

Siv gave her a thumb's up sign.

"Be careful against Banshee," Annalie said. "She's here to dig up the fire Steelterror, by the way."

"She's– the fire one's buried here?" Siv said.

"We need to go," Cassie said. She waved to Annalie, and the aerocopter ascended and moved away. Cassie and Siv resumed running. Three blocks later, they reached Sebastian. He crouched next to a house at the intersection of Ridge Avenue and Pierce Street and peeked around the corner at Banshee. They could see her from street level now, towering over homes. She was in a front yard three houses from the corner. Her laser blasts ripped apart the ground at ear-splitting volume.

"Did you join that voice-comm and hear what Banshee's up to?" Cassie asked Sebastian. He nodded.

"Reckon this calls for a soldier's plan," Siv said. "Tell us what to do, Big Man."

"Banshee has long-range weapons and flight capability," Sebastian said, "so we aren't nearly a match for her unless we even the odds. McCaig, go down one more street and loop around behind her. Use some of the grapple lines Fritz built to tether her to the ground. Cassie and I will attack her head-on, focusing on her eyes. Once she's blind and grounded, we pound the snot out of her. Any questions?"

"The two of you, head-on against her?" Siv said. "She has guns. Very big guns."

"We'll listen to our danger senses," Sebastian said. "And we heal fast."

Siv's look said he wasn't convinced. Cassie nodded. "We can do it. Sounds good."

"It actually doesn't," Sebastian said. "It's just the *least* suicidal plan I could come up with on short notice. But there's a fire Steelterror still in the ground, Sierra Monet will no doubt show herself soon, and Fritz isn't here."

Around the corner, something exploded. Had Banshee hit a pocket of natural gas in the ground? People screamed.

"Teufel will love how flammable you blood bags are!" Banshee cackled. She laughed as she destroyed homes and lives. Rage rose in Cassie's chest.

"That thing needs to die, *now*," Sebastian said.

"I'll holler when I'm in place," Siv said. He reached out and squeezed Cassie's hand.

"Be careful," she said.

Siv winked and clicked his tongue. "We ready?"

Cassie took a deep breath and nodded.

"Let's slag her," Sebastian said.

Together, the three of them scurried out from behind the cover of the corner house. Siv ran into the intersection and towards the next street down. Cassie and Sebastian moved towards Banshee, but paused, startled at their danger senses hollering for immediate attention.

Sheets of rock burst up out of the ground inches in front of their faces. They slammed into them and fell flat on their backs. Cassie tasted blood on her upper lip, dripping down from her nose. Near her on the ground, Siv and Sebastian groaned in similar pain.

Cassie blinked to stop the world from spinning. The rock sheets sank back down into the dirt. Small fires decorated the street like lanterns. They burned on the ground, in the rubble of the homes Banshee had destroyed, and in the homes that barely remained standing.

And across the street stood Sierra. She met Cassie's eyes and twisted her lip into a sneer.

"I'll wake up Teufel," Sierra said to Banshee. "Go wipe this city off my surface."

"Obliteration bombing," Banshee said. "I thought you'd never ask." She jumped into the air, refactored herself into a jet, and flew away towards the northeast.

Cassie climbed to her feet and aimed an arrow at Sierra, but the ground shook so violently underneath her she dropped her bow and lost her footing. She put her arms out to her sides to maintain her balance on the unsteady ground. A jagged mass of silver steel rose up out of the pit Banshee had been blasting. It was as big as three of the houses Banshee had destroyed to excavate it.

Sebastian had a pair of laser rifles strapped to his back. He swung one into his upper arms and the other into his lower arms, aimed at Sierra, and fired repeatedly. Sierra shuddered and shook under the assault. Sebastian didn't stop shooting until she collapsed. Her remains dissipated into dust, then another copy of her body rose up out of the ground a foot from where the first had fallen. Sebastian cursed.

"Sad thing about Teufel here," Sierra said. "He was the fourth Steelterror built, and his creators had gotten a little sure of themselves, as morons who think they're God do. By the time they realized his artificial intelligence was... flawed, he'd gone sentient and wouldn't let them terminate him. That's always the problem with chipware – the terrifying speed at which things go from 'What could go wrong?' to 'How could we have barking known?'"

The ground stopped shaking but only because the fire Steelterror had been fully excavated. It had no smooth surfaces and no sleek lines like the others. It was just a giant mass of scrap, crumpled and mashed and dented – a heap of metallic trash.

Sebastian ran ten steps closer and fired both of his laser rifles at it. Siv put away his sword and shot his laser rifle at it, too. Cassie launched a bomb arrow at it, then another. They blasted chunks of metal the size of Cassie's head off the metal heap, but Sierra remained indifferent to the assault. She picked up one of the too-many-to-count pieces of flaming debris covering the area and pressed it against a smooth, fist-sized, red-and-chrome ball embedded in Teufel's surface.

"Wake up, Teufel," Sierra sing-songed.

"We're out of time," Sebastian said.

The silver metal of Teufel's slag heap body turned orange, then red. Sierra turned back to Cassie and her friends and winked. Then her body turned to water and splattered on the ground. She didn't take a new shape. She was gone.

"Run!" Siv said. "As that thing gets hotter, it's gonna get softer."

Cassie's danger sense agreed. She turned back in the direction from which they'd arrived, stealing glances over her shoulder. Teufel's mass drooped and sagged until he'd dissolved into a lake of liquid steel. Glowing red, he spread out like flowing lava and covered Pierce Street. A haze of smoke and heat-distorted air hovered above him. The dirt road crumbled underneath him, and charred embers fell into the sewer system below.

The red ball – the part Sierra had ignited – skimmed across his surface. His undulating mass of burning steel followed. A river in hell likely looked no different. When Teufel got too close to a house, its proximity to his heat set it ablaze. When he touched a house, it collapsed into ashes and embers. He absorbed the remains of what he burned into him, increasing his already massive bulk.

Shrill, shrieking laughter cut through the air, and Teufel spoke with an almost comically high-pitched voice. "The fire loves me, and I love the fire! Steel will rise above the ashes of the dead world. And all shall burn! All shall *burn!*"

Sierra had said there was a problem with Teufel's artificial intelligence. "Great," Cassie said. "He's psychotic."

"And the others aren't?" Siv said.

A roar of engines came from somewhere across town far to the northwest. Banshee streaked across the night sky and buffeted the ground beneath her with bombs. Cassie startled at the shocking display of brutality, but Siv took her arm and urged her forward.

They sprinted across Ridge Avenue to the wooden sidewalk in front of a general store. Following Siv's lead, Cassie and Sebastian pointed the bracers on their left wrists towards the store's roof. Their grappling hooks took hold, and the attached lines pulled them up to safety above street level. They ran across the roof and jumped over the gap to the next building.

Teufel followed. The fire Steelterror had expanded himself out to a width of thirty, maybe forty feet. He burned bright red – even bright white in some places. The malleable metal of his body stretched like taffy upwards until he towered above the general store, then like a tidal wave of lava, he crashed down on top of it. The store burst into splinters and ash and collapsed beneath him. Teufel rode the wreck back down to ground level, but almost immediately he rose again and smothered the next building in his path, reaching out with tendrils of liquid metal to alight structures he didn't directly mow down.

The devastation reminded Cassie of an experiment she'd once done in a pre-med chemistry class. A drop of acid placed on a thin square of tin had moved across the metal at a rapid pace, bubbling, smoking, and eating it away until all that remained was ashy flakes and a pungent odor. Teufel was the acid, and the city was the dissolving tin. He moved like an amoeba on a specimen slide, except Teufel wasn't microscopic and harmless, he was gigantic and lethal.

Raucous laughter echoed from whatever part of Teufel transmitted his voice, but the constant sound of Cassie's danger sense screaming inside her head drowned it out. She, Siv, and Sebastian ran until they were nearly breathless. They used their grapple lines and leaped from one roof to another, swinging over streets. They gasped, sweat, and barely kept ahead of fiery death. Each time Cassie looked back, she saw Teufel's red-and-chrome ball head floating at the front of the liquid metal onslaught.

People scattered in every direction on each street they crossed. Terrified, they ran for their lives and yelled the names of loved ones. Guilt stabbed Cassie in the heart. Though Teufel was the one killing, she was helping choose his victims because Teufel followed her and her friends.

"Matter is neither created nor destroyed," Teufel yelled behind them. "It's just changed into ash, into embers, into dust. Oh, sweet fruit of the burn. Look at the flames, Omar! Hear their sweet crackle!"

"This one's a right bastard," Siv growled.

Somewhere in the distance, Banshee screamed overhead and dropped another series of bombs. *Boom boom boom boom BOOM.* Night had fallen, but so much of the city was on fire, the orange glow in the sky made it seem like twilight. Cassie wasn't sure how long they could keep running. Sooner or later, one of them was going to stumble, or one of their grappling hooks wasn't going to find a secure hold, or they were not going to be fast enough, and Teufel wouldn't just burn them, he'd melt them. Even she and Sebastian couldn't heal themselves if smothered by liquid steel. There wasn't any other way this could end. Their weapons were useless against Teufel's super-heated mass. She could call Annalie for an aerocopter lift, but Teufel would consume the copter and everyone in it before they could board.

They ran across the roof of an apartment building. When they were almost across it, the largest Steelterror Cassie had yet seen dropped out of the sky and landed on the street in front of them. He flattened a pair of nearby buildings, shook the ground, and shattered windows. He was so tall, his glowing red eyes were level with theirs, though he stood on the street three stories below. He had a person-like shape – two arms, two legs, even a metal mustache and beard.

Heat burned Cassie's back. Teufel formed a wall of fire stretching ten feet above the roof, but – thank God – he stopped short of consuming the building. "Gravitas!" he yelled with all the excitement of a kid who just got a new pony on Lenerstellen morning. "Gravitas! Gravitas! *Gravitas!*"

Cassie trembled as if her danger sense was trying to shake her into action. She heard it sounding an alarm inside her, but she made no effort to neutralize the threat, because what could she do? With the hellfire of Teufel behind them, and the new dreadnought of a Steelterror in front of them–

"You have nowhere to go," Gravitas said.

Chapter Twenty-One

Fritz panicked for the first ten minutes of burial, but if he hyperventilated, he'd just use up what little air he had left. He had to think rationally about his options. No – he had to stop thinking and feel. Use his power to figure things out. What could he do? What *should* he do?

There were no sparks left in his suit. Sierra's lightning bolt must have fried the sparkscube on his back. The suit's surge defenders and rubber insulation had saved him. He was lucky to even be alive. But was "lucky" the best way to describe being buried alive under a landslide? The steel armor of the suit had prevented him from being crushed, but his arms and legs were still pinned under rocks. If he tried to free them, it was likely he'd cause the rocks and boulders stacked above to flatten him, armored suit or not.

When she'd forced him to turn off the power plant, Sierra made it clear she'd beaten him. This time she hadn't stuck around to gloat, but once again, she'd beaten him. For good this time. The only question remaining was: would he die of suffocation or thirst?

He would never have imagined it but realizing and accepting he was going to die brought a calmness over him. Suddenly, he could remember only happy things. Lenerstellen celebrations with his family. Stacks of his mother's pancakes. His dad taking him into town to get new books from the library. Playing with Cassie – inside the house, of course. Feigning illness or fatigue or just hiding when his mother insisted they take their play outside. Years spent salvaging chipware and figuring out how it worked. The day it first occurred to him that the unique signal dispersal pattern of each chip contained the key to reactivating them. Meeting Siv and making a real friend for the first time in his life. Seeing Verde from space aboard Skylab. Waking up after the battle with Krulgoth, alive thanks to his new uncle, who had given up his human appearance to save him. Bringing light to his hometown's evenings. Every word of inspiration Harlan ever said to him.

And then there were his memories of Annalie. They were recent, but they were no less special. His amazement at realizing Annalie knew he'd chosen a lock code based on the circle ratio. Communicating with Felix in a non-verbal way. Working with Annalie every day for twelve days to lay the new sparksline to Earp. That purple dress she wore to the shindig celebrating the sparksline's completion. Getting Apple Juice battle-ready. Seeing her when he returned to Mondorf. Hearing she forgave him for the way he'd mistreated her.

The irony just kept coming; he'd gotten her back only to lose her again, though it was probably more accurate to say this time, she'd lost him. He wished at least his head was free of the rocks. If it were, he'd die of thirst instead of suffocation, though he supposed death also could come from exposure. He was on top of a mountain, after all, and it was late autumn, and it was night, and it would be very cold soon. But at least if his head were free, he could see the stars. He wasn't much of a stargazer, but if he saw the same stars she did, at least he'd die while having that connection with her. At least–

Click. Holy moly, what would happen if he dragged Sierra into outer space?

The night before the battle at the power plant, Annalie had said if Lady Verde won, the chipware restoration would have to move to one of the moons. The unspoken assumption was the moons would be safe because the spirit of the planet couldn't leave the planet. Since then Fritz had learned so much more about her, including her true identity, but that assumption still felt valid. So what would happen if he dragged the spirit of the planet *off* the planet?

Well, it would hurt her. Badly. Probably kill her. But could it even be done? Even though she'd buried him alive and left him to die alone, he still didn't wish her dead, but just in theory – would it work?

It wouldn't be easy, that was for sure. He'd specifically added features to his chipsuit to ensure he could survive in space, at least for a short time. He had an oxygen supply. He had protection from the vacuum. He'd found a solution to the icing problem. Except he hadn't found a solution to the "temperature reaching 3000 degrees during atmospheric reentry" problem. And he didn't know how to get Sierra up there with him. If he got close enough to grab her, she would turn to dust or water and slip away. What if he locked her in an air-tight container?

Click. Whoa, wait, if he could imprison her, he wouldn't have to hurt her. Imprisonment was a good middle ground between diplomacy and violence. It had worked against the demons. If he locked her somewhere air-tight, he could hold her indefinitely – maybe even long enough to finally talk some sense into her. It seemed like a good idea, but something bothered him about it. There was probably some flaw in it Sierra could exploit and render the imprisonment useless. There was also the whole issue of his chipsuit no longer having a power supply, and of him being buried alive under a ton of rubble.

Still – it was fun to think about. It beat thinking about dying.

At least once he was dead, he'd see Harlan and his dad again.

Wait. Just wait. Sure, he was pinned, trapped, buried, couldn't move, had no weapons, no defenses, no chipsuit-enhanced strength, no mobile to call for help, and no homing beacon to alert Annalie to his location. He was going to die trapped under these rocks sooner rather than later. So why not risk getting an arm or leg free? If he failed, he'd die by crushing instead of suffocation. What exactly did he have to lose, except several hours of suffering?

He closed his eyes and said a prayer. It felt like his right arm was pinned up to his elbow. Gently at first, he tried to pull it free. The rocks didn't budge, which was both good and bad. It was bad because he wasn't free, but it was good they didn't smash him to pulp immediately. When nothing crushed him, when it didn't sound like the rubble even shifted, he pulled harder and harder, but to no avail.

His left arm felt pinned all the way to his shoulder, but he repeated the same exercise anyway: tentative and fruitless pulling at first, followed by bolder, stronger, and still useless efforts. When both arms remained unusable, he tried his legs. He tried as hard as he could to pull his right leg free, and he yelled in alarm when there was a small shift in the rubble. But he remained trapped, and if anything, it felt as if the shifting rocks had pinned his leg tighter than before.

Well. He'd tried, but he was going to die under a pile of rubble on top of one of the Lavare Mountains. And Mom had always told him it wouldn't kill him to go outside. Ha.

At least it was better than being killed by the Celestines. He shivered and not because of the cold. While he wanted his last moments on Verde to be consumed with happy thoughts, maybe the best way to spend his remaining time was in prayer, begging God never to let them find his world. Or at the very least, to let it happen long, long after all his friends were gone.

How long did he have left? Hours? Minutes?

There was a terrible scraping of stone against stone. It was still pitch black, but he swore the rocks in front of his face shifted and moved closer to him. He screamed. Had a strong wind shifted the boulders? It whipped through the air outside his tomb. Was the whole pile about to collapse and flatten him? Was this the end?

More scraping, more shifting of rock. A blur of light – moonlight – punched through the snow covering him. The rocks shifted again. The light grew brighter. Gears and servomotors whirred and clicked. Has Gravitas returned to put him out of his misery? More light shined through the snow, then the mountain winds blew all the snow away. Fritz found himself staring up not at rocks, but at the stars, one of the moons...

And Samson?

The Steelterror Fritz had thought dead stared at him and stopped removing rubble. His arms and legs remained pinned. Samson's eyes glowed– Whoa. They weren't red. They were green, but there were disruptions in their glow. They quickly flickered to red, then back to green. The metal band wrapped around the back of Samson's head had come detached on one side. With a grunt of what sounded like annoyance, Samson ripped it off and discarded it. As soon as he'd completely removed it from his head, his eyes turned solid green, as did all of the trim lights up and down his arms and legs.

But the force of the throw seemed to take something out of him. He stumbled, grunted, then regained his balance. Was he hurt? He had to be. He'd been buried, seemingly inactive. Yet there he was, looming over Fritz. Not attacking. Not helping. Just staring.

"Hey, Samson," Fritz weakly offered in greeting.

"What is a farmer?" he said.

Fritz gasped. Samson had never spoken before. Fritz had assumed he couldn't. But he spoke perfectly. It wasn't a particularly deep voice. It wasn't all growls and snarls. It was just normal. It didn't even sound mechanical.

"What?" Fritz said. He'd heard Samson fine, but the confusion in his mind left him unable to say anything else.

"You could be a farmer. You know that?" Samson said – except he said it in Fritz's voice. It was a perfect recording of what he'd told Samson before Sierra had dug up Gravitas and brought the mountain down on both of them. "What is a farmer?" Samson repeated in his own voice.

"A farmer," Fritz said. "A farmer is someone who uses the land to grow crops. Plants. Food, usually. But also flowers for beauty. They fertilize the soil and make sure it has the nutrients it needs. They plant seeds that feed off those nutrients. They water the soil, and they make sure weeds get pulled. With your mastery of the soil and all those tools you can sprout out of your hands, you'd be a great farmer."

Samson raised his hands in front of him. His right arm had been flattened from the forearm down. He moved the fingers of his left, clearly trying to refactor his hand into a shovel or a drill or who knew what else he could change it into, but it wouldn't move. All it did was make a gooseflesh-inducing screech over the sound of gears slipping.

"I'll bet you could grow more than enough food for everyone on the whole planet," Fritz said. "You could end starvation. My dad was a farmer."

"Dad?" Samson said.

"My male parent. He was a farmer all his life. He died. He worked himself to death. He didn't mean to. But that's what happened. He might not have, though, if he'd had you to help him harvest. Not as his servant! I mean, as a friend."

"I had a dad," Samson said. "Sonne. Doctor Ada Sonne."

"A dad named Ada?" Fritz asked. "Do you mean a mom? Your creator? I thought the creator of the Stee– of the Verdant Wardens was Doctor Wilyam Albrecht?"

"Albrecht was not *my* builder," Samson said. He said it so suddenly, so harshly, Fritz would have flinched if he weren't so securely pinned. "Albrecht arrived after Doctor Sonne built me. He praised her. He smiled. He asked her to build others. And then he brought the men with the guns. Albrecht didn't want more miners. He wanted weapons."

Every Steelterror he'd seen was equipped with laser cannons and other chipware weapons, except Samson. Sure, he'd witnessed Samson do plenty of damage, but never with bombs or guns or lasers. Samson didn't have any of those things. He used the word 'miner.' What had Samson's original purpose been? Oh, he had so many questions. That metal band that had been wrapped around his head – removing it had turned his eyes and trim lights from red, like the other Steelterrors, to green. Had it been controlling him?

"Samson? Would you please get me out of here? I'm stuck."

Samson looked at him sharply, and Fritz was sure he saw the Steelterror flinch.

"I'm not going to hurt you," Fritz said. "There's no need to anymore. That band on your head made you one of them, didn't it? Now that you're yourself again, I'd like to be friends. And even if I did want to hurt you, I can't. My chipsuit is out of power. I think Sierra fried its sparkscube."

At first, Fritz wasn't sure Samson was going to do anything. But tentatively, carefully, he used his left arm to move the rubble off of Fritz. After he moved a few boulders aside, Fritz was free.

He took off his helmet. Once on his feet – oh he was *sore* – he climbed to the top of the stone heap, where he stood level with Samson's chest. A flattened right arm was the least of the Verdant Warden's troubles. He sat because his left leg had been snapped off. No wonder he'd nearly lost his balance when he'd tossed aside the controlling band. Huge pieces of his torso were gone, or broken off and sparking. And his eyes didn't glow anymore. They flickered – not between green and red, but between green and dark.

"Can you repair yourself?" Fritz asked.

Samson pointed to one of the larger dents near the middle of his chest. "My microbot cache is broken."

Fritz whistled. "OK, I don't know what a 'microbot cache' is, but you cannot just drop that kind of tantalizing jargon on me and not explain it. It sounds like something I *really* want to know about."

"Small robots – much smaller than even you," Samson said. "They work throughout my body, traveling to points of damage and making repairs."

Fritz tried to maintain his composure. "Are you saying you have robotic antibodies that heal you? Like a chipware immune system?"

Samson tilted his head. "Basically?"

Fritz pumped his fists. "That is – as Annalie would say – splendiferous! But they're broken?"

Samson nodded and lowered himself from a sitting position to laying down.

"I'm broken, too," Fritz said. He turned his back to Samson. "Can you see what's going on back there? Does my sparkscube look damaged?"

"Is it supposed to be black and burnt?"

Fritz sighed. "No. I was right. Sierra fried it. Now all I'm wearing is a suit of not-so-shining armor." Think, Fritz, think. He had to get to Harbrucken. Banshee was there. The fire Steelterror was there, possibly dug up and alive again by now. And Sierra and Gravitas were on their way there. It wasn't just his friends who would die trying to fight against those odds. Everyone in Harbrucken would die. He couldn't allow that to happen.

But even if *he* couldn't get back to Harbrucken, maybe someone else could. Someone else who had no love for the Steelterrors.

"Samson, I have some tools in my suit," Fritz said. "Tell me what I need to do to fix you."

Samson's eyes had gone dark, but they flickered back to light for just a moment. "I can't remain active," he said.

"Come on," Fritz said. "At least one of us has to get to Harbrucken and stop Sierra and her Steelterrors."

"I'm done being a weapon."

"You're done being *Sierra's* weapon," Fritz said. "And I don't blame you for not wanting to fight. I *hate* fighting. But some things are worth fighting for. Things like the right to be a farmer."

Samson looked at him for a long time. Occasionally, his eyes managed to glow again. Servomotors clearly not in fine-tuned operation rattled and creaked somewhere inside of him. "To be a farmer, I would," Samson said. "But I can't."

Fritz hung his head. Samson fingered a line in his chest, and after a moment's struggle, he managed to open a compartment there. The moons above only gave off so much light, so Fritz had to take several steps closer to him to see what was inside. He didn't recognize much of it, but he saw circuit boards, chips, wiring, and a sparkscube – a 345-volt sparkscube, just like the one on his back. This one, however, was bright yellow and didn't have a single scorch mark.

Samson's fingers moved towards it.

"What are you doing?" Fritz asked.

"You said at least one of us has to stop them."

"Don't you need that?"

Samson shook his head. "In forty seconds, no, I will not."

Fritz shook his head, his jaw hanging slack. "No. Samson, I... I don't know what to say."

"Say you'll stop Albrecht's creations," Samson said, "and the one who killed Doctor Sonne."

Fritz swallowed hard. "Thank you. Thank you so much."

"I wish I could see the look on Albrecht's face when he is destroyed," Samson said.

The look on *Albrecht's* face? "He's still alive?" Fritz said.

"He's Gravitas."

Fritz tried three or four times to start a sentence.

"Gravitas's neural code was patterned on Albrecht's," Samson said. "Having weapons wasn't enough for him. Albrecht wanted to *be* a weapon."

"He transferred his mind into a machine? Is that even possible?"

"Not a transfer, a copy," Samson said. "Albrecht's thoughts and memories formed the template of Gravitas's neural net so that his mind might live on after his body died. And when Doctor Sonne tried to stop him..."

Samson was the greatest source of pre-Blackout chipware information he'd ever encountered. The things he'd learned in just this brief conversation... And Samson was dying. It wasn't fair. It was so *not fair*.

"Break... them... all..." Samson said, his words drawn out, his voice's pitch sinking deeper.

"I'll try," Fritz said. "And when I stop them..." He shrugged. "*If I stop them, I'll come back for you. I'll fix you. I'll help you become a farmer, just like Doctor Sonne would want you to be.*"

Samson leaned forward as best he could, which wasn't much. Something in the way he moved made Fritz feel like he'd smile if he was physically capable of it. "You remind me of her," he said.

Fritz thought that was maybe the best compliment he'd ever received.

Samson yanked the sparkscube out of his chest, set it on the rock where Fritz stood, and collapsed to the ground with so much force Fritz feared another landslide. His busted gears stopped slipping. His broken servomotors stopped spinning. The green lights in his eyes stopped flickering and dimmed.

Fritz took off his glasses and covered his face with his hands. He almost made the Sign of God's Hand in blessing over Samson's body, but he stopped himself. Not because Samson was a supposedly soulless machine, but because it would be wildly inappropriate to bless the sleeping giant as if he were dead. He wasn't. He *was not!* He was just hurt. Comatose. And after Fritz put an end to the Steelterrors, he was going to do what he promised. He was going to come back here, and he was going to fix Samson. He'd already lost one farmer he cared about. He would *not* lose a second one.

"Good night, Samson," Fritz said, wiping his eyes and his nose. "You get some good sleep."

```
[1879-11-18 17:44] root@skylab:/bin > ALERT on
stationBroadcast0
Arrival calc reports ETA 1879-12-9 0843

[1879-11-18 17:47] root@skylab:/bin > .\servbot --
report
Job "Left Arm 1" complete as of 17:46
Job "Optic Array Final Test" complete as of 17:46
- 356/356 tests passed
Job "Duranium Sheeting Final Phase" complete as of
17:45

[1879-11-18 17:47] root@skylab:/bin > .\servbot --
startJob "Final Assembly" --all --now
All available Servbots will begin job "Final
Assembly" immediately

[1879-11-18 17:49] root@skylab:/bin > ALERT on
stationBroadcast0
Arrival calc reports ETA 1879-12-9 0843

[1879-11-18 17:52] root@skylab:/bin > .\servbot --
command "Prep pod for launch"
Parsing command....
A Servbot will immediately begin prepping the launch
of a pod to the surface. If this was not the
intended command, run "servbot --cancel 1039"

[1879-11-18 17:54] root@skylab:/bin > ALERT on
stationBroadcast0
Arrival calc reports ETA 1879-12-9 0843
```

Chapter Twenty-Two

Samson was soil, Leviathan was water, Banshee was air, and Teufel was fire. Wasn't that all four elements of the ancient world?

"Leave these Mantissa to me, Teufel," Gravitas said. "Go burn this city to the ground."

"*Wooooooo!*" Teufel said. He sank below the roof and moved away from them, off to burn more businesses and homes and people.

Gravitas raised his right palm towards them. Its center glowed with red light. "Bow," he said, and Cassie suddenly felt so heavy, she fell first to her knees, then flat on her face. The same force slammed down Siv and Sebastian. Cassie grit her teeth under the pressure. Gravity. This one's power was gravity.

"Feels like a horse sitting on me," Siv grunted.

"Too much for you?" Gravitas asked. He lowered his right palm and raised his left, which also glowed at its center. The invisible weight pinning Cassie to the roof went away, but so did normal gravity. She, Siv, and Sebastian floated an inch above the roof and slowly ascended even higher. Apparently, Gravitas's right hand increased gravity, and his left hand decreased it.

He pointed his right hand at the apartment building's foundation. The roof – and the rest of the building – shook. Rock and concrete rumbled like thunder, and the building fell away underneath them, crumbling under its own increased weight. Gravitas moved his left hand aside. Now in a field of increased gravity, Cassie, Siv, and Sebastian didn't just fall; Gravitas's power *pulled* them towards the ground three stories. Before their bodies cracked like eggs, they each managed to grab a hold on the adjacent building with their grapple lines and lower themselves to the street safely.

It was hard to see through the cloud of dust and debris stirred up by the apartment building's collapse, but the sixty-foot-tall Steelterror looming above them was impossible to miss. Sebastian and Siv fired at Gravitas's chest, but the Steelterror practically paid no heed to the damage. He pointed his right hand at the building opposite them. It practically exploded into powder. Gravitas pointed his left palm at the rubble of the three buildings he'd collapsed, and a cloud of wood, glass, metal, and concrete debris swirled into the air.

Warned by her danger sense, Cassie grabbed Siv and raced to the sidewalk. Sebastian also leaped from harm's way but to the opposite side of the street. Gravitas pushed his right hand towards the debris cloud and hurled it towards them. It was like a stampede of deadly projectiles – some bullet-sized, some cannon-sized. Cassie and Siv took cover inside a furniture store just before the detritus tore through everything on the street – carriages, hitching posts, gas lamps, wooden sidewalks, and porches. Thank God the street had been clear of people and horses; they'd already fled in panic.

Something hit the wide window at the front of the store, and shattered glass showered the showroom. The terrified shopkeeper lifted his head up from behind the cash register. "Is this the end times?" he shouted over the noise.

Cassie almost told him no, it was just a set of ancient robots hellbent on making steel the dominant life form on the planet. But calling it the end times was easier, simpler, and basically accurate. "Is there a back door?" she said.

The man seemed to nod, but he may have just been trembling.

"Get out!" Siv shouted at him. He obeyed.

When the tornado of rubble died down outside, Cassie looked to the other side of the street. "Where's Sebastian?" she said. "We lost him!"

An enormous sword made of blazing red energy slammed down through the middle of the shop's ceiling. Its deep, loud buzzing stabbed Cassie's ears. Dust and splinters swarmed like bees. Chunks of ceiling landed on the store's chairs and tables and sofas, smashing them to pieces. At twelve feet across, the sword took up nearly half the room's width; luckily, it was the half of the room she and Siv weren't in. Gravitas's foot stomped on the sidewalk outside the empty window pane, and he pulled the sword toward him through the front of the store.

Cassie felt like she'd suddenly gained a few hundred pounds. She and Siv fell flat on their backs. Cracks appeared in the parts of the ceiling still intact. Support beams groaned under the strain of increased gravity.

Siv shot his grapple into the store's back wall, and Cassie copied him. Their retracting lines pulled them across the floor, though not nearly as fast as they would have in normal gravity. The ceiling collapsed before they were entirely out of harm's way. Cassie saw a flash of red in her mind but couldn't get her extra heavy leg out of the way of a falling joist. It landed on her ankle and snapped the bone. A pile of rubble filled the center of the shop.

Siv helped her stand on her one good foot and put her arm around his shoulders. Their slide had taken them out of the field of increased gravity. "Can you heal?" he asked.

"Working on it." She gritted her teeth and breathed through the pain in short gasps.

They retreated through the same back door the shopkeeper had used, but when they reached the alley outside, bricks at the top of the building pulled loose from the mortar and rose into the air. Hundreds of bricks floated above the store, and the speed of their ascent quickened. Soon every brick that had made up the furniture store had soared into the air as if summoned to heaven.

Then nothing but that swarm of floating bricks was between them and Gravitas. He tilted his left hand towards them, and they ascended with the bricks until they hovered some thirty feet in the air. Behind Gravitas, Banshee zoomed over the western part of town. More bombs destroyed how many more homes, hurt how many more people, killed how many more children? Annalie and her aerocopter wouldn't be able to rescue them all.

Gravitas moved his hand, and she and Siv twisted around in the air to face north. Fire raged across a mile of the city. At the front of the fire was Teufel. He was only blocks away from the university – her school! The orange glow of the fires illuminated the night. The dark cloud of smoke hanging over the city blocked out the stars.

The gravity-controlling Steelterror spun them around to face him. "Your city will fall," he said, "because it does not deserve to stand. Only the fittest survive, and steel is far stronger than flesh."

His right hand withdrew his sword's hilt from a compartment in his forearm. He ignited its blade, which was half as tall as he was, and brought it to bear before him.

Cassie pulled a bomb arrow from her quiver, nocked it in her bow, and aimed for the spot right between Gravitas's eyes. He grinned at her, daring her to shoot. Out of the corner of her eye, she spotted a hole in the curb of the street below – a storm drain leading down to the sewer system. Suddenly she didn't feel so hopeless. After all, indoor plumbing was one of her favorite parts of living in Harbrucken.

She nudged Siv's arm and cocked her head towards a pole-mounted stop sign not far from the storm drain. "Grab me and pull us down to that sign." He wrapped one arm around her waist and aimed his grapple gun with the other.

Gravitas raised his sword above his head, preparing to strike. Cassie pointed her arrow at the storm drain and fired. Siv launched his grapple. Arrow and grapple traveled roughly parallel to one another through the air. Her arrow exploded against the storm drain. His grapple wrapped around the sign pole and pulled them down towards it. Everything – the arrow, the grapple, themselves – moved much faster than normal due to the field of reduced gravity.

With a roar, Gravitas swung his sword through the air where they'd just been floating. A handful of the floating bricks shattered. Cassie and Siv landed on the street and jumped into the hole she had blown in the curb. The sewer consisted of a round, metal tunnel roughly ten feet across and running parallel to the street above. It was dark; barely any moonlight reached the area. An inch and a half of foul-smelling water lined the bottom of the tunnel.

"Run!" Cassie ordered Siv. Her ankle had healed enough to join him.

A cacophony of shattering stone behind them told her Gravitas must have let the floating bricks of the furniture store crash down to the street. They had only retreated about ten feet from their point of entry into the sewer when the street behind them collapsed. Heaps of dirt and chunks of concrete curb splashed into the filthy water and echoed loudly off the metal tunnel. Then a second wide section of the street collapsed behind them. Dust stirred up by the destruction clouded the path ahead, but Cassie didn't stop.

"We can't outrun him, Cass," Siv said. "He's gonna bring the street down on us."

Cassie – and her danger sense – did not disagree.

"We have to get back up there," Siv said. "We're going to cash in if we stick around down here. We have to get out of the city."

There were four or five high-pitched screeches – they ran together so quickly, it was hard to tell exactly how many. But each one ended with a *boom* and with the ground shaking underneath them. Banshee had bombed the city, again. Teufel was still out there, too, setting everything he touched ablaze. And Gravitas was about to flatten her and Siv even if it meant tearing the entire neighborhood apart to reach them. How much of Harbrucken was even still standing?

"We can't leave," Cassie said. "It's a massacre out there. We're Mantissa. We have to help."

"There's no shame in us *not* being two of the massacred," Siv said. "Especially if we're running to get away and make a plan for how to come back and kick their–"

Danger! Cassie reached back, grabbed Siv's wrist, and tossed him in front of her, just as another section of the street collapsed behind them. Gravitas stood over the chasm he'd created in the road, his crackling, buzzing sword bathing his self-righteous face in a blood-red glow.

Siv got to his feet and gently pulled her elbow, urging her to continue running up the underground tunnel. Her danger sense similarly screamed at her to go, go, *go*. But it was useless. They couldn't outrun a sixty-foot-tall steel giant who commanded the powers of gravity and who was determined to see them dead. And they couldn't defeat him. This was it. The end. Or the beginning, depending on your theological perspective.

She found Siv's hand and squeezed it tightly, both to be close to him in their final moments, and also to steady her own. Her refusal to acknowledge her danger sense's urgings to flee caused her entire body to shake.

Gravitas raised his sword. He held it in his left hand. He pointed the palm of his right hand straight at them. Which would he do first – cleave them or crush them?

Cassie's shaking stopped abruptly. The danger screaming in her mind dissolved into calm. Great! But why? Gravitas was still poised to strike.

A volley of twenty laser blasts pounded Gravitas's back. For a moment, Cassie thought Sebastian had come to their rescue, but these blasts made the ones from his laser rifles look like spitballs. And they *hurt* the giant son of a gun. He convulsed under the assault until something crashed into him from behind and forced him to the ground. He dropped his sword, and its energy blade extinguished, leaving only the hilt to bounce and rattle down the road. He smashed through three parked carriages and slid for half a block with his face in the dirt before he came to a stop.

Fritz, clad in a suit of flying chipware armor, rose off the Steelterror and hovered thirty feet above him. In rapid succession, he fired three bombs from the launcher on his shoulder. Sparks and shrapnel exploded from the back of Gravitas's head. The Steelterror stopped moving, and his trim lights dimmed. Fritz flew higher, and the normally quiet voice of her socially awkward brother boomed both in confidence and in chipware-enhanced volume.

"People of Harbrucken, my name is Fritz Reinhardt. I am the leader of the Mantissa Reborn. Be not afraid. This city will be defended!"

Chapter Twenty-Three

Fritz flew over pure chaos. Every building in the city seemed to have at least one shattered window; some didn't have any glass intact. Overturned carriages, carts, and other debris littered the streets. Every breath carried the smell of burning. What happened in Earp was happening all over again, a thousand times worse. Fritz's throat threatened to close; his fingers went numb.

They'd found an abandoned carriage with three of its wheels busted. Siv and Cassie climbed onto its seat. Using his chipsuit's enhanced strength and grapple lines, Fritz carried it dangling beneath him as he flew. "Annalie said she'd lost contact with you," Cassie called up to him.

"I had a bit of technical difficulty," he said. "Got hit by lightning. Kind of fried my mobile."

"Beg pardon," Siv said. "I'm going deaf from all this hellabaloo. I thought you said '*lightning*'?"

After flying about a quarter mile, the three of them spotted Sebastian and touched down in front of a saloon. Siv and Cassie climbed off the carriage, and the four of them convened in the middle of the dirt road. "You all right?" Sebastian asked Fritz.

"Everything is everything," he said, lifting his visor and exposing his face. Across the street, a man approached a shop window and raised a foot-long piece of pipe towards it. Fritz blasted his mind using the Mantissa reader power emulator. The pipe clanged to the ground, and the man clutched the sides of his head, stumbling away with a splitting headache.

"Annalie?" Cassie said, her fingers pressed against her mobile's earpiece. "He's here. He's fine. His mobile was damaged."

"I have a simple radio broadcaster and receiver built into my suit," Fritz said. "If I adjust the frequency, I should be able to join in, as long as we're within a couple of miles of one another." He made the configuration change and his helmet filled with the sound of aerocopter blades. "Annalie?"

"You're alive!" she squealed.

He was fairly excited about that, too, which was a pleasant change. "You OK?" he said. "You're rescuing people?"

Her voice went softer as if she'd turned away from her microphone. "Get in! I'll get you away from the fire. All of you. That's it. You're welcome. Oh, this old thing? Just found it somewhere. Take a seat, and hold on!" The volume of her voice increased. "Yeah, I am. But not enough. This is bad. I ain't even nightmared anything this bad, and I saw Earp get ripped apart."

Distant gunshots echoed. A child screamed for her mother. Every time Fritz blinked, he saw Earp, too.

"Your *power* really told you to torque off Sierra? And cause all of this?" Cassie asked. "You know I'd do anything to make you happy, but if this is the cost of bringing back your project..."

"This isn't about my project," he said. "I get that now. Before he died, Harlan tried to teach me this is all about an idea. The chipware restoration will be a great thing, and it will improve life in so many ways. But it's just a means to an end. The first step towards a much greater goal – a much greater world. A world without misery. Without pain. Without fighting. Tomorrow can be better than today! Mistakes can be opportunities for learning, not blame. No one has to be hungry, sick, poor, downtrodden, or ignorant ever again. We can forgive one another. We can forgive ourselves. This is about *hope*, guys! It's still time to change the world, but in ways far greater than we ever imagined.

"I don't have all the answers. I don't know everything we have to do to get there. But I do know it starts by taking a stand here. Sierra is wrong. We're not trying to rebuild the past. We're trying to build a better future – for the planet *and* her people. That's worth fighting for, isn't it?"

"Reckon so," Annalie said over the radio.

"Yes, sir," Sebastian said.

"Amen," Siv said.

But Cassie just grimaced at the destruction surrounding them.

"Hey, sis," Fritz said, "there are some scars on my arm I just don't need anymore. Could you help me with that?"

A smile slowly fought its way onto her lips. She reached past his open visor to gently touch his cheek. He felt a tingling sensation in his forearms, and he knew the remnants of his self-inflicted wounds were disappearing. "We can heal the scars of the whole world," Fritz said, looking her straight in the eye. "The five of us. Look beyond. A revival is coming."

"Of what?"

"Of everything."

And she believed him. A steel came into her eyes, a look Fritz knew well. Cassandra Reinhardt had settled on a course of action. Neither hell nor high water – nor Steelterrors, nor a deranged, nearly all-powerful Mantissa – would keep her from it.

"What do we do, fearless leader?" Siv said.

"We destroy the Steelterrors," Fritz said. "Samson won't be here, Leviathan and Gravitas are already taken care of, and I have a trick in mind I think will work on Banshee. But I haven't even seen the fire one yet, so I don't have any ideas there."

"On your way into town, did you see the wave of lava washing over the city and heading north towards the university?" Cassie said.

"That was his work?" Fritz said.

"That was *him*," Cassie said. "Teufel. Fire and steel make liquid metal."

Oh. That made a certain amount of sense. Of *course* a fire Steelterror would be made out of superheated, liquid metal. Kind of brilliant, actually, if it wasn't so murdery.

"Wipe the smirk off your face," Sebastian said, "and admire the chipware later."

"Right," Fritz said. "The fire one may be a little tough. At that high a temperature, lasers, explosives, all of our best weapons will be pretty much useless against it."

"In my shop back home, I cool off metal in a quenching bucket," Siv said. "What if we lure Teufel to the river?"

Sebastian snapped his fingers. "That's it," he said. "I don't know that we can drag him into the Elde, but that does give me an idea. Good thinking, McCaig. Let Cassie and I handle Teufel."

"Sure," Cassie said.

"Siv and I will go after Banshee then," Fritz said. "Let's go."

"Wait," Sebastian said. "Siv said you want to talk with Sierra. Just in case that doesn't work, has your power given you any ideas about how to fight her?"

"We'd have to contain her," Fritz said. "Hold her prisoner until she hears me out. Maybe some kind of air-tight, water-tight compartment could hold her, but I don't know. I think there's something I'm missing. But it works in theory."

"And if you do contain her, and if she won't change her mind?" Sebastian said. "Let me be blunt. We need a way to kill her."

"I won't do that!" Fritz said. "She was once a person."

"I don't want it to come to that either," Sebastian said. "But what if she forces the issue? What if she makes it her or us? What if it's her or this whole town?"

Fritz exhaled. "Well. If we could get her into outer space, I'm fairly certain it would kill her."

"Separate the spirit of the planet from the planet," Cassie said.

"Could we use a teleporter for that?" Sebastian asked.

"We'd have to," Fritz said. "My chipsuit has enough power and oxygen to get into space, but not enough heat shielding to get back down, and we don't have a spaceship. But it will *not* come to that. It can't. She *has* to listen to me."

Sebastian gave him a strange look. "I wish Eroica could see this," he grumbled. "You're so much like Joseph it's scary."

"Who?"

"Joseph. My brother-in-law. Your ancestor. The reason you call me your uncle. The one Mantissa Sierra never managed to alienate. His friendship with Sierra was as baffling to me two centuries ago as your plan to reason with her is now. But I admit: he had a positive effect on her. When Salzhausen was flooded by torrential rains, she stopped the storms and used her power to create makeshift canals to drain away the flood waters. Then she and Joseph saved hundreds of homes and rescued thousands of stranded people, many of whom would have died without their help."

Fritz couldn't believe what he was hearing. The fact that Sierra's only Mantissa friend was his ancestor, Joseph Reinhardt, felt like important data to Fritz, but much like the realization that she could be anywhere but not everywhere, he wasn't certain what to do with it yet. "Wow," he finally managed to say.

"I still don't think she's going to have a friendly chat with you even if you sing her every verse of scripture in a baritone that makes the angels in heaven weep," Sebastian said. "But if anyone still breathing can get through to her, I think you can."

The moment was interrupted as, some miles away, Banshee screamed through the air and dropped more bombs on more people. "I need to go stop that. Siv, we're going to the university."

Siv nodded, wrapped his arm around Cassie's shoulder, and pulled her into a kiss. "Come back to me," he said.

"Always," Cassie said.

Sebastian and Cassie ran north, used their grapples to reach a rooftop, and disappeared from sight. Siv hopped into the broken carriage, Fritz tethered himself to it with his grapple lines, and the two of them took to the sky.

"What's the plan, Professor?" Siv said.

"Remember the satellite dishes at the university?" Fritz said. "They just collect rainwater now, but they used to communicate with Skylab and other orbiting satellites. We're going to give one of them some sparks, hook up my descrambler to it, and broadcast the Blackout signal."

"That gonna work against Steelterrors?"

"It was *made* to work against them," Fritz said. "Eroica told us so the day we first met her. The satellites transmit in a straight line, so we can't take out Banshee and Teufel at once the way the Blackout killed everything simultaneously. But if we shoot the signal into the sky, and if I bait Banshee into flying through it, we'll end her."

"What if it hits you? Won't it scramble your suit?"

"I put defenses in my suit specifically to protect it from the Blackout. It should be safe."

"Should?"

Fritz shrugged. "I never got a chance to test it. But in theory..."

They zoomed over the city as low as possible to reduce the chance of being spotted by Banshee until they were ready to deal with her. Approaching university grounds, nearly every building burned, and Teufel himself came into view. The rolling wave of living liquid metal was both awe-inspiring and terrifying, but Fritz was relieved to find he hadn't yet touched the courtyard containing the satellite dishes and he didn't appear headed towards them either. All five of the satellites looked physically intact, though fires burned as close as two blocks away. Fritz lowered the carriage to the ground, and he and Siv examined the biggest dish.

"This one was the most powerful of them," Fritz said. "They've probably severely degraded in effectiveness over two hundred years of non-use, but I don't need to send the signal into space. I just need to send it as high into the air as I can."

He opened a compartment in the upper arm of his chipsuit and took out his original descrambler – the mechanical one in a wooden casing. After adjusting the dials on its face, he handed it to Siv. "Wire that into the dish, please."

"What's our spark source?" Siv said. "You got a battery?"

Fritz shifted uncomfortably. "No. Not exactly. But your laser rifle's ammunition clip is a battery. It can power the dish. Though, umm, that will render your rifle a little useless."

Siv raised an eyebrow. "Oh. Well, thank God it will only be a *little* useless without ammo, as opposed to *completely* useless."

Fritz shrugged. "Sorry?"

Siv popped the energy clip out of his rifle and crawled underneath the largest of the five satellite dishes. "I'll manage. I like my sword better anyway, and at least I won't be the one playing rodeo clown with that steel bull up in the air."

"Rodeo clown, that's a good one," Fritz said with a laugh. "Because I'm going to distract the bull while you work to defeat it. Appropriate analogy."

"Rodeo clowns get gored, Professor."

"Yeah. Trying not to think about that part."

More high-pitched screeches and thunderous explosions marked another of Banshee's bombing runs.

"I'll be ready," Siv said. "Go get her."

Fritz engaged his rockets and ascended high into the sky. Banshee was about a mile away in her jet form, but her red running lights and the laser blasts with which she pelted the surface made her easy to spot even in the darkness of night. He sped towards her and cranked the volume of his external audio to full.

"Hey, Banshee!" he said. He pointed his left arm and fired several blasts from his laser cannons even though Banshee was out of his range – just to get her attention. It worked. Banshee veered straight towards him and increased her speed dramatically.

Fritz turned tail and hauled his rear end away from her. She fired at him. Red laser blasts flew past underneath him and above him, but *far* too close for comfort. He rotated to the right into an aileron roll, hoping to shake her off, but she stayed behind him and kept shooting.

She was faster, and she outgunned him, but he was much smaller so he should be more maneuverable. He dived straight down. Banshee followed. Once she was on his tail again, he tucked and rolled into an upward ascending position; then he gunned his rockets. The suddenness and sharpness of the maneuver left him light-headed, but Banshee was no longer on his tail. He'd left her in his contrails. A jet's size and aerodynamics rendered it incapable of making the same turn as suddenly as he had.

But Banshee wasn't just a jet. Still flying straight towards the ground, she refactored into her robot form, mimicked Fritz's maneuver, and refactored back into a jet. And just like that, she was right back behind him and firing on him again.

Blast it, but what had he expected? That after a few hours' worth of practice flights, he could outfly the Verdant Warden of Air? This wasn't a race, though. It wasn't even a fight. He didn't have to outfly Banshee; he just had to distract her long enough for Siv to pump the Blackout signal through the satellite dish, then lure her into its transmission zone. That meant this was nothing but an exercise in self-defense, and one of the most basic self-defense techniques Sebastian had taught him was: you run from a knife, and you charge a gun. Banshee was a gun – an enormously powerful, extremely fast gun, true. But a gun nevertheless.

So instead of running, maybe he needed to charge straight towards her?

He was a hundred yards away from flying right over the largest dish in the satellite farm. Though Banshee was still right behind him, he turned off his rockets, braked with his thrusters, and held his position in a mid-air hover. Banshee refactored into her robot form but didn't slow down. There was no way she could stop before colliding with him, and she wasn't veering out of the way. Why should she? She was nine times his size. His heads-up display filled with bright red warnings of an imminent crash.

With a silent prayer, he redirected all the power of the sparkscube Samson had given him into his suit's energy barrier. So much light surrounded him, he must have looked like a blue version of the frozen star to folks on the ground. He had one shot at this. It either worked, or he died.

Banshee rammed into his force field. Metal wrenched and screeched in agony. Shrapnel sprinkled the sky like stardust. Nuts and bolts dropped like hail. His force field flashed brilliant white before breaking apart into crackling and static.

The collision hadn't pulverized him. He and Banshee both hovered in place. He was fine – oh wow, *he was fine!* But she wasn't. The engines on her back kept her hovering in the air inches before Fritz, but her chest was bashed and smashed, and her abdomen had been obliterated. It was just gone. The collision had ripped her in two, and only her upper half remained. She was disoriented, and sparks crackled around her. Viscous blue fluid gushed down her face from the sides of her mouth.

And they were right above the main satellite! The impact had pushed them right into its transmission zone.

Except, no transmission. No Blackout. Banshee was critically wounded, but alive.

"Siv?" Fritz said over the voice-comm. Had Banshee's severed legs fallen on top of Siv? He looked down, and no – thank God – the legs had landed in the grass and on a dirt road. They had *not* smashed into the satellite Siv was working underneath, the one Gravitas was standing beside.

Turning back–

Gravitas?

Gravitas was still alive?!

Enraged, Gravitas swung a massive red energy sword and chopped a third of the satellite dish clean off.

Chapter Twenty-Four

After all the world's chipware fried in the Blackout, physical infrastructure remained intact. People could still walk on the roads. Four walls and a roof still provided shelter from the rain. And although chipware pumps, contaminant filtering systems, and pressure regulators were useless, the geniuses who taught and studied in the university's engineering department realized that with sufficient gravity-provided water pressure, the plumbing system was salvageable. Sinks could run, and toilets could flush just as they had before the world got sent back to the dark ages.

Therefore, the city of Harbrucken had built a water tower.

"Indoor plumbing is one of my favorite parts of living here," Cassie said.

"Siv's the one who said to drop Teufel into a quenching bucket," Sebastian said. "Dragging him down into the river isn't feasible, but–"

"But if we lure him to us," Cassie said, "we can dump the quenching bucket onto him."

Emptying the water tower of the darn near a million gallons of water inside it would shut down the city's indoor plumbing system, and it would likely create a drinking water shortage and messy sanitation problems. But it would stop Teufel from burning more of the city and killing more people. They hoped.

"Let's call in air support," Sebastian said.

Cassie tapped her mobile's earpiece. "Annalie?"

"You'll be fine," Annalie said, apparently to someone in her aerocopter with her. "I'm going to drop you off well away from the fire. Cassie, that you?"

"We need some help," Cassie said. "We need to get to the top of the city's water tower. We're a block away from it, but we can't reach it. We're cut off by fires."

"You say you need to get to the top?"

"We're going to dump the tower's water onto Teufel."

"Daisy," Annalie said. "I have a full boat here. I'll drop these people off, then come get you."

"See you soon," Cassie said. She disconnected her mobile from the voice-comm, then spun around, sensing danger behind her. So did Sebastian.

"Omar!" Teufel's high-pitched voice squealed. "I found them. I told you I felt the tingle-tingle of comm frequencies. I may be crazy, but I'm not *stuuuuupid.*"

Two blocks down the street behind them, a hill of lava raised itself above the buildings. Teufel's red metal head floated at the top. The lava surged into and through a building and flowed straight towards them. Teufel's head rode it down like a toboggan drifting on fresh snow.

Sebastian's translator changed one of his barks into a short, clipped curse word.

"Gravitas said to burn the city," Teufel said. "That he'd kill the Mantissa. But if the Mantissa are in the city, and I burn the city, then the hamster barks at yesterday. My logic is flawless! I'm sane after all!"

They were unable to reach the base of the water tower because the buildings surrounding it – university offices and classroom buildings – were consumed with flames. Munn Hall, which housed the university's school of engineering, had already collapsed. Fires raged everywhere around them, except the direction from which they'd arrived, which was where Teufel's liquid metal mass undulated towards them, blocking any retreat. Up? There were no buildings they could grapple onto within range. If there were, they wouldn't have needed Annalie to give them a lift. And they couldn't go down because there was no storm drains and no utility access holes in the area. No visible evidence of the sewer system meant even if she used a bomb arrow to make an entrance, there could be nothing but dirt and limestone underneath this section of the street.

Sebastian examined the wall of fire burning between them and the water tower with a strange mix of emotions on his face: afraid, hopeful, uncertain. All four of his hands shook, just noticeably. Was he afraid? Or ignoring the call of his danger sense? They stood right next to each other. If there was pending danger, she should be able to feel it, too, but she didn't sense–

No.

He wouldn't even consider it, would he?

"We can't," she said.

"It will hurt like all hell," Sebastian said, "but we'll heal."

"Maybe you would," Cassie said. "*Maybe.* You're wearing a fireproof Mantissa suit. And your healer powers are supercharged, cranked up to fifteen through Krulgoth's genetic engineering."

"My power can heal us both."

"We can't run through that much fire! Those are ten foot high flames. They're so hot, even the street is on fire. We'd have to run through as much as two hundred feet worth of hell before we'd be in grapple range."

"That sounds about right," Sebastian said.

Cassie threw her hands in the air. Why was he still considering this madness?

"Teufel will be here long before Annalie will," Sebastian said.

As if on cue, Teufel smashed through another building. Only one more stood between him and them. At least they didn't have to figure out how to lure him underneath the water tower...

"I know it's the craziest idea you've ever heard," Sebastian said.

Cassie sighed. Her body began trembling, too. "No. Craziest thing I've ever heard is letting that thing keep killing people." She ripped a strip of fabric off the tail of her shirt and wrapped it around her head, over her mouth.

"Speed will be the most important thing," Sebastian said. "Don't worry about anything else. Just run and don't stop."

Cassie bit the side of her mouth and looked into the fire. She nodded. "Is your mobile disconnected from everyone else?"

"Yeah," Sebastian said.

"Good. Keep it that way. I don't want Siv to hear us."

The look Sebastian gave her said he understood perfectly. She didn't want her fiance to hear her screaming in agony from her burns, even if she did end up being able to heal herself after some length of excruciating time. And that could only happen *if* she managed to get out of the fire alive. Fire she was about to *voluntarily* run through because it was better than being killed by Teufel and because it was their only shot at destroying that infernal machine.

Sebastian took off his translator device and secured it inside a zipped cargo pouch on his sleeve. Teufel crashed through the last building. He was sixty feet away from them, with nothing in front of him but wide open pavement.

Cassie made the Sign of God's Hand. "Let's go."

She and Sebastian jumped into the fire.

Fritz instructed his chipsuit to enhance visual magnification. Gravitas still had the hole Fritz's bombs had blasted into the back of his head, but bits of metal rapidly filled it. His microbot cache was repairing him.

That was a big problem, but Fritz couldn't deal with it yet. He had to keep what was left of Banshee in position over the satellite to buy Siv more time to transmit the Blackout signal – if Siv was even still alive, since he'd been working under the satellite dish when Gravitas had cut it apart. He extended his laser-enhanced knives – the ones he'd used to sever Leviathan's tentacles – from their wrist mounts and sank them down to their hilts into Banshee's bashed-up chest. When she tried to fly away, if she even could, he'd burn his rockets in the opposite direction and hope he could hold her in place for as long as he had to.

"You're not going anywhere," Fritz told her.

Banshee blinked, and her disorientation faded. "No, I'm not," she said, spewing blue fluid from her mouth and seizing him in one of her massive metal hands. "Not until I've squeezed you dry, blood bag."

What little of his force-field that still functioned prevented her from crushing him, but the field sparked and sputtered, and he feared it could die completely at any time. "Siv?" Fritz yelled over the voice-comm.

The voice-comm filled with the sound of Siv spouting expletives left and right.

"Just get out of there!" Fritz said.

Gravitas raised his energy sword for another cut.

Banshee hollered in rage and squeezed tighter. His force field system blared an alarm in protest, then died completely.

But so did Banshee's yell and the roar of her rockets. The light in her eyes extinguished. Her head and arms went limp. Siv had done it! He'd transmitted the signal straight up into the sky. They'd blacked out Banshee!

The Sky Steelterror plummeted from her domain. Fritz tilted away from her, and though he'd trashed his force field, the rest of his suit worked just fine. He gunned his rockets to maximum, and flew with trails of fire blazing behind him towards the place he'd last seen Siv.

A grapple line flew out from underneath the main satellite dish parallel to the ground and caught on the base of one of the other four satellites nearby. Gravitas swung his sword downward with massive machine-powered force. Siv slid out from beneath the dish like a shot out of a gun, his grapple gun dragging him to safety. Gravitas shattered the remains of the main dish into pieces, and since he still functioned, he'd apparently done it without the Blackout signal hitting him in the process. Darn.

Fritz landed next to the satellite dish Siv crouched beneath. He offered his friend a hand. The two of them scrambled away together.

Gravitas looked up just before Banshee's dead body landed on him like twenty tons of bricks. He raised his left hand towards her, and her corpse hovered in place a few feet above him. Fritz couldn't help but admire the chipware producing the quick range of emotions that cycled across Gravitas's face: confusion, shock, sadness, and *lots* of anger. He roared, extinguished and dropped his sword, and hurled Banshee's corpse through the air straight at Fritz and Siv, propelled by the increased gravity he generated. Fritz threw his arms around Siv's waist and rocketed into the air. Banshee's body landed in another satellite dish, which shattered upon impact.

About fifty feet away, Fritz put Siv on the ground, then flew away in the opposite direction, luring Gravitas away from his friend while also trying to keep ahead of the increased gravity field the Steelterror created. While dodging, he fired both his laser cannons at Gravitas's head and neck.

"Playing rodeo clown worked pretty well against Banshee," Fritz said. "I'll keep his attention. You attack him from behind, and focus on his right shoulder."

"Hack off his gravity-increasing hand," Siv said.

"If we can disarm him of that weapon – and that pun wasn't intended, sorry, I don't mean to make light of–"

"Keep moving!"

Fritz weaved through the air, faked right, flew left. Gravitas tracked his every move, turning at the waist, and kept his arms pointed towards Fritz. Each step he took across the university grounds shook buildings. Fritz stayed ahead of the Steelterror, but there was a flaw in their plan. If he was a moving target for Gravitas, then Gravitas was a moving target for Siv. Fritz had to make it as easy as possible for Siv to slash away at Gravitas's right arm.

So he "accidentally" flew right into Gravitas's field of power.

He dropped to the ground like a rock tossed into a well, pinned on his back by an invisible force. First, it felt like someone was sitting on him. Soon it felt like he was trapped under a house. Gravitas glared at him, one side of his metal mouth turned up in a snarl. But he did so while standing still, and that's what Fritz wanted.

"Anytime you're ready, Siv," Fritz groaned.

There was a flash of green light just beside Gravitas's neck. Siv had used his grapple to climb atop the Steelterror. Standing upright on Gravitas's shoulder, Siv was half as tall as Gravitas's head. With another flash of green, Siv slammed the energy-enhanced blade of his Dragon Slayer into Gravitas's right arm joint. Gravitas yelled, turned, and reached his left hand around to swat away the mosquito biting at him. With Gravitas's right hand pointed away, the extra gravity crushing Fritz vanished. He rocketed into the air and hovered at face level with Gravitas. Siv leaped away; his grapple was still attached to the back of the Steelterror's neck, so he fell quickly but safely to the ground. Once Siv was clear, Fritz bombarded Gravitas's right shoulder with laser fire.

Gravitas turned to face Fritz, and Fritz crashed to the ground, again pinned by increased gravity. Siv ascended to Gravitas's shoulder and hacked away at it. Fritz grinned when he saw the Dragon Slayer sink halfway into the shoulder joint. They were making progress, but they wouldn't be able to repeat this same sequence for long. Gravitas was smart and deadly. He'd adapt.

As soon as Gravitas spun and swatted at the pest on his shoulder, Siv leaped to safety. As soon as he wasn't pinned by artificial gravity, Fritz took to the air and took over the attack.

Fritz expected to find himself again pinned by increased gravity at any moment.

Instead, Gravitas used his gravity-reducing left hand to make the sword hilt he'd previously discarded float. He snatched it out of the air. His massive crackling energy sword blazed out of the hilt. Gravitas took a large step towards Fritz and hurled the blade towards him.

Fritz zoomed to the right but felt his flight slow, as if he'd suddenly come up against a strong headwind. At the same time, Gravitas's sword, turning end over end as it closed the distance between its owner and Fritz, increased in velocity. Gravitas had both his hands pointed at Fritz; one pinned him in place, the other propelled the sword towards him. Fritz gave more power to his thrusters, willing them to move him to safety, but it was as if he were stuck in a swamp.

He couldn't get out of the way, his protective force-field was gone, and his armor would be as soft as scrambled eggs to Gravitas's sword.

He was going to be cleaved in two.

This must be what hell felt like.

Everything around Cassie was so consumed with flames, even the smoke seemed to be on fire. Her face, her hands, her legs – every bit of her was in agony like nothing she'd felt in all her born days. The heat was overwhelming, like a tangible, physical force smothering her to death. What if her eyes melted, leaving her unable to see the way out of this inferno? She'd never have time for her power to heal herself if she couldn't escape.

She would have screamed, but she didn't dare stop holding her breath.

On all six limbs, Sebastian ran ahead at what seemed like double her speed. Good for him – at least one of them had to make it out of this alive. Ashes fell in front of her face, and she realized it was her hair burning away. Was she only halfway there? She was never going to make it.

Her peripheral vision turned from red to black. Sebastian aimed one of his arms, fired his grapple line, and shot up out of the fire. Good. She begged God that Sebastian's power could heal him before his burns killed him. Her vision lost focus. Everything went hazy, and not just from the heat distortions all around her. She stumbled but kept her balance. Her lungs yearned for more air. Run. Run. Run!

The next time she stumbled, she went down. There was air down low, but it felt like there was just as much heat, so it didn't matter. She tried to stand, but everything hurt. Her healing power couldn't keep up with the constant burning. Was she close enough for her grapple to reach the water tower? She dragged herself forward once, twice, three times. Raised her left arm.

Her vision went black.

This was the end? How could she have been so stupid? No – it wasn't stupidity that had led her to this. All she'd ever wanted to do was to make people better. She wanted to fight disease, and injury, and lies, and conflict, and anything else that brought people down instead of lifting them up. She never would have left Harbrucken, not while the Steelterrors were killing people. In every possible scenario, she would have stopped them or died trying.

Well. It seemed God had chosen the latter for her.

*   *   *

There was a gooseflesh-inducing screech of metal-on-metal, and sparks exploded from Gravitas's right shoulder joint. The Steelterror roared, and his right arm, severed from his body, crashed to the ground. The increased gravity holding Fritz in place vanished. He darted away from Gravitas's sword just a second before it would have ended him. Instead, it smashed through the front of Franklin Residence Hall and came to a stop with half the blade buried inside the apparently evacuated (*thank God*) building. Siv jumped off Gravitas, landed safely behind the Steelterror, and retracted his grapple line. Since his laser rifle lacked ammo, he darted for cover underneath one of the remaining satellite dishes.

Without his gravity-increasing hand and sword, Gravitas's only remaining weapon was his gravity-decreasing hand. That wasn't much of a threat to the flight-capable Fritz, but the Steelterror could easily use it to fling Siv into the air and let him fall to his death. Fritz had to command the Steelterror's attention. He hovered at Gravitas's eye-line, putting himself between him and the discarded sword. Let Gravitas charge towards it; Fritz would pelt him with laser cannon fire at point-blank range.

But instead of running towards his sword, Gravitas reached towards his severed arm. Huh? Fritz's mind raced through the data. Samson had taught him about microbot caches, the chipware antibodies that healed Steelterrors. Fritz had seen Gravitas's in action, healing an open wound on the back of his head that should have been fatal. *Click.* All the Steelterror would have to do was press the severed arm against his shoulder, and given enough time, his microbot cache would reattach it to his body.

Fritz shot Gravitas in the chest and face with his laser cannons. The assault pushed the Steelterror back but not enough. He remained only two steps away from his fallen arm.

Click. Fritz saw an entire scenario play out in his mind so suddenly, he knew it was a gift from his hyper-intuition. He descended to the arm and stood over it, just for a second, just long enough to let Gravitas realize he was there. As Fritz expected, Gravitas blasted the arm with a field of decreased gravity. He'd probably hoped the arm would bash Fritz in the face in its sudden rapid ascent. Instead, at the same moment Gravitas made the arm weightless, Fritz dove on top of it, wrapped his arms and legs tightly around it, and gunned his rockets. He'd never have been able to lift the arm on his own, even with his chipsuit-enhanced strength, but in the weightlessness provided by Gravitas, it was feather-light.

He wildly careened up and backward. He smashed through the second story of Franklin Residence Hall and emerged out the other side in a shower of wood, brick, and furniture. No longer aided by Gravitas's decreased gravity, he crashed hard into a grassy field between Franklin and another residential building. But at least he still had the severed arm.

"Professor?" Siv called through the voice-comm. "You alright?"

"Fine," he replied, once he got the wind back into his lungs. "Hide. Don't engage Gravitas. Let him come to me. I can end him."

It wouldn't take long for Gravitas to reach him. All he'd have to do is shove his way through the evacuated residence hall. Quickly, Fritz flipped open an access panel on the right forearm of his chipsuit and popped off a power outlet plug, exposing the bare wires underneath. Then he sorted through the bundle of dangling wires at the end of Gravitas's arm. There were two sets to choose from. One likely had powered the arm's movement, and the other had likely powered the gravity-increasing weapon. Fritz wanted the latter, and that was probably the set with the thicker, better-insulated cables. He picked out ground, hot, and return wires and spliced them into his chipsuit's power outlet. The severed arm hummed. The energy emitter at the end of it, on the palm of the hand, lit up with a red glow.

In front of Fritz, Franklin Residence Hall shook. Bricks rose off of it and into the air. Wood framing, windows, beds, desks, toilets, and chairs followed. The sea of floating building materials rose like a curtain revealing Gravitas behind it, dismantling the hall board-by-board with the gravity-reducing weapon he still wielded.

Fritz used his suit's grapple line to grab the fingers of the severed arm and pull them back with all his chipsuit-enhanced strength until the palm was angled up and pointed at Gravitas's chest. He issued the command to flood the arm with power from the sparkscube on his back, and a field of enhanced gravity slammed into Gravitas.

The Steelterror brought his gravity-reducing left hand in front of himself, neutralizing the enhanced gravity. Fritz increased the flow of sparks to the cut-off arm. Gravitas stumbled backward a step but recovered quickly. He must have raised the power of his gravity reducer to match Fritz's attack.

"You insolent pissant," Gravitas said. "When I get back my arm, I'll shove it–"

Fritz increased the sparks. For a moment, Gravitas fell to one knee, but he recovered and stretched his intact arm out towards attacker. Fritz felt himself rise an inch off the ground. He increased the sparksflow into the severed arm even more. The two of them went back-and-forth, each raising the power output of their weapons to match, then beat, the power output of the other. Fritz couldn't remember the power remaining in his sparkscube when the standoff began, but he thought it was somewhere in the low 80% range. The power meter on his heads-up display now read 62%. He didn't have enough power to drag this on indefinitely, so he jacked up the power output suddenly and significantly to end it.

The blast knocked Gravitas on his rear. The armor on his chest crumpled. A chunk of it fell off. He yelled, and the red glow coming from the palm of his left hand intensified. Fritz's legs floated backward and up, away from the Steelterror, but he fired his chipsuit's thrusters to compensate and keep him in place. He increased the power to the gravity-increasing weapon. Remaining charge in his sparkscube: 44%.

"I won't fall to *flesh*," Gravitas hollered. He stood, pulled back his left arm, and slammed it forward again, dramatically increasing its power.

Fritz saw the increase and raised it. Gravitas's severed arm vibrated and hummed from all the sparks flowing through it. White light shone out through cracks in its armored shell. Gravitas fell to his knees and struggled not to fall farther. Remaining power: 36%.

Enraged, Gravitas's left hand trembled. Fritz flooded so many sparks into Gravitas's severed arm, red alerts from his power system appeared on his suit's heads-up display. He was at risk of overload, and the suit was about to blow its fuses in an emergency attempt to protect itself. As dumb as it was from a safety perspective, Fritz overrode that command. Remaining power: 18%.

He swallowed hard. This had seemed like a great idea. His hyper-intuition had suggested it, but his power was only as good as the data he could provide to it, and he hadn't realized how many sparks Gravitas's weapon would consume. Now his sparkscube was almost empty, while Gravitas showed no signs of stopping. His stolen gravity-increasing weapon would falter, and in a powerless chipsuit, he'd be easy prey for Gravitas, who must have had multiple sparkscubes encased inside his chest, or some other, even stronger power source.

Remaining power: 10% and draining fast.

Chapter Twenty-Five

Something yanked Cassie into the air. It took her a moment to realize she dangled from the end of Sebastian's grapple line like a rag doll. She still felt like she was burning, and she probably still was. Air flooded into her lungs, but she wished it didn't because it hurt to breathe.

Sebastian was on a platform about fifty feet up the water tower. Sickening red and black wounds covered his face and hands. They made her stomach churn, but at least that meant her eyeballs hadn't melted. He released his grapple's claws from around her forearm and pulled her close to him, smothering her against his chest. Smoke hissed as the last of the flames were extinguished against his fireproof Mantissa uniform. He lowered her to the platform, and though his translator was still tucked away, she understood the meaning of his growls easily enough from the way he pressed all four of his hands against her body. *Heal*, he told her. *Heal!*

She felt cold all over, and she shook from the chills. The rational part of her mind knew if she was cold after having been bathed in hellfire, she was deeply in shock. Both her power and Sebastian's were working to heal her, but she wasn't sure it would be enough. She instantly regretted looking at her hands, the sight of them was so vile. The black wounds on Sebastian's face turned crimson, then pink, then they were replaced with normal chalk-white skin. He could heal himself, even while expelling some of his power to help heal her? The demon bodies Krulgoth had made before his death, the ones with Mantissa abilities, possessed unbelievable levels of power. Cassie dared another look at her hands. They actually seemed a little better.

Eventually, she managed to sit up. She was short of breath and felt like she wanted to sleep for a week, but her skin had healed. Her hair felt more like Siv's short crew cut than the tresses she'd had three minutes earlier, but she could almost feel it growing. It tickled. She looked into the white, bone-like snout of the man who'd just saved her life for the second time. First five months ago on Skylab, when he'd given up his human body to do it, and now here. She almost said, "Thank you," but those words seemed pitifully weak.

Sebastian took his translator from the pouch he'd stored it in and tied it around his neck. "I expect you and Siv to name your firstborn after me," he said. "Come on. We have to get to the top."

Teufel flowed down the street below, closing in on the water tower. With Sebastian's help, Cassie stood. Using their grapple lines, they ascended to a balcony surrounding the tower at the base of its giant tank. The high vantage point gave her a wide view of the city; there was far more destruction than she'd imagined, and she'd imagined a horror. Smashed buildings and carriages, human and equine bodies in the streets, and so much fire, the evening was lit like mid-morning. The sound of screaming was endless.

Sebastian gave her one of his laser rifles. Its metal surfaces were still warm to the touch. For safety, they secured the hooks of their grapples to the railing surrounding the outside edge of the balcony. Then, with their rifles set to fire a steady stream of energy, they worked together to cut a rectangle the size of a barn door out of the water tank. They began at the same spot and worked in opposite directions. When their cut had reached its desired width, they moved their beams upward. Water spilled out of the gashes as soon as they cut them.

They had reached the desired height with their cuts when a loud *clang* sounded far beneath them. Teufel rose from the fires at the base of the water tower and undulated his way up. A dozen tentacles of red-hot steel circled the legs of the tower and reached higher. His head bobbed at the top of the thickest part of his mass.

"Come on, come on," Sebastian muttered.

Cassie and Sebastian completed their cutting, and a gusher of water poured from the tower, flowing like a raging waterfall onto Teufel and the fires surrounding him. His laughs turned to howls. Steam and smoke rolled off of him like a thick fog. As his temperature dropped, his bulk turned from glowing red and molten to gray and solid. The rapid cooling welded his tentacles to the legs of the water tower, strengthening and supporting it as gallon after gallon of water poured from its tank. It streamed off in every direction and extinguished every fire it touched, leaving an ashen cloud hovering over the entire area.

Falling to her knees, Cassie wept – not because she was sad, but simply because it seemed the only way to release the bundle of emotion twisting her insides into knots. Elation at Teufel's defeat. Terror at the memory of the fire that had burned her. Gratitude that she was still alive. Outrage at the number of people who weren't. Adrenaline still coursed through her veins like sparks, too. She trembled and braced herself against the railing.

Sebastian patted her on the back. "Nice work," he said, sounding as spent as she felt.

"Stupidest thing I've ever done," Cassie said.

"Me, too," Sebastian agreed. "Idiotic."

Cassie ran her fingers across her scalp. Some of it was covered with prickly stubble; the rest sprouted thick clumps of burnt hair. Her clothes were blackened rags. "I look like hell."

"Nah," Sebastian said. "I've seen hell. *Very* recently. There's no resemblance."

"Think we need a drink."

"Ice water?" He laughed. She did, too.

"Whiskey," Cassie said. "A bottle. A case."

"Now you're talking." They both laughed again, not at any joke but just at having survived. Minutes passed. The flow of water out of the tower slowed to a mild trickle. Sebastian pointed down at the ball Cassie had come to think of as Teufel's head. It sat motionless as if it had been welded in place. "Let's blow that up and be done with this. Go find your betrothed and your brother."

Cassie nocked her last bomb-tipped arrow–

Teufel's head sank and disappeared into the metal mass beneath it.

A glowing red spot appeared on him and grew larger and brighter. Cassie and Sebastian's laughter died. Something between a sigh and a moan escaped Cassie's lips instead. They'd drained the tower – the whole tower! Every last drop. And it hadn't been enough. Sebastian cursed, then repeated his curse in a yell.

Beneath them, Teufel reheated.

Fritz moaned. When his sparkscube drained, Samson wasn't going to show up and offer him another one. Just like back on the mountain, he'd be in a suit of armor, but nothing more. All Gravitas would have to do is fling him into the air and let him fall to death.

"Professor?" Siv said over the voice-comm. He spoke so softly Fritz almost didn't hear him. "Do not look, but I'm behind that oak over yonder. I got a shot lined up, but when this monster gets angry, his eyes get squinty. Give me a moment to trust my aim."

Fritz turned his head just enough. Siv crouched behind a tree, calm and still as if hunting deer, but with the grappling hook launcher on his wrist pointed at Gravitas's face. If the Steelterror even knew he was there, he paid no attention to him. Fritz had never been so relieved to see his friend.

"Maybe I can get you an easier shot," Fritz said. He raised his helmet's visor. "I know what you did!" he shouted at Gravitas. "You murdered Doctor Ada Sonne. Didn't you, *Albrecht?*"

Gravitas's red eyes widened dramatically.

"That'll do," Siv said. He fired.

His grapple pierced Gravitas's right eye.

Instinctively, Gravitas reached his one remaining hand towards his face to pull the grapple away.

And the moment he did, he removed the field of decreased gravity protecting him.

He must have recognized his error the moment he made it, but Fritz had the power output on his commandeered weapon cranked so high a moment was all he needed. Gravitas was instantly pushed onto his back. He shook and trembled, and pieces of him rattled and fell off. A chasm opened in the center of his chest as the armor there crumpled. His left arm snapped and flattened. It was as if a month's worth of sledge work Siv could have done in his blacksmith shop all happened in a matter of seconds. His sheet metal cheeks popped off of his face. The top of his head caved in as if the fist of God had bashed it to hell.

"Crush that son of a gun!" Siv hollered.

Gravitas's screams became grunts, then gurgles. Oil and coolant liquid sprayed out of his mouth like a geyser. When it dried up, a long, drawn-out rattle escaped his mouth. He went limp and still. Smoke rose from all over the pile of scrap metal that had once been the Steelterror leader.

Fritz cast aside Gravitas's severed arm. "That was for my friend Samson!"

"How many bomb arrows you have left?" Sebastian asked.

"Just this one," she said.

Sebastian turned away and hissed in frustration.

Cassie could feel the heat emanating from the hunk of metal beneath her. Teufel would be liquefied enough to be capable of moving soon and would be superheated again not long after. "We have to separate his head from the rest of his mass," she said. "I think the head controls everything else. We wait for him to show his head, then we grab it with our grappling hooks and yank it away from the rest of him. If I'm right about how he works, then his body will stop moving immediately and will eventually cool down and harden on its own."

A steady, oscillating noise grew louder. Annalie's aerocopter approached from the south.

"That might work," Sebastian said, "or our grapples might melt before we can grab his head. We need to get out of here before he heats back up. Regroup and come back with a new plan."

The aerocopter hovered above the water tower. A rope ladder dangled down from it. Cassie grabbed its bottom rung and climbed. The Steelterror beneath them bubbled and burned bright red. The vast majority of Teufel's mass was back in a liquid state. His head rose three feet out of the mass, lifted by a bundle of steaming red tentacles. "You think you can ice me?" he yelled. "I'll cremate you alive and incinerate your ashes!"

Cassie reached the top of the ladder and climbed into an open area of the aerocopter behind the pilot's seat. The sight of her stubble-covered head and ragged, burned clothes made Annalie's eyes as wide as the moons. "What in the name of all that's–?" Annalie said. "You alright?"

"I'm fine," Cassie said. "We couldn't wait for a lift. We dumped all the water on him, but it wasn't enough. We need to figure something else out."

Annalie glanced out the window. "What's Sebastian waiting for?"

Cassie gasped. Sebastian remained on the water tower's balcony. He looked up at her, but he made no effort to even reach for the ladder.

And he trembled violently.

"No," she whispered. "Don't you dare."

He looked up and shrugged as if he'd heard her. "You know this is the only way."

She wanted to argue. She wanted to beat this nonsense out of him. But he was right. She knew.

Annalie called out the window beside her. "Get up here! Hurry!"

Teufel's red ball head was just thirty feet beneath Sebastian, sitting on a rising column of molten metal. Arms of dripping red-hot steel stretched out of his bulk and reached towards the top of the water tower. "Burn, baby, burn!" Teufel hollered.

"You give Eroica a great big kiss when you see her," Cassie said, choking on the words. "That's an order, soldier."

"Yes, ma'am," Sebastian said. "Now here's one for you. Don't miss."

Sebastian jumped off the platform.

Annalie screamed.

Cassie nocked her last bomb arrow.

Sebastian landed directly in front of Teufel's head and sank to the waist into the molten metal of the Steelterror's body. He roared in agony.

Teufel's head retreated away from him.

Sebastian lunged for it. Though his arms burst into flame, he seized it in the palm of his hand and tossed it high into the air.

Cassie judged the head's arc of descent, aimed, and released her arrow.

Tentacles grew from Teufel's mass and desperately stretched towards his falling head. He shrieked.

The arrow hit his head and exploded.

Sebastian had stopped screaming. He'd stopped moving, too. He was sinking.

Cassie dropped her bow and launched her grappling hook towards Sebastian's arm. "Please!"

Before it reached him, he sank beneath the surface of the liquid metal. When the grapple reached the same spot, it melted.

Teufel's body drooped into a shapeless glob. His movement up the tower stopped, and his remains slowly sank to the ground.

"Oh my gosh, oh my gosh," Annalie mumbled from the pilot's seat.

"Easy," Cassie said. She took two steps forward and placed a hand on Annalie's shoulder, willing her to calm. "Need you to keep control of this copter, OK?"

Annalie's shoulders relaxed. She nodded and breathed. "OK."

"Let's go find Fritz and Siv."

"Yeah."

Annalie moved the aerocopter away from the empty water tower and the cooling hill of metal underneath it. Cassie collapsed into a seat and found her grunblume in her pocket. The wooden beads were warm, but they hadn't burned. She fingered the beads but didn't bother saying any prayers. Instead, she leaned her head against the window and didn't take her eyes off the spot she'd last seen Sebastian until she couldn't see it anymore.

Just like Bernice when she was a little girl.

Just like Eroica when Krulgoth killed her.

Just like Harlan.

Just like her father.

His death hadn't been her fault. But it hadn't been hers to fix, either.

Fritz disconnected the severed arm's sparkslines from his suit. Remaining power in his sparkscube: a mere 7%. Siv ran across the field to meet him.

"I told you to hide from him," Fritz said. "Thank you very, very much for not listening."

Siv grinned and squeezed Fritz's shoulder. "Welcome," he said. "Do Cass and Sebastian need our help?"

Fritz opened a voice-comm. "Cassie, Sebastian, can either of you talk?"

"I'm here," Cassie said. Siv – who had also heard her response via his earpiece – looked up sharply and met Fritz's eyes. The tone of her voice was wrong. Extremely wrong.

"What's going on?" Fritz asked. "I hear the aerocopter. Are you and Sebastian with Annalie?"

"I am," she said. "Sebastian didn't make it."

Fritz gasped.

"But Teufel's gone, too," Cassie said.

Then they'd done it – they'd destroyed *all* the Steelterrors. But celebrating was the farthest thing from Fritz's mind. He felt like he'd been knifed in the chest, and he struggled to breathe. Sebastian was *gone?*

"Where are you?" Cassie said. "Where's Banshee?"

"Umm. Uhh. Banshee's dead," Fritz said. "And Gravitas came back, but he's dead now, too. We're..." The two front doors of the residence hall behind him hung limply on their hinges. A sign in front displayed the building's name. "Do you know where Lewand Residence Hall is? We're in the yard between it and where Franklin Hall used to be."

"Annalie and I are on our way," Cassie said.

"Professor?" Siv said. He was looking over Fritz's shoulder at the bare-limbed elm trees standing in a row between Lewand Hall and the sidewalk. Their branches swayed, but there was no wind. In a flash of instant growth, they tripled in length and seized Fritz, wrapping themselves around his arms and chest.

Then they flung him fifty feet into the air. He closed his visor, engaged his thrusters to hover in place, and aimed his laser cannons at the trees. "Power: 7%" flashed red in the bottom right corner of his heads-up display.

The air in front of him swirled. Breezes coalesced and took on a tangible shape.

Sierra flashed him a wicked grin.

And with all the force of a thirty-five mile-per-hour gust of wind, she slammed her shoulder into his abdomen and sent him sprawling across the sky.

Chapter Twenty-Six

Fritz soared through the night sky a couple hundred feet above Harbrucken and all its wounded and terrified residents, but his chipsuit wasn't what propelled him. Sierra pushed him on a turbulent series of high-powered winds and flew along with him, right in his face. Lightning crackled around her hands, and she pounded him with punches that felt like thunderstorms. He hit back, slamming his metal-covered fists into her body and belly and face, though the assault didn't seem to faze her.

Before he could talk to her, before she'd listen, he'd have to cut her off from everything natural – from the soil, from water, even from the air. What container could meet such criteria? Even a sealed wooden crate would be porous enough to allow water to soak out through the wood. If he put her in a metal container, she'd turn into lightning and conduct her way out. Was it even possible to imprison her?

They flew higher. Sierra dissipated into nothingness; a moment later, she slammed into his back and sent him tumbling forward. He glanced around in time to see her dissipate again.

She reformed right in front of him and gave him a right hook that dented his helmet and veered him off in a new direction, but she was ready and waiting for him there, too. She seized his upper arm and repeatedly bashed his visor with her fist.

When she let up for a moment, Fritz fired his laser cannon at her abdomen at point-blank range. It blasted a hole the width of his arm in her mid-section, and it didn't bother Sierra a whit. Dirt filled the wound, and she was healed in seconds. She dissipated and appeared behind him and bashed him in the back of his head. It *hurt*.

She spun him around so he flew horizontally on his belly with her arms locked around his torso, holding him in place. They sank together toward a city street filled with scattering, screaming people. "I beat you," she said. "Again! You think any of these people are going to let you restore chipware now, you privileged, sheltered little piece of crud? They'll hang you if you even try."

"I'll take my chances with them," Fritz said. "You're just one person. You don't speak for the world."

Sierra pushed him ahead of her and gaped at him in complete disbelief. She blinked and shook her head. Then her eyes narrowed, and her hair turned an even fiercer shade of red.

"Oh crud," Fritz whispered.

She *slammed* into him and pointed him downward. The metal of his suit thudded and groaned under the lacing she delivered. The vibrations of each blow rattled Fritz's teeth and gave him a splitting headache. She steered him towards a park. It was a mostly open, grassy area peppered with benches, paved paths, gas lamps, and trees. Moments before crashing, she turned him horizontal and put him on his belly again.

He hit the ground and skidded over the grass at... well, Fritz had no idea what his speed was, because so many red alerts covered his heads-up display, his normal dashboard wasn't immediately visible. But it was *fast*. Buried two feet under the surface, he dug a huge rut into the ground as Sierra dragged him. Grass and dirt showered the surrounding area.

"The ground is my body," Sierra said. "People have buried toxic waste in it and gutted it for landfills so they could have a convenient place to discard beer bottles and fast food wrappers. They've cut down trees and replaced them with metal and concrete."

Sierra dragged him halfway across the park before she yanked his head backward and carried them both back into the air, soaring straight up. Above the trees. Above the buildings. Above the haze of smoke from all of the fires. Through the clouds. Water vapor covered his dented visor.

"The sky is my mind," Sierra said, "and people have stuffed it so full of chemical pollutants, tobacco smoke, and chlorofluorocarbons they ripped a barking hole in my ozone layer!"

She pointed him towards the Iller River and brought him down again. Fritz scanned his heads-up display, which was now cracked and pixelated in some places. He dismissed several damage reports to clear the visible space and finally uncovered what he needed on his dashboard. Suit containment seemed to be intact. Then again, he'd taken such a beating, his internal sensors could be damaged, and their data could be unreliable. The only way to find out would be to see if he got wet in about three... two...

Click. His *chipsuit* was an air-tight, water-tight container! It had kept him dry when Leviathan dragged him underwater. The rubber insulation within had kept him from being fried by Sierra's lightning. Could he somehow stuff Sierra inside his suit?

Sierra slammed him beneath the river's surface. Completely submerged, he felt Sierra on top of him, holding him down and rocketing him forward at the same time. And he could hear her, too, the same way he'd been able to hear Leviathan underwater.

"The water is my heart," she said, "and industry has treated it like a toilet. People have covered the river beds and ocean floors with litter. They've over-harvested water life until food chains decayed and whole species died."

She brought him straight up out of the water and back into the air. He wasn't wet inside his suit! The suit's containment held. Now how could he get *her* contained inside it? Up she dragged him until they were a couple of hundred feet above the river, almost smack dab above the middle of the city. She slammed a particularly vicious uppercut into his chin, then grabbed him by the arms and yanked him close to her until they were nose-to-visor.

"And after all your species has done to me, you have the sand to tell me I don't speak for the world?" she hollered. "*I am the barking world!*"

She punched him. *Hard.* He flew ten feet through the air before she grabbed him and resumed pummeling him.

"*My* species?" Fritz said between blows. "You're human, a Mantissa, and–"

Click.

Click click click click click click click click!

It made perfect sense. Why hadn't he seen it before? She could be anywhere, but she couldn't be everywhere at once. She might be nigh invulnerable, infinitely repairable, and capable of appearing anywhere, but she couldn't be conscious and present in multiple places simultaneously. Why? Because her planet-based body was tethered to her *human mind.*

He used his Mantissa power emulator to slam her with a mind blast.

And for the first time, he hurt her.

Sierra clutched the sides of her head and screamed in agony. He hit her with a second blast. When he hit her with a third, a chunk of dirt blasted away from her as if he'd put a bullet through her skull. Fritz turned on his suit's thrusters to stay airborne because Sierra couldn't keep him up any longer; she sank towards the ground like a boulder on its way to the bottom of the sea.

This was his chance! He had to land, take off his suit, and put it on Sierra. Then he'd have her contained, and he could finally get her to listen.

Except that still didn't feel right. Talking to Sierra, listening to her concerns, sharing ideas, making compromises – all of that felt as right as his right hand. That was everything Harlan told him he'd have to do: work with his critics to make them partners. But Sierra wouldn't talk unless he *made* her talk, so he'd have to...

Wait. Was he actually considering putting Sierra into a prison cell and *forcing* her to talk? No, no, no. *That's* what felt wrong. Forced dialogue was no way to gain an ally. Besides, what had she ever done that made him think she'd *ever* want to talk? The night she destroyed Earp, she'd made it very clear: words meant nothing to her. Actions–

Insight from his hyper-intuition came to him, but not as a *click* like usual. It came more like the gentle heat of a sip of cocoa, radiating outward from his midsection until the warmth consumed him. He breathed deeply and thought through the details of the idea coming to life in his mind. It could work. It belonged on the Stupid List, maybe right at the very top. But it felt right. It felt so thoroughly right.

"It's time to change the world," he said.

Fritz soared underneath Sierra and caught her, stopping her descent.

"Fritz?" Annalie said over his voice-comm. "Where are you? You all right?"

"Everything is everything," he said. "I've got Sierra. She's barely conscious."

"You beat her?" Annalie said. "Let's get her contained!"

"No," Fritz said. "I'm taking her into space."

They ascended towards the moons. Sierra threw a weak elbow into his abdomen. He hit her with another mind blast. She moaned in pain and vomited water. Fritz felt her soften underneath him. She was trying to turn into air, or water, or something else he couldn't hold, so he blasted her mind again. She fell limp in his arms, barely moving.

"Into space?" Annalie said. "You're gonna kill her?"

"Of course not," he said. "I'm going to talk to her. Just not with words."

"But you go up there and you can't get back down!" Annalie hollered, and before she could protest further, he flew out of range of the voice-comm's signal.

He gave every bit of sparks he could pull out of his rapidly diminishing power supply to his rockets. The clouds fell away underneath him and Sierra. The sky got blacker, and the stars glowed brighter. His emergency oxygen supply pumped air into his helmet.

When he stopped ascending, he recalibrated his force field to emit itself outward, away from him instead of around him. The system, still beaten to a pulp from his collision with Banshee, put a list of errors and warnings as long as his good leg onto his heads-up display. But he didn't need it to hold off a ramming jet. He just needed it to hold a little air, and it seemed up to that meager task. A bubble of blue energy surrounded him and Sierra. He opened his visor and allowed some of his air supply to escape from his helmet and fill the bubble.

"Sierra," he said. He gave her shoulder a gentle shake. "Sierra."

Her eyes fluttered open. When she realized where they were, she startled. She glared at Fritz and spat muddy water on his face. Tiny particles of her blood-red hair drifted away like wind-blown sand. She was losing cohesion, falling apart. But her defiant scowl had vanished. She seemed genuinely afraid.

Wow. Leaving her in outer space really would kill her.

Fritz turned her around and showed her the beautiful ball of life underneath them. Verde. Clouds swirled above her blue and green surface. Continents floated in her oceans. The view was a thousand times better than when he'd seen it from the deck of Skylab because this time there was no glass. Nothing but a thin air-containing force field separated him and Sierra from their world.

"The first time I saw our home like this," Fritz said, "it inspired me to take Harlan's advice and get out of my bedroom and bring my chipware to the people. I suppose that means *you* inspired my restoration. Which is ironic. But just look at it! That's where we work and play and love and laugh and cry and *live.* Look how peaceful it is. I believe that if it can be this peaceful from up here, then it can be just as peaceful down on the surface. But *we* have to make it that way."

Sierra didn't spit. She didn't swear. She didn't make obscene hand gestures. She just stared down at planet Verde.

"You know, you've never bothered to ask me my name, but I'm Fritz *Reinhardt*."

She looked at him sharply.

"I'm told you once did great things with my ancestor, Joseph," he said, forcing himself to look her in the eye. "You saved towns. You stopped flooding. You helped people. I have something I want to ask you, but you once told me words don't mean anything to you. You need to see action. That's why I'm not going to leave you up here to die.

"I'm going to take you home."

He closed his visor and turned off the force field. With quick bursts of his thrusters, he flew behind her, wrapped his arms around her waist, and rocketed straight back towards Verde.

"But there's one small problem," Fritz said. "My chipsuit can't survive the friction heat of atmospheric re-entry. I *can't* get us back."

The atmosphere grew thicker. And hotter. Much hotter. Sierra stiffened in Fritz's grasp, though she didn't fight against him. Gently, he pushed her away, and she didn't leave. She kept pace with him and descended alongside him. Her expression was unreadable, but it wasn't her normal mask of aggression and contempt.

"But *you* can," he said, reaching his hand out towards her. "You can move the hot, burning air away from us, and let us descend safely. Please help me get back down alive. You don't have to do anything else. Just take this one small step towards peace."

His chipsuit glowed red; then flames erupted across it. His heads-up display screamed critical warnings about his suit's temperature. Before he could read them, they disappeared – the entire heads-up display shut down due to overheating. His sparkscube died, and his rockets extinguished, but his descent continued. Verde's gravity had him in its grasp. He was no longer flying down to the surface. He was *falling* towards it. And it was hot *inside* his suit, too. Sweat poured off every inch of his skin. It wouldn't take long before the heat became painful, then deadly.

"I could have killed you, but I put myself at your mercy instead," Fritz said. "If this little stunt doesn't prove I sincerely want to work with you, then I don't know what will."

The red haze Fritz saw everywhere disappeared from Sierra as if a heat-shielded, invisible bubble had suddenly formed around her. She'd done it, just as he'd known she could! But she only protected herself. He still fell. He still burned.

"Please!" he yelled over the rush of the wind, the roar of the flames. The heat was unbearable. He could barely breathe. He stretched his hand farther towards her, seeking both a friend and a lifeline. His intuition still told him this was right, even as the three *g*'s of gravity slamming into him bashed away at his consciousness. He probably only had a few more seconds before he fainted.

Well, if these were to be his final moments, he didn't want them to be filled with melancholy or worry. He wanted them to be happy. He imagined being with Annalie. And Cassie, and Siv, and his mom. And his dad. And Harlan and Sebastian. They were all having a serious breakfast together. Pancakes and scrambled eggs. Sausage. Bread and jam. Chocolate milk. It was splendiferous. And then he found the courage to tell Annalie she was smart, funny, caring, and beautiful and that he loved her.

If he ever woke up – *when* he woke up – he'd tell her for real.

But that would only happen if Sierra helped him. Trust. Trust!

She wouldn't let him die.

She wouldn't let him die.

She–

Everything changed from fire red to pitch black.

Chapter Twenty-Seven

Fritz woke up.

Everything around him was white except the green metal of his chipsuit, large swaths of which were scorched black. Where was he? Had he died? Cassie once told him after Krulgoth had... well, had killed her on Skylab, she'd seen a tunnel of white. She'd been heading towards it, and when Sebastian revived her, she'd suddenly been pulled back to her body.

He blinked and looked for Harlan, Sebastian, and his father.

When the cold hit him, he knew the white around him wasn't heaven's light; he was laying on his side in a snow bank, surrounded by powder and ice and the glare of early morning sunlight. Had he landed somewhere in the frozen north? How long had he been unconscious?

Sierra. Was she here? Had she helped him? He was alive, so she must have!

He sat up and found her fifteen feet away sitting with her back to him. She looked like she should have been freezing, what with the thin cardigan and t-shirt and skirt and ripped tights she wore, but of course, she didn't even shiver.

"I died," she said without turning.

"Oh," Fritz said, his heart sinking. "I thought so at first, too, but then I thought all this whiteness was just snow. But we died?"

"No." She snorted and raised her eyebrows at him. Wow. She looked like a completely different person when she was in a pleasant mood. Pretty, even with a metal ring pierced through her lip. "Not just now, goofus. Before. A long time ago." Her smile inverted. "I died."

It took him about a minute of very careful and very painful movement, but Fritz managed to stand, walk over, and sit down next to her. He was sore everywhere, and the cold in the air felt so nice because he was fairly certain he had minor burns – and some not-so-minor – over much of his body. He opened his visor and let in more of the frigid air. Except for when the gentle breeze crescendoed into a biting howl, the wind soothed his scorched skin. No new snow fell, but that which was already on the ground drifted and blew with the breeze.

Sierra hugged her knees close to her chest. "The night of the Blackout, one of the aliens got me. Destroyed me. I bled all over the dirt, and the next thing I knew I couldn't feel my body anymore. But I could feel *everything* else. The Iller River. The hill country. The oceans. The sky. And it wasn't even that I could feel those things. It's that I *was* those things. For a long time after that, I sort of... lost myself. Forgot who I was. I don't believe in God or heaven. I believe when we die, we just become one with the planet, so I just assumed I was dead. And after a long, long time, I realized I wasn't, and, man, I don't even know who I barking am anymore. I remember who I used to be, and *maybe* that's who I still am. But I don't know. I don't know."

She gave him a piercing look. "And yet you trusted me. With your *life*. I can count on *one finger* the number of people who have ever trusted me."

Fritz shrugged. "Now you need two."

She looked back out over the horizon, which was just more snow, more ice, more tundra, and a dreadful realization came to Fritz. "This is the frozen north, isn't it?" he said.

"Yeah," Sierra said. "Your re-entry trajectory brought us here."

"So," he said, licking his lips, "about the white demons you mentioned, I should probably let you know we exiled them–"

Sierra pointed behind them. "About a hundred miles that way. I know. You left the wreckage of the teleport pad you blew up just sitting there. Might want to clean that up when you get a chance. Barkin' litterbug."

Fritz breathed a sigh of relief that the demons were nowhere nearby and that Sierra was actually joking with him. At least he was fairly certain her demand to clean up the abandoned teleport pad was a joke.

She fidgeted with her hands. "What's gonna happen to me?"

Fritz winced under another biting wind and only spoke once it died back down. "You mean how are we going to punish you for your crimes?"

She nodded tersely.

"You know I'm not going to kill you," Fritz said. "Whipping you on a pillar wouldn't do you any harm. I could throw you in prison, but first I'd have to create one that could hold you. I guess that leaves 'stern lecture,' but talking to people isn't really one of my favorite hobbies."

"Shut up," she said. "I'm serious."

"So am I. You want to do penance for your sins? Good. Forgive yourself, and do better in the future." He shrugged. "That's all any of us can do."

"You *cannot* just let me walk. People *died* because of me. I'm a burning murderer."

Her voice broke on the last word.

"Yeah, you are," Fritz said. "And some of your victims were my friends. Death is absolutely what you deserve." He shook his head. "But I don't want to live in a world of vengeance and anger and punishment. I want to live in a merciful one."

"I don't deserve your mercy."

"Teach me about where chipware went wrong in the past," he said, ignoring her all-too-familiar sounding self-punishment. "Counsel me on what should be different this time. Chipware and nature don't have to be at odds. Each can benefit the other. We can make tomorrow better than today – you and me and my friends, together. I need you to be a part of that change."

For a long time, the only sound was the gentle breeze, which eventually built up into another harsh wind. Until abruptly, it stopped – just fell flat, like a rubber balloon that suddenly lost its air. Fritz blinked. Had Sierra made the wind gentler for his sake?

"You know what happened to Joey?" she asked. "After the Blackout?"

Fritz shook his head. "Only that because I'm here, he must have somehow survived."

"I sent him away. Chipware gone, aliens on Verde, the Mantissa wiped out. Might as well have been the end of the world. I had to make sure it got rebuilt by someone like him." She stole a quick glance at him, then looked away. "Or like you."

He existed only because Sierra had once saved Joseph Reinhardt? Wait until he told Cassie. "Wow. That practically makes us family." He tentatively opened his arms. "I'm not much of a hugger, but this feels like–"

"I don't hug."

Tension left Fritz's shoulders. "Oh thank goodness."

Fritz flipped open a small panel on the upper right arm of his chipsuit and revealed a flashing yellow light. "Look at that! My sparkscube already soaked up enough solar to activate my homing beacon! Annalie will find us in no time."

"She the redhead with the glasses?"

"Yeah."

"She's cute."

Fritz shrugged. "I don't really pay attention to–"

"Yes, you do. You're blushing."

"I'm not," Fritz said. "Re-entry was wicked hot before you saved me. These are burns on my cheeks."

"You're such a liar," she said, shoving a handful of snow at him.

"But seriously," Fritz said, desperate for something, anything, that could change the subject, "I bet she's on her way right now."

"I can answer that," Sierra said. Her face fell flat, and her body went rigid, which Fritz now recognized meant her mind was somewhere else. Probably scanning the landscape, however she did that, for Annalie's aerocopter, searching to see if it really was–

"Barking *crud*," Sierra said as she practically jumped to her feet.

Fritz stood, too, but much slower. Sierra looked all around them, sparks of lightning crackling at her fingertips. The wind returned, stirring up the snow.

And three white demons burst up out of the powder thirty feet from them. Then five more. Then *twelve* more. Instinctively, Fritz pointed his arms towards them, but there were too many to target, and his suit didn't even have enough power to raise his laser cannons out of their compartments, let alone fire them. The demons formed a wide circle, surrounding him and Sierra.

"I've seen your kind before," Sierra muttered at the demons. "*Slaughtered* you before."

A few of the demons growled at her, but none made any move to close in, even as more of them joined the scene, jumping down from atop a ridge some fifty feet from where he and Sierra had sat. Their glowing red eyes stood out starkly against their white skin and the white snow. Most slunk low, down on all sixes. Some stood only on their back four legs. All of them hissed and growled at the man who had exiled them, but they didn't attack.

Why the heck not? His helmet's visor was up. They could *see* it was him. What were they–

From the top of the ridge came the sounds of servomotors and hydraulics. The sounds of a Steelterror. But the Steelterrors were gone. Unless... Unless! Please, God, had Samson revived himself?

One blur of motion later, a final demon jumped down from the ridge, joining the others on the plateau, but this one was different from the cloned homogeny of the rest. It was larger – larger even than Sebastian. And it was the source of the Steelterror-like sounds because it wasn't a *white* demon. It was built out of gray metal.

It stomped across the snow on all six of its limbs, and the flesh demons parted to give it deferential passage. It looked unfinished. Many of its inner workings and circuit boards were exposed. Bundles of wires hung loosely at its elbow joints. Gears and pistons inside its legs, with no metal plating covering them like skin, moved the monstrosity closer to him. Sierra raised her hand, preparing to strike out with her power.

"Wait," Fritz told her.

The metal demon raised its upper body and stood before them on its back four legs. Just like a flesh demon, its eyes glowed red.

It? *He*. Fritz knew exactly what this was, *who* it was. It couldn't be him, but nor could it possibly be anyone else.

"You're dead," Fritz said. "Siv killed you."

Krulgoth tilted his steel head and emitted a low electronic growl.

"Krulgoth!" the demons chanted. They were unable to speak the human language very well, but they could certainly speak their own language and their leader's name, even if all of their words sounded like a cat gagging on a hairball. "Krulgoth! Krulgoth! Krulgoth!"

"How?" Fritz demanded.

Krulgoth threw back his head and made several high-pitched barking noises. Even when replicated electronically, white demon laughter chilled Fritz more than the brisk northern wind.

Samson had told him about how the Steelterrors' creator had used his human mind as the template for Gravitas's artificial intelligence. Before Krulgoth had died, had he somehow made a chipware copy of his mind? He'd possessed multiple Mantissa powers, including mind reading and mind transference. He'd died aboard Skylab, which was practically the chipware capital of the planet. That had to be what had happened.

And *still* the assembled demons didn't attack. That made even less sense than Krulgoth resurrected via chipware. They had killed Annalie's father simply because he was exhausted. Fritz was best friends with the man who'd killed Krulgoth. He and Siv and Cassie had ended their quest to pillage Verde. He'd captured their city. He'd exiled them to the frozen north. For all he'd done to them, they ought to have been tearing him apart, ripping him to–

Click.

No.

Oh please, God, no.

"You're not here to kill me, are you?" Fritz asked with a callow voice, dreading the response he knew he would receive.

"No," Krulgoth said. White demons made out of flesh and bone couldn't speak human words, but ones made out of steel and chipware apparently *could.* His voice was electronic and sounded like a harsher, less refined version of Sebastian's, but it was delivered in the same emotionless monotone Fritz remembered from when Krulgoth was in a human body.

There was only one reason the demons wouldn't kill him on sight.

"They're coming," Krulgoth confirmed.

Fritz checked the last handful of wires connected to the main circuit board, then closed the access panel. "All good here," he said.

On the other side of the teleport pad, Annalie read diagnostic numbers from a small screen. "Daisy," she said. She took a steadying breath and checked another readout. "And our guests signal they're ready."

Standing out of his crouch, Fritz stepped across the barn wearing the boots of his chipsuit, so he didn't require his cane. The barn was well-stocked with hay and ready for winter. Their cow was content in her stall. Annalie's two youngest siblings, Elise and Felix, chased the chickens. And above it all, Sierra sat on the edge of the loft, her combat boots danging over the side. Her hair was green now, as green as the Lenerstelen decorations that would soon cover his mom's home and the nearby village. Fritz flashed her an exaggerated, goofy smile, a non-verbal admonition for her to stop scowling.

She scrunched up her nose, stuck out her tongue at him, and caused a cold wind to blow in through the open barn doors. Fritz tightened his jacket and vest around his chest.

"Elise, Felix, time to go inside," Annalie said. "Mrs. Reinhardt is baking cookies."

Elise whooped with joy and ran from the barn. Felix followed her silently, pausing only to brush his fingers against the hand Fritz reached out to him.

"And there are muffins left over from this morning, too," Fritz called after them. He turned to Annalie. "Say, if brinner is breakfast-for-dinner, what's breakfast-for-snack? Snackfast?"

"Stop," Annalie said. "You're making me hungry."

On their way out, the kids nearly bowled over Cassie and Siv, who were on their way in. Cassie held her bow, and her quiver was fully loaded. Siv wore a long-sleeved jacket to protect himself against the late Autumn cold, and he had the Dragon Slayer in its scabbard across his back. "Are those weapons necessary?" Fritz said.

"Are you about to teleport white demons onto our father's property?" Cassie said.

"Yes," Fritz said.

"Then yes," Cassie said.

Fritz shrugged and joined Annalie behind the teleport pad's control panel.

"Before we welcome back the monsters we worked so hard to exile," Cassie said, "I want to ask one last time. Are we sure about this?"

"Before he used Skylab's robots to make his metal body, Krulgoth's mind spent five months inside the chipware aboard Skylab," Fritz said. "The way he consolidated data from all of the station's sensor networks and the algorithm he came up with to analyze it all were works of brilliance. And Annalie and I have each triple-checked his numbers. There is a fleet of Celestine spaceships headed towards Verde. They're coming to capture their fugitive battalion of troops: the white demons. But the Celestines do not send enough ships to carry thousands, maybe a *million* Shakren soldiers just to fight a couple hundred renegades. They intend to conquer us."

"They can try," Sierra grumbled.

Fritz spread his palms. "It's simple math. The demons need us, and we need them."

"The enemy of my enemy is my friend," Siv said.

"Except our 'friend' is still a gang of pillaging monsters," Cassie said.

Fritz rubbed the back of his head where he'd bashed it on his workbench weeks earlier. He'd thought it had just been a nightmare, but the gray-skinned man whose hand had passed through his furniture really had been physically present in his bedroom – or at least as physically present as his kind ever were. So had the other one, the female with the knife that formed out of smoke. They'd already invaded his home – his *bedroom* – once, and they were on their way back.

"Neither the white demons nor the Shakren army are the worst part," Fritz said quietly. "The two creatures who call themselves the Celestines are. Even if Krulgoth is a pillaging monster, I want him on my side. He's the only person in the galaxy who's ever killed a Celestine." Fritz swallowed hard. "Which is a pretty remarkable feat considering they're ghosts."

"I don't believe in ghosts," Sierra said.

"How'd he do it?" Cassie asked. "How'd he kill a ghost?"

Fritz shrugged. "The white demon that once invaded my mind didn't know. I guess we can ask Krulgoth when he gets here."

He reached for the teleport controls.

"Dark days ahead, y'all," Siv mumbled.

"No!" Fritz said, pointing at Siv so suddenly it startled Annalie. "There are long days ahead. Hard days. Busy days. Days of strife. Certainly not days of peace – not yet. Days of danger. Deadly days. Not all of us may survive what's to come. But *dark* days? No. Not as long as we don't lose hope."

Siv considered that then nodded once in agreement. Annalie rested her head against Fritz's shoulder. Sierra dissipated into wind, then reformed out of dirt from the barn floor directly in front of the teleport pad, cracking her knuckles. Cassie cast a glance back towards the house sheltering her mother and Annalie's siblings and closed the barn doors.

"It's time to defend the world," Fritz told them.

He activated the teleport pad.

Acknowledgments

Jesus, Mary, and Joseph, I love you very much. Save souls. St. John of God and my dear friend St. Therese of Lisieux, my writing patron saints, thank you for your prayers. *Ad maiorem Dei gloriam.*

To my beloved and beautiful bride, Rose: I'd be lost without you. Thank you for being my partner, my business manager, my best friend, and my everything.

To my six treasures to whom this book is dedicated, Todd, Joseph, Gianna, Rose, Giovanni, and Mary-Elizabeth: you know I love stories. Watching the six of you grow up into adults is the best story I could imagine. Daddy loves you.

To the five best parents a guy could ask for: thank you for your endless love and example.

To Editor Cassandra, who once again had the answers I needed to make this book better: you are so very much appreciated. Or put another way, since I know you like Siv's country twang: "Gratitude."

To Tommaso Renieri: I *love* your cover art! You brought Fritz out of my mind and into a visual medium. *Grazie!*

To my beta readers JWL, my nieces Kaitlin and Emily, Richie Franklin, and Will Munn: thank you so much for your time and honest opinions.

To my brothers and sisters in prose, my writing group friends Will Munn, Drew Gerken, KM Alexander, Shannon Bradshaw, Richie Franklin, J. Rushing, and Scott Drakeford: thank you for your advice, encouragement, friendship, and camaraderie.

Special thanks to fellow writer Lauren Sapala. She believes writers are meant to share their wounds, write from their souls, and be of service to the world. Taking her advice deeply to heart made this a much different book, and one that means a lot more to me. Thank you so much, Lauren!

This book was written to a soundtrack of songs by Matt Maher, Foo Fighters, the Sex Pistols, No Doubt, Smashing Pumpkins, Fifteen, Green Day, Ingrid Michaelson, Even in Blackouts, Idina Menzel, Guns N' Roses, and Ned's Atomic Dustbin. See my website (michaelripplinger.com) for the specific songs and their meanings.

Gevalia Columbian coffee, I still adore you and each and every person in any small way responsible for getting you into my mug. People often say "this book wouldn't exist without so-and-so." But this book truly wouldn't exist without Gevalia Columbian coffee because I wouldn't have been awake to write it.

Finally, thank you once again for supporting my work and allowing me to take you away to Verde for a while. I hope you'll come back for one last trip.

Deus vobiscum.

–Michael Ripplinger

Fritz Reinhardt, Annalie Krieger, Cassie Reinhardt,
and Siv McCaig will return
and **The Verdant Revival** will conclude in Book 3:

Today's Saints

Keep reading for a preview

They were halfway across the farm from the forest back to the house, and no one had said anything. Not even Sierra. They were returning to the house for dinner, which meant Annalie, at the very least, should have been raving about how hungry she was. Instead, she kicked at the dirt as she moped along. Fritz was so distracted, he nearly wandered off course three times.

"Say something," Cassie said to Siv in an undertone. "They need a distraction."

"What should I say?" Siv whispered back to her.

Cassie shrugged. "Anything. We just need to get their minds off of practice failure number fifteen."

Siv nodded and thought for a moment. "Who's done with their Lenerstelen shopping?"

"Haven't even started," Annalie said. "Not used to shopping for it."

"You've never celebrated Lenerstelen before?" Cassie asked.

"Celebrated, sure," Annalie said. "But living up in Demons' Town, we didn't *buy* nothing for it. Demons didn't exactly operate stores. We made gifts for one another instead. Guess I could go buy things now, this being me and my siblings' first

Lenerstelen free of the demons. But I think I'd still like to make my gifts. Feels more personable somehow."

"I made Mom a chipware mixer," Fritz said.

"For serious?" Annalie asked.

Fritz nodded. "Well, I repaired and restored an old one. I didn't make a new one from scratch. But still, now it will be easier than ever for her to make bread dough."

"Or *cookie* dough," Annalie said, rubbing at her stomach. "Mmm. I'm hungry."

"What about you, Sierra?" Fritz asked.

She raised an eyebrow at him. "Me? Lenerstelen shopping?"

Fritz shrugged.

"I'm both atheist and anti-capitalist," Sierra said. "In what universe do you imagine I go Lenerstelen shopping?"

"I wasn't going to get you anything anyway," Cassie told her.

Sierra kissed her palm and blew it towards her. Cassie glared back.

"I just want to get y'all to my sister's place over in Gorman," Siv said. "Or bring her and her family here. The place don't matter. The food does. Sammy's the only one who knows how to make the traditional McCaig family five-course Lenerstelen feast, and that's what I want my gift to y'all to be."

"I'm *so* hungry," Annalie said.

"Beg pardon," Siv said. "Five courses *plus* the prickly pear pie."

"I'm completely famished," Annalie moaned.

Fritz reached out and took her hand.

"How about you, Cass?" Siv said.

Lenerstelen wasn't the distraction topic she would have chosen, especially as they tromped across the farm's fallow wheat field. Less than two months earlier, her father had died in that field.

It had happened in the middle of her first semester of med school, so she'd been away in Harbrucken. If she'd been home, certainly her healing power could have saved him. Except she *had* been home just one day earlier. She'd made an emergency visit to help Fritz through a tough time. The day after she'd left – the very next day – a blocked coronary artery had killed their dad.

She *was* looking forward to her first Lenerstelen with Siv, but she was *not* looking forward to the first one without her father. Her grief was still a raw wound. And perhaps even worse than the grief was the nagging question that lingered underneath it. She tried to dismiss it, but she couldn't let it go.

Things had worked out just right for her to find out about Fritz's depression and to make it home to help him. She knew that had been the work of God's Almighty Hand, and she was so grateful he'd made sure she was there for her brother. But why couldn't he have made sure she stayed home just one day longer so she could have been there for her father, too?

"Cassie does all her shopping on Lenerstelen Eve," Fritz said.

"The woman with the plan waits for the last minute?" Annalie said.

"Too busy studying," Cassie admitted with a shrug.

"Guess I oughta ask what *you* want then," Siv said, putting an arm around her shoulders. "Other than a handsome fella, since you already have that."

"Honestly, I'd be OK with skipping Lenerstelen this year," she said, "so long as it got me back to Harbrucken. My professors and fellow students are working hard to rebuild the university, and I want to help them. Keep my plan moving forward. *That's what I want.*"

She practically dared Sierra to give her a look or make a comment, but she didn't. The crank just kept her mouth shut and her head held high, and she didn't so much as glance at Cassie. Did she have *any* remorse for what she'd done to Harbrucken? For the people she'd killed?

"You'll get back there," Siv said. He planted a quick kiss on her cheek.

"I know I will," Cassie said. "I just want to be back there *now.*"

Past the wheat field was the chicken coop and the house. They approached it from behind, so Cassie couldn't see the front door yet, but she heard its squeaky hinges creak open and heard the door slam back against the frame. A moment later, a young girl, barely a teenager, barreled around the corner and ran towards them. She had red hair like her older sister Annalie, a too-thin frame, and a wide smile.

"Hey, Doctor Cassie," Elise said after skidding to a stop in front of her.

When Annalie had come to live here, to prepare for the Celestines' arrival, she'd brought her two youngest siblings with her. Elise had taken to Cassie like oxygen to the lungs. Cassie had never had a little sister before Elise began following her around. She could gladly get used to it. Having Elise around had been the best part of all this Celestine invasion preparation. It was like getting an early Lenerstelen present.

"Hey, Nurse Elise," Cassie said to her. "How you been?"

"Helping your mama," Elise said, falling into step next to Cassie. "I read how to make a tourniquet."

"Ooo, advanced stuff," Cassie said. "Why would you use one?"

"If bleeding is severe and direct pressure alone won't stop it."

"Good," Cassie said. "But why could it be dangerous?"

"If left on too long, your patient could lose the limb."

"But used correctly?"

"You stop someone from bleeding to death."

Cassie patted her back. "You keep this up, and they're gonna give you a job teaching at the med school when it reopens."

Past the house was a small pasture. Cassie's horse, Mandolin, and Siv's horse, Rebel, both grazed here. Cassie gave Mandolin a wave, and Mandolin flopped her tail in response. Beyond the pasture was the barn. Its exterior had once been red, but now it was half-faded and half-weathered.

The only sunlight left in the sky was a thin strip of orange on the western horizon. Still, the barn's inside was visible even from a hundred yards away because of all the chipware lights Fritz and Annalie had mounted from its ceiling. The reaper, the tractor, and every other piece of heavy equipment that should have been inside was parked outside, which cleared up plenty of floor space inside.

For the spaceship.

Two hundred years earlier, the Blackout reverted Verde to a pre-industrial society overnight. It had been the Mantissa's final, desperate attempt to fend off the white demons, and it hadn't worked. The Mantissa didn't survive, but the demons did, and they immediately began stockpiling broken, scrambled chipware in anticipation of one day repairing it. They had all kinds of ancient chipware in their stash up north: screens, mobiles, dispark ovens, weapons, comm systems. They even had a spaceship.

The cargo ship was once used to transport molecularly unstable goods and teleport-phobic passengers up to the Skylab space station. Now it was a physical symbol of the Mantissa and demon alliance. Everyone worked together to restore it, except when practicing their cathedral-ship assault.

The white demons bounded into the barn and swarmed over the ship like bees around a hive. Hundreds of engine parts lie scattered across the barn floor. The demons resumed the work of meticulously cleaning, inspecting, and rebuilding each one. Chipware diagnostic tools buzzed and beeped. Somewhere on the other side of the barn, metal clanged against metal in a steady rhythm. Open panels exposed degraded interior wiring. There was still a lot to be done to make the ship space-worthy, and they were short on time.

Krulgoth and the last of the demons were almost in the barn when Annalie called out to them. "You sure we can't bring y'all some dinner?"

"We can go a month without eating," Zethken said. Or was it Merkg?

"And we just ate five days ago," Rarkh said.

"Well, that's one way to live your life," Annalie mumbled.

Sierra also wouldn't be joining them for dinner since she didn't eat. The color disappeared from her body, revealing its dirt composition. She leaned forward, stretched, and elongated. Additional dirt rose up out of the ground and augmented her existing mass. When her body shimmered and took on color again, it was in the shape of a horse – a black horse with a lush green mane. And with piercings in her ears and lips. How charming. After a quick glance back at Cassie and Siv, she galloped across the pasture, and Mandolin and Rebel gave her chase.

"That is the oddest looking horse I ever dang seen," Siv said.

"Creepy," Cassie said.

Everyone still in the pasture turned towards the home's front porch. While they were out in the forest, it seemed Mom had put up some Lenerstelen decorations. She'd wrapped garland around the porch rail, and two of the front windows were painted with green soap.

Sitting on the first step and waiting for them was a ten-year-old boy with wide eyes and a mop of messy brown hair. The youngest Krieger sibling, Felix, kept his mouth closed, but he took three nervous steps towards Fritz.

Without a word, Fritz waved his hand.

Felix nodded.

Fritz pointed his index finger at the boy, then put up his thumb, tilting his head to the side in inquiry.

Felix rubbed his stomach.

"Yeah, I'm hungry, too," Fritz said, opening the front door and letting Felix enter first.

Cassie and Fritz had grown up together in this house. It was mostly a single room with a kitchen on the right side and a sitting area on the left. Three doors led off to the bedrooms. Ruth, Cassie and Fritz's mother, stood before the brick oven, stirring broth in a pot hanging over the fire. She smiled at her children as they came into the house. "Well, how'd you do?" she asked.

"We lost," Annalie said. "Again."

Ruth groaned then side-nodded towards the barn and the demons within it. "Can't *they* do anything to help you?"

"They are, but don't worry, Mom," Fritz said. He pulled a chair back from the table and dropped into it. "We'll figure it out."

"You're not wearing that crazy suit of armor to my dinner table, are you?" Ruth said.

"You're making me change?" Fritz asked.

"Don't talk back to your mama," Annalie said. She scooped a stack of bowls from a kitchen cupboard and began placing them around the table. When Fritz didn't retreat to his room to change fast enough, she took the dishtowel off her shoulder and threatened to swat him with it.

He stood up. "I'll change, I'll change."

Ruth came up beside Cassie. "I love her," Ruth whispered. "Can we force Fritz to marry her already?"

"Not legally," Cassie said. She snatched a piece of chopped carrot off the cutting board and tossed it into her mouth. "Shouldn't let that stop us, though."

Elise, hovering nearby, mimicked Cassie and took a piece of carrot for herself. Cassie took another and tossed it towards Elise's open mouth, but it bounced off her bottom lip and landed on the floor. Both women laughed.

"You two," Ruth said, "stop playing with the food."

The front door opened and a one-armed man with white hair, a weathered face, and a tired smile stepped inside. "Hey, Daddy," Siv called to him. "You been working out there all day?"

"Yep," Duncan said. "Got all the port aft hull plates repaired, though."

"*All* of them?" Siv said.

Duncan nodded.

"There were twenty-three of 'em needed work this morning," Siv said.

Duncan just nodded again. He stood beside Cassie. "How's my future daughter-in-law?"

"Causing trouble and playing with food," she admitted.

Duncan laughed. Cassie put her arm across his back, resting her left hand on the stump that ended four inches past his left shoulder. "Mind if I work on that arm a little before dinner?"

He released a contented sigh. "Please do."

Elise gave a small jump of excitement and settled in to watch.

A white demon had ripped Duncan's arm off nearly twenty years earlier. After she'd met Siv, and then his father, she'd quickly read everything she could find in the university library on the science behind amputation. Following the traumatic injury, a blood clot closed the wound, then skin cells closed in to form a mass of scar tissue over the top of it. That much was true of many animals – humans, horses, dogs, cats. Except lizards were capable of something more. They were able to grow epithelial tissue on top of the clot, putting the amputated limb into what Cassie thought of as "embryo mode." Cellular processes not used since before the lizard hatched were dug out of nuclear memory and reactivated, and the lost limb regenerated.

Being the sister of the guy who restored broken chipware meant Cassie had access to an additional resource. Fritz could pull pre-Blackout medical texts off of old hospital proc-boxes he restored and descrambled. That opened her studies to areas lost even to the university, such as genome mapping. The ancients had mapped out the DNA of humans and just about every other living organism on Verde. It turned out humans possessed all the same genes lizards used for limb regeneration. But in humans, those genes typically remained dormant and unused.

Cassie saw no reason to remain typical, especially not when she had a patient she could help. All Mantissa powers were psychic in nature. She didn't heal people with magic juju. Her mind reached out into her patient's mind and somehow instructed it to do things it usually didn't do, like heal at ten times average speed. Or put those sleeping genes to work and regrow a lost limb.

It took lizards about sixty days to regrow a tail. Cassie reckoned it would take her a lot longer than that to regenerate Duncan's entire arm. But she managed to scrounge up some time here and there, and it was slowly working. His arm was growing back under her healing power.

Cassie closed her eyes and felt for the end of the stump underneath the mostly empty sleeve of Duncan's flannel shirt. She reached out with her power, and a familiar calm fell over her. She always felt most at peace when she was healing. It was one reason she knew it was her calling.

"Cassie, I almost forgot," her mother said. "You got post today."

She opened her eyes but kept her hand on Duncan and kept her healing power flowing. "I did?"

Ruth motioned behind her towards the table. "Over there."

Siv found the letter and brought it to her with a wide smile. "It's from the university."

"They finally know when I get to come back!" Cassie said. She nodded towards Elise. "You want to open and read that to me, kiddo?"

Elise tore open the envelope and unfolded the letter inside. "To the most amazing doctor in the whole world," she read.

"It does not say that," Cassie said, though her heart swelled at the compliment. She winked at Elise.

Fritz emerged from his bedroom wearing – what else? – a button-up shirt, vest, and trousers. He returned to his seat at the table, and Felix returned to Fritz's side, hiding behind him.

"Dear Miss Reinhardt," Elise said. Then she cleared her throat and repeated herself in what she must have imagined was the tone of an uppity university administrator. "Dear Miss Reinhardt. In the immediate aftermath of the horrific November 18 attacks, our faculty and students were focused on one thing: caring for thousands of casualties. We are all still in mourning, for there were far too many deaths. Yet there is no doubt the death toll would have been much higher if not for the efforts of our medical school family who selflessly aided the first responders overwhelmed by the scope of the Steelterror assault. It was our city's greatest hour of need, and we responded with our finest moment."

Elise gave an exaggerated bow to Cassie, her big sister, Siv, and Fritz. It was the four of them – plus Sebastian, who hadn't survived – who'd stopped the Steelterrors, but no one outside that kitchen knew it. There were still too many myths and lies about what had happened in Verde's past. All most people "knew" was once upon a time, there had been Steelterrors and Mantissa. Then after the Blackout nearly destroyed the world, there was poisoned land – Terrascorcha – and white demons. Many folks believed the Mantissa had likely been just as much a part of the problem as the Steelterrors. And so the Mantissa Reborn kept tight-lipped about their accomplishments. They had enough to deal with. No need to add potential persecution to the list.

"Three weeks have passed," Elise continued reading. "The dead have been buried. Wounds have begun to heal. And the university faculty have begun to assess the damage. It is..." She resumed her normal voice. "I don't know this word."

Annalie happened to be sweeping past her while putting napkins on the table. She squinted over her sister's shoulder. "Calamitous."

"Calamitous," Elise repeated. "Food, potable water, and medical supplies are scarce. Both the main university library and the medical school library were total losses."

"*Total* losses?" Cassie said. She couldn't have heard that right.

"Half our tenured professors perished," Elise read. "Buildings can, of course, be rebuilt. However, the sheer amount of knowledge lost in the attacks is unfathomable and irreplaceable."

Since helping Elise with the word she didn't know, Annalie hadn't resumed setting the table. She'd continued reading the rest of the letter over Elise's shoulder. Suddenly, she gasped, then looked up at Cassie in disbelief.

Cassie's hand slowly fell off of Duncan's arm.

"Two hundred years ago," Elise read, "the university at Harbrucken survived the Blackout and emerged carrying the torch of light and learning for all that remained of the civilized world. This time, Harbrucken and her university were not so lucky. It is simply impossible to comprehend how the university could possibly recover. Therefore, we regret to inform you that the medical school and all other colleges at the university are indefinitely, and quite likely permanently... closed?"

Cassie gently took the letter from Elise's hand. The crinkling of the paper was the only sound in the room. It seemed like even her mother's soup had ceased to bubble and boil. She found the letter's final paragraph. *Refunds for tuition and room and board for November 18 through the end of the semester will be issued. However, because of the extraordinary nature of our current situation, please understand this could take some time and may, in the end, prove financially impossible. With deepest regrets, Percy Holt, Dean of the University Medical School.*

Refunds? Who gave a damn about refunds? Like that even mattered.

Fully-trained doctor by age twenty-four. Cure cancer. Start a new village. Serve as its physician. *That's* what mattered. But without a university, none of it would ever happen. None of it *could.* Not anymore. Not ever.

Her plan.

Her *dream.*

"Darlin'?" Siv asked softly. His brown eyes were so gentle, but they weren't the only eyes watching her. Everyone in the room looked upon her with a mix of dread and pity on their faces. The main room suddenly felt the size of an outhouse, and the walls seemed to be moving in closer still.

"Excuse me," she said, and she pushed open the door and stormed outside.

Michael Ripplinger writes both novels and computer software. He is a certified introvert who enjoys breakfast cereal and a variety of indoor activities, but he'd rather be at Disneyland. Michael, his wife Rose, and their seven children make their home in south Texas.

Michael would love to hear from you. Please visit his website at mripplinger.wordpress.com or contact him at michael@ripplinger.us

Also by Michael Ripplinger:
Yesterday's Demons
Today's Saints